For my Daughter,

I want you to grow and know your worth and value. Never let a man tear you down or use you, you my beautiful girl are no one's doormat. Go slay this world with your imagination and sass, take no prisoners on your way to achieving your dreams.

Mummy's got you always and forever.

SAVAGE
LIES

SAMANTHA BARRETT

Cover design by Amber Withers
Editing by Amber Withers
Proofreading by Willie Field at Darmara Grammar

First Printing, 2022

SAVAGE
LIES

CHAPTER ONE
Jessica

Do you ever feel like you're a piece on a chess board?

All my life I have felt like I am a pawn in a game, I know deep down inside me my life must mean more than this. My destiny cannot be scrubbing restrooms all over the country as my mom and I never stay in one place for long. The closer I get to my eighteenth birthday I become more impatient toward my mom, she hides stuff from me and it's frustrating. I'm always the new kid at every school and I hate it. Over the years I have learnt to ignore the staring, whispers and all the bullshit that goes with it. I have begged her for years to home-school me but apparently, she's too busy. The woman changes her jobs as often as she changes her panties.

"Come on Jess, if you don't hurry up, you'll be late." I roll my eyes and curse beneath my breath. I take one last glance in the mirror to make sure I don't have anything in my teeth. It takes me all of two seconds to reach the kitchen, thanks to my mom's current job we live at the local motel. The owner allows us to stay in one of the old two-bedroom cabins out back; it's so damn small I feel claustrophobic half the time. I know my mom is doing her best, I just wish sometimes she'd hold a job down long enough so I can stop being the new kid every year!

"I'm here, now can we go so I can get this awkward first day crap over with?" My mom narrows her eyes and places her hands on her hips. Great, she's about to give me another lecture.

"Don't you sass me young lady. I know this sucks, but one day when everything settles down you will understand." Frustrated, I throw my hands in the air.

"Understand what mom? You have been preaching that same line for years and I'm over it." She arches a brow at me, for a small woman she sure as shit can hold her own. Her full lips turn down and sadness enters her eyes, she shakes her brown hair from her face, takes one long look at me and turns away. I release a long sigh; I need to stop doing this to her. It's not her fault my dad is a dead beat and skipped town when she told him she was pregnant with me. I close the space between us and wrap my arms around her from behind and rest my chin on her shoulder. "I'm sorry mom, I was out of line."

She breaks out of my hold and spins around and cups my face between her tiny hands and smiles at me like I'm her favorite person in the whole world. I really need to stop being so ungrateful.

"You have nothing to be sorry for, Jess. When the time comes, I swear I will tell you everything, but for now I don't want to complicate things any more than I have for you." I can hear the truth in her words, what is she hiding from me? She pats me gently on my cheeks and smiles wide. "Come on I'll drop you off since it's your first day."

Pulling up in front of Rosewood High I can feel everyone's eyes on me. I try to shrink down in my seat but the feeling of being watched remains. Mom stops near the stairs that will lead me to the admin building, I take a few deep breaths and collect myself before turning to her. A look I can't decipher passes across her face.

"What's wrong?" Mom's eyes begin to mist, worry starts to seep into my bones. She reaches across and clasps my hand in hers.

"Promise me something, Jess."

"Why?"

"Promise me" I start to panic; she's trembling and it's freaking me out.

"Okay, I promise?"

"Anyone tries any shit, you use your training and you run, do you understand?" I reel back shocked, my mom has never let me use my training on anyone, let alone encouraged it.

"What the hell is going on mom?"

"Not everything is as it seems here Jess, this town has more secrets than the Bible." My mom's ominous tone scares me. She didn't give me a chance to ask more questions, shooing me out of the car and speeding off. I'm now standing at the bottom of the stairs clutching the strap of my pack like a lifeline, I keep replaying that strange as shit conversation with my mom over and over again in my head. I'm so lost in my own thoughts I didn't notice the girl standing in front of me, until she clicks her fingers in my face. Her blonde hair shines in the sunlight, her piercing blue eyes and skin-tight outfit complete her Barbie doll look. Either side of her stands her clones, I release a long sigh knowing these three are obviously the bitch-squad who are here to warn me off. I square my shoulders and brace myself for their onslaught, this isn't my first rodeo.

"You're new." I cock my brow in answer, Queen Bee narrows her blue eyes, her two minions do the same. "You don't belong here; Rosewood is for the pure not for riff raff off the street-"

"Piss off Kayla and go find someone else to torment!" The three blow up dolls turn to the newcomer; I refuse to take my eyes off them and acknowledge whoever spoke.

"Mind your own damn business, Kelly." I snap my gaze to the newcomer when I hear a growl, a freaking growl! The new girl is stunning, long brown locks hang down her back, bright green eyes, she's around the same height as me and her style is on point. Ripped jeans, Doc Martens, a flannel shirt tied around her waist and a tank top that reads 'I'm a TWIhard.'" Being a Twilight fan myself I instantly feel a kinship with this girl.

"Really? We're still trying to play the 'say my name

wrong' game? Grow up and buzz off Kayla, what my brother sees in you is still a mystery to me." Queen Bee tries to take a step toward the newcomer, I move in front of the girl and block Kayla's path.

"Oh, you've got balls." I hear the venom that laces her words, I think I've just painted a target on my own back. Awesome.

"The only ballbag around here is you. You may climb my brother's dick each night but you're still beneath us! Leave now while you have the chance." I'm shocked that some guy has come to our defence, the three bimbos glare at him before stomping past us, Kayla makes sure to shoulder check me as she makes her way back to the car park with her minions in tow. Once they're gone, I spin around and eye both my defenders, the guy is jaw-droppingly gorgeous, wait is droppingly a word? He has the same-colored eyes as the girl and the same shade of brown hair, he is tall and built like a wrestler. He has such a sweet aura about him, he doesn't give off I'm hot and I know it vibes.

"Right, well if you're done checking out my brother, my name is Callie." I focus on the girl and smile politely. "This brute is my brother Colton."

"Cole." He cuts in; Callie rolls her eyes and smiles. "What's your name?"

"I'm Jess." They each hold their hand out for me to shake,

which I do. They both seem like good people.

"Well Jess, it goes without saying but you should stay out of Kayla's way."

"What my brother's trying to say is Kayla's a royal bitch, she won't get over what just happened." I sigh and nod my head, I guessed as much.

"I don't want any trouble; I just want to finish my last year of high school and haul ass to college." The pair look at me like I'm some strange being. "What?"

"You don't plan on sticking around?" Are they nuts? I shake my head.

"No, I want out of here as soon as possible. I've already sent out applications to pretty much every college in the country."

CHAPTER TWO
Jessica

Callie and Cole were kind enough to take me to get my class schedule and help me find my locker. Callie and I have English together in first period and couple other classes as well, Cole is in a few of my periods too. I'll admit I'm glad that I won't be sitting alone in any of my lessons. Callie and I make it to our English class just as the bell rings, where she introduces me to our teacher, Mr. Briggs. He seems kind or quirky but looks way too young to be a teacher.

"Welcome to Rosewood high Miss Hastings." I smile politely.

"Thank you, Mr. Briggs."

"With our hei--Callie taking you under her wing I'm sure you will be fine."

"Ummm, yeah thank you?" I'll admit I'm slightly taken back; I feel like there is a double meaning to what he just said. I shake it off and follow Callie toward the back of the room and we manage to snag a couple of seats side by side. As the lesson drags on, I start to zone out, English was never one of my top subjects. The bell rings and snaps me out of my daydream, I follow Callie to our next class which Cole has with us. The three of us take up the back row, I pull my pad and pen from my pack and place it on my desk. As I look up my gaze lands on God himself, okay maybe not God himself but this guy looks like he could give the Greek gods a run for their money. My breath hitches in my throat, he's beautiful. Chocolate brown hair with tints of blond through it, he has striking hazel eyes; he stands there just staring at me. I can't pull my gaze from him, as if my body is on autopilot, I stand from my seat. He squints his eyes and cocks his head to the side, I see his nostrils flare as if he smells the air then his eyes darken, I gasp.

Callie and Cole rise to their feet beside me, everyone and all the noise in the room begins to fade as I stand here transfixed in this gorgeous stranger's gaze. I feel this unexplainable pull toward him, I'm about to make my way over but the spell I'm under is broken when Kayla aka Queen bitch wraps herself around him. His gaze remains on me for a second longer before she grips his face so he is looking down at her. I shake my head and take a deep breath, I drop down into my chair, Callie and Cole do the same. I can feel both their gazes on me but don't acknowledge them. What the heck would I say?

I lift my eyes as discreetly as I can and watch as Kayla leads the giant god to the other side of the room. When he takes his seat, he turns to stare at me, I quickly drop my gaze to my desk. What the hell was that? I felt like I wasn't even in control of my own body, my mind was saying not to move, but my body had a mind of its own. I can feel his gaze on me, and it takes everything I have not to look at him. Something deep inside is urging me to walk over there and rip that bimbo off him. I quickly shake away that thought and try to focus as the teacher begins to speak.

Throughout the whole lesson, we continue to sneak small glances at each other. It was hard to concentrate through most of the lesson, but Callie is kind enough to offer me her notes to copy. As the lesson draws to a close and we begin to exit, Mrs. McCredie asks me to stay behind.

"Is everything okay?" I ask once the classroom is empty, Callie and Cole said they would wait for me outside the class.

"Yes of course, I just wanted you to know that I'm here if

you need help." I scrunch my face in confusion.

"Um, I think I got the gist of what you were teaching just fine." She shakes her head and smiles sadly.

"When you learn about all of this, you will understand why I offered." I nod my head and thank her, then make a quick exit from the room. What a strange woman. I stop dead in my tracks when I see Callie and Cole talking to the beautiful stranger that stole my attention throughout the whole class. They all turn to me; Callie and Cole smile invitingly while the strange guy looks at me like I'm an equation he can't quite solve.

"Hey Jess, everything all good?" I stop a few feet away from them, when I let my eyes roam freely, they land on Mr. tall, dark and handsome. His gaze is firmly on me, when I rake my gaze down his glorious body, I notice another hand linked through his, a throat clearing has my gaze snapping up to land on the owner of said hand. Great.

"Keep your eyes off my mate!" All eyes turn to Kayla, I scoff and roll my eyes.

"Taking the Twilight thing a bit far aren't ya?" Callie and Cole chuckle but I can tell it's forced, seriously though what a weirdo calling someone your mate.

"Who. Are. You?" I gasp at the sound of his voice, it's so deep and raspy. Hearing him talk sends a shiver down my spine, what is it about this guy that has me so transfixed? I lift my chin and look him in the eyes as I answer.

"I'm Jess and you are?"

"Come on baby, you don't need to waste time on that mongrel." I let the bimbo's words blow straight over my head and wait for him to answer. Seconds tick by and still he doesn't speak.

"I'm gonna head to the cafeteria." I don't wait for their reply, I turn on my heel and make my way to the exit.

"Smooth Creed, real fucking smooth. Jess, wait up!" I hear Callie say, I slow my pace and within a few seconds Callie and Cole are both beside me. We head toward the cafeteria in silence. After loading our trays, we claim one of the empty tables outside. "Sorry about that, our brother--"

"Brother?" I interject; they exchange a look before turning back to me.

"Yeah, Creed is our older brother."

"If he's older, how is he in our classes?" They both chuckle before Cole answers me.

"We're triplets, Creed is the oldest, I'm the middle child and Callie is the baby." Holy shit, I would never have guessed that. But I will say being able to put a name to a hunk of male specimen is great, Creed. That name suits him to a tee.

"Trust me, I'm the prettiest out of the three of us." I chuckle at Callie while Cole glares at the side of his sister's head. Cole and Callie They spend the rest of our lunch hour filling me in on all things Rosewood and fun things to do. Apparently, there is a party this weekend at some guy Toby's house and Callie is demanding my presence there. I'm not really a party kind of gal but it is my senior year so I may as well live a little right?

"Okay, I'll come but I don't have a car."

"We got you Jess; Cole and I will pick you up at seven. You live at the motel on the edge of town, right?" I reel back shocked; Callie's eyes widen before she quickly schools her features.

"H-how did you know that?" Cole cuts in before Callie can answer.

"Callie helps out in administration sometimes and took a peek at your file before you arrived." I don't know why, but I can tell Cole is lying, how the hell did they know where I lived? Before I can push this issue more the bell rings, signally it was time for the last part of the day.

The rest of the day passes by quickly, only Cole is in my last period class. As final bell for the day rings Cole and I make our way out the front doors of school I come to a stop at the top of the stairs. Standing down the bottom and glaring up at me is none other than Cole and Callie's brother, Creed. Why is he glaring at me? Cole slings his arm around my shoulders casually, I swear to God, I hear someone or something growl!

Cole's chuckling snaps me out of my moment of insanity, of course humans can't growl only animals can Jess, get it together!

"Don't worry about Creed, he's just salty because he can't figure you out." I look up at Cole in question and ask.

"What do you mean he can't--"Before I can finish Cole's arm is slapped away from me, I turn to the front and gasp, shocked to see Creed standing in front of me vibrating with rage.

"The fuck, bro?" Cole snaps. Creed turns angry eyes to me, I stumble back a few steps until I smack into something or someone, a quick glance over my shoulder shows me I just backed into Cole.

"Stay away from my brother!" Is this guy for real? I'm not a confrontational person but I'm also not a meek mouse. I square my shoulders and meet Creed's angry stare.

"You do not get to tell me what to do you overgrown...eggplant!" Eggplant? Seriously, I mentally facepalm myself. I ignore the laughter from behind me, Creed closes the space between us and holy crap, I didn't realize how tall he was until I'm now looking directly at his chest having to crane my neck back to stare up at him. He has a smug look on his face which only fuels my irritation.

"You're lucky you have no idea who you are speaking to. When you do find out I will enjoy putting you in your place." Get a look at this guy, his ego is freaking huge and what is up with people telling me I don't know something today?

"I don't care who you think you are, you do not get throw your weight around like you're some damn king!" I grit out, a cruel smile crosses his face as he bends down so we are eye level.

"I'm close enough to a king, princess." Did he seriously just call me princess?

"That's enough Creed, back off now!" Callie pushes her way between us and breaks us apart, Creed's gaze remains on me as he takes a few steps back. "Leave her be, now is not the time for this."

CHAPTER THREE
Jessica

I'm sitting in my room trying to finish my homework, but I can't for the life of me concentrate. My mind keeps drifting to the strange day I have had, Creed and three other teachers hinted to the fact that I don't know something and it's bugging me! I hate feeling like everyone knows something and I don't. As soon as Callie broke up mine and Creed's little disagreement I took off and pretty much ran home. Running helps me think, I haven't gone for an early morning jog since we moved here over a week ago. My mom tells me it's too dangerous for a young girl to run through the woods around here but what would she know, it's not like she has ever lived here before.

"Kitten, dinner!" I groan and roll my eyes at my mom's pet name for me. I have begged her for years to stop calling me that, but she refuses. I drag my sorry butt out of bed and head to the dining slash kitchen and plonk down onto one of the stools at the breakfast bench. I sit there and watch as my mom dishes our plates. "Tell me about your day."

"There's not much to tell."

"Come on, there has to be some cute boys." I groan, loudly.

"Mom!" She waves her hand and smiles as she serves me my plate. I'm starved, I dig in and shovel the yummy goodness into my mouth.

"Jessica Delta Hastings! If you want to eat like an animal, then you can eat outside!" Mom abolishes me. I grin at her sheepishly. "Now tell me about your day, did you make any friends?"

"Yeah, I even met triplets today." My mom pauses, her fork full of mac'n'cheese suspended mid-air. Shocked eyes turn to me.

"What triplets?" The harshness in my mom's voice has me

stiffening.

"The ones I met at school today?" It sounds like more of a question than I want it to.

"What are their names?"

"Why? What's wrong mom?" She drops her fork, and it bangs loudly against her plate.

"What are their names Jess?" I stare at my mom stunned, what the hell is going on?

"I'm not telling you. Ever since we moved here you have been cagey and closed off from me!"

"Stay away from the triplets Jessica, I won't say it again."

"How do you even know them?" I shout.

"That's not your concern, just do as I say. We will only be here for a few more months and then we'll be gone." I deflate in my seat; I don't want to move again.

"Mom, please. This is my second school this year, let me finish my senior year here please." I can tell from the stubborn tilt of her head and how her eyes are crinkled at the sides, she's about to say no.

"You will thank me for this one."

"You're lucky you don't know who my dad is, or I would have chosen to live with him." I hightail it to my room and slam the door shut, the look on my mother's face as I said those words will haunt me for life.

I awake the next morning to the house being empty, mom already went to work. I check the bench for a note or something but there isn't one, I went too far last night. I barely slept, I could hear my mom crying from her room and it tore me up inside. I should never have lashed out at her like that but I'm tired of her always speaking in riddles and never telling me the truth about anything. How does she know the triplets? Why do we have to move? So many different questions are swirling through my head and it's driving me insane. I just wish someone could be honest with me for once in my life.

The walk to school is uneventful. I spent the whole time replaying the conversation between mom and I last night repeatedly in my head. She looked worried as soon as I mentioned I was friends with the triplets, well I'm good with two of them. I make my way up the stairs and head toward my locker, I scan the halls but there's still no sign of Cole or Callie. I just met them yesterday, but I feel a bond with them, almost like we were meant to be or something. I know that sounds stupid but it's true, I feel like I know them somehow. I grab my books from my locker to put them in my bag when a loud bang from my locker slamming shut has me dropping my books. I jump back and automatically drop into a crouch and hold my fist's up in front of me like my mom trained me to do. When I see that I'm not in danger and it's just Kayla and her minions staring at me like I'm a freak I stand and collect my belongings from the floor.

"Go near Creed again and I will tear your throat out, you little slut." I zip up my bag and sling it over my shoulder; I face the three bimbos and glare at each of them. Kayla has her top lip pulled back in a snarl.

"One, don't tell me what to do. Two, I didn't go anywhere near him so get your facts right." Kayla closes the space between us and looks down her pointy nose at me like I'm a piece of shit.

"I saw his sister pushing you away from him yesterday.

Creed would never look at a plain low life like you when he has me, learn your place--fast." I'm about to give her a piece of mind when I'm suddenly pulled backward by my backpack. Next thing I know Creed, Cole and Callie are standing in front of me facing off against Kayla and her minions.

"I told you, stay away!" I shiver at the anger lacing each of Creed's words.

"The alp--boss never gave a direct order about her, so she's fair game!" Holy shit, they're talking about me!

"Get over yourself Kayla, you were never going to end up with my brother."

"Fuck you Kelly!" Kayla shouts, I see Creed's back muscles tense and out of nowhere I hear a loud as shit growl. I snap my gaze left to right to see where the hell that came from, but I can't see an animal anywhere, students line the halls staring at the commotion going on in front of me. Creed takes a menacing step forward toward Kayla.

"You speak to my sister like that again and you know what will happen. Stay out of my sight and stay away from her." Wait, what will happen and by her he meant me right? The bell rings and that snaps me out of my stupor, I don't stick around and wait to see what will transpire between the six of them. I head to my elective History class, which as luck would have it is right next to my math's class. I make my way inside and choose to head for the back row. I plonk down beside a jock looking type of guy and pull my history book, pad, and pen out. As I settle in and look to the front of the room, I see Cole and Creed walk in. Creed's gaze somehow finds me straight away, he spots the guy beside me and then he narrows his eyes but doesn't stop moving till he gets to the middle row on the other side of the room. Cole drops down next to his brother then turns around and smiles and waves at me, I return his gesture then quickly avert my gaze to the front.

"Hey, I'm Josh." I turn to the side and see the jock guy with his hand extended out to me, he looks like a really nice young man. I might have misjudged him; I place my hand in his and say.

"I'm Jess." He chuckles.

"I know."

"You do?"

"Yeah, we have chem. together." Oh, I don't remember seeing him yesterday in the chem. lab.

"Oh, sorry." He pulls his hand back and waves it in the air dismissing my apology.

"Don't sweat it, I probably have one of those faces you tend to forget." I snort and quickly cover my mouth in horror, Josh's brows raise, and I can see he is trying hard not to laugh at me.

"Can we forget that I just did that?" I mumble out, Josh bites down on his lip and nods his head.

"Only if you agree to be my chem partner for the upcoming exam?" What the hell, right? Y.O.L.O. and all that shit so why not.

"You have yourself a deal Josh."

The lesson passes at a snail's pace, I can feel Cole and Creed's eyes on me most of the lesson, but I choose to ignore them. I have no idea who they are but after my mom's ominous warning last night I feel like I need to stay away from them. Callie and Cole were nothing but kind to me yesterday, am I being too harsh? I jolt in my seat when the bell rings, Josh stands and smiles down at me.

"See you in chem. Partner." I smile and nod as I collect my things and head to my next class. By the time I exit the classroom it's empty, just as I clear the threshold of the door I'm yanked to the side by my arm and then pinned against the wall by a huge hulking body. I act on instinct and strike out with my fist, but it's captured and held against my side, I try with my other but end up in the same position. I glare up at my captor.

"Let. Me. Go." He bends down till we're eye level.

"Stay away from Josh." I narrow my eyes to slits and yank my hands free, then push against his chest until he steps back.

"You don't get to tell me what to do, I told you that yesterday, Creed. Now stay the hell away from me!" I don't stick around for his reply, I high tail it to English. I drop into my seat seething with rage, how dare he man handle me like that! I'm snapped out of my thoughts when Callie drops into the seat next to me. I take a few calming breaths, so I don't lash out at her, after all it's not her fault that her brother is a pig.

"Hey, you okay?" I plaster a fake smile on my face and nod. "You need to learn how to lie better than that." I slump back and groan, today is proving to be a shitter already.

"Sorry, just having a rough morning." Callie's smile slips, understanding enters her gaze.

"Don't worry about Kayla, she's a grade A bitch and we'll make sure she backs off."

"Why?" Callie's face scrunches in confusion.

"Um, because it's the right thing to do?" I have no idea why I'm getting pissed off but it's getting annoying feeling like I'm the only one left out of the know. So, I decide to try a different approach. I turn to face Callie, so I can look her in the eyes.

"My mom warned me to stay away from you and your brothers." Callie's only give away is that her right eye twitches, but other than that her expression remains neutral.

"I don't even know your mom."

"But my mom somehow knows you three, or about you all at least. How?" Before our conversation can continue, the teacher walks in. I sigh and resign myself to the fact that I'm just going to have to wait till lunch.

Callie and I grab our trays and head out to the table we sat at yesterday, I can feel tension between us, and I don't like it. I feel like a crazy person, I only met her and her brothers yesterday and here I am accusing her of hiding something from me. Maybe I'm reading too much into what my mom said, she may have just heard some gossip from the people who stay at the motel. I give myself a mental pep talk and take a seat; I need to let this go and not act like a dick.

"Callie?" She snaps her gaze up from her tray to look at me. "I'm sorry I accused you of knowing my mom and being an ass."

"Don't sweat it, I really don't know how your mom knows me or my brothers." After clearing the air, she and I fall into easy conversation. The rest of the day passes quickly, I get to know

Josh a bit better in chem. He is such a funny guy and easy to talk to. Since being here I have made three friends in my first two days which is an achievement for me. When the final bell of the day rings, Cole and I exit our class and he walks me to my locker. Cole has football practice today and told me he is the quarterback, no surprise there.

We head out the front to meet his sister after leaving my locker, we come to a stop when we see Kayla and a few others facing off against Callie. A feeling of protectiveness washes over me. I'm shocked. I have never felt the need to defend or protect anyone aside from my mom before. When Kayla shoves Callie something inside me snaps, I don't hesitate. I march over to them and insert myself in front of Callie and scowl at the Queen Bee. Kayla's face changes from anger to glee when she meets my heated stare.

"You just can't stay away, can you?"

"Don't you dare lay your hands on my friend like that again." Kayla and the four girls with her begin to cackle like hyenas which just pisses me off more.

"Stay out of my way, you bottom feeding slut, or I'll make you!" The venom and hatred in her tone doesn't deter me.

"If I'm a slut, then you must be the fricken brothel! My god aren't you tired?" By now we have gathered quite the crowd, I ignore all the stares from other students and focus on Kayla, I can feel Cole and Callie standing close behind me which gives me a small amount of comfort.

"Tired of what?" She snaps, I cock my brow and place a hand on my hip.

"Having that stick so far up your ass?" I don't see it coming, I don't even have time to react. It's like she moved at lightning speed or something. One minute I'm standing there staring at her thinking I just won this verbal war and the next minute her fist is in my face and I'm falling backward.

CHAPTER FOUR
Jessica

I wake to the sound of raised voices.

"This is all your kid's fault!"

"Calm the hell down, Katharine. This was a random incident."

"I never should have brought her here! I've just put my daughter in more danger than ever before." I blink my eyes open and look around to see I'm in my room. How the heck did I get here?

"She needs to be with us, you know this." I have no idea who the man is that my mom is arguing with. Whoever he is it sounds like he and my mom know each other---well.

"Get your pack under control, or I'll take her and run." I hear a growl sound outside my room and gasp, I hear footsteps and then my bedroom door swings open to reveal my mom standing in the doorway with a worried look on her face. "Jess!" She breathes my name like a prayer, she rushes over to me and drops down on to the side of the bed. She pulls me up then wraps me in a bone crushing hug, I return her embrace.

"Mom?"

"Hmmm?"

"Who the hell is the guy standing in my doorway?" She pulls out of my embrace and looks me in the eyes. Her face is an emotionless mask, a feeling of dread begins to pool inside my belly. My gaze goes back to the man when he clears his throat, he's a large man who looks like he takes care of himself. Shaggy brown hair, brown eyes, and a sweet smile. This man looks innocent and plain, but I have a niggly feeling that the nice look is all fake.

"My name is Jacob Michelson." Rigghhhht, because that's

supposed to mean something to me? I turn back to my mom to see she is torn; I implore her with a look of mine to not lie. Minutes tick by as we sit there staring at each other in silence. "Why don't I make some coffee and we can chat in the lounge room?"

"Thank you, Jacob, we will join you in a moment." As soon as he is out of sight, I start asking questions, but she places a finger against my lips to hush me. "Please just know, everything I have done Jess is because I love you." I reel back shocked.

"I know you love me, I love you too, but who is that man?" She sighs loudly then drops her gaze to her lap.

"Your father's old...friend." She whispers.

After mom dropped that bomb, she made some excuse about going to help Jacob, while I head to the bathroom to check out the damage. Perfect word to describe my face, I have a huge black bruise surrounding my cheek and eye, Bimbo bitch packs quite the hit, I'll give her that. Years of defense training with my mother has taught me how to block out the pain and focus on something else, no doubt if I didn't have this training it would hurt like a bitch.

"Jess, can you come out here please?" I splash some water on my face and quickly tie my hair in a messy bun atop my head. I take a few deep breaths then exit the bathroom.

I enter the loungeroom to find my mom and Jacob on the sofa, so I choose to pull one of the dining chairs over and sit on that rather than stand.

"It's nice to finally meet you Jess." Jacob says after a moment, I dart my gaze to my mom to see her twiddling her hands in her lap.

"I wish I could say the same, but I only just found out about you." Jacob doesn't falter, he smiles kindly and nods his head in understanding.

"Well, nevertheless I'm glad your mother finally brought you home." Huh?

"Home?" Her gaze finally meets mine; unshed tears cloud her eyes.

"You were born here Jess." If I was standing, I would have fallen on my ass.

"Say what now?" I grit out.

"Kitten--"

"Don't you dare kitten me right now mom." She drops her gaze to her lap.

"Maybe if I could explain?" I turn and glare at Jacob.

"No offense but I want to hear this from her not you." If I offended him, he doesn't show it.

"I'm so sorry, as time went on it got harder and harder to tell you the truth and come clean." I stiffen in my seat. "You were born here."

"I know there is more to this story, so please put me out of my misery. You told me you didn't know my dad and now all of sudden his friend is sitting on our couch." She flinches and Jacob just smiles kindly which rubs me the wrong way.

"Your father was--"

"I said I want to hear this from her!" I snap, my mom narrows her eyes at me, but she does not get to be mad right now when I have just found out that she has lied to me my whole life.

"Pull your head in Jess! Jacob is not to blame here."

"Then who is mom? You?" I'm vibrating with rage; I feel like an absolute fool.

"We did it to protect you!"

"We?" I grit out, she sighs and then looks to Jacob who gives her a reassuring nod.

"Your father was an incredible man Kitten, kind, loving and above all he adored you. He was the...boss of a lot of people which put a target on his back. To make matters worse he had a daughter, someone that could be used against him."

"What the hell. You made him out to be a deadbeat who didn't want anything to do with me!" How freaking dare she?

"I had to so you wouldn't go looking for him."

"Why?"

"Because your father was murdered, and I was afraid his killer would come after you!" I sit there stunned and silent. My father was murdered, he loved me. He didn't abandon me, he wanted me. So many thoughts are swirling through my head, I feel like I might explode. I always wondered about my dad and who he was, my mom has told me since I was little, I look like him. She would say 'you have his blue eyes' or 'you get your blonde hair from your father'.

"Your mother did what she thought was best for you." I cast my gaze to Jacob and glower at him, he really needs to stay silent right now.

"With all due respect Jacob, I don't really care what you think." I turn to look at my mom. "I honestly don't know what to say to you right now. You lied to me and turned my dad into something horrible in my mind and now you want me to think of him differently?" I rise to my feet; she does the same, so I cut her a look that tells her to leave me the hell alone and head to my room. I slam my door shut and head to my dresser mirror and look at myself, like really look. I have sky blue eyes; long blonde hair and I have curves. I'm proud of my curves and wear them with pride, I'm definitely not a stick figure.

Do I look like him?

Do I have family here, aunts and uncles?

I turn away from the mirror and flop down on my bed. I have never been able to look in the mirror for too long because I always felt disgusted that I look like my dad. Now, I don't know whether I should be proud or saddened by the fact that I have always hated what I look like. Guilt is eating at me for all the horrible thoughts I have had over the years about my father, he was murdered. He didn't choose to leave me; he was taken from me.

Lying here staring up at the ceiling I make a vow, I will find out everything I can about my dad. I'll find who took him from me and make sure justice is served, whoever is at fault with this won't get away with it.

CHAPTER FIVE
Jessica

The next morning, I get up and feel like crap. I didn't get much sleep last night. No matter how hard I tried I couldn't get my mind to shut off, I feel so betrayed. My mom is the only family I have and my only constant friend, she betrayed my trust and broke the bond we have built. She is my world, my rock, my everything, and all because of some stupid fight at school my life has changed forever. The one bonus is with what happened last night, I haven't had a chance to process what went down yesterday with Kayla. How did I even get home? I brush those thoughts away, have a quick shower, and change. One look in the mirror and I'm not shocked to see the bruise has faded to a dull yellow. According to my mom I'm super lucky because I can heal fast, I broke my arm as a kid and the bone healed within a couple of days. Doctors have never been able to explain why this is, mom said she took me too many different doctors as a kid and none of them could explain it.

I apply some makeup to cover the yellow bruise, I don't need people whispering about me more than they probably already are. I wish I wasn't embarrassed that my ass got handed to me but that would be a lie. I'm not used to being the one to get laid out, I don't like fighting, but I have had my fair share of them throughout the years and always came out the victor, but not yesterday. I finish my makeup and quickly tie my hair into a high ponytail. With one final look at my reflection, I deem myself ready for the day. I head to the kitchen to get some breakfast before heading to school, but as soon as I round the corner and see my mom in the there, I opt to skip eating and go straight to school. I grab my backpack and head for the door, but her voice stops me.

"Can we talk?" I stiffen but don't turn around and face her, I can't.

"I have nothing to say to you right now."

"Jess, we need to talk about this. There is so much more you don't know." I wheel around and glare at my mom, she at least has the decency to look sheepish.

"And whose fault is that mom? You kept me in the dark all these years, you lied to me! You betrayed my trust; you could have come clean years ago, but you didn't. Give me some credit here, it wasn't hard for you to tell the truth, it was just easier for you to keep living a lie." I quickly rush out the door and ignore her calling me back. I run as fast as my legs will carry me and don't stop until I see the front of the school. I'm a panting mess but right now I just don't give a flying hoot. I feel so many pairs of eyes on me but ignore them and quickly make my way inside to my locker. I'm shocked to see Josh leaning against it. When he sees me, he stands up straight and scans me from head to toe for injury, not that he will see any thanks to the makeup I'm wearing.

"Hey, I didn't think you would be in today." I shrug my shoulders and open my locker. "What my sister did wasn't--"I wheel around so fast I nearly lose my footing, and I would have if Josh didn't reach out and grip my arm.

"Kayla is your sister?" He reaches around and rubs the back of his neck; his face is contorted almost like it pains him to admit who Kayla is to him.

"Uh, yeah." Well, this day is proving to be eventful already, isn't it?

"Great, just...great." I mutter as I slam my locker shut and stomp the whole way to first period. I'm not shocked to see Callie standing outside the classroom. When her eyes land on me they fill with concern and worry. She rushes over and wraps her arms around me and pulls me in for a hug. I snap out of it after a second and return her embrace, even though I'm not sure why we are even hugging. She pulls back and holds me at arm's length and runs her gaze all over me.

"Thank god, I was worried Kayla the bitch tit had done some serious damage." Oh, she was hugging me because of yesterday, now it all makes sense.

"I'm okay, are you okay?" Callie scrunches her face in confusion.

"Seriously, you're asking me if I'm okay? You're the one who got knocked out, not me, thank you by the way. I'm not used to people...sticking up for me." She sounded so baffled at the fact that someone would want to defend her, it was weird.

"Don't sweat it, I honestly don't know what happened. I didn't even see her fist till it was too late." Her face becomes a mask of anger.

"We don't treat pac---people like that where I come from, Kayla is a disgusting vile bitch who needs to be put down." I'm slightly taken back by the tone of her voice; she isn't kidding she really wants to hurt Kayla. Next time though, I'm staying the hell out of it. "Anyway, are we still on for Friday?" I cringe, I doubt my mom is gonna let me go out if we don't sort things between us but I'm not ready. So, I hatch a plan. I'm gonna stay at Callie's house on Friday and we'll go to the party from there. I didn't relish in the idea of lying to my mother but at the end of the day she lied to me for years. I have always been honest with her, and she couldn't give me the same courtesy.

The day passes by so fast; my teachers have given me all the stuff I need to catch up on which blows my freaking mind. This shit is going to take me ages to get through! I'm at my locker getting the books I'll need for my homework when I feel a presence behind me. I spin around and come face to face with a guilty looking Josh. I release a long sigh, I avoided him today in chem. Which I know I can't do forever because starting next week we will be partners, but I feel like him hiding the fact that he's related to that mole is not okay. Okay, maybe he didn't hide it but still, his sister hit me!

"I'm sorry I didn't tell you about my sister, but I didn't think I needed to." I deflate, he's right and it's wrong of me to take this out on him.

"You're right, I'm sorry I shouldn't have ignored you today. I just don't need more trouble from her." Josh moves a step closer which makes me slightly uncomfortable. He reaches out and tucks a stray hair behind my ear, I stiffen at the contact. I try to step back but he follows suit, I'm starting to worry that Josh has the wrong idea here. I don't even know him, and he doesn't even know me. The fact that he just touched me so intimately and has invaded my personal space doesn't sit right with me. "Josh, can you take a step back, please?" His mouth kicks up into what I'm sure is supposed to be a sexy smirk.

"Come on Jess, live a little." He places his hands either side of my head, caging me in. I'm pressed so hard against the lockers I'm sure I'll have an imprint of them on my back. Josh leans his head down and I snap my arm out to push against his chest, but it doesn't deter him.

"Josh stop!" He leans even closer, I lift my knee ready to slam it into his balls when he is suddenly ripped away from me, I gape at the strong muscular back now standing in front of me.

"You just royally fucked up Reeves."

"Touch her against her will again and next time I won't stop to chat." Not wanting to cause another scene I reach down and grab my bag off the floor and grip Creed's arm. He won't take his eyes off Josh, so I tug on his arm a couple of times until he finally looks down at me. He stands there with nothing but rage shining in his eyes, a moment passes before he sighs, grips my hand, and drags me out of the building and doesn't stop until we are standing beside a huge pickup truck. I stand there staring up at him but remain silent, his gaze is locked on mine but the way he is looking at me is different. It's like he's not seeing me as a person, he's looking at me like he wants to devour me. That thought alone sends a shiver down my spine. Creed's nostrils flare and then he drops my hand like it's on fire.

"Bro, Josh just declared war on the pack because of that stunt. Dad is goi--"Cole stops speaking as soon as he rounds the side of the pickup and sees me and Creed standing there staring at each other. "Oh, um, hey Jess." I hate to admit it, but it took more strength than I'm willing to admit to tear my gaze from Creeds. Cole's cheeks are slightly red like he just ran here, his gaze keeps darting between me and his brother. Cole moves to take a step toward me but stops when Creed spins around and blocks Cole's path to me.

"Don't." is all Creed says, that one word holds so much

power behind it and I don't know why.

"Jess." I turn to see Callie jogging toward us, she completely ignores her brothers and wraps me in another hug. "What the hell is it with you and the Michelson's?" I know she's joking but I stiffen in her embrace which has her pulling back and looking at me with concern.

"Wait, Michelson's?" Callie looks to her brothers and then back to me.

"Yeah?"

"I don't suppose their father is Jacob Michelson by any chance?" The tension ramps up between the four of us, one minute I'm facing Callie then the next thing I know my back is against the truck and Creed is looming over me. My anger soars. "Seriously? Did you not just throw a guy back not five minutes ago for having me in the exact same position?" I snap, Creed smiles smugly.

"Difference is, you want to be in this position with me, not him." My mouth drops open in shock.

"You have a huge ego, don't you?" I push against his chest, but he won't budge. I lift my knee ready to knee him in the balls, but he must anticipate the move because he drops his hand down to stop my leg. Heat surges through me where his hand touches, I gasp, and Creed's eyes widen before he yanks his hand away and steps back. I stand there stunned until Callie steps in front of me, I shake my head to snap myself out of it.

"How do you know Jacob?" Her tone has me on edge, I can hear bitterness as she says his name.

"I don't know him per se I just met him last night."

"Where?" I turn to Cole and cock a brow, what the hell is this, twenty questions?

"Jess, Jacob isn't a good guy." I sigh and smile politely at Callie; I don't want to keep talking about this.

"Okay, I'll take your word for it then. I'm beat and have a lot of work to catch up on so I'm gonna head home."

"We'll give you a ride." I thank Cole but decline his offer, I'd rather walk to clear my head.

"Stay out of the woods, it's not safe." I eye Creed up and down and give the confident jerk a two-finger salute as I turn and walk away.

CHAPTER SIX
Jessica

The rest of the week goes by quickly and without any more incidents. I found out Kayla was suspended for the fight but will be back on Monday, yay...not. Josh has kept his distance and has tried to apologize so many times for the misunderstanding. I told him I would forget about it if he just left me alone which he has, thankfully. Mom and I are still not speaking, I left her a note on the bench this morning that I would be staying at a friend's place. She's texted me a couple of times to ask what friend and where, but I ignored her messages. I told myself that I would talk to her on Sunday and clear the air, I just need more time to try and process this.

Callie, Cole, and I have gotten to know each other better and they are really kind decent people. I see Creed in class and in the hallways, but we haven't spoken since the other day. I can feel his eyes on me whenever we're whenever we are near or when he passes me, but I choose to ignore it.

The last thing I need right now is to fall for a guy and get distracted, I have too much on my plate as it is. Plus, when a guy who looks as good as Creed gives you some attention there is almost always an ulterior motive or something for them involved. My phone vibrating in my pocket pulls me from my thoughts, another text from my mom.

Mom: Jess, I'm not kidding. Where are you staying?

I may be mad at her, but I also don't want her up all night worrying about me, so I reply.

Me: At Callie's!

She tries to call but I ignore it and tap out another text.

Me: in last period can't answer!

Mom: YOU ARE NOT STAYING THERE!

Mom: Come home after school.

Mom: I mean it Jess.

Me: Why do you hate them?

Mom: They are not good people; I will tell you everything when you get home...Today!

Yeah, no. I know what she is trying to do, and it isn't going to work.

Me: That's funny they said the same thing about your friend Jacob. You also failed to mention that Jacob's daughter is the one who hit me!

I turn my phone off after I click send. I will not let her bait me with information that she should have told me about a long time ago.

After the final bell I follow Callie out the front of the school and head toward the black pickup Creed had me pinned against the other day. I hate to say it, but I kept replaying that moment over and over again in my head the past couple of nights. I know it was just a hand on my leg, but it sent heat rippling through my body. I'm no sex expert or anything like that but if it felt that great to just have a hand on me then what would kissing Creed feel like? Yes, I have been thinking about kissing Creed since that moment as well. I have never dreamed about a guy let alone thought about doing things with him!

"Hello?" I shake my head and turn and smile at Callie who narrows her eyes playfully. "What's got you so distracted?" I can't fight the blush that heats my cheeks, I'm so not going to tell her I was just thinking about her brother, so I go with something else.

"My mom and I are fighting, and we have never fought like this before." Callie's eyes soften, once we reach the pickup she stops and turns to face me.

"If there is anything I can do let me know. I want to be a good friend Jess; I don't know how to be a friend if I'm honest." I furrow my brow in confusion.

"What do you mean?" She drops her gaze and then begins to shuffle from foot to foot.

"My...dad is kind of a big deal, so people use me to get to him. Needless to say, my dad being the...boss has made making friends hard for me. My brothers don't have that problem though, they are both popular as I'm sure you have gathered." Yeah, I have, Creed and Cole constantly have guys and girls all over them throughout the day, the guys look at them like they want to be them, and girls look at them like they are their ticket to life. It's weird but I guess it's how they do things in this town. I reach out and clasp Callie's hand in mine and smile at her.

"I have no idea who your dad is so rest assured, I just want to be your friend because I think you're great." Callie's face breaks out into a huge grin from ear to ear, she squeals and wraps me in a hug which causes us both to break out into laughter.

"Well don't you both look cozy." Callie and I break apart and turn to face Josh and two of his friends. The guys standing either side of him have sinister looks on their faces. The looks send a cold shiver down my spine. I look to Josh to see him locked in a glaring match with Callie.

"I think you might be lost Michelson." Josh's mouth lifts into a nasty smirk which has me stumped. I have never seen him look so...scary. He comes off as such a nice guy, you know like boy next door kind of vibe.

"You seem to forget who belongs to whom, Reeves." What the hell are they talking about?

"We forget nothing, now back the fuck away from her." My gaze snaps to the side, Creed, Cole and a couple of other hulking guys either side of them walking toward us.

"Which her? Your sister or Jess?" Josh sounds like a cocky dick right now and I don't like it. I'm starting to get a bad feeling about him.

"Both." Creed's words hold so much weight and power. I even want to obey what he's saying.

"Get out of here Josh, we don't need to hash this out in the open." Cole says. Josh, Creed and Cole flick their gazes to me and then back to each other. Josh nods at the guys and then turns to face me.

"I'll see you tonight, Jess." I don't know what to say to him, so I just nod my head and watch as he and his friends walk away. I stand there watching their backs for a few more seconds before I turn and face the others. The triplets and the other guys I have seen around stand there just staring at each other like they're having a silent conversation. I wait a few minutes and watch as their facial features constantly change, and they gesture with their hands but still no words come out of their mouths. Tired of standing here like an outsider I clear my throat; all eyes turn to me.

"Planning on meeting up with your boyfriend at Toby's?" I reel back shocked at the disgust in Creed's voice. I refuse to let his tone and the angry look on his face make me squirm, I square my shoulders and meet his gaze.

"I don't need to explain what I do or who I see to you, thank you very much." Creed breaks away from the guys and stalks toward me. I refuse to listen to the voice in my head telling me to run. The way he moves is like a predator stalking his prey. I hold his gaze as he stands directly in front of me with only a sliver of space left between us. I breath in and I'm immediately assaulted by his alluring scent, he smells like soap, honey and...home. What the hell? The small voice inside my head is now screaming at me to claim him. I know people say their subconscious tells them to do crazy things, but I have never had that issue--until now.

"You will learn that everything you do or who you see, I have a say in." I stare up at him in shock, who the hell does he think he is?

"Well until hell freezes over that will never happen. Get down off your high horse and pull your head out of your--"

"Eggplant?" I narrow my eyes at the dick, he smiles widely and my word. Seeing Creed angry is hot but seeing him smile is something else. I fight the urge to crumble and melt on the spot at the way he is looking at me, I latch on to my anger and ignore the blush I know is coating my cheeks.

"I said eggplant one time! One bloody time, let it go man." I can see he is trying hard not to laugh which just angers me further, I hear Cole and the others coughing trying to mask their laughter. I drop my gaze and deflate; I am such a loser. Creed's hand grips my chin and lifts my head until I meet his gaze, all forms of humor is wiped from his face.

"Don't look down, don't let what others say or think make you feel less. If only you knew how truly special you are." I stand there utterly stunned staring at him, as what he just said registers his forehead creases and he drops his hand then turns away from me.

The ride to the triplet's house passes in a blur, the tension in the truck is suffocating. Callie and I sit in the back seat and remain silent, Creed and Cole are both tense and quiet in the front. No one has said a word the whole ride. When we pull into a long drive that has trees lining either side, my face is squished against the window staring out in wonder, the driveway is freaking long. When we finally break away from the trees, I gasp. Spread out everywhere are cabins --like the one I live in. These cabins look new and cared for, but there are so many of them scattered around here, people are walking around, children run freely through the grass laughing. I'm stunned to see a couple of girls from my gym class standing near one of the cabins. Creed keeps driving past all the people and the cabins. We drive for another couple of minutes and when Creed stops the truck, my mouth drops open. If this is their house, I'm making their parents adopt me!

It's a newer style cabin but...it's all black. The roof, the wood, the porch railings, and the stairs! It's so beautiful, I open my door and jump out of the truck and stare open mouthed at my dream home. I have always wanted to live in a house that is black themed.

"Close your mouth babe or a bug will fly in." I snap my mouth closed and turn to playfully glare at Cole, Creed shoulder checks his brother on his way to the house.

"Come on, I'll introduce you to mom and dad." I grab my bag and follow Callie and Cole inside.

Oh. My. God!

It's like someone went inside my head and found the design of my dream home and built it. High ceilings with black pillars, black carpet lines the entryway, the further you move inside everything is different shades of black, when we enter the lounge room I stop and spin around in a circle, all the furniture is black, the massive faux fur rug is black.

"Your house is freaking...bonkers!" Callie and Cole chuckle.

"Here I was thinking my house was dull and dark." I spin around so fast I nearly slip until Cole reaches out to steady me, I smile up at him gratefully and I'm about to thank him when I hear a low growl. I snap my gaze around the room but can't see any dogs, I'm losing my mind I swear! I keep randomly hearing growls since I moved here. "She's very pretty." I snap my gaze to the doorway and see Creed and a stunning woman standing there. The woman is beautiful, her hair is cut short into a bob style haircut, she has a soft welcoming smile on her face, her brown eyes hold nothing but warmth and love in them. She looks way too young to be a mom! She even dresses amazing; she's wearing a pure white lady suit and by God does she rock it.

"Mom, meet Jess. Jess this is our mom, Meg." I smile politely and wave like an idiot, Meg saves me from further embarrassment by waving back and winking. "Jess is coming with us to Toby's tonight." Callie announces to Meg.

"I thought Toby's get together was tomorrow night?" Callie rolls her eyes at her mom before answering.

"No mom, I told you the other day he changed it because of the full moo--"

"Because we have practice tomorrow afternoon." Cole cuts in, I look at the pair of them, they're acting weird. Meg doesn't miss a beat.

"Okay, we'll be safe and don't engage any of the--others Credence, I mean it. Colton, make sure you watch over your brother and keep him calm. California, I expect you to keep both of them in line and return home safely, your father and I will be out for the night and back in the morning." Holy cow, these three have freaking cool as hell names!

CHAPTER SEVEN
Jessica

After Meg left, Callie showed me around their huge as crap house, her room is massive! Her room is the same as the rest of the house, black. Callie has brightened her room up by decorating it with a white rug, white bedding, curtains and colorful pictures on her walls. We have been chilling out and talking, getting to know each other better. I was shocked to learn that Callie and her brothers are already eighteen, she declared that it is a must that she throws me a party for my birthday. I tried to talk her out of it, but she wasn't listening. I'm starting to realize that Callie loves to plan and decorate things so throwing me a party is right in her element. I hate to admit it, but I don't want a party because I have no one to invite, my only friends are Callie and Cole. I wouldn't exactly count Creed as a friend, he's more of an...associate.

"Right, you go take a shower and I'll lay out some outfits for you to try on." I do as I'm told and follow her directions to the bathroom down the hall. I open the door and stop dead in my tracks, I quickly snap my eyes closed and turn around to leave but then smack into something hard.

"Shit!" I pull back and rub my forehead, the deep chuckle behind me has me turning around again. Creed stands there in nothing, but a towel wrapped around his waist, holy lord above. Credence Reeves has a body that could only be described as a work of art, he has abs and holy shit he even has the V, you know the V I'm talking about. He clears his throat which has my gaze snapping back to his, I feel the blush creeping into my heated cheeks. Creed crooks a brow at me, his hair is wet and sticking to his forehead, I have the strange urge to run my fingers through it.

"You do curse." I snap myself out of my lustful thoughts and try to gauge his meaning.

"Huh?"

"You said shit."

"Oh, um, yeah." He moves toward me and reaches up to run his thumb over my forehead where I just banged it on the wall. His touch soothes the ache but, in its place, I start to feel hot, just like when he touched my leg. Our eyes meet and something inside me opens, I don't know how else I can explain it, but I feel like a piece of me has been returned or restored. "What's happening?" I whisper, Creed slams his eyes shut and takes a deep breath then opens them again, I stifle a gasp. His eyes! They are no longer hazel, they're blue. I blink rapidly a few times to make sure I'm not dreaming, and sure enough his eyes are still blue!

"You're starting to learn you're more than what you were made to believe, so much more."

After Creed dropped that cryptic as hell line, he left. I chose to file what the hell just happened in my I'll deal with you later box. When I get home, I will unpack that box and try to decipher the meaning of what just transpired between us.

"I love that outfit on you, now get over here so I can do your hair and makeup." I look down at the outfit I let Callie dress me in, and honestly this is an outfit I would never choose for myself. I'm more of a jeans and shirt kind of girl not jean cut offs and a strappy barely-there crop top. I feel so exposed, I have so much skin on display and the world really doesn't need to see all of this. "Stop bloody fidgeting with that top, you look hot babe." I try to let her words give me some confidence that I don't feel.

"Holy shit on toast!" Callie burst out into fits of laughter behind me, I can't stop looking at myself in the mirror. I may have complained and moaned for sitting here for the past hour while Callie plucked and poked my face and pulled and ripped my hair but my god the end result is astounding. I have never thought of myself as attractive let alone beautiful but looking at myself now I'm stunned. I look...beautiful. Tears begin to build; I have never felt like this before when I've looked in the mirror. Callie has given me a smoky-eye look which enhances my blue eyes more and applied a nude lipstick, my hair is straightened and hangs down my back.

"Don't you dare cry, that mascara is not waterproof!' Callie abolishes me light-heartedly. I jump to my feet and wrap her in a hug.

"Thank you, Callie." We break apart and she smiles lovingly at me.

"For what babe?"

"For being my first real friend and for making me look...beautiful." I whisper the last part; Callie's eyes fill with pity.

"Jess, all I did was enhance your natural beauty. You, my friend, are beautiful without all of this makeup, you just need to believe it." I blink a few times to try to clear the tears from my eyes and give Callie a quick hug again. I perch up on her bed while she finishes getting ready, we chat some more, and I tell her about my life and where mom and I have lived.

A knock sounds at the door a while later.

"We're leaving in five."

"Okay, I'm nearly done." Callie shouts back to Cole. Suddenly, nerves course through my body, this is my first ever high school party and I'm scantily dressed. What if people laugh and mock me? Who am I kidding? I never should have agreed to this party.

"Callie, I can't go. I've never...I don't think...look at me." I whisper.

"You look beautiful Jess, what's the problem?"

"I've never looked like this or worn anything like this before in my life, what if they all laugh?" Callie scoffs and makes her way over to me, she looks stunning. She is also wearing a pair of cut offs and if you thought my top was revealing, it has nothing on hers. Her top is literally like a rope criss crossed over her chest and barely conceals her girls. We're both wearing chucks, I put my foot down when she suggested heels. I never expected her to dress like this when I first met her on Monday, she's definitely surprised me.

"If anyone laughs or says anything to you, I'll punch the fucker in the nose." I snort laugh which causes Callie to giggle. I take a few deep breaths and close my eyes. Tonight, I'm going to embrace this and enjoy this new me. Since moving here, I have felt a strength inside me I didn't know existed, I feel more comfortable in my skin and why shouldn't I wear an outfit that makes me feel...sexy?

Callie and I make our way toward the living room. As soon as she walks through the door, I hear the guy's groan, clearly, they don't approve of her outfit. I take a deep breath and then follow her through a moment later. Both the guys stand there staring at me, I look to Cole who smiles wide and whistles at me which causes me to blush.

"Fucking hell, Jess. Wow." I bite my bottom lip to stop myself from smiling, I look at Creed and the look in his eyes confuses me. He runs his gaze down my body and when he finally reaches my eyes again, heat fills his gaze. That one look from him has my body heat skyrocketing, my confidence begins to grow the longer he stares at me. A sensation inside of me is urging me to go to him and wrap myself around him. As if my body has a mind of its own, my feet carry me to him on their own accord. I stop when there is a smidge of space left between us and stare up into his once again hazel eyes. What the hell is going on, I have never behaved like this toward anyone let alone someone I have only known for a few days. I just feel this unexplainable pull toward him like I'm on a string and he's constantly pulling on it.

"I...I--what's happening?" Creed's gaze flicks to Cole then a moment later his eyes are back on me, and the look of lust is gone and is replaced by sadness.

"Nothing, you don't belong here." My eyes widen in shock, Creed brushes past me and leaves. I spin around to face Callie; her face is a mask of irritation, not toward me but toward Creed.

"My brother is an idiot Jess, ignore him." I just nod my head, unable to speak. I appreciate Cole trying to comfort me, but it doesn't lessen my embarrassment.

CHAPTER EIGHT
Jessica

Once again, the car ride is silent all the way to Toby's, the tension is suffocating, and I can't help but fidget the whole way there. As soon as Creed slams the truck in park, he leaps out like it's on fire and storms into the party. People are all over the place, some are even passed out on the lawn, the music is blaring so loud I can hear it from out here.

"I'll keep an eye on him, any trouble you know the drill." Cole says as he gets out and follows Creed into the crowd of people. I turn to Callie who reaches over and places her hand atop mine.

"Let's get in there and have some fun, maybe after a beer or two you might loosen up and even dance with me." We both laugh and get out of the truck. I take a steadying breath and wait for Callie to come around to my side. I look at all the people milling about on the lawn and wait for them to point and stare, but none of them seem to notice us or even care, which makes me feel more at ease. Callie and I make our way toward the house, we have to push through a group of guys to get through the door, once inside the music is ten times louder. There are people dancing and some guy doing a handstand on a keg while his buddy's watch. Callie interlocks her fingers through mine and leads me through the throng of partygoers toward the kitchen, we each grab a red solo cup and fill them from the keg in the corner. We head outside to the backyard and I'm shocked to see even more people out here, guys and girls are in the infinity shaped pool swimming, half of them are only in their underwear. I follow Callie across the yard to a group, seen a few of them around school but have not yet spoken to them.

"Guys, this is Jess, Jess this is Tommy, Chris, Asher, Selena,

Carmi and Chloe." I smile and wave at the group, Callie dives right into chatting with them while I spin around and take in my surroundings and sip my beer. I've never been drunk before, mom has only allowed me to try some wine and a few beers, but nothing extreme. My eyes land on a familiar face and I smirk, Cole stands at the end of the pool surrounded by a group of girls. He looks like he's in his element, all the girls are vying for an ounce of his attention. Let's be real, Cole is hot and easy on the eyes, but his carefree down to earth personality is what makes him even more beautiful. I pull my gaze from him and look around when I spot another familiar face, leaning against the fence with his arms crossed over his chest and a few guys standing around him is none other than Creed, he looks like a bad boy. Dark jeans, black shirt and chucks, his hair is a hot mess, but he suits it. Even standing in a dark corner he oozes confidence and...power. One of the guys must have said something funny because he smiles, and that smile is so disarming. I don't know him and yet I have this feeling inside me like I know everything about him, whenever he is near, I want to go to him. I lose my train of thought when I see Kayla and her two minions approach them. Creed narrows his eyes when she places a hand on his chest, but he doesn't push her away. It angers me to see her hands on him, but it pisses me off more that he won't push her away! Wait, am I...jealous? How the hell could I be jealous when I have just met him?

"Hey." I turn my head to the side to see one of the guy's Callie introduced me to standing next to me. He smiles invitingly. "I'm Tommy."

"Jess." He chuckles.

"I know." Oh yeah, duh Callie just introduced us.

"Sorry, blonde moment I guess."

"All good, how you liking Rosewood?"

"Uh, it's been good, I have a lot of schoolwork to catch up on though."

I'm on my...wait I don't know what number beer I'm on, but I'm feeling loose and buzzed. I've been sitting down on one of the outdoor chairs for the past couple of hours talking to Tommy, Asher and some of their friends, who are really cool. One of the girls I met, Ashley, is pretty amazing and is a diehard Twilight fan as well. We've been sitting here for the last twenty minutes trying to get Asher and Tommy to agree to watch the movies, but they won't budge.

"If the dude is a wolf, I have to choose his team!" I groan.

"No way, you have to watch the movies! Team Edward is the best Tommy." He rolls his eyes.

"Jess, vampires are not real babe." I cock my brow at him.

"And neither are wolves Tommy boy, it's all fiction." Tommy, Asher, and Ashley exchange a strange look, it looks like they're having another one of those weird silent conversations like the triplets did earlier. "Why do you all do that?" All eyes turn to me.

"Do what babe?" I give Ashley a dry stare.

"Exchange weird looks and then, have like a silent conversation with your eyes." Tommy and Asher tell me I'm seeing things but the fact that Ashley doesn't dispute my claim makes me think I may be right.

"Well, if Jess likes Edward, then so do I." We all turn and standing at the end of the table is none other than Josh and the two guys he was with this afternoon. He smiles at me and winks. "Told you I'd see you tonight Jess." I give him a small smile and nod my head; my mind is a bit fuzzy at the moment thanks to the alcohol I have consumed.

"What do you want Josh?" Josh looks down at Ashley like she is nothing but a nuisance.

"From you smashley, not a goddamn thing."

"Don't be an asshole, you know where we are." Josh waves off Asher's concerns and focuses back on me.

"Yeah, we're in human territory." Asher and Tommy growl, I snap my gaze to them in shock. They just fucking growled! Instead of running or demanding answers my drunk idiot self starts to laugh and point at them.

"You just growled like a dog and Josh said human." Uncontrollable laughter bursts out of me, I look around our group and find none of them are joining me, they all look at me like I'm some strange being. "What?"

"You want to know the truth about what we are and what you really are, come find me." The laughter dies in my throat at how serious Josh sounds.

"What do you mean?" Josh's eyes fill with sadness.

"You're not what you think you are Jess, none of us are." I

look to Asher, Tommy and Ashley and find them all glaring at Josh.

"What am I?"

"Nothing Jess, he's drunk." I ignore Tommy and keep my gaze on Josh, urging him with my eyes to answer me.

"You're a--"

"Shut your dirty fucking mouth now, Michelson." I snap my gaze to the side and see Creed, Cole and some guys storming over to us. Creed doesn't stop until him and Josh are chest to chest, glaring at each other. "I told you to stay away from her."

"I told you she is our pack, now back the fuck off Reeves." Huh, what the hell are they talking about and why are they saying pack? Plus, they do not get to talk about me like I'm an object. I stand on wobbly legs; Asher reaches out to steady me, but I bat his hand away.

"You both can kiss my ripe cherry; I am not an object to be fought over. What does pack mean? Oh Josh, you're not on team Jacob, are you?" Creed and Josh both turn to face me and both wear looks of confusion, until Josh's face breaks into a wide grin.

"Nah babe, I told you if you're team Edward, so am I." I clap my hands and smile widely.

"You're drunk." Creed snaps, I turn and smile at the grump of a man.

"And you're a mean eggplant." Everyone laughs except for Creed, Cole and the three guys standing beside them. Callie breaks the moment when she comes over and tugs on mine and Ashley's hands, so we'll follow her to the dance floor. We dance like there is no tomorrow, the strange conversation from outside is forgotten as I sway my hips to the beat and laugh with my friends. This has to be the best night of my life!

CHAPTER NINE
Jessica

That was the worst night of my life!

I woke this morning to a splitting headache and my mouth feels like it is full of cotton balls. I am never, ever drinking again. I don't even remember getting home or how I even got to bed. Callie assures me that if I have a shower and brush my teeth, I would feel alive, I do just that, and I admit I feel slightly better. She gives me some aspirin and a large bottle of water, apparently, I need to eat as it will help the hangover pass. After tying my hair up and checking my reflection in the mirror to make sure I look better than I feel, I follow her into the kitchen. Cole and Creed are sitting at the table already. Meg is bringing in dishes loaded with food. The aroma is making my mouth water, I drop into the seat beside Callie and avoid looking at the guys.

"Morning Jess." I meet Meg's gaze as she sits down.

"Good morning, thank you for allowing me to stay last night." Meg smiles brightly, she seems like such a nice woman.

"You are welcome here anytime sweetheart." We each load our plates full of food, and as we eat, we engage in conversation. It's nice to sit around a table and listen to stories about the triplets growing up, Cole and Callie laugh and join in on telling me about their childhood. Creed remains silent and doesn't even so much as break a smile.

"Creed got into so much trouble from dad when he stole Josh's clothes from the locker room--"Creed drops his knife and fork, and they clang loudly against his empty plate. He looks around the table at his family and then settles his cold hard stare on me.

"We shouldn't be discussing this shit with the enemy." I reel back shocked at the venom in his voice.

"Credence--"Meg tries to intervene, but Creed won't let her.

"No mom, she isn't with us." Creed's gaze meets mine and his eyes are filled with nothing but mistrust and anger. "She's against us, she's theirs!" I don't know whether it's the need to defend myself or the because of the accusation in his tone but I snap, I snap like I have never snapped before. I push back from the table and stand; Creed does the same.

"You have some freaking nerve! I am tired of everyone speaking in fucking riddles around me. I am no one's! I am not a freaking object to be spoken about or passed around, I don't know why you hate me or why you're treating me this way, I have done nothing to you or anyone!"

"You and your people never do anything wrong do you? It's always us that fuck shit up, I want to end whatever this is. You don't belong here!" I fight back the tears that want to fall, I will not allow Creed to see me break.

"My people? I have no idea what the hell you are talking about, I just moved here. You're right though Credence." His eyes widen at the use of me using his full name. "I don't belong here, I'm the poor kid whose mother is a maid, I won't ever forget my place again." I see the anger flee from his eyes but ignore him and face his mom who looks absolutely horrified at what just happened. "Thank you very much for having me in your home Meg, it was a pleasure to meet you." I look to Cole and Callie and find them both glaring daggers at their brother. "Callie, Cole, thank you both for your friendship. It was really nice, and I appreciate you both so much." I turn and leave, grabbing my bag that's sitting next to the front door, I sling it over my shoulder and walk out.

Once I hit the main road, I cave and called my mom to come and get me. I have no idea where I am to give her directions, when I told her I was at the triplet's house, she assures me not to worry and she will be here in twenty minutes. I didn't bother to question her about how she knew where they live. I'm too angry to care. I'm used to people not wanting to know me because I'm not rich or because my mom doesn't have a great job, but none of that has ever bothered me until now. Creed made me feel like I was trash, worthless, beneath him and that is not okay. I'm embarrassed that I swore in front of his mom, but I can't change that, what's done is done. I'm still trying hard not to cry, but when I see my mom's car approaching the first tear falls.

As soon as I'm inside the car she pulls me to her and wraps her arms around me as I sob, she doesn't say a word as she holds me and lets me get all my tears out. When I finally breakaway from her, she pats my cheek and smiles lovingly at me.

"Let's get home and you can tell me everything."

The ride home was quiet, I spent the whole time trying to process what just happened. Memories of last night and the strange things said start to come back to me.

You're not what you think you are Jess, none of us are.

I told you she is our pack, now back the fuck off Reeves.

Yeah, we're in human territory.

I can't stop playing those sentences over and over in my mind. What did Josh mean? Am I reading way too much into this and wanting to see and believe things that aren't even there? I know I love Twilight and God I wish Edward was real, but he isn't, it's all fake...right?

"Come on, I have a tub of ice cream with our name on it." I follow mom inside the cabin and drop down onto the couch, she returns with a tub of Ben and Jerry's double chocolate fudge and two spoons. No words are exchanged while we dig in and stuff our faces full of goodness.

"I'm sorry." I blurt out, mom grabs my hand in hers and squeezes.

"Don't be kitten, I should have been honest from the start."

"Why didn't you just tell me mom? I have hated a man who I've never known because of the things you have led me to believe." Regret and hurt fills her eyes.

"Your father was an amazing man, Jess and I loved him so very much. He was my best friend; you only get one happily ever after in life and he was mine." Tears leak from my mom's eyes; I had no idea she felt this way. "I was scared that whoever hurt your father would come after you, I couldn't risk it. So I ran, I never told a soul I just put you in the car and left." Tears trail down my cheeks for the man I never got to know, for my mom and the life she has lived so I could be safe. "There is so much more Jess, I want to tell you, but I can't." I pull my hand back and shake my head.

"Why not? I have known my whole life that you have kept things from me, I want to know why. Why did we come back here, if this is the place my father was killed and the very place you just said you ran from?" I can see it in her eyes she's about to close off and not say anymore. "Don't shut me out mom."

"I'm sorry Jess; it's too dangerous for you to know the truth. Things are different and not all is as they seem, I swear I will tell you, soon." I'm too exhausted for this crap, I stand and ignore her protest as I head to my room.

I stay in my room all weekend, even when mom goes to work Saturday night I don't come out. I spend the whole night looking out my window, I could hear wolves howling in the woods out back. Sunday passes in a blur. When Monday morning rolls around I got up earlier to sneak out, so I don't have to see her before I leave. The whole way to school I feel nothing but sadness inside me, Creed's words still hurt, mom not telling me the truth stings. I have always felt like I'm a pawn in a game of chess my whole life, and I'm done being played with by others. From now on, I'm going to do what I want, and consequences be damned. I'm sick of being the good girl with manners and always doing as I'm told; I think it's time I let my inner devil out to play.

CHAPTER TEN
Jessica

I walk through the doors of Rosewood high with my head held high, I keep repeating my mantra in my head.

Embrace it and live your truth.

I wave to some people I met Friday night and continue to my locker. I have almost caught up on my schoolwork. I spent Saturday and Sunday powering through it. I still have a few more papers I need to do, but I'm proud of myself for getting through what I did so quickly. After exchanging books, I close my locker and turn toward my first period class when I spot Callie, Cole and Creed walking through the doors. The old me from twenty minutes ago would have tucked tail and hid but not the new me, I will not allow Creed to make me feel ashamed. Just before they reach me, Josh appears in front of me.

"Morning Jess."

"Hey."

"Can I walk you to class?" A part of me wants to say no because I'm annoyed at how he behaved the other day, but the new Jess is all about taking risks.

"Okay." We make our way toward my class, Callie and Cole look toward me, but I don't acknowledge them. I thought they were my friends and after thinking it over all day Saturday I realized, neither of them once came to my defense when he was belittling me.

"How was the rest of your weekend?"

"Uh, good. I caught up on most of my work."

"I can help you if you like. You can come over and we'll work together." The new Jess is about taking risks, but she isn't stupid, after the stunt Josh pulled, I wasn't going anywhere alone with him.

"Thanks for the offer but I'm good. Like I said I'm nearly done now." The bell rings and I wave goodbye to Josh as I go in and take my seat. A minute later Callie walks in and when her eyes land on me I see some of the tension in her shoulders ease. She makes her way to me and claims the seat beside me. It begins to get awkward when neither of us says anything. Someone dropping into the seat on the other side of me draws our attention, I'm shocked as hell to see who it is.

"You're not in this class." I grit out. His eyes narrow to slits.

"Actually, I'm now in all your classes." What the...? I spin to Callie to see she is just as shocked as I am.

"What the hell are you doing Creed?"

"What has to be done little sister." I look between the two of them, both remain locked in a silent staring contest. One's set of eyes will narrow, the other one's forehead will crease, sighing I give up and focus my attention toward the front. The new Jess doesn't care about what she doesn't know. The whole lesson is filled with tension, not from me but from the siblings sitting either side of me. Creed would move and I'd make sure I was far enough away so there wasn't a chance of him touching me. I want to be as far away from Credence Reeves as I can, he has no idea how much his words hurt me. It wasn't even the words really; it was the way he looked at me and the way he said them that hurt. He meant each and every one of the cruel words he said. As soon as the bell rings I race out of the class like it's on fire, I'm not ready to talk to Callie yet. Honestly, I am hurt that she or Cole didn't stick up for me or even try to call. What I'm more worried about is do they think about me the same way Creed does.

I groan silently when I round the corner and see Kayla walking into my next class. I forgot her and the triplets are all in this class as well, great. I take a seat at the back of the class, Cole, Callie and Creed walk in just after I get my books out. Callie spots me and makes her way toward me with Cole following behind her. She drops into the seat beside me, and Cole is about to claim the other when Creed's words stop him.

"Don't brother."

"Seriously?"

"Yes, Seriously Cole, move." I can't take it. I turn and glare up at Creed, his gaze still locked onto Cole.

"Would you stop!" I whisper shout, I don't need the whole class to hear this. He tears his gaze from his brother to stare down at me. "After the way you spoke to me Saturday morning you have--"

"She was with you Friday night?" A shrill voice shouts, I turn to see Kayla standing from her seat in the middle row on the other side of the class. How the hell did she hear me?

"Mind your damn business Kayla!" Callie seethes back.

"When a whore is staying at my ma--boyfriends house I have a right to know!" I stare at her in shock, she just called me a whore! I rise from my chair slowly and make sure she can see the rage in my eyes.

"I'm not the one flogging a dead horse you brainless bimbo. Don't you ever call me a whore again!" A cruel smile stretches across her face, I can tell from the way her eyes light up that she is ready to spew some hurtful words my way.

"Keep running that mouth and next time I'll make sure you

don't get up. Creed won't be able to save you from me when that time comes!" Before I can process what she means about Creed saving me, I feel a body press against my back and stifle the gasp that wants to escape. I don't know how I know but I can just tell from the way my body wants to melt into him and how heat spreads through my body that its Creed pressing against me.

"Touch her and then you will see what I am really capable of." He doesn't raise his voice but the weight and power behind his unveiled threat is as strong as if he shouted those words. Kayla's face turns red with rage before she can volley back the teacher walks in, she glares at me, and I can tell from the look on her face she will not let this go. We take our seats. Cole moved down one so Creed could sit in the chair next to me, as soon as he moved back and took his body heat with him, I felt cold and...incomplete.

Callie and I head outside to our usual table. I'm shocked to see Asher, Tommy, Carmi and Ashley sitting there. Each of them smiles up at us, I return the gesture and sit between Asher and Tommy, Callie takes the seat opposite me. Her and I haven't spoken to each other, and I know I should give her a chance to explain, after the way she acted toward Creed today I can tell she and Cole don't think about me the way their brother does. Creed is confusing the hell out of me, one minute he hates me and thinks I'm worthless and then the next thing I know he is defending me.

"So, what did you think of your first Rosewood party?" Asher asks me, I grin wickedly at him.

"I had a blast, met a few cool people." Asher snorts and starts bouncing his eyebrows.

"You mean me right?" I chuckle.

"Of course, you're like the coolest guy I know."

"Hey! What about me." Everyone laughs at Tommy.

"And you too of course, I'll say you're the best guy in this school if you admit you're on team Edward?" Both the guy's groan and mutter stuff under their breath, the girls and I laugh. My laugh stops abruptly when I feel a presence behind me. I know who it is when Callie looks up and rolls her eyes.

"Who the hell is Edward?" I ignore the irritation in his voice and choose to stuff a grape in my mouth instead of answering him.

"It's just a mov--"

"I didn't ask you Tommy." The fact that he just spoke down to Tommy annoys the hell out of me. I won't let him bully me or my friends.

"Edward is hot as fuck," everyone gasps, yeah, I know it feels weird to curse so freely but hey, new Jess and all that. "And not an ass, so trust me the two of you would have nothing in common." My bravado flies right out the window the moment he leans down, and I feel his full lips against the shell of my ear, I fight the shiver that wants to run through me.

"Edward sounds like a little bitch, stop saying fuck." I gulp.

"Why?" I'm so damn proud of myself because my voice doesn't waver.

"Because it doesn't suit you. You're not like the rest of the girls here, so stop trying to be." My eyes double in size, stuff this, I stand and turn around to face him.

"Why Creed, because their mothers aren't maids?" His brows furrow in confusion.

"That's not--"I cut him off.

"I don't want to hear what you have to say. I think you made your point on Saturday, so if you don't mind my friends and I were having fun until you showed up." I don't wait for his reply, I turn around and give him my back. Everyone at the table is staring at me with their mouths agape. "What?"

"Girl if you were on the market, I would be howling up your tree." I look at Callie in question while the others laugh. What the hell does Callie mean?

The rest of the day passes by quickly, I ignore Creed in every class. He even sat next to me in chem and glared at Josh the whole time. Josh ignored the brooding male beside me. Creed was annoyed to learn that Josh and I were partners, and he wouldn't be able to work with us, I'll admit seeing the angry look on his face when the teacher told him filled me with satisfaction.

The walk home was refreshing, and it was the first time I felt like I could breathe freely. Whenever Creed is near me, I'm constantly fighting my body's urge to go to him or touch him in some way. I'm so annoyed at myself because of it; I wasn't raised to let a man talk down to me or have a man dictate what I can and can't do. So why the hell am I allowing Creed to do that to me?

"Jess, dinner is ready." I drop my pencil and stand from my bed. I have homework to do, and I haven't written a single thing because I'm thinking about Creed instead, argh. I need to get over this stupid infatuation I have with him. Callie texted me earlier as well and asked if she and I could talk before school tomorrow, I agreed. I drop down onto the stool and thank mom for dinner, we eat in silence until there is a knock at the door. I look at mom in question who just shrugs her shoulders and goes to see who it is. Mom opens the door, but I can't see who it is.

"We need to talk, Katharine." Then she walks outside and closes the door, who the hell is that?

CHAPTER ELEVEN
Jessica

I've been sitting here for ten minutes waiting for mom to come back inside. I'm beyond tempted to eavesdrop, but I know if she catches me, I'll be in huge crap. Before I contemplate this any further the door opens, and mom walks inside with a distressed look on her face. Jacob follows her inside and closes the door behind him. The three of us stare at each other in silence, seeing how tense my mom is I'm starting to worry that something bad might have happened.

"I can do this if you like Kathy." Kathy? Since when did mom allow anyone to call her Kathy, she hates being called that?

"No, she's my daughter and I will be the one to tell her." I stiffen in anticipation. "Jess, why is Credence Reeves following you around school?" I reel back shocked, why would she care?

"He's not following me around."

"Josh says otherwise." I turn to glare at Jacob, something about him just isn't sitting right with me. I don't know what it is but I'm getting a bad feeling.

"Well, Josh is wrong. Josh and Creed don't get along so maybe he's just making up tales." Anger flashes in Jacob's eyes before he quickly masks it, I knew he wasn't as nice as he portrayed himself to be the first time we met.

"My son does not lie, unlike that mongrel Credence." The way he spits out Creed's name is shocking, why does he hate them so much?

"Mom, what is going on?" Sadness covers her features.

"Kitten, I think it might be best if you finish school from home.

"No way, mom I have finally made friends--"

"The wrong friends from what I hear." Jacob snidely cuts in.

"Who I am friends with is none of your damn business!"

"Jessica! Apologize now, that was out of line." She must be joking right?

"I can't do that, he's wrong mom. I don't know what he has told you but it's not true. Callie, Cole and the rest of the gang are great and they're good to me."

"They can't be that great if they let you get drunk, and Credence Reeves had to carry you out of a party! This is the second time that boy has carried you home."

"Second?" I question.

"Yes, how do you think you got home after that incident at school?" Holy crap, Creed brought me home? And now I'm just learning he was the one to carry me out of Toby's and back to his house. "You're grounded for lying to me and going to a party behind my back and you're banned from seeing any of those Reeves kids." I gape at her in shock.

"You can't do that!" I exclaim.

"I can and I just did. This is for your own good Jess and one day you will thank me." I scoff.

"Yeah, that will be the day you actually tell me the truth and stop lying to me! You can ground me, but you cannot stop me from hanging out with my friends at school."

"Maybe if you told her why--"Mom cuts her gaze to Jacob and pins him with a deathly look.

"You may have been my br---husband's best friend Jacob but you were never mine. Do not mistake my need to be here for anything else, once this is over, I will be leaving--with Jess." An unreadable expression crosses Jacob's face.

"She needs to be here Kathy, so do you."

"I think it's time you leave Jacob." Jacob nods but doesn't say another word as he lets himself out. Mom and I remain silent, the tension between us is palpable I refuse to be the first to speak. She needs to explain everything--now!

"It's getting late Jess." I throw my hands in the air, she can't do this!

"No, you can't brush me off, I have a right to know mom!" She glowers at me and puts her hands on her hips.

"Jess please, I am asking you to trust me."

"I used to trust you, but now...I don't. What is so bad that you can't tell me?" Mom sags in defeat, her face is a picture of unease. Worry seeps in, I can tell from the look on her face that whatever she isn't telling me, is going to turn my world upside down when she finally comes clean.

"It's not that I can't Jess, I just won't tell you until I make sure I can get us out of this."

"Out of what?" I shout.

"This town, I never wanted to come back here--I never wanted you to come here. This town and the people are not what they seem Jessica, they're all wolves dressed in sheep's clothing. I am not trying to hide things from you; I am only doing it because I'm trying to keep you safe. The triplets and their parents are not good people--"

"And Jacob and Kayla are?" I cut in, she sighs and shakes her head.

"Your father trusted Jacob, as for his daughter, she can go take a flying jump for all I care." I smile, mom smirks devilishly at me.

"I'm glad we agree on her being a bitc--"A knock sounding at the door stops my insult about Kayla. Mom and I share a look before she opens it.

"Can we come in?" Holy mother of mercy.

"Why?"

"I think it's time we have a chat." Mom stiffens.

"Anything I had to say to you died along with my...husband when you lot killed him!" I jump to my feet; four sets of eyes meet mine. Creed pushes his way inside until he is standing in front of me. The look in his eyes worries me, did they kill my father? I beg him with my eyes to tell me that my mom is wrong.

"We never hurt your father." Before Creed can say more my mom comes over and shoves him back until she is standing in front of me, I peer around her to see Callie, Cole and Meg are now standing beside Creed.

"Stay the hell away from my daughter!" Mom snarls, Meg moves forward so she is slightly in front of the triplets and looks at my mom with...pity.

"Given the circumstances I will let that go, but if you ever touch my son again, you and I will be the ones at odds."

"We are at odds Meg and have been for years! You chose a murderer over your own blood." What the hell? Meg looks at mom then darts her gaze to me before she can answer, Callie speaks.

"We never hurt him, we tried to help him Mrs. Hastings. My Dad and Austin became friends."

"I don't believe that for a second." Mom snaps.

"Then you are fools, both alphas agreed for peace when you

left our pack to marry your mate. The Reeves pack never killed your mate, Jacob did."

I look to Creed waiting for him to laugh and say he was joking but he doesn't.

Alphas, pack, mate?

I'm going crazy, this can't be real. There is no freaking way that werewolves exist. They can't, it's all fiction or a myth; they only exist in movies and books. Why is my mom standing here and listening to this crap? I move out from behind mom and stand beside her, Callie, Cole, and Meg look at me with guilt in their eyes, Creed though, looks at me like he would rather be anywhere but here.

"What the hell is going on?" Meg's gaze jumps from me to my mom in shock.

"You haven't told her yet? She turns eighteen on Saturday Kitty, she has a right to fucking know before then!" I reel back in shock by Meg's outburst, what is even more shocking is my mom doesn't say a thing to defend herself. I turn to her and ask.

"What does she mean mom?" Mom starts to shake her head.

"Oh for god's sake Katharine, she has a right to know!" I throw my arms up in the air and release a loud groan of frustration.

"Would someone please tell me what the hell is going on?" Cole, Callie, Meg and even my mom won't meet my gaze. I turn to the person I know who doesn't give a shit if they hurt my feelings. Creed stares back at me, I plead with my eyes that he tells me the truth.

"You're the first person to be born from the Reeves and

Michelson pack. This makes you the rightful alpha to both packs and the first ever female alpha. Your father died trying to protect your birthright."

CHAPTER TWELVE
Jessica

After Creed dropped that bomb last night, I excused myself and hid in my room. My mind has been a mess since then, I don't even remember the walk to school. I keep darting my eyes around the hall expecting someone to turn into a wolf or for Edward Cullen to walk in and bite me. Standing in front of my locker for the last ten minutes just staring; I can't focus on anything for more than a few seconds. Snapping out of my thoughts when I'm shoved forward, I manage to snap my hand in front of me to stop myself from head butting the metal door. Spinning around I glare at the person, when I see who it is I grind my teeth together to stop myself from saying something stupid. Kayla leans in closer and I stiffen when I feel her breath against my ear.

"Rightful alpha or not, you will not take Credence from me." I reel back in shock; Kayla is a wolf. Oh my god, does that mean everyone in the school is? All of a sudden, I feel like the walls are closing in on me, is my mom a wolf? Did the triplet's dad really kill mine? I feel bile rise up my throat, pushing past Kayla and her minions I head for the bathroom, as soon as I lock the stall door behind me, I drop to my knees and empty what little I have left in my stomach into the porcelain bowl. Wiping my mouth with the back of my hand; I need to get myself together. I need answers and I need to find out the truth once and for all. I head to the sink to rinse my mouth and splash some water on my face. Standing there and staring at my reflection in the mirror, how could someone like me be this amazing mythical creature, I'm no one. If I am what Credence says I am then why have I never changed into a wolf? I'm startled out of my thoughts when the door crashes open and see Josh standing there.

"Wanna get out of here?"

"I...maybe...I."

"Jess, Jacob is my dad and I know all about this stuff. I'll answer any questions you have." I look at Josh and I can see he means every word he just said. He is the first person to offer me the truth and I would be stupid to pass up this opportunity.

"Okay."

Josh drives us to a lake on the outskirts of town, we sit on the grass watching the ducks swim back and forth for a long time. Josh doesn't push me or even try to talk, he's giving me time to think and come to him which I appreciate.

"Is it all true?" I ask, too chicken to look at him. I keep my eyes on the ducks.

"Yes." I release a whoosh of air, holy shit on toast.

"Are you a--"

"Werewolf?" I finally turn and meet his gaze; he smiles kindly as I nod my head. "Yeah Jess."

I wish I could say I was scared or in shock but truthfully, I just feel numb. Josh is the only person that has dropped little hints about werewolves since Toby's party. He is also the only person to offer answers any questions or even tell me about any of this. Mom won't tell me and as far as I can tell the triplets didn't come to school, I didn't see their pickup in the car park when Josh and I left.

"Have you always known what you are?"

"I was raised on pack lands; we have all known what we are since the day we were born."

"Why didn't anyone tell me sooner?" Josh releases a sigh and looks out at the lake.

"Because Kane and my dad put out an alphas order that no one was to tell you. In a way it was their way of showing respect for your mom and what she lost. Plus, when an alpha issues an order it must be followed no matter what."

"What does that mean?"

"Kane's pack blames my pack for your father's death and vice versa. Truthfully the only two people in this world that really know what happened to your father is them."

"Who is Kane?"

"He's the alpha to the Reeves pack and the triplets father." I reel back in shock; I didn't expect that.

"So, your father is the alpha as well?"

"Yeah."

"Why do the packs hate each other?"

"Honestly, it has been going on since long before I was born. Apparently, our pack killed someone from Kane's. We nearly achieved peace once when your mother and father mated."

"Huh, what do they have to do with any of this?" Josh turns to face me with a serious expression on his face.

"Your father was the original alpha of the Michelson pack, back then it was called the...Hastings pack. Your mother is the daughter from the original alpha of the Reeves pack." My mouth drops open in shock, what the hell? "The packs started to come back together and live-in harmony until your father was killed.

You see Jess, you are the first to ever be born from two alpha lines and you just happen to be female. There has never been a female alpha before, your mom hid you to keep you safe. If other packs find out about a female alpha, they will want to claim you."

"Claim me?"

"Like take you as their mate, wolves are all about power and dominance. If a male alpha was to claim you, then whatever pack you come from would fall under him. So, mating with you would give him power over two packs." My head is starting to hurt from all this new information. I'm still finding it hard to believe any of this is real.

"I don't want a mate and I don't want to be alpha. I don't want any of this Josh, I'm not built to be strong and lead people. I just want to graduate, go to college and live my life." Sadness enters Josh's eyes; he reaches over and claps my hand in his larger one.

"We all wish for the same thing Jess, but we can't have that. None of us are normal and we have to stay with our packs." I wrench my hand free and stand, I pace back and forward along the grass. I am not giving up on my dreams. I refuse to do that; I have worked too hard to give it all up for some hocus pocus crap.

"Can you take me home please, there's something I have to do."

Josh dropped me off about fifteen minutes ago. I'm pacing the living room waiting for mom to walk in any minute. My phone vibrating in my hand pulls me from my thoughts, I look at the caller ID and see its Callie. Should I answer or let it go to voicemail? I decide to answer it.

"Hello."

"Where were you today?" I gasp, I double check to make sure I didn't read the caller ID wrong.

"Why do you have Callie's phone and why are you calling me?"

"Where were you today?" I grit my teeth in frustration.

"I don't have to answer you Credence, you are not my keeper." I hang up and I must say I'm quite proud of myself. Credence Reeves scares me, but some mangled part of me loves to provoke him and see how far I can get. I know that sounds stupid and crazy, but it feels great to know that I can push his buttons and in a way I guess have some form of control over him. I'm pulled from my thoughts at the sound of the loud knock at the door; mom probably forgot her keys again. I swing the door open and I'm about to give her the lecture again about making sure she has her keys but the words die in my throat, it's not mom. Credence stands there breathing hard and glaring down at me, I notice then he's shirtless! Oh lord have mercy on my poor heart, my gaze travels down his naked bronze skin. The abs on this man could melt butter they're that hot, he's wearing a plain black pair of basketball shorts and he's barefoot. I'll admit the sight of him is making me hot and bothered.

"You ever hang up on me again and you will regret it." He

snaps, I snap my gaze to his, confused. Oh, that's right I hung up on him, I forgot about that, due to his glorious body distracting me.

"You don't get to demand things of me--"I stop speaking as soon as Creed begins to crowd me, I move backward until I smack into the wall. His eyes are burning with anger and...worry. He closes the space between us until his body is pressed against me. An involuntary moan escapes me, I quickly bite my lip to stop it from happening again, Creed looks down at me and my eyes widen, his eyes are blue! I wasn't going crazy when I saw them change the other day. He leans down and runs his nose from the shell of my ear to the crook of my neck. I'm panting and shivering from his touch, then he growls and I still.

"Why do you smell like Joshua Michelson?" I scramble to answer him, but no words come out, he hasn't stopped growling and I'm woman enough to admit I'm petrified right now. "Answer me."

"B-because, I was with him today." Creed cages me by placing his hands either side of my head, his eyes swimming with anger.

"Stay away from him!" His voice sounds strange, it's like it isn't him speaking. I reach out and place my hand on his naked chest, I gasp when a feeling of warmth travels through my body. His gaze snaps to mine, his eyes are back to their normal hazel color. Whenever I touch him a feeling of completeness settles over me.

"Why does that happen every time I touch you but not anyone else?" His relaxed expression changes to anger in a second. A loud growl rips free from him and I drop my hand in fear.

"Get the fuck away from my daughter if you want to live to see tomorrow Credence!"

CHAPTER THIRTEEN
Jessica

He doesn't flinch or move his gaze from mine, I hear my mom walk toward us and stiffen. I see her out the corner of my eye, she looks so angry, but her anger is directed toward Creed not me.

"Step away from her now Credence before you do something you will regret." Indecision shines in his eyes; it looks almost painful for him to pull away from me. He takes a reluctant few steps back and I release the breath I didn't know I was holding. "You need to leave now." Creed turns to face my mom.

"Tell her everything before her birthday or I will. There's only so much I can do to keep my wolf in check." Understanding shines in my mother's eyes as she nods her head. Creed doesn't spare a glance as he makes his way out of the cabin and shuts the door behind himself. Mom rushes over and checks to make sure I'm not hurt or injured.

"Did he hurt you?"

"No mom."

"Why was he here kitten?" I sigh.

"Honestly, I have no idea. Can we talk about that later, I need to ask you something?" Mom nods her head for me to continue. "I want to go to college and do the things I have always planned. Am I still going to be able to do that?"

"I will make sure that you go."

"Why did we come here mom?" She remains silent for so long; I start to think she won't answer.

"So, you could either accept your birthright or not."

"What does that mean?"

"A wolf has till their eighteen to shift or not, if you don't,

then you will never be a wolf, but if you do, then you have to remain with a pack. We had to come back here so both packs could see with their own eyes that you would choose not to shift."
I reel back in shock.

"So that's it? You just get to say I can't be a wolf and I have to listen." Mom has the nerve to actually look confused.

"I thought that's what you would have wanted Jess!"

"If Creed didn't spill the beans, would you have told me any of this or even given me the choice?" Shame coats her face; she was never going to tell me. She would have let me live my life without ever knowing the truth. I'm so angry at her, that was never her choice to make, it was mine!

"You don't want that life Jess. There is so much more to this story than you know, and it isn't a happy one it's all lies and tragedy."

"How would you know mom; you never gave me the option! You just did what you thought was right for you, I only want to go to college so I can lay down roots and stay in the same place for more than a year. I'm eighteen on Saturday and for the first time I actually have friends, I've never been able to have those before."

"They are not your friend's kitten, each of them wants something from you."

"Like what?" Her eyes take on a harsh edge.

"If you shift, then you will be crowned alpha, Kane and Jacob will have no choice but to step down. Your friends want that so they can each claim something from you when you're alpha. This isn't some fairy-tale Jessica, this is real and it's dangerous. I am begging you to not shift, we can leave first thing Sunday morn--"

"Why did we move around so much?" She deflates at my blatant brush off.

"Because your scent is strong and if a male alpha caught wind of you, they would claim you so they could have your packs."

"They can't do that!"

"They can and they will Jessica. Wolves are assholes, they always think the males are superior and females are always treated as lesser. If you are an unmated female alpha, any male can claim you Jess."

"I won't let them." I say stubbornly.

"Then you must fight to the death in wolf form." I gasp, how barbaric.

"No one would claim me." She shakes her head sadly.

"Jess in case you haven't noticed you have the heirs to both packs sniffing around you."

"Huh, who?"

"I can smell Josh on you." I smile sheepishly. "And Credence was just here." I exhale loudly, I need my mom's help to understand all this. I now know why she tried to protect me because she was worried about me, but I can't let her worries cloud what I want.

"Mom, I know you're worried and scared but it's my choice."

"What if you choose wrong Jess?" I try to smile reassuringly but from the distraught look on her face I think I failed.

"Then that's my problem, I want to know the truth and I want you to be the one to tell me. Josh filled me in on some of it today--"

"Don't trust a word that comes out of that boy's mouth." I'm shaken by the venom in her tone. "He is just as power hungry as his father."

"That may be true, but he is the only person who has even tried to answer any questions and explain all of this to me." Mom flinches, I didn't mean to hurt her but it's the truth. If she had been honest with me and forthcoming with information, I wouldn't have had to seek it elsewhere.

"Fine, sit down and get cozy, I'll order pizza and tell you everything."

Mom and I are sitting on the couch eating pizza. I'm nervous to hear what she has to say but I want--no need to know the truth.

"I will tell you this once and once only Jess. Re-living these memories is hard for me."

"I understand mom." She nods her head and takes a deep breath.

"My father--your grandfather was alpha of the Reeves pack; my dad wasn't like the other alphas. He treated everyone equally, men weren't above women, the way he ruled pissed a lot of other packs off because women wanted to leave and come to ours so they could be treated better. My dad fought a lot of battles and won, my mom was just as fierce and strong as my dad. Whenever alphas came to try to claim me, he refused, he told me it was my choice not his or any other mans. When I turned sixteen my best friend and I went with my parents to a summit, once a year all alphas would meet up. It was just bullshit really; it was a place they could go to brag about who's stronger and who has the bigger pack. Anyway, that was where we met the alpha of the Hastings pack--your grandfather." Goose pimples skirt all down my arms. "Long story short, my dad agreed to let them move into town near us."

"Why?" Mom smiles sadly at me; her eyes are glassy with unshed tears.

"Because at that summit I met your father and told my dad that he was my mate." I gasp. "My dad agreed to divide up his territory so my mate could be closer to me. Also, because he knew after the mating ceremony, I would have to move to my mate's pack and he wanted me close. Your father was an amazing man, so kind and courageous and oh so beautiful. He had blond hair and blue eyes like you." Tears build in my eyes as I listen to how my mom talks about my dad with so much love. But something is off, she doesn't talk about my dad like he is the love of her life. I can tell she loved him but in a different way. "Years passed and your father and I were happy and in love."

"Wait, Josh told me there was never peace between both packs." Mom narrows her eyes and grits her teeth.

"He is a lying little shit, some of the members of your fathers pack tried to cause trouble with mine but it was dealt with. When your father became alpha after his father passed that's when things took a turn." Tears fall from my mom's eyes; I reach over and clasp her hand in mine offering my silent support.

"Someone from the Hastings pack murdered my father, I demanded that your father seek vengeance for my father, and he tried. He set up a meeting with the newly appointed alpha, Kane Reeves. While your father, Kane and each of their seconds were away, Kane's wife was murdered." I gasp in horror.

"Oh my God."

"It gets worse Jess; Meg isn't the triplets biological mother. Meg was their nanny; the tw--triplets were only a few months old when their mother was killed." My heart hurts for them. "Needless to say, peace was never achieved, the packs went to war and many lost their lives. Things changed, I found out I was pregnant with you, you would be the key to peace. You are from two alpha bloodlines and come from each pack so rightfully you are the one to lead. Your father tried to reach out to Kane to stop this fighting and form peace like my father had wanted. The night he went to meet Kane you were only a baby." A sob breaks free from my mom. "He loved you Jess so much. When Jacob came back and told me what Kane had done, I knew I had to run. If I had stayed here, he would have come for you and killed you." I gape at my mom; dread fills my veins. Kane killed my dad. "I didn't want you to have anything to do with any of this kitten that's why I never told you. You were supposed to be oblivious to all of this, Kane and Jacob were supposed to watch from afar and see that you wouldn't shift on your birthday, then you would be free."

"What happens if I choose to shift?" I whisper, mom sucks in a sharp breath.

"Then you have to change in front of the alphas and council, be prepared to fight Jess. They will challenge you for their position and if any male wolves come forward to claim you, then you have to fight. You have to be prepared to take on your role as alpha."

"What if I just want to shift and not be alpha?" Mom furrows her brow in confusion.

"I...I don't know, do you want to shift?" The thought has crossed my mind.

"I don't know, I haven't really had time to process all of this properly. I have four days to come up with an answer, if I do, can I give up being alpha?"

"That is something we would have to discuss with Jacob and Kane."

"When?"

"On Saturday, there is no way to get the both of them together until then. You have to remember they don't like each other, I don't exactly relish the thought of seeing Kane either." An idea hits me, it's probably a bad one but at this stage it's worth a shot.

"What if we go to Kane?" Mom looks at me like I've lost my damn mind.

"Are you crazy! I just told you that he killed your father."

"I know mom. I'm sorry, I'm not trying to be insensitive. I swear I just need to speak to him so I can make a decision."

CHAPTER FOURTEEN
Jessica

After a lot of begging, pleading and mom getting in contact with the alpha of the Reeves pack, somehow we manage to arrange a meeting with him. Mom let me skip school today so we can attend the meeting. We have been a ball of nerves all morning, we may be nervous and scared but at least the tension between us is gone. We stayed up for hours talking and teaching me things about the pack. She tells me stories about dad and my grandparents, somehow, I feel closer to her now. My mom is my rock and my only family. I love her more than anything, if this meeting with Kane doesn't go well, then I won't shift. I refuse to be a slave and claimed by some male pig, I am not an object. As we pull up to the alphas house my nerves skyrocket, mom turns the car off and we sit there staring at the home that I thought was my dream house.

"We can tuck tail and run?" I snort at her crappy joke. "Okay, are you sure you want to do this?" I meet her gaze; mom is the best person I know and will support whatever I decide. I reach over and grip her hand in mine.

"Let's do this, and tonight we'll have a girl's night."

We stand in front of the ominous black door and wait; mom grabs my hand and interlocks our fingers. I close my eyes and try to calm my nerves; I have to do this for myself and for my mom. When the door opens a pristinely dressed Meg stands on the other side, she smiles invitingly at both mom and I, and mom squeezes my hand reassuringly.

"Hello kitty." Mom releases a whoosh of air.

"Don't do that Meg."

"You're still my best friend, so why shouldn't I?" I look between them shocked.

"Wait, Meg was the best friend that went to the summit?" Mom nods her head stiffly while Meg smiles warmly and invites us in. We follow her toward the back of the house and down a long hallway, she opens a door and ushers us in.

I want to look around at the bookshelves that line the walls, but my eyes are glued to the four people behind the desk. Creed stands in the middle of his siblings; sitting in front of him is a handsome looking man. Creed and Cole look exactly like their dad. Kane Reeves looks nothing like a murderer, he has a powerful presence about him, but all I can see in his hazel eyes is nothing but genuine kindness, he's wearing a suit which tells me he's more of a business man. His dark brown hair is slicked back flat against his head, not a hair out of place. Mom stiffens next to me when Kane's eyes turn to her, remorse is clear in his eyes, but he still says nothing. Meg enters and ushers us to the seats in front of Kane's desk, I can feel Creed's gaze on me the whole time. It takes everything inside me not to look at him, we sit down to face Kane and his family, Meg moves around the desk and stands on the other side.

"I'm not one to drag shit out; I know this is hard for you to be back here Katharine. If you're here to ask if I killed your br-
-mate, the answer is no." A growl sounds from beside me and I turn so fast I nearly tumble out of the chair. Mom sits there vibrating with rage, her gaze is locked onto Kane, neither of them willing to drop the intense stare off. I can feel the tension in the room amping up the longer mom stares at Kane, I flick my gaze to Kane and his face contorted like he doesn't want to be angry but it's hard for him not to be.

"Katharine, unless you would like to challenge him for alpha, drop your gaze now!" I'm still new to this wolf thing but the urgency in Meg's voice tells me mom has to stop or things will go bad. Growls still tumble out of her; I have never been scared or even feared my mom before, but right now I'm nervous. I tentatively reach over and place my hand on her forearm, the growling stops, and her gaze slowly turns to me. A whoosh of air escapes her, I bite my bottom lip to stop the screech that wants to tear out of me, my mom's eyes are yellow! I make sure to keep all emotion off my face, and a few seconds later her eyes return to their normal color. She places her hand on top of mine and smiles gratefully. I don't know what would have happened if I didn't intervene and I'm glad I won't have to find out.

"I know you're angry and hurt--"Mom cuts Kane off.

"Do not sit there and act like you care how I am feeling Kane." Kane slams his hand down on top of his desk, I jump back in my seat. His eyes narrow in anger, his fists clenched on top of his desk.

"I know exactly how you feel! My wife was slaughtered by your pack; I'm about the only person who can relate to how you are feeling!" Mom slumps back into her chair in defeat, Kane is right they have both suffered such a horrible loss. My heart constricts for both my mom and Kane, as if my mouth has a mind of its own, I blurt out.

"I am so sorry for your loss." I try to keep my expression neutral and act like I totally planned to say that. A grunt behind Kane tells me Creed knows it was an accident, the fact he isn't calling me on my bullshit is shocking. Kane twists in his seat to give me his full attention. I thought I would crumble under the full gaze of the alpha, but the truth is I'm more afraid of Creed than his father. Kane doesn't look at me with pity, he looks at me like he's...honored. Weird.

"Thank you, Miss Hastings, it is a pleasure to meet you. I am sorry I missed you last weekend." I'm in shock at how formal he sounds; he seems like such a...human. I can't believe I'm now referring to people as humans; this is going to take some getting used to. Before I can answer Callie steps in, and I am honestly grateful for her interruption.

"Everything I have ever said to you Jess is the truth, I just couldn't admit to who and what I really am." I can hear the unease in her voice and judging by the look in her eyes she never wanted to lie to me. I don't blame her; I like Callie and she is the first real friend I have ever had. Am I annoyed that she hid things from me, yes but will I get over it, yeah.

"I know Callie, this is...just going to take some time to get used to." Callie nods her head but doesn't reply.

"You better get used to it fast, you only have a few days to decide." My gaze snaps to Creed, I can hear the anger and annoyance in his tone. Why the hell is he so hot but such an...ass? Choosing to be the bigger person, I square my shoulders and jut my chin out while looking at the beast of man that has been playing havoc with my emotions since I met him.

"I will decide when I am ready, not when you demand it Credence!" Creed's upper lip pulls back to bare his teeth, a low growl vibrates his chest. I refuse to cower; I will not let him or any other wolf scare me.

I meet his heated angry gaze with one of my own. The air thickens in the room, I feel a weird heat start to creep up my spine. The feeling from the first day I met Creed comes barreling back, I need to touch him!

I jump to my feet, I'm no longer in control of my body it has a mind of its own. Never breaking eye contact he begins to move toward me, I feel this pull inside me urging me to him, everything fades away I get lost in the depths of his beautiful eyes. When I'm only two feet apart, I'm wrenched backward, I glare at the person who dares to stop me from going to my...my...I don't even know what I was about to say. I spin back toward Creed to see Kane and Cole holding him back, Creed is thrashing against their hold growling. I spin back around to face my mother and cock my brow in question.

"He's angry because I stopped you from reaching him."

"Why?" Her eyes soften as she reaches out to touch me, a loud long growl has her pausing and dropping her hand back to her side.

"You try to take her from me, and I will hunt you down!" I spin around startled at the anger and possessiveness in Creed's voice. He still pushes against his father and brothers hold; Callie tries to help pull Creed back, but he's too strong. Meg comes into view and the pleading look in her eyes makes me tense.

"Either go to him and calm his beast or take your mother and run Jess. He will hunt you until he finds you, you will need to stay inside and wait till you hear from me." Does she mean Creed wants to eat me? I shudder at the thought. "He won't hurt you Jess but he will take away your choice if you don't run." I'm so confused, none of this makes sense! I dart my gaze between

Creed and my mom, she looks so torn. I move toward her but stop when a guttural growl reverberates around the room. I know it's Creed warning me not to flee. My mom's eyes are round with shock.

"Choose now Jess, they won't be able to hold him back much longer!" The urgency in my mom's voice puts me on edge, I start to shake from fear.

"What will he do?" I whisper hoping that he won't be able to hear me over his loud growls. I was wrong to assume that, after all, he is a wolf so of course he has great hearing. He chuckles but it's hollow and scary, I turn slowly so I can face him, all four of his family members are fighting to hold him back from---me.

"Run little alpha---I dare you!" The challenge in his eyes and gruff tone of his voice puts me on edge. I won't lie, a part of me is thrilled at the thought of this Adonis chasing me down but another part is also shit scared of what will happen when he does catch me. I decide to take a chance, I see the moment he recognizes that I have made my choice. A devilish glint enters his eyes, and a hungry smirk graces his beautiful full lips, he stops struggling against his family. "Run, run as fast as you can princess, the big bad wolf is coming for you." I gulp then quickly spin around and grab my mom's hand as we race from the room, Creed's cruel laughter follows us the whole way to the car. I still hear his laughter ringing in my ears as we leave his pack lands.

CHAPTER FIFTEEN
Jessica

As soon as mom shoves the car in park, we both spring from the vehicle and scramble inside. We race around the cabin to make sure all the windows are locked, and close the blinds, mom pulls the couch in front of the door to barricade the only entry point. We stand across from each other panting, I can feel the sweat lining my brow not from the heat but from fear. Mom looks at me, but I can't quite decipher the look before she can speak the shrill sound of my phone ringing distracts us. I pull it out of my pocket and nearly drop it twice from how much my hand is shaking, my gaze snaps to mom when I see the caller ID.

"Answer it." I take a deep breath and do as she says, I push the green button then put it on speaker.

"Hello."

"Jess, stay inside. We tried to hold him back, but he fought Cole and Dad, we're on our way to you now. We'll set up a perimeter around your cabin but only dad, mom, Cole and I can come. We can't involve the pack or Jacob's pack will see it as a threat, I'm so sorry Jess."

"Why is he coming for me Callie and please---don't lie to me." I hear her sigh and I can hear someone in the background cursing. I hear some muffled sounds and look at my mom in question, she shrugs her shoulders as Meg's voice filters through the speaker.

"Jess, we're about five minutes away. He will get there before us, don't let him in. Stay inside and we'll get Creed away from you, but it may be safer for you until you decide if you don't go to school and stay away from my son." I reel back not in shock but anger, did Meg just threaten me? Before I can lash out at her there's a loud bang. Mom makes her way over to me and just as she is about to reach me, we hear the window shatter in my room, I scream in fright. "Jess! What's going on?" Mom grabs the phone from me and takes it off speaker.

"He's here, he just broke her window. Get here fast, or I will put him down before he touches my daughter." Mom doesn't wait for a reply as she hangs up, she pushes me behind her and crouches slightly ready to spring into action. I stand behind my mom unsure what the hell I am supposed to do, I'm so confused as to what the hell is going on and why Creed is chasing me. What changed in such a short amount of time, Creed couldn't stand to be near me, now he's chasing me down like I'm---prey.

Holy shit, I'm his prey!

"Mom, we need to run." I whisper shout, I can hear the tremble in my own voice. We haven't heard another sound since the glass shattered, the silence worries me and has put me on edge.

"He's a predator kitten, if you run it will thrill him more to be able to chase you." I stiffen, this is so not how I saw this going. Mom won't take her eyes off the hallway; her body is coiled tight and ready to strike at any given moment.

"What the hell does he want mom?" If possible, her entire body stiffens more.

"You Jess, he wants you." Before I can answer a loud thud comes from my bedroom, mom subtly tilts her head back and...sniffs.

"Stay behind me Jess, he's inside." I stifle a gasp, fear shoots through my body and all the horror stories of what wolves can do to people run through my mind.

"I can scent your fear little alpha." I freeze at the sound of his voice; Creed sounds more beast than man. I hear the floor creak under his weight and know he is making his way out of my room toward us. A growl tears from my mom in warning.

"Your family is on their way, Credence and will be here soon, leave now!" Creed steps into the hallway and I shiver, his eyes are a piercing blue, and a cruel smirk graces his beautiful face. He's only in a pair of black basketball shorts, no shirt and he's barefoot. Mom begins to growl loudly, Creed doesn't even look at her, his gaze is locked on me. "Stop Credence, I will not let you take her!" Huh?

The front door bursts open, I sigh in relief thinking that Meg and the others are here, Creed growls so loud. I turn slightly toward the door and gasp when I see Kayla, Josh, Jacob and two others standing in our doorway. Suddenly mom moves from facing Creed to standing shoulder to shoulder with him, like they're now on the same team. Jacob pushes past both his kids to come in but at the sounds of mom and Creed's growls he stops just as he passes the threshold.

"Son, take Jess out of here." I gape at the audacity of the giant peacock; he does not get to order me around. Before I give Jacob a piece of my mind, Creed moves to the other side of me so I'm now in the middle of him and mom.

"Your son lays one hand on her, and I'll kill him." The venom and hatred in Creed's voice has ice filling my veins. I can hear the truth in his words, he really will kill Josh.

"Enough, Credence, take Jess back to your house. I'll catch a ride back with Meg and Kane when they get here." At the mention of Creed's parents, Jacob narrows his eyes, clearly he doesn't like them. Creed reaches for me, but I dodge him, I will not leave my mom. The look in my eyes must convey my thoughts; he drops his gaze and sighs.

"Sorry princess, this isn't our fight." I cock my head to the side confused at his meaning, before I can even process what happened, Creed has me slung over his shoulder caveman style.

"Keep her safe Credence." I lift my head up and push against Creed's back so I can see my mom. She has tears in her eyes and a sad smile on her face.

"Mom!"

"I love you kitten."

Creed dashes back down the hallway toward my room, I hear shouts and a scuffle coming from the lounge where my mom is. I scream and pound my fist against Creed's back as he leaps out the window with me still slung over his shoulder. Just as we're about to enter the woods I hear a gut-wrenching scream come from inside the cabin and deep down in my soul I know that sound came from my mom.

After what feels like hours of me bouncing up and down on Creed's shoulder, he finally puts me down. My legs feel like jelly, I begin to sway a little. Creed reaches out and places both his hands on my shoulders to steady me. I haven't been able to stop the tears streaming down my face, the scream I heard has been playing over and over in my mind. The scream was pure agony. Creed reaches into his pocket and pulls out his phone, he dials a number and puts it to his ear. He curses under his breath and then dials another number. I assume he's trying to call his family; I spin around and see that we're on a hill, I can see all the towns lights and houses. I have no idea where in the hell we are, but one thing is for sure this place has an amazing view, I just wish my mom was here to share it with me.

"I can't reach my family." Oh, so now he wants to talk. I ignore him and just stare out at the lights. Creed being the overbearing ass that he is won't tolerate my silence, he reaches out and spins me so I'm facing him. His eyes narrow to slits so I do the same! "You should be thanking me." He grits out, my hand is itching to slap his face.

"If you hadn't chased us, none of this would have happened! This is your entire fault; my mom could be hurt and that is on you Credence." I shout, his eyes widen but not with anger or shock. He looks down at me with so much remorse, he reaches up and cups my cheek. I hate that I want to melt into his touch and let him hold me, I'm angry as heck and blame him for all of this, but his touch seems to settle my anger and calm me.

"I'm sorry princess, I tried to fight my beast, but I wasn't strong enough to keep him at bay. Even if I didn't chase you tonight Jacob still would have come." I look at him in confusion.

"How did Jacob know you were at my house?" Creed shakes his head and furrows his brow.

"He wasn't there for me."

"Who was he there for?" He strokes my face with his thumb, and it takes everything inside me not to melt at the feeling of his hand on me.

"You, he was coming to claim you as his Luna." Now my brow furrows in confusion.

"What's a Luna?"

"The female equivalent to an alpha, he wants to claim you as his mate." My eyes double in size, I stumble back from Creed in shock. He has to be joking, Jacob is nearly double my age.

"W-why?" Creed's kind, caring moment is gone and replaced with his normal emotionless mask.

"Because he wants to rule both packs and you are the key to that."

"I won't do it!" Before he can answer his phone rings, cutting our conversation short.

"Yeah. She's with me; we'll meet back at the house." He ends the call then jerks his head; the movement tells me he wants me to follow him. I'm not going to do what he wants! I turn around and attempt to head back the way we came; I am not leaving my mom behind. Not knowing if she's ok is killing me inside. I don't make it three steps before an arm bands around my waist and he hauls me back against his chest, a loud gasp escapes me. Being this close to him short circuits my brain, heat rushes through my body at how close he is to me. Half of me wants to melt into his hold but the rational part of me knows that none of this between us is real. Creed is like the iceberg that sank the Titanic, beautiful to look at but deadly as hell.

"Let me go!" I snap, his arm tightens around me as he leans down and whispers in my ear.

"I will never let you go little alpha." His words stun me, his mood swings are giving me whiplash and I'm so close to losing my cool at him.

"You don't own me! I am not a toy you can play with whenever you feel the need and then discard when you're done." His deep chuckle sends a shiver down my spine, the sound has my insides turning to mush. I don't understand this pull between us, whenever he is around, I feel like I'm a magnet to him. My mind screams at me to stay away and that he is nothing but trouble, my body--ignores my brain and wants to climb him.

"Oh, you have no idea princess, when you learn the truth, you will know then just how much of a say I have over everything in your life." His words hold a promise that scares the crap out of me. Instead of trying to process what he said and the underlying meaning, I struggle in his hold to break free, he's to freaking strong. I'm frustrated that he is only using one arm to restrain me, and I can't even manage to get free. "Stop struggling, you can't go back there."

"Why not?" I grit out, as I continue to struggle against his hold. He moves so fast I don't even have a chance to comprehend what the hell is happening. I'm now facing him with my chest plastered to his front. I crane my neck right back to glare up at him. His arms are like a vice wrapped around me, and I hate to admit it but being held by him like this feels so right. His hazel eyes stare down at me with such sadness that I cease my struggle.

"Your mom isn't there Jess." The tone of his voice and the look in his eyes has my blood turning to ice. There is a double meaning to what he is saying, I need him to spell it out for me, my mind is conjuring up horrible thoughts and I'm praying that

I'm wrong, deep down I know I'm right.

"Where is she Creed?" I feel tears beginning to build behind my eyes and a lump form in my throat. He removes one of his arms from around my back and cups my cheek, his touch is so tender and sweet. He runs his thumb across my lips in an intimate caress as he answers me.

"Jacob took her."

CHAPTER SIXTEEN
Jessica

After Creed dropped that world shattering bomb I followed him silently, I have no idea where we were going. I just knew that if I wanted to get my mom back, he is my best chance--my only chance. I realize where we are when we break through the dense trees and Creed's huge black house comes into view, I release a long sigh. I didn't think I would end up back here, after running out a couple of hours earlier with my mom. The thought of her being held against her will has a strangled sob tearing from my throat. All the adrenalin drains from my body, and I drop to my knees and cry. This is the first time I have cried since all this information was dumped on me. I'm not just crying for my mom; I'm crying for the dad I will never get to know because someone took him from me. These tears are for the lie I have been living all my life, my whole world has been tipped upside down in a matter of hours. Ugly sobs tear through me. I clench my hands into fists and start hitting the ground.

"Why me, why did this have to happen to me." I choke out, I don't expect anyone to answer me. I said it more for my own benefit than anyone else's. I keep pounding my fist into the ground, tears continue to streak down my face as sobs tear from me. Before I can slam my fists into the hard earth again, strong arms wrap around me from behind, we fall backward and I land on his lap. I don't need to see who it is to know it's Creed, the heat that always runs through me whenever he touches me is a clear giveaway. His arms are tight around my midsection, he buries his face in the crook of my neck. He doesn't whisper a word as I break down, I can't find the will to stop the sobs or the tears. Creed moves one of his arms from around my waist and grips my chin so he can turn my face. I stare at him from over my shoulder. He has an emotionless expression on his face, I don't mask the pain from my eyes. There isn't any point, he knows I'm hurting. Instead of using words Creed leans in closer, the sobs stop when I realize what he is about to do. The air between us seems like it's charged with an electric current, he stops a hair's breadth away, I begin to inhale his exhales. The tension between us is palpable, the heat coursing through my body turns from warm bearable heat to an inferno. He leans down and just as our lips are about to touch in what I am sure is a soul shattering kiss, a loud shout has us pulling apart. We both turn our gazes to see his family members jogging over to us.

The closer they get to us the clearer I can see their faces, Cole and Callie both look worried, Meg and Kane seem distraught. Realization hits me like a truck, of course they're worried, they know my mom was taken against her will, and here I am trying to make out with Creed. What the hell is wrong with me? I try to break out of his hold and get off his lap, but he won't let me, the hand that was holding my face is now wrapped around my waist again. I huff in annoyance and decide not to make a scene like a child and just sit here--On Creeds lap...in front of his whole family.

"Well don't you both look nice and cozy?" I stiffen in Creed's embrace, embarrassed to be found in such a compromising position. Creed lets loose a low frightening growl, my eyes double in size while Cole just chuckles at his brother.

"Don't antagonize him, his wolf is too unstable at the moment." Kane's voice holds so much authority, that I even want to obey him. Kane shifts his gaze from his younger son to

Creed and me, I can feel the blush creeping up my neck. I have never and mean never been in such a position like this in my life, let alone in front of the boy's family! "Creed, why don't you let Jess up so we can go in the house and discuss our next move." Creed doesn't so much strain or even grunt, he stands and pulls me up with him, both his arms are still locked around my middle. I'm trying so hard not to blush as I stand here with Credence plastered against my back and his chin resting on the top of my head. I know I should feel uncomfortable, but I don't. I feel confused and---safe. In his arms I feel like a part of me that I didn't know was missing has finally returned. It's such a strange feeling but at the same time it's so welcoming. I don't know what this thing is between us, but I want to explore this as soon as I find my mom. Kane motions for us all to head inside, I consciously try to wipe my face and hide any sign of my tears. I move forward to follow Meg and the others, but he isn't having any of that. I huff out my frustration.

"Give us a minute, we'll catch up." Kane nods his head and follows Meg and Callie, Cole shoots us a devious smirk before following his parents, once the front door to their house closes behind them Creed spins me around so I'm now facing him. I lift my gaze slowly to meet his. I can't get a read on his emotions; he has his mask of indifference back in place and it annoys me. "Do you trust me?" His question baffles me, he has to be kidding right? I shake my head as I answer.

"No, what reason would I have to trust you?" His eyes harden but I refuse to lie. Creed has given me no reason at all to put my faith or trust in him. He has been so hot and cold with me since I met him and now, he has the nerve to ask me this!

For goodness' sake he literally just broke into my house and tried to...I don't know but that is a major red flag.

"You are out of options on who to trust. My family and I are the only ones who are able to help you, remember that." Before I can think of a good retort, he grips my hand in his and drags me behind him.

We find Kane and the others in the lounge room, Creed leads me over to the vacant couch opposite Cole, Meg and Callie. Kane is standing by the large window with his back to us, Creed drops down and by default thanks to his grip on my hand I flop down next to him with the grace of a giraffe. I turn and glare at the side of his head, I can tell from the smirk he's trying to hide that he knew exactly what he was doing when he pulled me down. I try to shuffle away from him to put some distance between us, but he refuses to let go of my hand. The more I struggle the tighter his grip on my hand gets.

"Would you let go of my freaking hand you....you..."He turns to face me, and I can see the mischievous glint in his eyes.

"Eggplant?" I groan and narrow my eyes at him, he is never going to let that go! Before he can gloat, I snap back.

"I was going to say asshole." Creed's eyes narrow to slits, I hear Callie and Cole both snort then try to cough to hide their laughter. Before I can bask in my glory of stunning him he yanks me back, and then wraps his arms around me so I'm now sitting on his lap facing his laughing siblings, and Meg who is trying so hard not to laugh, I dart my gaze to Kane mortified that I am once again in this position in front of them. He doesn't seem annoyed, he seems...pleased.

"Of course, the first friend I make, Creed has to go and claim." I dart my gaze back to Callie; I know she was joking, but I don't want her to think that Creed has somehow taken me from her. That will never happen. Creed doesn't get to claim any part of me; he is an overbearing ass who is obviously not used to being told no.

"Callie, your arrogant ass of a brother hasn't claimed jack. He obviously just wants what he can never have, it will pass." I sit up a bit straighter feeling triumphant when I feel Creed stiffen beneath me. I believe I just got one over on him. He leans forward so his lips are against the shell of my ear, I will admit, it takes more willpower than I want to admit not to shiver and let my eyes close.

"Never say never princess. You already belong to me; you just don't know it yet." I turn my head so I can look him in the eye, he looks satisfied with himself but I'm about to burst his bubble.

"I don't belong to anyone, FYI once I get my mom back, we are leaving." A crestfallen look encompasses Creed's face, his eyes scan my face no doubt trying to see if I'm lying but I'm not. Why does he look so sad at the prospect of me leaving?

"Jess you can't!" I snap my gaze to Cole in shock, his eyes aren't on me though they're on his brother. I look between the two of them confused, clearly they are locked into one of their silent conversations again and that grates on my nerves.

"Why can't I Cole?" Cole doesn't get a chance to answer, his father cuts him off.

"That is not important right now, we need to focus on getting your mother back." I deflate in Creed's embrace and slink back against him, a low rumble sounds in his chest which I choose to ignore, because I have a feeling that rumble was in appreciation at my close proximity. Our heads are now side by side, I refuse to acknowledge that though. His arms loosen slightly around my waist, I don't even know if he notices, but his thumb is stroking my forearm that rests across my abdomen.

"What do we do, Kane? We can't leave her there!" I can hear the slight tremble in Meg's voice which worries me.

"I know darling, I'm trying to think of a way to save her without starting a pack war." I have no idea what Kane means so I ask.

"Why can't we just go and get my mom? Call the police or something, they kidnapped her." Kane's eyes soften when he looks at me.

"The police can't help with this matter. Technically your mother has just been contained by her alpha, if we go there and demand her back it is seen as a challenge."

"So, what do we do? I won't leave my mom there, I can't. She's...she's all I have left." Creed's arms band tighter around me, I feel his lips against the crook of my neck. Cole, Callie and Meg ignore Creeds actions, they look at me with utter heartbreak. They all know I only have my mom, I cannot and will not lose her.

"You have my world as Luna to the Reeves pack. We will do everything in our power to get Kitty back." I can hear the conviction in Meg's voice, I know she means every word she is saying. I smile timidly and nod my head in thanks, years ago mom and Meg were best friends, but I don't know much more than that. I feel like there is more than just friendship between them but neither of them have exactly come clean with the information.

"I'll call Jacob and try to set up a meeting; I don't think he is going to hand her over easily." I grit my teeth in frustration, she is not some object to be handed around, she is a freaking person!

"He doesn't own her--"before I can finish speaking, my phone begins to ring in my pocket. I wiggle in Creed's lap to try and get it out of my back pocket, but I grip something else. I freeze while Creed chuckles.

"That definitely isn't your phone princess." I cringe but ignore the fact I just gripped Creed's junk and fish my phone out. I let out a relieved sigh when I see it's my mom calling and answer it.

"Mom, where are you? Are you okay?"

"Your mother is occupied at the moment Jess." I freeze at the sound of his voice; I know without even asking that it's Jacob.

"Why are you doing this?" I grit out through clenched teeth.

"Because it's what your father would have wanted. You need to come back to your people; I can have Josh come collect you and bring you home." Before I can answer, the phone is snatched from my hand, I turn and glare at Creed. as he brings my phone to his ear.

"Send your son to collect her, we don't want her or the trouble that she is worth." A sharp pang hits me square in the chest at his words.

CHAPTER SEVENTEEN
Jessica

Creed ends the call after Jacob agrees to have Josh here within an hour to collect me. I feel so used and disposable. I've tried to wiggle out of Creed's hold for the past ten minutes with no success, now I know why he won't let me go. It's not because he wants to keep me close, it's to make sure I won't run away. How could I have been so dumb, here I was thinking that these people can help me? Tunning out the others conversation I get lost in my thoughts, choosing to ignore the fact that my body is melted against Creeds. Another five minutes pass before I blurt out.

"I need to pee, either let me go or I'd be happy to urinate all over you." Creed loosens his grip and before he can change his mind I jump to my feet.

"It's just down--"I cut Callie off.

"I remember." I snap, she recoils slightly but I refuse to feel bad about hurting her feelings. Her and her family fooled me; I won't let that happen again.

After finishing my business, I wash my hands and stare at myself in the mirror. How can my whole life be a lie? Crap like this only happens in movies, for the love of spicy Cheetos, werewolves are real! I have never seen one in person--yet. If werewolves are real, does that mean vampires are too? Splashing water on my face and re-tying my hair into a high ponytail, while giving myself a mental pep talk.

We just need to get mom back and then we'll leave and never look back.

I steel my spine and hold my head high as I open the door and attempt to step out, but the door is blocked by a brooding and angry looking Credence. I refuse to cower and shrink away from him, I narrow my eyes and let him see the anger in the depths of my blue eyes. The air seems to charge and thicken around us, I fight my body's reaction to him and stay rooted to the spot. I don't have to fight for long, Creed closes the space between us and grips my chin roughly in his hand, he moves us until my butt hits the vanity sink behind me. I try to slap his hand away, but he catches it with his other hand and pins it to the basin beside me. I strike out as quick as possible with my other hand and slap his face, his head jerks to the side for a moment before he slowly turns back to me. I'll admit I'm as shocked as he is that I actually went through with that.

An angry red handprint stares back at me, when I look at his cheek, a small sliver of satisfaction courses through my body at the sight of the mark. After all the crap he has pulled and put me through for the past week, he deserves that. He strikes out so quick I don't even have time to prepare, he has both my arms pinned behind me and his head drops to the crook of my neck, I still when his tongue darts out to taste my flesh. An involuntary shudder tears through my body, biting my bottom lip to stop myself from making embarrassing noises. He makes a trail with his hot tongue from my neck all the way to the shell of my ear, he nibbles my lobe then bites down--hard. I curse loudly before I can continue with my insults. He sucks my lobe into his mouth and soothes the ache he caused. A small whimper escapes me, I quickly bite my bottom lip to stop myself from doing that again. Creed releases my lobe, and pulls back so he's looking me directly in the eyes, I could get lost staring into those hazel eyes for days.

"I said what I needed to say in order to get us some leverage." It takes me a moment to figure out what he's talking about, thanks to my mind drifting to the gutter.

"What leverage? You agreed to get rid of me." He releases my hands and cups my face.

"I told you before little alpha, I won't let you go. I said what I had to so he would send his heir to get you; you won't be leaving with Josh." I furrow my brow.

"I won't?" He smiles wickedly.

"Not a chance, and just so we are clear princess. If I so much as see Josh lay a single hand on you again, harmless or not I'll break every fucking bone in his hand." I gasp at his words, from the look in his eyes I can tell he means every word.

"You don't own me Credence, you cannot tell me what I can and--"

"Keep telling yourself that, try me Jess. Push me too far and you might not like what you see." He releases me and steps back, I follow him numbly back to the lounge room still trying to process what the hell he meant. Before I can sit down my phone pings with a message, I pull it out of my pocket to see it's from Josh.

Josh: I'm here, do you want me to come to the house or wait out here?

I look up and relay the message to the others.

"The house." I do as Creed says and reply to Josh. "Princess?" He grits out as I pocket my phone and look up to meet his angry glare.

"Yeah?"

"How the hell does Josh Michelson have your number?"

"I gave it to him." I say as I shrug my shoulders, Creed growls and his eyes flicker to blue. Instead of being scared, I'm intrigued at how his eyes change and how he is able to growl like that while standing on two legs.

"Calm down brother, she's here, with you and you need to cool it. He's here." Just as Cole finishes speaking, I can hear a car approaching.

"If we do this, there is no more peace and Jess will have no other option except to shift in order to ensure peace amongst the packs again."

"We'll deal with that later darling." Kane says in answer to his wife's worries. I can't even focus on what any of that means, my heart is beating so fast I think it might burst out of my chest. I follow the others as they make their way to the door, I feel a trickle of sweat drop down my back. I'm nervous and scared, Josh doesn't deserve to be out in the middle of this, but if it's the only way to get my mom back then I don't have a choice---right? Creed follows behind me as I trail after the others, he walks so close that I can feel the heat radiating off his body. Sitting out front in a dark green Jeep is Josh, his eyes land on me and he smiles kindly. I have no idea what part he played in the capture of my mom, half of me wants to claw his face until he gives her back, the mature side of me knows that hurting him won't solve anything.

"I want assurances." Creed shouts, Josh rolls his eyes and gets out of the idling Jeep. I feel Creed press closer to me, for someone who is trying to play the she means nothing card he is doing a bad job of acting. Josh takes two steps toward us but stops when Callie lets a low growl loose, I spin toward her and gape. I know she is a werewolf but I have never seen her act like one. I sound like a total moron but I don't give a flying hoot. This is all new to me.

Josh keeps his gaze on Callie as he asks. "What assurances?"

Creed moves so he is now standing beside me. "When you leave here no war will ensue. We are done with your pack, we will agree to meet you on Saturday to see if she shifts or not." Creed sounds so cold and detached, the coldness in his tone sends a shiver down my spine. Josh turns his gaze to me and checks me out from head to toe, not in a sexual way but like he is checking me over for injuries. Creed and Cole move to stand in front of me and block Josh's view, Josh chuckles which just annoys Creed. I see his back tense and his shoulders stiffen, I don't know why I do it but I reach out and place my hand on his back, he goes stiff then a second later he relaxes. It's like my touch has the power to calm him, I'll dissect that info later.

"Fine, now can you move so Jess and I can get out of here. We have a lot of planning to do." I can hear the glee in Josh's voice and it rubs me the wrong way, what the hell could he be excited about.

"Planning for what?" Callie snaps, why are their parents not saying anything?

"Oh California, for the mating ceremony of course." Creed goes as still as a statue, growls are tumbling out of him, they are low and deadly and hold a promise of pain.

"Who's mating ceremony?" Finally, Meg says something. I look around at the five Reeves and see they are all standing tall and stiff.

"Well, mine and Jess's of course." It all happens so fast, one second my hand is on Creed's back and the next second my hand flops to my side. Creed is down the porch steps and standing in front of Josh with his shirt clutched in his fist. Josh doesn't attempt to fight back or even stop Creed; he just stands there smiling at him. "Careful now Reeves, don't do something you will regret. With Jess out of the way, you can finally claim my sister." He strikes out so fast I don't even register Creed has punched Josh until he hits the ground and has blood trickling from his nose. I gasp as I look between them, Creed is coiled tight and ready to fight. Josh smiles up at him from the ground.

"Touch her and you die!" Josh laughs so loud and long that you would think he just heard the funniest joke in the world. What the hell is going on here?

"You were never going to hand her over, were you? I told dad that you were too attached, and this was a trap, lucky for me he listened." I stiffen as Josh climbs to his feet and turns to me. "Come with me Jess." Creed goes to grab him again, but Kane and Cole are there to stop him.

"Don't do it!" Creed snaps, he looks so wild and ferocious, seeing him like this has heat filling my veins. My body is begging me to go to him and calm him--.

"Don't listen Jess, your mom is waiting for you." The mention of my mom snaps me out of my thoughts. "Come home and be with her, these people are not your family or your pack---we are." Growls break out from the Reeves family; I look around and notice more people have come out to see the show. This must be some of their pack.

"You cannot force a mating bond, it's against the laws of-"

"California, you sound like a jealous ex, Jess will accept the bond, won't you?" Something seems off, almost like Josh knows I won't have a choice, then it hits me square in the chest.

"Before I go with you." I ignore the growls coming from Creed. "I want to talk to my mom." Josh's eyes flicker and his body turns rigid for a second before he quickly masks his reaction.

"You can see her in like twenty minutes." The tremble in his voice sets me on edge, something isn't right. I make my way down the porch steps and move toward Josh; I stop a few feet away and look him in the eyes. He tries to keep his features blank, but I can see fear in his eyes, perspiration begins to dot his brow, his left eye twitches. My heart begins to pound in my chest, tears threaten to spill as I watch him take quick rapid breaths. I breathe in through my nose and try to stand tall as I ask the question that I know will break me, I already know the answer I can feel it in my bones and my heart.

"I'm asking you as her daughter, Is my mother alive, Josh?" His eyes dart around me to look at the others, his mouth opens and closes and my temper spikes, I can't take the silence. "Fucking answer me!" I scream, Josh jolts and stands tall, his eyes snap to me like he's a puppet.

"No."

CHAPTER EIGHTEEN
Jessica

My whole world falls down around me, I can't focus or think straight. What am I supposed to do now? I can't live without her. My mom--my best friend is gone. The rational part of my brain switches off and the unstable side of me begins to take control, my vision narrows as I zero in on Josh. Everything else is white noise, nothing else in this moment matters except for me and Josh. I don't think or hesitate. I launch myself at him and begin to claw, bite, punch, kick. I do anything I can to hurt him. He tries to throw me off, he's ripping my hair backward, but I feel no pain, I'm numb. All I feel is the need to hurt him. He manages to hit me across the face, but I don't feel it, I claw his face and relish in the hiss of pain he releases, I jump and wrap myself around him. He tries to shift and fling me from his body, but I lock my legs around his waist and clamp my mouth on his ear, I bite down--hard. He screams out in pain and flails his arms around, someone grips me from behind and pulls me back, Josh screams louder the more I'm pulled away from him, I refuse to let go. I'm tugged back hard, and Josh's cartilage gives way, I just bit through the top half of his ear, he clutches it and screams in pain. Arms band around my midsection, my feet dangle above the ground, I look Josh in the eyes as I spit out the rest of his appendage from my mouth, I feel his blood running down my chin and relish in the look of pain on his face.

"You crazy bitch!" I throw my head back and laugh, rationally I know I'm having some sort of mental breakdown, but I don't care. I look him in the eyes with an unhinged smile on my face and say.

"Tell your father, I'm coming for him and his pack. Anyone who had anything to do with harming my mom will die. I will kill every fucking last one of you!" I scream. I struggle against the arms around my waist; I'm placed on my feet gently and spun around. Creed looks down at me with so much remorse and sadness, a strangled sob burst out of me. He engulfs me in an embrace and cradles me against his chest as I breakdown.

"I'll see you Saturday for the mating ceremony--mate." Creed doesn't respond to Josh, instead he picks me up and I wrap my legs and arms around him as he walks inside the house. I close my eyes and bury my head in the crook of his neck and let the tears soak him. Sobs continue to tear from me; my chest feels like it's caving in. I'm struggling to breathe; she's gone, my beautiful fearless caring mom is gone! She was fucking taken from me; I cling to Creed tighter, I grip the back of his hair and pull, and he hisses in pain but says nothing. I hear a door slam shut, and then a few seconds later Creed is trying to lower me, but I won't let go. He spins around and sits down; I open one eye and see he's sitting on a bed. He runs his hands up and down my back while I continue to cry. I tighten my hold on him and tug on his hair harder as I dig my nails into the back of his neck, if I never met him or his family my mom would still be here!

"I hate you." I choke out, he releases a loud whoosh of air.

"I know."

"This is your entire stupid fault."

"I know."

"She would still be here with me if you didn't chase me!" He sighs and then reaches around to untangle my arms from his neck and hair. He pushes until I'm sitting back looking down at him, it's now I realize what a compromising position I am in, I am literally straddling his lap. He claps my face between his hands and uses his thumbs to wipe away my tears that refuse to stop falling.

"I can't undo what I have done but given the choice, I would do it all again Jess." I reel back as if he slapped me.

"Why the hell would you say that?" His eyes turn blue, I don't care if he changes into a dog right now, I will not back down.

"Because if I didn't chase you then you would be at their mercy right fucking now. You would be mated to that fucking slimy weasel Josh, before you even knew what was happening. You should be thanking me!" It's a reflex I swear. Okay maybe not, but he deserves it. I struck out so quick he didn't get a chance to stop me, as I slap him. I reach out with my other hand and slap him again. He still won't do anything, so I start to pound my fist against his chest and shove him. Gut wrenching sobs tear from me as I break apart in the arms of the man I blame for my mother's death.

"I hate you, I fucking hate you so much!" He wraps his arms around me and hauls me toward him, in one swift move he turns us, so I am lying flat on the bed as he hovers over me, I ignore the heat that courses through my veins at his close proximity. His eyes are back to their normal hazel color, he looks at me with so much pity, I narrow my eyes and glare up at him.

"Hate me all you want Jess, just know that I will trample through any barriers you have between us, and I will demolish you if I have to until you see that I am your only choice. When all of this begins to make sense, you will understand why I am doing this. I don't have a choice or a say in any of it, just like you.

I'm sorry about your mom, we will help you seek vengeance for her but before that, you need to make a choice."

"W-what choice?"

"If you're going to shift or not, if you are then we will help you and guide you. If you don't, then after your birthday on Saturday you are free to go, and I will make sure no one ever comes for you." He moves back and takes a couple of steps back; I quickly sit up and track his movements with my eyes. "There is a bathroom through there; I'll get Callie to bring some of her clothes." I dart my gaze around the room, I see clothes, and posters, a desk in the corner and some trophies on a shelf.

"This is your room?" He nods. "Wait, if you have a bathroom in here, why were you using Callie's?" A devilish glint enters his eyes as he answers.

"In the hopes of you joining me in the shower." I gasp at his crude words while he chuckles at my unease. He turns around and stalks out of the room while I just sit here and stare at the closed door he just left through. His mood swings are giving me whiplash.

I snoop around the room and try to see if I can find anything to give me a better insight into who Creed really is. Aside from a few posters on the wall there are no other personal touches, his room doesn't tell you anything about who he really is. I give up and decide to have a shower. I'm taken back when I see my reflection in the mirror. I have dry blood crusted to my chin and chest; my shirt is ruined. Not wanting to dwell on it, I jump in the shower and am standing under the massive rainfall shower head. My mind won't stop reeling. I'm trying to process what I have learnt and deal with the fact that my life has changed forever. On top of all that, my mom---she's gone, just thinking about never seeing her again has a horrible gut wrenching sob tearing from me. I crumble to the shower floor and wrap my arms around my knees and rest my head on top of them, there's this pain inside my chest that feels like I'm tearing apart from the inside out. I feel like I'm suffocating and can't breathe, I have never felt pain like this--ever. It's excruciating and debilitating, I can't move or even think straight.

The pain morphs into anger, I dig my nails into my skin and bite hard on my bottom lip. Why did they have to take her from me? She wasn't just my mom she was my world, my best friend. I release a loud long scream.

"Why her?" I choke out between sobs; I have nothing left now in this world. I hear voices from outside the bathroom, I don't care what everyone in this house thinks. I just lost my mom, and right now nothing else matters to me, I don't give a shit about any of this werewolf crap, I just want to leave and never look back. Strong arms wrap around me, and I let out a squeal, once the heat surges through my body, I know who it is, he sits down behind me and wraps his arms around my sobbing body and pulls me back against him. He's still fully clothed and right now I don't even care that I'm naked, I'm too focused on trying to hold myself together and not break apart. I'm so angry at everything and everyone, I want to turn around and lash out at Creed but at the same time I want him to hold me. This unexplainable pull and feelings I have whenever he is near or touches me isn't healthy, I need to sort my crap out and come up with a plan.

"You know, my mom tells us that tears are our body's way of cleaning our souls." I stiffen at the sound of his voice. I'm okay with him being in here and holding me but I am not okay with him talking to me and being nice. I want him to be rude and mean like he has been so it will make my choice easier.

"What does that mean?" He chuckles huskily. That sound has my heart beating faster and my body craving to hear it again.

"Honestly, I have no idea. Mom is all about saying weird cryptic shit, I just thought it might be the right thing to say given what's happened." I turn my head slightly and stare at him over my shoulder. His eyes shine with lust which makes no sense.

"Why are you here Credence?"

"Because apparently I can't stay away from you." I'm reeling at how honest he is being.

"Why?"

"My wolf won't allow me."

"How come you, Callie and Cole can change or whatever you call it into a wolf, but I can't?" He releases a long sigh and brushes loose strands of my hair behind my ear.

"Because you weren't given the choice, we all grew up knowing what we are. We were taught how to shift by our parents, without guidance we would be like you."

"I want you to teach me how to shift." Creed's eyes widen.

"You want to shift?"

"I want vengeance for my mom, and if becoming a wolf is what I need to do for that to happen, then so be it." His brow furrows as he begins to shake his head.

"If you shift you will be bound, you will be sought after until you are claimed. Is that what you want?" I grit my teeth and make sure he can see the seriousness in my eyes.

"I am not an object to be claimed, I want justice for my mom and that's it. I don't want to be alpha or the boss or what the hell it's called."

"It doesn't work that way Jess--"

"I don't care, I won't stay here either." Creed's eyes change to blue, and a rumbling sound comes from deep inside his chest.

"You can't leave."

"Watch me, I have no reason to stay here." A look of hurt crosses his face, before I can dwell on it the look vanishes, it was so brief I would swear it didn't happen if I wasn't paying such close attention. He drops his arms from around me and stands, he looks down at me with an unreadable expression.

"Your loss little alpha." He breathes out then stands and stalks out of the bathroom dripping wet. I refuse to sit here any longer and wallow in my own self-pity, I stand and quickly wash my hair then get out.

After I exit the bathroom and head into the bedroom, I see clothes laid out on the bed for me. I quickly change and then run my fingers through my hair, I don't have a brush so this will have to do. Now that I'm out of the shower and in Creed's room alone I start to feel awkward about being here. Honestly, it's not like I know Callie and Cole all that well, I don't know Kane at all, and Creed is just an ass ninety percent of the time and screws with my head. Meg seems really nice and genuine but it's not like I actually know her.

I lay down on the bed and stare up at the ceiling lost in my own thoughts for so long I don't know how much time has passed. A knock sounds at the door, I sit up and lean against the headboard as I call out to whoever it is to come in. I'm not surprised to see it's Callie and Meg who drew the short straw to come and check on me. Both women wear pitying looks and it irks me, I don't need their pity, I know my anger toward them is irrational but part of me blames them for what happened to my mom. Callie and Meg each take a seat on the end of the bed, they share a look before Callie releases a long sigh and turns to face me.

"Babe, we are all so sorr--"

"Please don't. I don't need your apology or your pity, I just need a solution." The firm tone of my voice has Callie stiffening.

"What solution sweetie?" Meg asks.

"The solution on how the heck I get justice for my mom!" Meg's features harden and she sits up straighter and says,

"Then let's start brainstorming because I won't let those sons of bitches get away with what they have done to my friend."

CHAPTER NINETEEN
Jessica

After talking to Callie and Meg for a few hours and coming up with a plan, that we all seem happy with, they bid me goodnight and leave. I know what we have planned is tricky and complicated, if we work as a well-oiled trio, we can make this work. Callie was really unsure and apprehensive at the start; this plan means she would have to lie to her father and brothers. I know she hates the idea of lying, but I need her to do this, she doesn't owe me a single thing and we have only known each other a short amount of time. We agreed that the hardest one to fool and keep in the dark would be Creed. I know they are both hiding something from me about him. Honestly, I just don't care right now, my only focus and concern is getting justice for my mom.

I close my eyes and try to clear my mind and focus on trying to sleep rather than lay here and think about my grief. I release a long sigh and scoot down the bed until my eyes peek out of the blanket. I'm so exhausted it takes me no time at all to fall into a dreamless slumber.

I jolt upright in bed gasping for air, I look around the strange room and panic seeps in, where am I? Arms wrap around me and let out a shriek, I thrash around to get free but still when he speaks.

"It was just a dream, you're okay princess." I gulp in a large lungful of air then sag in Creed's embrace. I will the tears that are threatening to spill from my eyes not to fall, it's at this exact moment that my mind finally catches up. Why is Creed in bed with me?

"What are you doing in here?"

"Sleeping."

"Why?"

"It is my bed ya know?" I grit my teeth and try to pull away from him, his arms lock around me and I growl in frustration which just causes him to laugh.

"Let me go." He leans down so his lips brush against my lobe when he speaks.

"Never. I thought I was pretty clear when I told you that. You run; I chase." Anger sparks inside me.

"You chasing me cost me my mom." He releases a loud whoosh of air before sitting back, he hauls me back against his chest, I'm now sitting between his legs with my back plastered to his chest. The silence between us stretches for so long that my lids begin to get heavy, and I feel sleep pulling me under just before I fully succumb to it, I hear him say.

"I'm so sorry princess, if I could change it I would, but she knew from the start."

When I wake the next morning Creed is gone, which I am grateful for. Dealing with his moods first thing in the morning is not something I think anyone would enjoy. I sit up and notice there is a pile of clothes at the bottom of the bed. I hate that I have to borrow Callie's clothes, but I'm going to change that today. I take a quick shower and use the toothbrush that was sitting on the basin, I change into the clothes laid out for me and quickly exit the room to go in search of the others. I hear voices coming from the kitchen and as soon as I round the corner and they see me, everyone falls silent.

Awkward.

"Uh, I'm gonna go now but thank you all...for you know." Before I can turn, Creed is out of his chair and standing in front of me glaring at me like I just pissed in his cereal.

"Where are you going?" He grits out, his demanding tone irritates me.

"None of your business Credence, I don't answer to you." I move to step around him and then everything goes south really, really quick. Creed grips my upper arms then moves so quick across the room until my back slams against the wall. I gasp in shock as his body presses me harder against the wall.

"Back away from her now Creed!" I turn my head slightly toward Cole, I stop as soon as Creed releases a long deadly growl that sends shivers down my spine. I snap my gaze back to him and bite my bottom lip to stop the shriek that wants to tear out of my throat. His eyes are a deep blue, his lip is pulled back in a snarl and the look in his eyes tells me he is angry, really angry. "Credence." I can hear the panic in Cole's voice but this time I don't attempt to look toward him in fear of pissing Creed off again.

"Son, let her go." Creed looks me directly in the eyes as he answers his father.

"Never." That one word holds so much weight and meaning, the longer I stare into his eyes the warmer I become. I'm starting to get accustomed to this feeling of warmth whenever Creed looks at me or touches me, but right now the way he is looking at me is more concerning than the heat coursing through my body.

"Jess sweetie, you're gonna have to calm his beast before he releases you. If we try to approach, especially the guys, he will attack us." I don't miss the slight tremble in Meg's voice, I keep my gaze on Creed as I ask.

"Why would he attack you?"

"Because his wolf is an alpha male and sees other males as a threat, standard wolfy things you know." Even I know Callie is full of it, but I don't call her on her blatant lie, I keep my gaze on Creed as I reach up and place both my hands against his chest. He shivers at the feeling of my touch and his body loses some of its tension. The heat within me begins to rise in temperature, whatever this is between Creed and me, I know he and his family are hiding what this really is from me.

"I need you to move back Black." His brow furrows in confusion and his eyes narrow.

"What does that mean?"

"Black?" He grunts, I smile up at him wickedly. "Well Jacob Black is a werewolf, so I thought it fitting to give you a pet name after him." Creed looks at me like I have lost my mind, I fight to hide the smirk that wants to break free.

"Who the hell is Jacob?" Oh my lord, how does he not know?

"You my friend need a Twilight marathon."

"I'm not your friend." I hate to admit it, but his words kind of hurt.

"Well, non-friend can you back up please because people who are not friends definitely do not stand this close to each other." If possible, he presses in closer, I hold my breath and stand still.

"We are past the point of being friends, we are so much more." I have had enough of his cryptic crap; I shove against his chest and don't stop until he finally moves back. I release the breath I was holding and quickly move away from him toward the others, Kane and Cole move as far away from me as possible. Meg and Callie try to reach out to me as I pass them to head for the front door. I don't stop to say goodbye. I grip the handle and pull the door open and make my way down the porch stairs to start the long walk back to the cabin.

The walk back to the cabin took a lot longer than I thought, but nevertheless I made it here in one piece. I've been standing outside for ten minutes staring at the closed door trying to work up the strength to go in. I'm scared. What if I walk in and it's a crime scene, I will never be able to unsee that. What if there are signs of a struggle and I see how hard my mom fought, a lump begins to form inside my throat at the thought of her fighting for her life. I clench my hands into fists at my side, anger courses through my body like lava. I will get justice for her even if it costs me my life, I will not let them get away with this. A car approaching has me spinning around, I tense and wait for whoever it is to show themselves. I'm in shock when the doors open and see who it is.

"What are you all doing here?" Kane, Meg, Cole, and Callie stand before me with unreadable looks on their faces. Callie approaches me and clasps both my hands in hers and meets my gaze.

"Losing my real mom was hard to swallow, we didn't exactly get a chance to know her, but the loss still hurt. I can't imagine what it must be like for you to have known her your whole life and then to lose her. We want to be here for you Jess, no strings attached I swear. We care about you and only want to help." I can hear the truth in her words.

"I-I don't know what I'm gonna do Callie, I can't stay here or--"

"Then don't stay here, come home with us and stay until you figure out your next move." I snap my gaze to Cole in shock.

"I can't do that." Cole scoffs.

"Why not?"

"Because I...uh...I shouldn't" I stutter out which just causes Cole to roll his eyes.

"Sweetheart, we would love it if you would come home with us. Plus, if you don't my son won't come home." I cock my brow at Meg not understanding her meaning, she sighs. "Come out now." Huh, I look at the car, but no doors open. Then I hear a rustling sound from the bushes on the other side and see a huge gray and white wolf, I clamp my mouth shut to stop the scream from tumbling out. The wolf moves toward us, and I watch in shock, its fur looks like silk and its paws are huge! When it nears us, it stops and turns to look at me, I gasp. Deep blue eyes stare at me with such intensity that my knees nearly give out. His ears stand up and he tilts his head back slightly and sniffs the air, a low rumble sounds from the wolf. I feel this compelling urge to go to him and touch him, this is such a weird moment standing here staring into the eyes of this animal. But he isn't just a wolf though, I know with every fiber of my being that this wolf is Credence.

"There's clothes for you in the back of the truck, change and let's help Jess pack." I turn to Kane in shock, I never agreed to stay with them. When his gaze lands back on me he smiles and shrugs his shoulders. "Like my wife said, if you don't come back our son will end up staying out in the woods and it's not safe for him to be away from his pack right now. Please listen to Cole and Callie, stay with us for as long as you need." I mull his words over for a moment, even though I think Creed is a tool, I would hate for him to get hurt because of me.

"Okay, but on one condition."

"Name it." I meet Kane's gaze, so he is able to see the seriousness in my eyes.

"After my birthday on Saturday when I turn--change and I get justice for my mom, I'm leaving, and you will promise not to stop me." I ignore the loud growl coming from the back of the SUV. Kane and Meg share a look that I choose to ignore and wait for him to answer.

"You have our word that Meg and I will not stop you if you

choose to leave. But if you decide to stay, you are welcome in our home as long as you like."

I stand here with my key inserted in the lock and my hand on the handle working up the courage to open the freaking door. I take a few deep breaths and close my eyes. I have to do this for her. She wouldn't want me to be weak and cry all the time. She would want me to finish school and live the life she always wanted me to live. I stiffen when I feel him stand behind me, my eyes snap open when his hand lands on top of mine. I wish I could say I didn't shiver at the feeling of him pressed against me, but then I would be lying. Having no idea what the hell is going on between us or what this feeling is but it's a distraction I can't afford right now.

"We're with you--I'm with you. You don't have to face this alone little alpha; we'll help you through this."

"Until you decide we're not friends again and be an ass." His low chuckle stirs something inside me, rather than focus on what that feeling might be, I open the door to the cabin and gasp.

"The fuck are you doing here?" Creed snaps.

CHAPTER TWENTY
Jessica

"That's not exactly the greeting I was going for, but okay." I stare at her open mouthed and shocked, what the hell is she doing here?

"Don't play coy with me Kayla, it doesn't suit you." I can feel the anger radiating off Creed, Kayla darts her eyes around the room. I can tell she is nervous; I make my way inside and don't get more than two feet before I'm tugged backward and pushed behind Creed. The rest of his family pile inside and form a blockade around me.

"What the hell are you doing here?"

"I came to help Kelly." I scoff and push between Creed and Callie, so I can see her. I see remorse and regret clear as day in her eyes, her shoulders sag.

"Why?"

"Believe it or not Jess, I am not your enemy." I narrow my eyes.

"Your left hook would say otherwise!"

"You stole my boyfriend." I gasp, she has to be kidding.

"Creed was never yours to begin with, you knew that." I stare at Cole in disbelief; anyone with eyes could tell they were a couple.

"It wasn't just an arrangement to me." Kayla looks to Creed, and I see the devastation in her eyes, she's in love with him. "It was real to me." Creed completely ignores her statement.

"Why are you here?"

"Because what happened was wrong and it was never meant to go down like that. I swear I didn't know." I snap, the anger takes hold of me, and I lose it.

"You lying bitch! My mother is dead and it's all your fucking fault." I try to launch at her, but arms wrap around my middle, and I'm hauled back against Creed's chest, I try to wrangle out of his grip to no avail. "My mom is dead because of you!" Kayla darts her gaze over all of us in confusion.

"What the hell are you talking about you dimwit?" I glare at her, and growls sound from the others at her insult.

"The death of her mother." Meg grits out, Kayla's gaze lands on me and her brow is furrowed in confusion.

"Your mothers not dead you idiot, who the hell told you that?" I go completely still in Creed's arms. Could she be right?

"If you are playing some game Kayla, I will kill you, your problem is with me not with her."

"Fuck you Credence, you broke my heart for a girl who doesn't even know what she is or who she is to you."

"Enough!" Kane's voice booms throughout the cabin, the weight of that one word has everyone standing straighter and wanting to obey him. "Where is Katharine then Kayla, and for your own sake you better tell the truth." Kayla squares her shoulders and stands tall.

"I want your word."

"My word for what?"

"That as...alpha of the Reeves pack you will grant me sanctuary." I hear Callie and Meg gasp.

"Why would you need sanctuary in my pack?" Kayla stiffens for a moment before turning around and lifting her shirt. I begin to glare at her thinking she is about to strip or something but stop. My mouth hangs open in shock when I see the scars lining her back, thick welts of skin are plastered all over her, I can tell some of the marks are new.

"What the hell happened to you Kayla?" Creed sounds so torn; how could he not know about those scars? Kayla pulls her shirt back down and turns to face us, a sad smile crosses her face as she stares at Creed.

"That's why I would never take my shirt off, I never wanted you to know."

"Who the fuck did that to you Kay?" Cole demands.

"You are not the only ones who think my dad is a monster." Gasps ring out around the room; this poor girl has been abused by her own father for God knows how long. My heart hurts for her, no child should ever be treated like that.

"Jacob did that to you?" I hear the anger that laces Kane's tone.

"Yes, and others. Being born a female isn't a gift in our pack, it's a curse, Dad hates that I'm older than Josh."

"But you're in the same year?" I question, her gaze darts to me as she shakes her head.

"Josh is a year younger; dad made the school put him up a year. If I graduate before Josh, I bring shame to my family because I have a vagina and not a dick." Callie moves toward Kayla and places both her hands on her shoulders.

"I am so sorry this happened to you Kayla, your father is a fucking monster and will pay for what he has done."

"As alpha of the Reeves pack I grant you sanctuary. Now we will discuss this further once we return home, but we need to collect Jess's things and leave before your father is alerted that we are here. The council will not tolerate a pack war over a non-shifter." He's talking about me, I'm the *non-shifter.*

We load what we can fit into Kane's SUV and my mom's car, the rest stays here until I figure out what to do with it. Creed chose to ride back with me in my mom's car while his family and Kayla rode back in their SUV.

"Do you believe her?" I release a whoosh of air and grip the steering wheel tighter.

"I don't know. I want to believe her, but after what Josh said--"

"Technically Josh didn't exactly admit to it. Kayla might be right." I grit my teeth in anger.

"So just because your girlfriend says something, then it's automatically the truth?"

"Call her my girlfriend again and see what I do to you princess." I look at him and the smug dick just grins at me, I turn and glare out the windshield wishing I could slap that look off his face.

"Has anyone ever told you that you're the worst triplet, your brother and sister are so much nicer."

"My brother and sister have the luxury of having fun, I don't." Bitterness coats each of his words.

"What does that mean?"

"Nothing."

"Fine then answer me this, what did Kayla mean when she said I don't even know what I am to you?" I see him stiffen out of the corner of my eye.

"If your mom wasn't taken, would you have wanted to shift?" I don't miss the fact that he ignored my question.

"I don't know, I thought about it but then my mom told me that I wouldn't be able to leave."

"Why do you want to leave so bad?" This is the longest conversation Creed and I have had without one of us going off, it's...different.

"My whole life I have moved around every few months, going to college means I get to stay somewhere for years. I have always wanted to go to college and live out the American dream, staying here means I have to give it up."

"Then don't shift, go live your dream and forget about all of this." I'm taken back by his answer, we both remain silent the rest of the drive back to his house. I keep playing his words over and over in my head, I feel like there is a double meaning to them, but I can't decipher it. As we pull up behind his dad's SUV, I start to feel awkward, I pretty much just moved myself into their home and I don't even know them all that well. Before I lose myself in my own thoughts, Callie opens my door, kneels beside me, and looks across at her brother.

"You have to go now; this is girl talk." Creed grunts and then exits the car to go help the others unload my things from the SUV. Callie turns to me and places her hand on my leg and smiles. "I, California Reeves, swear to be the best roommate and best friend ever, if you'll have me." I can't keep the smile off my face, so I get out of the car and wrap my arms around Callie.

"Thank you." She returns my embrace.

"We'll make this work Jess, I swear."

CHAPTER TWENTY-ONE

Jessica

After unloading both cars and taking my stuff into Callie's room, Kane and Meg offered to store my mom's belongings that I brought with me in the basement, I was grateful that they allowed me to bring some of her things with me, I couldn't leave it all behind. Creed has been MIA for a while, I haven't seen Kayla either. I hate to admit it, but a small part of me is jealous and worried that they may be off somewhere shagging or doing God knows what. I know I have no right to think like that, but deep down inside I know I'm lying to myself when I say I'm not attracted to Creed. I don't know what it is, but ever since the first day I saw him I have felt this pull or whatever you want to call it. Whenever he is near, my body alerts me and wants to saddle up next to him. This type of thing cannot be healthy, I shouldn't even be thinking about this right now when there is a chance my mom could be alive. I snap out of my thoughts when Cole throws a pillow at me, I turn and glare playfully at him.

"What was that for?"

"I have been calling your name for ages and you never answered." I smile sheepishly.

"Sorry, got a lot on my mind."

"Yeah, I figured. Look it's Wednesday today and I know your birthday is on Saturday so how about we celebrate early?" I appreciate him trying to cheer me up but right now I couldn't think of anything worse. Before I can voice that Callie cuts in.

"I know you're worried about your mom, dad is trying to get in contact with the council see if we can do anything about it. In the meantime, try and take your mind off it and let us throw you a party Friday night?" I want to say no, but then a part of me that has never had friends is screaming at me to let them do this for me. I should be focusing on getting my mom back and not thinking about my stupid birthday.

"I want to hear what happens with your dad and this council first." Both Cole and Callie high five each other while I continue to unpack my stuff. Callie cleared some space in her wardrobe for me and Meg brought in a dresser, they are all being so nice and welcoming. I need to find a way to pay them back, I know this is only temporary, but I don't expect them to feed me and put a roof over my head for nothing.

We're all sitting around the dinner table as Meg serves the food, it smells amazing. I look around and notice Creed and Kayla are still missing, I push the spark of anger that flares inside me down. Creed isn't my boyfriend so he can do whatever he likes, I have no right to tell him what he can and can't do. If the tables were turned, I'm sure he would have no trouble telling me what to do.

"I got the principal to send over your class work, you will all be home-schooled until further notice." Callie and Cole nod their heads.

"Does that go for me as well?" Kane smiles kindly and nods his head.

"Yes, you will remain here with us until we know the outcome of Saturday."

"Callie told me you were trying to call the council

concerning my mother." Kane's face is unreadable, but I can tell from the way he stiffens that whatever he is about to say isn't good news.

"Yes, I spoke with them, and they are not prepared to get involved until you shift. Technically they don't see what Jacob did as wrong because he is your mom's alpha."

"What the heck, seriously?"

"I'm sorry Jess, my hands are tied." Tears begin to well in my eyes. "I tried to reach out to Jacob, but he is ignoring my calls. I've sent a couple of men to his house to ask if he will agree to a meeting." I don't want to cry here at the table, so I stand.

"Sorry, I just need a minute." I turn and hightail it out the front door, I freeze when I see Creed and Kayla making their way up the stairs. Anger surges to the surface, I latch onto the anger. The last thing I want to do is cry in front of these two. Creed holding me the other night while I broke down was bad enough.

"What's wrong?" I ignore the concern in his voice and move to shove past them when his hand snakes out to grip my wrist, I spin around and glare up at him.

"Let her go, clearly she doesn't want to tell you." Kayla reaches out and places her hand on Creed's chest and I see red. I snatch my hand out of his grip and send him the frostiest look I can manage.

"Listen to your girlfriend Credence, leave me alone." I turn and stomp down the first two stairs but then squeal when I'm hauled backward by my shirt, his arm wraps around my middle and I'm slammed against the front of the house. I yelp when my head hits the wall behind me, I glare up into deep blue eyes. He presses in close to me and I turn my head to the side, bad move. He drops his face into the crook of my neck and inhales.

"What did I tell you about calling her that?" I wrack my brain for what the hell he is on about then it hits me, he told not to call her his girlfriend again.

"Let her go, come on let's go eat. I smell how good it is from out here." Creed doesn't even attempt to move as he answers Kayla.

"Go, Jess and I have some things to discuss." I can feel her eyes burning holes into me, but I don't dare move. After seeing Creed as a wolf today and having all this madness confirmed I'm scared to piss him off. He has really sharp teeth when he's a wolf and the last thing I want is for him to bite me if I annoy him too much. Kayla lets out a loud moan and then storms inside and slams the door behind herself. My heart begins to pound inside my chest now that I am standing out here alone with Creed, he could eat me, and no one would know. "Why are you shaking?" I swallow a couple of times before I answer him.

"You want the truth?"

"Lie to everyone else but not me Jess." He says as he runs his nose up and down the length of my neck. Goosebumps break out over my skin; I hate that my body reacts to him this way.

"Because you scare the shit out of me." Creed pulls back and stares down at me, his eyes are back to their normal hazel color, his hair falls onto his forehead, and I have to shove my hands in my pockets to stop myself from reaching up and pushing it out of his face.

"You're scared of me now because you saw me as a wolf?" I nod my head. "Well princess, a little newsflash for you. If you decide to shift you will be a wolf as well, your mother and father are both shifters."

"Wh-what happens if I choose not to shift, will this wolf council thing hunt me down?" His face morphs into anger in a split second.

"If they come for you, it will be their worst mistake. The choice is yours Jess, if you shift you have to lead and claim a mate. If you don't then you can never come back, you will never be allowed contact with your friends or family."

"What? Why?"

"We cannot risk humans finding out about us, you will be monitored by the council to make sure you don't pose a threat to our race for many years. Either way, whatever you choose you will never be entirely free."

Creed led me back inside, when we enter the dining room all conversation stops. I can feel Kayla's gaze on our joined hands. I try and pull my hand out of his so I can take the seat between Callie and Cole but he won't let me go. One look from Creed has Cole standing and moving around the table with his plate to sit between Kayla and Meg. I roll my eyes and this time when I pull my hand away, he lets go, I slump into the chair next to Callie. while Creed sits next to me. Meg offers a plate with delicious food on top to Creed, conversation picks up again, but I remain silent and basked in the normality of how this family is together. I envy Callie right now, the way her dad looks at her with so much love, I will never have that. You can tell how proud Kane and Meg are of their children. Cole and Kane began to talk about his upcoming football game and what strategies his coach is implementing. Callie nudging me in the side pulls me from my thoughts.

"Sorry, what did you say?" Callie grins at me and shakes her head.

"I was just saying about how we want to throw you a party on Friday."

"What party?" Creed interjects, Callie ignores her brother's question and continues.

"Mom wants to help plan as well."

"Callie, I told you and Cole--"

"You knew as well?" Creed snaps at his brother, Cole shrugs his shoulders and leans back in his chair.

"Course I did, it was my idea. Not my fault you were busy with her." Creed growls low in his throat at Cole's insinuation that he was up to no good with Kayla. Before Creed loses his cool, I quickly cut in.

"If we can find out about my mom--"

"What do you want to know?" I grind my teeth in irritation at being cut off for the second time and glare at Kayla.

"For starters, is my mom alive?"

"She was the last time I saw her." I clench my hands into fists at how blasé she sounds when referring to my mom.

"Is she okay?" She pops a piece of bread into her mouth and chews slowly before answering me, she's enjoying this way too much.

"Bit roughed up but she's fine." I push back from the table so fast my chair topples over behind me; Kayla is on her feet as well and ready to fight if it comes to it. Creed and Callie stand beside me, I can feel the anger radiating off both of them.

"Cut the shit Kayla and tell her everything you just told me." I stare at Creed in shock, his gaze meets mine, a knowing smirk crosses his beautiful face. "You didn't think I wanted to spend time with her did you? I needed information and the only way I knew how to get that was for her to think I wanted to be near her." I gape at him in shock, Kayla begins to growl but stops when Kane slams his fist down on the table.

"Everyone sit down now! Kayla, you will tell us all, what you have disclosed to my son."

CHAPTER TWENTY-TWO

Jessica

We all take our seats again; tension ramps up in the room. I begin to fidget with my hands in my lap as I wait for Kayla to speak, I stifle a gasp when I feel Creed's large hand land on top of mine beneath the table. The look he gives me has me relaxing slightly, I can tell from the look in his eyes that what she is about to tell us is important.

"Kayla, now would be a good time to start talking." Kayla nods her head to Kane and takes a deep breath before she speaks.

"That night, we were only supposed to go and collect Jess and her mom. Dad wanted Jess to see the pack and what she could have if she joined us. He knows that she is close to the triplets and that Creed has a...fascination with her, he worried that she would be swayed to join you lot instead of us. When we got there, things went south when we scented Creed in wolf form, dad thought he was there to claim her. After Creed took Jess, dad sent Josh and Billy after them to try to bring her back. Her mom fought us and put up a great fight." Her eyes dart to me and I'm shocked at the look of admiration in her eyes. "Your mom didn't go down easily; she fought against three shifters and gave them a run for their money. She is strong, and you are bloody lucky to have a woman who would fight like that for you. Anyway, after dad and the others subdued her, Billy and Josh returned empty handed, dad decided to take her as leverage."

"Why?" I cut in.

"Because he knows she is your weak spot and plans to exploit it."

"Exploit it for what exactly?" Her eyes harden.

"So you will agree to be claimed by my brother." Growls

sound out around the table; Creed's hand begins to grip mine tightly.

"That isn't going to happen!"

"How do you propose to stop him then Colton?" Cole glares at her, if looks could burn you alive, Kayla would be on fire right now.

"By sneaking in and releasing her mom." Kayla shakes her head and looks at Cole like he's thick.

"I tried to set her free and all that got me was more scars." I flinch at the coldness in her tone.

"Why would you want to help my mom?" Kayla drops her gaze to the table as she speaks.

"I may not like you, but I can respect any woman who would go through the lengths that your mother did to keep you safe. Plus, she told me if I freed her she would convince Meg to allow me into the Reeves pack."

"Your dad beat you for that?"

"Yes Kelly, not everyone has a parent who loves and adores them like you do. My father despises me, he won't kill Katherine. He'll use her to sway Jess on Saturday; if she doesn't choose Josh I honestly don't know what he will do. My father is obsessed with power and being the biggest pack, having Jess mated to Josh will give him what he's always craved."

"I am not mating or whatever the hell it is called with your brother." Her sad eyes meet mine.

"Then prepare to say goodbye to your mom for real, because he won't let you mate with Creed. He would rather kill you and your mom than see that happen." I still in my chair, I'm too shocked by her words to voice my retort. Did she just say mate with Creed? Why the hell would I do that? "You have no idea what you are to him, do you?" I stare at her in shock, my mouth opens and closes but no words come out. Her eyes double to the size of dinner plates as she looks between the both of us.

"Don't." Is the only word Creed utters, I dart my eyes to Cole and Callie, they both refuse to meet my gaze and find their food more interesting.

"I can smell you all over her and so will they come Saturday. How do you expect to hide it?"

"Shut your mouth Kayla and stay out of it."

"Creed, you're going to get her mother killed!"

"I said stay out of it!" Creed yells, Kayla slinks back into her chair and I flinch from his harsh tone. What the hell is he hiding from me that will get my mom killed? I turn to Creed and wrench my hands out from under his grip.

"What the hell is she talking about?" His face hardens and an angry glint enters his eyes.

"Nothing for you to worry about princess, you don't want to shift so you don't have to know." He has some nerve to sit there and speak to me like this.

"You have no right to judge me, I just found out about all of this." I gesture around wildly with my hands.

"You were the one who told me you wanted to be free."

"Isn't that what everyone wants? Who are you to judge me for that, you have no right!" Creed slams his fist down on the table and I jump in my seat.

"I have every damn right, your choice effe-- you know what,

don't even worry about it. Get your mom back and you can both ride off into the sunset and be free of all of this. Just don't regret your decision because you won't get a second chance. You want your mom back, Tell Jacob you won't shift and give up your claim to both packs. It's fine, you can leave and be happy, while we stay behind and fight to the death." I flinch from the cold harsh tone of his voice.

"That's enough son, Jess owes us and the packs nothing. Katherine chose to keep her in the dark for her safety and if she chooses to leave, we will deal with it." Kane sounds defeated and that worries the hell out of me, I see looks of resignation on their faces. I am missing something big here.

"Why do you all look so distraught?" A sinking feeling settles inside my stomach when Meg meets my gaze. She tries to mask the look of sadness on her face but fails.

"We all knew that you would come back to Rosewood before your eighteenth birthday, it wasn't an if it was a when. Jacob and Kane have been on the knife's edge so to speak for years awaiting your return. The council has forbidden any attacks from each pack until you make a decision."

"A decision about what?" Meg smiles but it doesn't reach her eyes.

"About if you will shift or not. If you shift you will become alpha, Kane and Jacob will have to stand down."

"And if I don't shift?"

"Then Kane and Jacob will go to war, neither of them will allow the other to lead their packs so it will be to the death." I gasp in horror, how freaking barbaric!

"Tell her the best part though mom." Sarcasm is thick in Creed's voice; Meg gives him a disapproving look before meeting my gaze.

"If one alpha falls, then their whole bloodline will have to be eradicated. Kane wouldn't do that to Josh and Kayla no matter the circumstances, but Jacob would." I dart my gaze to Cole and Callie and both smile at me, I see no anger or malice in their gaze, just understanding. I turn to Creed who is staring right at me with a cruel smile on his beautiful face.

"You see, your freedom costs my family their lives. So run away little princess and don't look back, if anything and I mean anything happens to my family because of you, I will kill you." I hear the truth in every single one of his words, I don't cower under the intensity of his gaze. I had no idea that my decision or wants would cost someone their life. Right now, at this moment I need to make a choice: live my life, or save theirs? I hold Creed's gaze as I ask.

"What if I choose to stay, what will I have to do then?"

"College is out of the question." I narrow my eyes at him.

"I get that jackass; I mean what would I have to do to be alpha?"

"Being alpha means hundreds of people depend on you. It's a full-time job and a way of life Jess." I swivel around to meet Kane's gaze. "You will be responsible for merging two packs that have hated each other for years. You will need Beta's and Delta's to help you with day to day running of things--"

"Will you be okay to give this all up to me?" I cut in. Kane smiles and lays his hand on top of Meg's as he says.

"I'm ready to pass the torch over so to speak. I'm tired and

I long to have time with my wife and kids, I have been doing this for years Jess. If you decide to do this, I will help you, don't make a decision based on what Creed has just said. You have to be sure; you cannot do this for anyone else but yourself. This must be your choice, there is no going back after this."

CHAPTER TWENTY-THREE

Jessica

Laying here next to Callie in her bed while she sleeps, I stare up at the ceiling wondering what to do. If I shift then I lose my dreams, I'll be stuck here. If I don't shift, I risk the lives of others. Right now, the only thing I want is to talk to my mom, she would know what to do. Today is Wednesday which means come tomorrow I only have two days to decide what I'm going to do. I know myself and if my leaving causes Callie, Cole, Kane, Meg or even Creed harm I would never forgive myself. I don't particularly like Kayla, but I would hate for her to get hurt, as for Josh he will get what's coming to him the slimy snake.

After laying here for another hour tossing and turning and not being able to sleep, I grab my phone and notice a message. It must have come in while we were eating dinner, it's an unknown number. I open the message and freeze. It's a picture of my mom...chained in a cage. The look in her eyes is pure fear, tears leak from my eyes as I sit up in bed. I can't stop looking at the way her body is cowered in the corner with her arms wrapped around herself, she has chains on her hands, ankles and neck. Those assholes are hurting her! I look below the picture and see one word that sends ice through my veins.

Shift!

This is clearly from Jacob or one of his minions, threatening me and leaving me no choice. I attempt to call the number but it's an automated response saying the number is no longer in service. I grind my teeth together and wipe the tears from my face, I throw the covers back and slip out of bed. I decide to head toward the kitchen to grab myself a glass of milk and turn to head back toward Callie's room but freeze when I see a shadow standing in the doorway. I gasp and nearly drop the glass but manage to grip it tighter at the last second. I should have turned some lights on, but I didn't in case I woke someone up. As the shadowy figure moves closer, I don't need to see who it is, the heat that fills my veins tells me who it is.

"What are you doing up princess?"

"What happened to little alpha?"

"Since you decided not to shift, that name no longer applies to you." I ignore his angry tone and try to move past him but stop when he blocks my way. I can't see his features in the dark, but I can feel the heat of his gaze on me.

"Please move."

"No."

"Why? You made it clear you hate me, and will kill me, so why not just pretend I don't exist?"

"Believe me, I would if I could."

"Why are you always so cryptic?" I can hear the hurt in my own voice, I don't have the emotional capacity right now to deal with Creed and his bullshit.

"What's wrong?" He has to be kidding me right?

"Don't pretend like you care, Credence." He chuckles and it grates on my nerves.

"I like how you say my name." Oh my gosh, his mood changes are doing my bloody head in.

"I don't care, just let me pass please." He doesn't reply, just grips my free hand and tugs me along after him. He passes Callie's room and heads toward the end of the hall where his room is. I try and yank my hand free, but he won't let go, he opens his room door and drags me in after him. He flicks the light on. I slam my eyes close to try to fight off the shock of the light on my eyes, after a moment I blink them open, and I see him standing before me in only a pair of black basketball shorts. My eyes travel up his body slowly and I'll admit I am fully checking him out. He has washboard abs and that V, oh lord that V that women dream about on a man is right there. When my gaze finally lands on his, a smug grin is plastered across his face, I mentally groan. He so knew I was just checking him out and he didn't do anything to stop me. I feel the blush creep up my neck and the heat in my cheeks, feeling awkward at the fact I just got caught ogling him. I bring the glass to my lips and take a sip. Once I'm done, I lick my lips and find his gaze transfixed on my mouth, before I can process what is happening Creed closes the space between us. The tension in the room amps up, the heat that travels through my veins at his close proximity is stifling. He reaches out and grips the back of my neck, just as I open my mouth to ask what the hell is he doing; he slams his lips against mine and holy crap cakes!

Fireworks explode inside me; his tongue enters my mouth and I whimper at the feeling He explores my mouth slowly, the sensation of having him kiss me is short circuiting my brain. His free hand grips my waist and pulls me flush against him, I get lost in ecstasy of him kissing me. He deepens the kiss and moves us backward until the backs of my legs hit the bed. He grabs the glass from my hand and places it somewhere without breaking our kiss. He reaches up and cups my face between his hands, I cling onto his arms like they're my lifeline to keep me from floating away. I'm so consumed in this kiss that the ringing doesn't register at first, but when Creed pulls back and looks down at me in annoyance it snaps me out of my daze.

"You gonna answer that?" I cock my brow in confusion until I realize the ringing is coming from my phone in my pocket. I quickly fish it out and see it's an unknown number again, I ignore the feeling of unease inside me and quickly answer it.

"Hello?"

"Jess, so good to hear your voice dear." I snap my gaze to Creed, he grabs the phone from my hand and puts it on speaker. "I hope you received my message I sent you earlier?" Creed looks at me accusingly, I shake my head and mouth I'll tell you later.

"Let her go and I promise I will shift." I'm proud of how strong I sound.

"Now, now, let's not get ahead of ourselves dear. You shift and then your mother goes free."

"Why do you want me to shift so badly? Don't you want to remain alpha? Isn't this what it's all about for you, to remain the big bad wolf?" Jacob chuckles, which just pisses me off, Creed grips my phone so tight I'm afraid he might crush it.

"I have other plans dear; you shift on Saturday and your mom will return to you."

"What's the catch?"

"No catch, the council will be present so rest assured no one will be harmed. You have my word." I scoff.

"No offense but your word doesn't mean shit to me right now." I hear him growl on the other end of the phone.

"You will learn in time to listen to what I say, I will see you Saturday--"

"Wait! I want to talk to my mom." He stays silent for a moment, and I start to panic that he will refuse to allow me to speak to her.

"Fine, but only for a minute." I dart my gaze to Creed; he nods his head reassuringly. We hear movement and then the sound of metal clinking.

"Kitten?" I have never been more relieved in my whole life to hear that pet name.

"Mom, it's me. Are you okay?"

"I'm fine, Kitten, I don't have long." I swallow past the lump in my throat and keep my tears at bay.

"Okay."

"Do you remember that summer in Utah?" What the hell does that have to do with any of this?

"Yeah, but mom--"

"Remember what I told you in the car on the way there?"

"Yeah, but mom--"

"Remember what I told you Jessica." I flinch, she never calls me Jessica unless she is worried or scared. "I'm okay, I have loved being your mom kitten. You gave my life meaning again after I thought I had lost everything. Run Jess, don't you dare stay RUN!" Then the line disconnects.

"Mom? Mom?" I shout, tears leak from my eyes as I snatch my phone back and try to redial the number, it goes straight to voicemail. After the third attempt Creed snatches my phone and wraps his arms around me. I push against him, but he won't let me go, sobs wrack my body. Creed continues to hold me as I break down in his arms...again.

"We'll get your mom back princess." I can't talk past the

lump in my throat, so I nod my head against his chest. He picks me up and I wrap my arms and legs around him like a Monkey, he doesn't complain as he maneuvers us to the bed and rests his back against the headboard with me still wrapped around him. I don't know what the hell this thing is between us but being here in his arms makes me feel safe and secure. That phone call has my mind racing a million miles an hour as I wrack my brain for what conversation she was talking about. We had millions of conversations but the one she is referring to must have a hidden meaning to it. We discussed so much on the trip to Utah, my non-existent love life, school, dad, safe sex and what would happen to me if something ever happened to her--.

"Oh my god!" I blurt. Creed's hands stop stroking my back and he stiffens beneath me as I pull back and stare down at him in shock. Worry lines mar his beautiful face and I reach up to smooth them.

"Why did you say oh my god?" I drop my hands to his chest and just stare at him for a moment. I know what my mom wants me to do but I can't do that. That conversation in the car finally makes sense, at the time I thought she was smoking some happy grass but now I know she was preparing me for if something like this ever happened. Creed grips my waist with both hands and squeezes gently to get my attention. "Care to fill me in?"

"My mom doesn't plan to make it till Saturday." Creed reels back shocked, clearly that's not what he thought I would say.

"What do you mean princess?" I ignore the stupid nickname.

"The trip she's referring to we talked about what if one of

us got taken hostage. I thought it was stupid ya know, but now it makes sense. She told me if she was ever taken and if I was made to do something I didn't want to do I was to run and not look back because she wouldn't let her life affect mine. I didn't get what it meant so in layman's terms she told me she would take her own life before someone ever used her against me. I can't let her do that Creed; I won't let her." Creed shushes me and wraps his me in his embrace well simultaneously stroking my hair.

"We won't let that happen; we'll get her back. What did Jacob mean when he asked if you got his message?" I pull back and grab my phone to show him the message I received earlier.

"They have her chained like a common animal."

"That's because she is princess, the chains on her hands, legs and neck prevent her from shifting. Your mom is a beta wolf."

"What's a beta?" Creed doesn't get annoyed at my lack of knowledge, instead he spends the next hour telling me about pack dynamics and how everything works. It's all so fascinating but I can barely keep my eyes open. I'm tucked into Creed's side with his arms wrapped around me and my head against his chest.

"I'll tell you more about it in the morning, get some sleep. It's nearly three in the morning." I nod against his chest and just as I'm about to lose consciousness he leans down and places a kiss to the top of my head and speaks. "Whatever you decide, you will always be my little alpha."

CHAPTER TWENTY-FOUR

Jessica

I'm so hot, I feel like I'm burning up. I try to move but I can't, I snap my eyes open and begin to panic until I turn to look over my shoulder and see the source of the heat that is burning me alive. Creed has his arm draped across me and one of his legs thrown over mine, I can't help but stare at him. He looks so peaceful and...not so grumpy when he's sleeping. I want to reach out and touch him but in the light of day I'm scared. Last night was amazing, the way I felt when he kissed me was life changing. I can't describe the feeling I felt, it was like...home. I let my gaze travel down his naked torso and silently groan because I can't see the V because he is spooning me.

"I can roll over if you want so you can check me out properly?" I shriek and quickly turn the other way embarrassed. How did he know I was looking at him, he was asleep damn it! "Don't get all shy on me now princess." I feel the blush heating my cheeks and it only intensifies when he laughs. His laughter cuts off when the door opens.

"Have you seen Jess; I woke up this morn--"Callie stops speaking as I quickly push away from him to sit up. Creed shakes his head and chuckles; Callie smiles widely, to make matters worse I can hear Cole coming down the hallway shouting.

"I can't find her, maybe she's with--"Cole's cut off by Creed as soon as he enters the room.

"With me? Yeah, she spent the night here, now how about you both get out." Both Cole and Callie have knowing grins on their faces, I want nothing more than to face palm myself.

"So, should we move her stuff in here?"

"Shut up Colton and get out!" Creed snaps.

"I give her till Saturday, and I bet my roommate ditches me

for our brother." I groan and cover my face with my hands. Could this get any more awkward?

"Oh, you found her, morning Jess." Oh my god, yes it can get more awkward. I drop my hands and try to smile at Meg but fail miserably, the three of them stand there trying to fight the laughter that wants to burst out of them. I have never been more mortified in my life! I bury my head in my hands and mumble out a greeting, I can hear them snickering but don't even lift my head.

"Okay you've had your fun now get out."

"Come on bro--"

"Get out!" Creed shouts.

"Fine."

"Geez okay."

"Breakfast in ten." Meg says as they leave the room and close the door behind themselves. I'm even too much of a chicken to face Creed, memories of last night flash through my mind of the way his lips felt against mine and how he had my body filling with need. He pulls my hands away from my face then grips my chin and turns my head toward him. I look up into his hazel eyes and I can see he's trying so hard not to laugh. I grit my teeth and try to turn my head away, but he won't let me.

"Princess, you have nothing to be ashamed of." I scoff.

"Your mother and siblings just caught me sleeping with you!" I screech, a devilish glint enters his eyes as he says.

"If we were sleeping together princess, I'm sure I would know about it." I feel the blush coat my cheeks, that is not what I meant and he knows it.

"Don't be a douche, you know what I meant."

"I don't actually, care to explain it to me?"

"Argh, you are such a male head strong pi--"

"Eggplant?" I groan and bat his hands away so I can get off the bed, he begins to laugh, full on belly laugh and I can't help but stare at him. He looks so carefree and relaxed right now, it's such a contrast to the uptight on guard all the time Creed that I am used to.

"Will you ever let that go? I said it one freaking time, one time Credence!" He clamps his mouth shut and looks at me, I can see he is still trying to contain his laughter which makes me groan and roll my eyes. "See you at breakfast you ass plant." I say as I storm out of the room with his laughter following me.

After heading back to Callie's room, I grab a quick shower and change then head to meet the others for breakfast. May as well get this awkward moment over with, I think as I enter the kitchen and see everyone. I avoid eye contact at all costs as I take my seat next to Callie, I thank Meg without looking at her and ignore Cole's laughter. I peek up through my lashes and notice Creed is missing before I can think on it more the chair next to me scrapes as it's pulled out and I know immediately who is about to sit there. The heat in my veins amps up and I quickly shovel the eggs into my mouth for something to do. Creed drops down next to me and he sits so close his leg rests against mine, I try to move my leg but his hand lands on top of my thigh under the table and it takes everything inside me not to squeak out in surprise.

"Why are you trying to move away?" I feel the blush coat my cheeks, I ignore Creed and focus on eating so I can get the hell out of here--fast. As I'm about to shovel the last forkful into my mouth something happens. An inferno begins to burn inside, I gasp and jolt in my seat. My body feels like it's burning, you know how you get too close to a fire and it feels like you are about to be burnt? It's like that but times ten! I grit my teeth to stop the scream from tearing out of me but fail when the heat kicks up. My vision blurs and ringing begins in my ears, I lose my sight and my hearing as I begin to panic. I flail my arms and try to grip something to ground myself, my hand clasps something, and I latch onto it and dig my nails in as a scream tears from deep inside me.

The pain is nothing I have ever felt before, my skin feels tight and restricting. I begin to claw at my body and try to shred my clothing, I need to cool down! I can't focus or hear anything above the ringing in my ears, I try to plead for someone to help me, but I can't even hear my own voice. I feel my arms being pinned to my sides and I try to fight against the restraints, I kick out with my legs and then I feel myself falling and try to prepare for impact, but I don't feel it. My head begins to pound, I feel like my skull is splitting in two. I thrash against the restraints on my arms and try to kick out again, but my legs are held immobile by an invisible force. I call out for help, but no help comes, my pleas are falling on deaf ears!

Oh my God, I'm going to die.

CHAPTER
TWENTY-FIVE
Credence

I stare down at her helplessly as I watch my family hold each of her limbs down while she screams for help. I don't know what the hell is happening. One minute she was fine and then next thing I know she's screaming and withering in agonizing pain. I still feel sting from where her nails dug into my arm, I feel helpless. Kayla rounds the table to stand beside me and her presence alone angers me, she is a snake in nice clothes. I don't trust her, and neither should my family, she only cares about herself and climbing the pack ladder. A horrible gut-wrenching scream from Jess pulls me from my thoughts; Dad exchanges a loaded look with mom before he says.

"We need to move her out of here and take her to the living room, so she has more room."

"Why dad?" My sister asks, I can see the tears in her eyes. She's worried for her friend, and I love that she is so protective over Jess. Callie will do anything for the people she loves, and Jess has no idea how lucky she is to have that kind of loyalty from a friend. Dad reaches over with his free hand and places it on her shoulder.

"Because she is about to shift. This shouldn't be happening until Saturday, but something has brought the change on sooner." I can hear the worry in dad's voice and that snaps me out of my stupor. I make my way toward them and when they each move away from Jess's writhing form I bend down and scoop her up. She feels like she is on fire, her skin is flushed and blotched with red marks. She's trembling in my arms, sweat is slick all over her body, her hair is stuck to her forehead. I walk briskly toward the living room but stumble when a piercing scream tears out of her. Do you know what it feels like to hold the other half of your soul and watch it in unbearable pain and there isn't a fucking thing you can do about it? It's the worst feeling in the world, and it makes you feel more useless than you could ever imagine. Even if this is all my fault, I still hate seeing her in pain.

Mom and dad clear everything out of the way and lay some cushions on the rug, I place a writhing Jess on the ground and rest her head gently on the pillows. Her body is covered in sweat, her shorts and shirt cling to her body. Callie comes toward me with a bowl and cloth, she puts the cloth in the bowl and then squeezes the excess water out before she begins to dab the cool liquid over Jess's face. Dad grabs her wrist and then watches the clock on the wall--he's checking her pulse. Mom and Cole both grab a bowl and cloth each and begin to dab Jess's body, she's still shaking and clenching her jaw so tight I think it might break. I'm kneeling next to her head just watching my family try to calm her, I don't know what I'm supposed to do to help. This is all new for me, I've only ever had to worry about my family and my pack, not some...girl.

"What do we do dad, she's burning up?"

"We need to try and regulate her body temp. She's an alpha heir, I can't force her shift or control it, Colton."

"Then what do we do? If we can't help her shift, she will die!" Dad turns to me instead of looking at Callie and the look in his eyes tells me I'm not gonna like what he has to say.

"You will need to guide her shift." I stare at him in shock, how the hell am I supposed to do that?

"Why Creed?" Dad keeps looking at me instead of Callie and it's unsettling.

"Because he is the only one that has a bond with her--"I cut him off.

"But you're better at this than me, why can't you just override her?" He shakes his head before answering.

"I can already sense her wolf and it's too strong, it would cause her more harm than good if I did that. Her wolf will fight me the whole way and it could cause Jess more harm. You can do this Creed, you're of alpha blood and your wolf is strong enough. Once her wolf senses yours it will allow you to guide the change, if you don't do it, she will die."

"She never wanted this dad! If I help her change, she will hate me for this."

"If you don't help her Credence, you know the consequences!" His ominous words hang in the air for a minute, a harsh scream rents the air and snaps me out of my stupor. I look down at her and the contorted look on her face has my chest aching. My wolf whimpers inside me, I feel him pressing against my mind and urging me to shift to allow him to take over. Part of me wants to let my wolf out and allow him to help Jess but I know inside myself that I need to be in the flesh and not fur to guide her. I reach down and cup her cheek, touching her is like a healing balm to my soul. I never thought I would find her and the fact that she is here now in front of me, all the plans that we made for her are out the window. After getting to know her these past few days I can never do that to her, we were so wrong, she isn't anything like Jacob and his pack.

"Tell me what I have to do so I can help her."

"Everyone, back away." The others listen and move back toward the doorway, I see Kayla standing there and growl out a warning. She darts her gaze to mine and stiffens, she shouldn't be here!

"Leave." I grit out.

"I can help--"

"I said leave!" I shout, she flinches and looks to my family for support, when none of them meet her gaze or even try to help she huffs and stomps out of the house. She may preach she is here to help but my wolf doesn't trust her as far as he can throw her and after all these years, I have learnt to trust him, he has never steered me wrong. Dad kneels down next to me; he places his hand against her forehead to check her temp. She is still writhing and shaking, whispering pleas for help fall from her delectable mouth every few minutes.

"She's still too hot, son, you need to find a way to make it through her walls." The worry in his voice spikes my own internal panic.

"What happens if I can't?" The fact that he won't meet my gaze has a pit of dread settling inside me.

"Sweetheart, try to focus on getting through. Jess is a tough kid and has been through a lot, she is far from weak."

"Mom, if I do this, she will hate me." I know it's selfish but now that I do have her, I can't risk losing her. Even if she doesn't hate me for guiding the change, she will hate me when she finds out what I had planned.

"No honey, she has too big of a heart for that. She may not know what she is to you, but I have seen the way she looks at you and the way your touch comforts her. She could never hate you even if she tried." My mom's words fill me with a renewed sense of strength and pride, dad moves away and leaves me alone next to Jess. I don't know how I'm supposed to do this or what is the right way, so I just go with my gut feeling. I gather her in my arms and shuffle us back until my back is against the wall, she huddles into me as I reach up and stroke her hair.

"I'm gonna help you princess, you have to let me in, okay?" She whimpers at the sound of my voice; I would give anything in the world right now, just to take her pain away. I close my eyes and try to clear my mind of everything else but her. I focus on the rise and fall of her chest; I listen to her ragged breathing and the small whimpers that escape her. I focus on the feeling of having her in my arms, I think about how content I feel holding her close to me. I don't know how long we sit in silence before a small niggling feeling in the back of my mind begins to take place. I try to latch onto the feeling and explore it, I ignore the scream that tears from her. The feeling intensifies inside my head, the stronger it gets for me the louder her screams become.

"Make it stop!" I hear her scream, but I ignore her plea and pull on the tether that's building inside my chest. I feel a snap and then heat surges inside me, it's so intense I groan and grit my teeth to stop myself from shouting. Minutes tick by as the heat burns through me, Jess continues to scream and thrash in my arms.

"Let me in princess!" I grit out through clenched teeth. She stills in my arms, then the heat burning a path inside me stops, my body deflates, and I release a relieved breath.

"Oh my god it hurts, make it stop."

"Princess?"

"Creed?" I gasp in shock; I can hear her inside my head.

"It's me--"

"How are you here?" We may be communicating telepathically but I can still hear the strain in her voice.

"I'm going to help you shift."

"Wait, no! I have till Saturday."

"Not anymore princess...something triggered the change and if you don't let me help you it won't end well."

"What the hell...Arrrggghhh." I flinch at how loud her scream sounds inside my head.

"Shhhh, let me guide you. The more you fight it the worse it will be."

"Creed?"

"Yeah?"

"Please don't let me die."

"Never."

The fear in her voice has me focusing harder and wanting nothing more than to guide her through this. This might not be what she wants but she has no other choice, I just hope helping her now will hopefully sway her into forgiving me later when she finds out the truth.

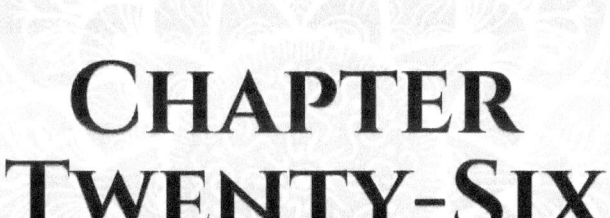

CHAPTER TWENTY-SIX

Jessica

The pain is something I can't even explain, it feels like my body is splitting in two. The more I try to fight it or block it out the worse it becomes. My body is blazing like an inferno, and I have no idea how I am supposed to regulate my body heat to cool myself down. I have read somewhere if a person's body heat remains high for too long, they can stroke out and die, I really don't want to die.

"Creed?"

"Yeah?"

"Please don't let me die."

"Never." Hearing the conviction in his voice gives me a renewed sense of hope. I have no idea how I am able to hear him inside my head or why I trust him right now to help me. Something inside me is telling me I can trust Creed with my life, right now I don't have any choice. I need him to help me fix whatever this is because I don't think I can handle this pain much longer; I already feel dizzy and light headed from all the screaming and pain radiating throughout my body. *"I need you to surrender to me, princess."*

His words shock me but what other choice do I have?

"Why do I feel like there is more to this than you are saying?" I grind my teeth together to stop myself from screaming. It's a struggle to even have a coherent thought let alone speak to Creed through my mind.

"There is, right now we don't have the luxury of time for me to explain it. You need to let me help you or you will die. I am asking you to trust me Jess, I know I haven't done anything to earn it, but I'm asking anyway." It takes me only a second to think about it before I answer.

"What do I have to do?"

"I need you to let go, stop fighting. Once your wolf comes to the surface mine will guide her out."

"Wi-will I still be me?"

"Yes and no. We don't have time princess; your body heat is too high and your pulse is dropping."

"Okay."

"Let go, I promise I will bring you back princess. Trust me."

I do exactly as he says, I let go and stop fighting the pain coursing through my body. I let the heat envelope me and allow the dizziness to cloud my mind and ravish through my body. Time passes so slowly, the pain doesn't immediately subside or disappear, it intensifies and then as suddenly as it appeared it stops, I'm not hot or in pain I'm just...stuck.

"Come to me little alpha, it's time to meet." Creed's words penetrate my mind, but I'm unable to respond, before I panic a sense of calm washes over me. Then I feel it, I feel this presence inside myself that I didn't even know was there. This presence inside me makes me feel complete. It's like a piece of myself I didn't know was missing has finally returned. *"Let her out princess, it's gonna hurt, but I'll be here with you every step of the way. I promise."*

I don't understand what he means, let who out?

My train of thought is cut short when a searing pain tears through me. I feel my arm break and scream out, I don't get to recover from that pain before I feel my ankle snap. I cry out again, fear grips me, and panic begins to override my senses, who is doing this to me? Why are they doing this to me?

"Stop!" I scream out, and then I feel my other arm break.

"*Don't fight it Jess, the more you fight it the worse it is. Let her lead the change and stop fighting it.*" Creed's words boom inside my head, I want to trust him, but the pain is so unbearable. "*I swear princess, I will never let anyone harm you. Trust me.*" I hear the truth in his words and take the biggest leap of faith, I let go. I surrender to the darkness and allow it to overtake me, I just pray I haven't put my trust in the wrong person. I feel every muscle in my body stretch and tear then reform. My bones break and repair, my body thrashes around for what seems like hours, I am beyond exhausted from the pain and fear. I don't register the pain anymore, I'm numb to it. If this is what death feels like, then I'm ready to let go of the living. I can't take much more of this.

My ears pop and then my hearing returns but everything is so loud. I can hear cars and voices; I hear birds chirping and the wind rustling the leaves. Am I outside? I blink my eyes a few times hoping my sight will come back, I fear it won't when minutes pass and still nothing. I try to blink once more and then it happens, I can see. I dart my head around the room and see Callie, Cole, Meg and Kane standing in the doorway with looks of awe on their faces. I turn back in front of me and that's when I see him, Creed is kneeling with his hands on his thighs and a broad smile stretched across his face. His hazel eyes meet mine and then something inside me snaps into place.

Mate.

I stumble back in shock when a strange voice speaks that one word inside my head. I trip over and crash to the ground, I try to stand again but I can't find my balance. I look down and freeze, I can't see my hands and feet. All I see is white paws, oh my god!

What the fuck is going on? I think to myself.

You have become your true self; we are now whole.

I gulp and dart my gaze around again to make sure no one else is here.

Who are you?

I am you; I am Sheba your wolf half.

Wait, so I'm a wolf now?

You have always been a shifter; you just didn't know it.

Oh my god, I'm talking to myself, I'm going crazy!

You are not crazy Jess; I am going to take over now. I will teach you everything you need to know; I will help you. We are one now and must work together to ensure the safety of our pack.

I don't get a chance to respond, I feel a barrier of sorts rise up and block off my thoughts as Sheba stands--gracefully I might add. Once she is at her full height she turns and pins a look on the four Reeves standing in the doorway, they all drop their heads in a respectable bow. Once she is satisfied with their submission, she turns back toward Creed who has no trouble meeting her gaze and not dropping his. Sheba lets out a low warning growl which just causes Creed to smirk. I can feel that Sheba doesn't like that Creed won't bow to her and show her the respect she *thinks* she deserves.

"I will never bow to you little alpha, it's not in my nature." Sheba stalks slowly toward Creed and stops directly in front of him, when her nose is nearly touching his, she pulls her lips back and snarls right in his face!

"Dad, do something!" Callie pleads, I'm also trying to get out of this mind cage she has locked me in to help Creed, but I can't!

"She won't hurt him, she can't." Sheba's growling stops, she turns toward the others, and it fills her with glee when she sees Creed stiffen from the corner of her eye.

"Touch them little alpha, and you won't like what Corbin does to you." I--Sheba spins back toward Creed and growls.

"Are you threatening me?" A devious smirk spreads across Creed's face as he looks at Sheba--us. This is going to take a long time to get used to.

"I'm warning you, do not touch my family. You can push my patience and snap at me but do not ever think you can touch them without consequences. I don't give a fuck if you are an alpha heir, I will challenge you!" Oh lord, I tense while Sheba does--we both do! I can hear the threat in his voice and for some reason the way his words challenged Sheba has her wanting to rub up against him.

"I want to see the pack and lands."

"No, they cannot know you have shifted until Saturday."

"I said now!" Wow, Sheba is the complete opposite to me. She is fearless and doesn't care whose feelings she hurts; I can feel the dominance inside myself, and it all comes from her not me. Creed narrows his eyes, and a small growl comes from him in warning, Sheba spins toward him and snaps her jaws. Holy crap, she just tried to bite him!

"Fine, go look around, but when your mother is killed because you're impatient, don't come crying to me." Sheba stops growling and stands tall as she processes Creed's words. I feel the cage she has placed around me drop.

That was freaking rude! Don't ever do that to me again.

If it means keeping us safe, then I will do it a thousand times. We have to shift back.

Wait what? Will it hurt?

Yes, the more we shift the easier it will be. The first is always the hardest but the second won't be as bad. I will remain with you always.

Sheba closes herself off from me, the change back isn't as painful. By the time I am back in my human flesh, I am beyond exhausted, I flop forward but before I can hit the ground Creed wraps his arms around me and lifts me from the floor. He doesn't say a word as he carries me from the living room and walks toward his bedroom, I don't fight him. Partly because I am too tired and also because it feels good being in his arms. Once inside his room he kicks the door shut and then places me on the edge of the bed, he turns around and rummages through his draws. I look down at myself and gasp, I'm naked!

"Here." He says as a shirt slaps me in the side of the face, he keeps his back to me as I hastily pull the shirt over my head. I'm trying not to dwell on the fact that Creed's family have now seen me naked, but it's bloody hard. Once I have the shirt on, I quickly crawl under the covers to hide my bare legs from him while his back is still to me. I clear my throat to indicate that it's safe for him to turn around, which he does but he remains across the room leaning against his dresser. His gaze travels up and down my body; the way he is looking at me sends shivers down my spine.

"Thank you." I blurt out, he snaps his gaze to mine in shock.

"For what?" I sigh before saying.

"Helping me, I-I don't know if I could have done that without your help." He smiles sadly and makes his way over to me, he sits at the end of the bed and rests his large hand on top of my legs, even through the covers the feeling of him touching me sends heat through my body.

"I shouldn't have had to help you, this should have happened years ago princess. The pain you felt today could have been avoided if you shifted earlier."

I drop my head in shame, Creed and his family witnessed everything today. They watched me writhe in pain and didn't even try to help me. They stood at the exit and watched as Creed tried his best.

"Your family didn't help me, you did." I whisper, Creed reaches out and lifts my chin until my eyes meet his.

"My brother and sister were worried out of their minds, they and my mom were rubbing you down with cloths to bring your temp down. Dad monitored your pulse and helped me guide you through the change. They stood back so when you did shift you wouldn't attack them; we all helped you today. Do not think for a second my family would let you lay there in pain screaming out for help and not do a goddamn thing!" The anger in his voice spikes a rage inside me, I don't like the tone he is using! A low warning growl sounds inside me, my eyes widen with shock as I stare at Creed.

"What was that?" Creed releases a long sigh before answering.

"Your wolf is pissed at me; you're going to have to learn

how to control her before going near any norms."

"Who are norms?"

"Humans, normal people." I furrow my brow.

"What makes you think they are the norms? What if you all are, but just don't know it?" Creed cocks his head to the side studying me, I've confused him.

"I've never actually thought about it like that."

"Well maybe you should start viewing it that way. Can I ask you something?"

"Yeah, sure." I take a deep breath and meet his gaze.

"When I changed, my wolf told me her name is Sheba--"

"And my wolf is called Corbin." Wow, that is freaking cool.

"Okay, well Sheba called you, her *mate.*" Creed stiffens then jumps to his feet, he paces the bottom of the bed and keeps sneaking side glances at me but won't say anything. I'm about to ask if he's okay but then he turns around and leaves, he freaking leaves! He didn't even answer my question, he just left and slammed the door behind himself.

CHAPTER TWENTY-SEVEN

Credence

I didn't know how to answer that without having to tell her the whole truth. How do I tell her that I lied, we all lied to her. She has lost the only person she cares about and trusts, if we break that trust, I have no idea what she will do. Her wolf will go nuts without a pack, she's an alpha and needs to lead. Sitting there and staring into her blue innocent eyes I could see the fear, she is terrified of what just happened. Her mother should have taught her to shift and told her everything about herself instead of lying to her. Now that she has shifted, Jacob will challenge her, and she is too much of a novice to even stand a chance against another wolf. Jacob may be a slimy asshole, but he is a strong wolf, he will make her submit to him and that is worse than death for any alpha, let alone an alpha heir. I scent the air and follow it toward my dad's office, I don't bother knocking as I enter. The four of them are all sitting around talking but when they see me, they all stop and stare.

"Is Jess okay?" I smile and nod, Callie slumps back into her seat relieved that her friend is okay. I drop into the seat between Callie and Cole, my parents are sitting opposite me, both of them wear looks of concern.

"Her wolf told her that I'm her mate." No one is shocked to hear this.

"We knew that would be a possibility once she shifted, what do you plan to do?" I meet my dad's gaze and can see in his eyes that he will follow whatever I suggest.

"We stick to the plan, she cannot know the truth, it will ruin everything." Mom shakes her head.

"I know you all want your revenge and I support that, but at what cost? Everyone has sacrificed a part of themselves in this family, and I fear you will sacrifice your heart Credence. Do not let this revenge cloud your chance to love, that's not what she would want." I know my mom worries and thinks she is overstepping when she speaks about our bio-mom, but she isn't. We love our mom, blood couldn't make her more of our mother, she raised us and loves us more than anything.

"I know mom, but I can't let Jacob get away with this. Cole, stick to the plan and get on Kayla's good side. Callie stick with Jess and get her to open up to you." I see the looks on both my siblings' faces, and it irritates me. "What?" I snap.

"She doesn't deserve this Creed; she isn't like the Michelson pack. I believe her when she says she knows nothing." I glare at my sister; she drops her gaze to her lap in submission.

"Well I don't, I want to know the truth and I want to know who did it. Come Saturday whatever trust she had in us will be shattered." Cole stiffens beside me; I wait for him to say what's on his mind.

"I want to know the truth just as much as you do, but I don't want to become *them* in the process." I growl in warning; he is about to cross a line.

"Creed!" I snap my gaze to my dad; I hold his gaze until he relents and looks away.

"We all have a job to do, don't let an innocent act fool you." I stand and head toward the door, but my brother's words have me pausing.

"We'll all do our jobs like you command, but from what I saw today you're the one lying to yourself."

"How so, brother?" A humorless laugh comes from him,

but I still refuse to face him.

"You didn't fake shit today when you helped her shift. Your feelings for her are real, and whether you admit it to yourself or not, you're falling for her."

I avoid the house all day and busy myself with pack business, also making sure to go over a game plan with the deltas for Saturday. We want everyone to be on guard and ready for anything, I won't let him get away again. This is our chance, now that he is distracted with Jess, his guard is down. The council will be present and with them there he will not be able to back out and get away with what he did.

When daylight fades and it turns dark, I make my way back to the house. I open the door and immediately I'm assaulted by the smell of venison, potatoes, and other foods. I follow the scent and the sound of laughter to the dining room, when I enter all the light-hearted chatter stops. Jess doesn't even turn around to see who entered before she stiffens. From the slight tilt of her head, I can tell she has just scented the air and her wolf has alerted her to my presence. I keep the smirk off my face and claim the seat next to her, I can see how tense she is out of the corner of my eye, she's showered and changed. My wolf is pissed that our scent has been scrubbed from her. I push him down and ignore his ramblings inside my mind, Corbin doesn't get to take the lead on this one.

"Why so tense princess?"

"Creed, Jess and I--"

"I was asking Jess, sister." I growl out, Jess snaps her gaze to me and if looks could kill I would be six feet under. Her upper lip is pulled back in a snarl, a low growl rumbles inside her chest and I'm impressed at how fast she is accepting her wolf.

"Don't talk to her like that." I raise my brows and clutch my chest in mock offense, she rolls her eyes at my antics.

"She is my sister--"

"And she is my friend, so don't be a dick. If you had a bad day, then that sucks for you, but don't take it out on anyone else." I stare at her in shock, does she really not know? "If it will help, do you want to talk about it?" The concern and genuine curiosity I hear in her voice has me stunned. Can they be right? Am I looking at this all wrong? I shake my head to clear those stupid thoughts from my mind, I can't go down that path. We have come too far to let her derail this plan.

"I'll pass." Conversation resumes around the table; I note that even Kayla joins in, and it grates on my nerves. She was a means to an end, but I'm still pissed, I allowed myself to let it go on as long as I did. I thought I could get close to her in the hopes Jacob would drop his guard or retrieve information from her, but it all proved useless. I finish my meal and head to my room to shower and change. I'm pissed about living in my old bedroom, part of me wants to drop the act and just demand it of her, but then a part of me thinks Callie is right, if she did know the truth she would run.

I grab my tablet from my side drawer and settle down in bed, the shower helped relieve some of the tension from my body. After a couple of hours have passed and I have finished emailing out all the notifications and invoices, I shut the tablet down and place it on the bedside drawer. I lay there and stare up at the ceiling getting lost in my own thoughts. A knock at the door snaps me out of it. I call out to come in expecting it to be my dad bringing me the reports and numbers, but it isn't. Her scent surrounds me as soon as she steps inside the small space. It takes more restraint than I want to admit not to go to her and smooth the worry lines from her face. My wolf perks up inside me and I scold him for being such a sappy asshole.

Don't push her away.

Don't start with me Corbin, she is the enemy.

She is not our enemy; she doesn't know anything.

She knows something!

"I didn't mean to interrupt you; I just wanted to return your shirt and say thank you again for what you did today." Her humble tone shocks me, she is the biggest mind fuck I have ever encountered. The innocent act she has going isn't fooling me, she may have my family fooled but I'm not as gullible as they are.

"Don't mention it." She walks briskly toward me with the shirt and drops it on the bed, before she quickly turns and leaves. She opens the door and is about to exit when my words stop her. "If you could change everything and learn from birth what you are, would you do it?" She stands there silently pondering.

CHAPTER
TWENTY-EIGHT
Jessica

I stand there and let his question sink in, would I change it?

Would I give up the normal life mom and I had to be part of this world?

Before I give him my answer, I want him to answer a question of my own first.

"I'll tell you, if you answer my question first?" I still refuse to turn and face him; Creed seems to have some kind of effect on me, and I'm not okay with that. Every time we make eye contact, or he is near, I tend to become unfocused and only concentrate on him.

"What's your question?"

"*Why can I only communicate with you and no one else?*" I ask through my mind link, I tried it with Callie and Cole, but they couldn't hear me, and I couldn't hear them. I find it so freaking strange that Creed of all people is the only one I can hear, I just know there is a reason behind it.

"Look who is learning quickly."

"Don't patronize me." I spin around and face him; his eyes bore into me, but I refuse to give in. My body heats and wants to be near him, it takes every bit of self-control I have to remain rooted to the spot.

"No idea." I narrow my eyes and a small deep growl loosens from my chest. I make sure to keep the shock from my face, I want him to think I meant to do that.

"Unless you want me to put your wolf in its place, pull her back--now!" I, of course, have no freaking idea how to do that! I try to take calming breaths and close my eyes to focus. After taking a few calming breaths and centering myself, I open my eyes and squeal in shock. How the hell does a man of his size move so silently? Creed is now standing directly in front of me, and I didn't even hear him shift off the bed. He doesn't look happy; I tentatively take a step back but stop when I hear Sheba growling and snapping her jaws inside my head.

We never back down!

Have you seen the freaking size of him?

We do not flinch for a bitch.

My mouth drops open in shock at her crude words. We may have to share the same body but we are nothing alike.

"Either let her out to play or pull her back." Sheba doesn't like Creed's tone or the fact that he is demanding something of us. I feel her inside me trying to take over, but I fight back, I have no idea if what I am doing is right, but I have to try something. Creed releases an irritated breath then cups my face, just the physical contact from him has her settling. "Breathe, push back against her and don't let her control you. Over time it will get simpler to work with her and share, but right now she is fresh and fierce and wants dominance." I nod my head in understanding.

"She seems to have settled." He nods but doesn't drop his hands from me, an intense wave of heat rushes through me and I gasp. Creed's eyes change to blue, and his nostrils begin to flare.

"I don't want this." He grits out, I don't think he was meant to voice that thought. I can see a war in his eyes like he is torn, I reach up and place my hands flat against his chest. He stills under my touch, but then his breathing begins to even out and his eyes slowly change back to their normal hazel color. I get lost in the intensity of his gaze; feelings begin to surface inside me. I have this strong sense of longing and rightness as I stare at him. As if my body has a mind of its own, I move forward and close the space between us, his hands drop to my waist and my body begins to thrum with need. I stare up at him in question hoping he will have some answers as to what is going on. Creed is an enigma to me; he is so hot and cold, but my body still craves his touch. Before I can ask him anything he leans down and smashes his lips against mine, an inferno builds inside me. I feel his tongue prod my lips and I open for him; I think it is time to admit the truth---I have feelings for Credence Reeves, and I don't know if I'm okay with that.

He moves us back until my back hits the wall, he deepens the kiss and all trains of thought flee, the only thing I can focus on is Creed and how good his lips feel against mine. He consumes me, I explore his mouth with my tongue and moan at the taste of him. He runs his hands down my body then grips my thighs and hoists me up, I wrap my legs around him and lock my arms around his neck but never break our kiss. I moan when he begins to run his hands up and down my body, he leaves a trail of heat everywhere he has touched. Sheba purrs like a cat in the back of my mind.

Mark mate.

She keeps purring, I have no idea what that means and right now all I care about is how amazing Creed's hands and mouth feel. He breaks our kiss and begins to kiss a trail down my neck, I throw my head back and whimper. I need more, I don't know what *more* is, but I just need it. I squirm against him and gasp when I feel his hard length prod against my jean clad centre.

Holy shit, Creed is hard for...me. He begins to kiss and nip at the other side of my neck. I run my hands through his hair and drag my nails along his scalp, he releases a groan which spurs me on. A sudden urge to take charge tears through me, I grip the back of his hair and tug hard enough for him to pull back and stare up at me in shock, I don't give him a chance to question me. I slam my mouth against his and take control of the kiss. He moves us away from the wall and places both his hands on my ass, so I don't slip as he walks back toward the bed.

Creed places me gently down on the bed after he untangles my limbs from him. I lay here sprawled out on my back and look up at him. He is beyond beautiful and has the body of a god but his eyes, I see the war of indecision within himself. I have no idea what has that haunted look in his eyes, but I want nothing more than to wipe that look from his face. I reach up and grip the front of his shirt and tug him down to me, he braces himself on his elbows either side of my head. We lose ourselves in the others gaze for a moment, time seems so irrelevant at this moment. He leans down and kisses me, this time it isn't messy or rushed, it's slow and sensual. Running my hands up and down his back enjoying the moan that escapes him when I drag my nails along his spine. He grinds against me which causes me to gasp, his hard length is pressed firmly against me and oh my god the pressure against my clit paired with the seam from my jeans and panties is perfect. I moan into his mouth as he grinds against me, I can feel that I'm wet for him, and I can't find it within myself to even care. Something inside me is telling me this is right and not to question what is happening between us. So, I don't, for the first time in my life I live in the moment and don't get lost in my own head over thinking. I wrap my legs around him and lock him against me which earns me a satisfied groan from him. He breaks our kiss and pulls back to look down at me, I'm afraid he's about to end this and turn back into his usual cold detached self.

"Are you sure?" Relief floods through me that he isn't ending this, warmth fills my chest at his concern.

"Yes." As soon as the word leaves my mouth, he smashes his lips against mine and begins to run his hands under my shirt, I sit forward and allow him to slip it off. I grip the hem of his shirt and do the same. I run my hands down his naked chest and marvel in his beauty, his body is amazing and sculpted to perfection. He brushes my hands away and leans down to kiss me again, my nipples harden and poke against the padding of my bra. An ache begins to build between my legs, he reaches behind me with one hand and unclasps my bra like a pro. I brush the thought of him doing this many times with other girls out of my head. He pulls back and rips the garment from my body and chucks it over his head. He looks down at me with such intensity I begin to squirm beneath him.

"You're so fucking perfect." His words have me softening and melting back into the mattress. He drops down and captures one of my nipples in his mouth and I cry out in pleasure. His mouth is freaking amazing, he laps and nips at my nipple until I'm a writhing mess beneath him. He swaps sides and plays with my other nipple, by the time he releases it with a pop I'm a highly strung panting mess. He trails kisses from my throat all the way down to the top of my jeans, I wiggle beneath him and push my hips up urging him to relieve this ache he has caused. He chuckles and lays one of his hands against my stomach to push me back down and hold me still. "Patience princess."

I growl out my frustration. "We're not trialing out for a marathon here." My reply causes him to laugh, I stare at him in awe. Seeing Creed laugh is something else, he looks so relaxed and calm, it's a stark contrast to his normal brooding self. Once his laughter subsides, he bends down and places a feather light kiss to my stomach, he works his way down again and then reaches up to undo my jeans button. He looks up and meets my gaze as he slides my zipper down, the look in his eyes tells me that he will stop if I say the word. No part of me wants him to end this, every fiber of my being wants this moment with Creed. A deep-seated part of me feels like this moment has always been meant to happen, whenever he is near me, I feel strong and confident. Sheba has been so calm since Creed kissed me; she has been screwing with my emotions all day except for now. It's almost like she has been waiting for this since she awoke today.

Creed begins to peel my jeans off my body, once he has them off, he stands back and looks down at me with such a lustful stare that my body shivers. The only piece of clothing I have left on, is my red lace panties. I don't feel vulnerable, I feel empowered and strong that this man is captivated by me. As force inside me is driving me to make an intimate connection with him, I honestly don't think I would be here right now if I hadn't shifted today. Sheba may be calm and quiet, but I can feel her urging me silently from the back of my mind.

"If I take these off, there is no turning back princess." The look in his eyes makes me pause, so much remorse shines inside his beautiful orbs. Sheba pushes me to answer and agree to his terms.

"Take them off." My voice doesn't sound like my own, it's huskier and the way Creed's brow just raised I guess he caught the change as well. He runs his hands up and down my legs then grips my panties and tugs them off in a smooth fluid movement. His nostrils flare and a satisfied groan escapes him, did he just scent my arousal? He grips my ankles and pulls me forward until my ass is balancing on the edge of the bed, then drops to his knees. I rise up and rest on my elbows and stare down at him, seeing how transfixed his gaze is on my pussy and the way he is licking his lips in anticipation sends a shiver down my spine.

CHAPTER TWENTY-NINE

Credence

Her scent is driving Corbin crazy, her pussy is slick with her arousal. I can't wait any longer, I have given her every chance to back out of this. I shouldn't have even given her a chance to back out, but a part of me knows what I am about to do to her is beyond fucked up. She will hate me, it's inevitable.

I lean forward and part her pussy with my fingers, her tight wet hole is clenching and unclenching in anticipation. I flick my tongue out to taste her and we moan in unison, she tastes like heaven, I hear Corbin growling his approval and urging me to feast on her. I do as my wolf desires, I circle her clit with my tongue, then suck the enlarged nub into my mouth, she cries out in pleasure, I slip two fingers inside her and begin to pump. After a few minutes I feel her begin to clench my fingers and know she is close to her climax. I pull out and stand, her lustfilled gaze stares up at me in question, I wink at her as I begin to slide my pants down, her eyes trail my movements and when they land on my hard aching cock, her eyes double in size and her breaths come in hard fast pants. I step out of my pants and palm my cock; I line myself up with her entrance. I don't give her anytime to prepare or any warning, I slam inside her and rejoice in the way she cries out. I'm not a complete asshole, I give her time to adjust to my size as I can see her face is etched in pain. After a moment she gives me a jerky nod and I begin to move inside her, her pussy fits my cock like a glove. The feeling of being inside her is more incredible than I could have ever imagined, she moans, and I reach down and tweak her nipple which draws another loud cry from her.

"Creed...shit...fuck." I smile at her cuss word but don't slow my pace. "I'm gonna come!" I reach down and use my thumb to swirl around her clit, she tenses for a second then screams my name loud enough for the fucking house to hear. I pull out of her and quickly flip her so she is on her stomach, I kick her legs apart and line my cock up slamming inside her, I can feel my balls tightening, I'm not gonna last much longer. Indecision wars inside me, I know I shouldn't do this to her, but I have to. I lean forward and wrap my hand around her throat and pull her up until she is flush against me. I continue to fuck her like there is no tomorrow, just as I'm about to reach my climax, I let Corbin out. I feel my teeth lengthen and my vision sharpen, I brush her hair out of the way and clamp my jaws on the crook of her neck, she cries out, in pain before her pain turns to pleasure and I feel her grip my cock again, a second later she screams my name and I follow her grunting. I release my jaws and lick at the droplets of blood.

She falls forward face first panting with my cock still inside her. I can't tear my eyes from the mark on her neck. What the fuck have I done? When he finds out what I did to her he is going to skin me alive, I can't do this. I pull out of her and quickly locate my pants and pull them up, I feel her gaze on me the whole time. I am such a fucking asshole for doing this to her, I don't even have the balls to face her after what I just did. I grab a shirt from my dresser and quickly pull it on before I turn toward the door and grip the handle, then pause when she speaks.

"Have I done something wrong?" I can hear the devastation in her voice, and I want to throat punch myself for all of this. I just used the only person in the world who can ever truly love me for who I am, not what I am.

"No." I whisper.

"Then why are you leaving?" I release a long sigh and steel my spine, I have to play the game and play it right. This girl has a way of getting under my skin and making me become something I'm not, if things were different, I would hold her in my arms and love her like she deserves, but they're not.

"Because we're done, I had an itch and you scratched it. Don't make this out to be something it's not princess, we fucked--end of story." I open the door and step out, before I close the door behind myself, I hear a sob tear out of her and hate myself even more if that's possible. As I turn to head toward the kitchen, I see my brother and sister standing at the end of the hall glaring at me. I make my way toward them and ignore the sobs coming from inside my room, I try to move around them, but Colton blocks my path. I release a warning growl for him to move but the shit head just stands there.

"I want revenge as much as you do but hurting her to get it isn't the way Credence!"

"You know nothing Colton, she has a part to play like we all do. She is the key to taking him down and if I have to use her to get it I will!"

"You're a real piece of shit Creed, she has done nothing to you or any of us. She told you the truth, she knows nothing about any of this!" I know my sister is upset and angry that her friend is being used but this has to be done. I meet each of their gazes so they can see the seriousness in my eyes, I will not budge on this.

"What happens when all of this comes out on Saturday?" I

ignore Cole.

"Don't question me again, Jacob will go down on Saturday, and she will deal with this. She doesn't have a choice now." They both gasp, they know what I just did and disgust fills both their gazes. I go to move past but Cole's hand slams against my chest, I turn and snarl at him. Brother or not he doesn't get to lay hands on me like that, he knows better.

"You have been so consumed with this that you can't even see the truth. Your anger is misplaced. If *he* hears about her and let's be real here, there is no way *he* hasn't heard she is in town. He will be coming for her on Saturday." I growl long and loud, Corbin is pissed at the threat of someone taking Jess. I may want to use her, but Corbin doesn't.

"She will do as she is told, I can already feel her heartbeat and how she mourns for me. She craves me brother and believe me, you have to get over this crush you have on her, she isn't yours." I growl the last part out and I know my eyes have changed to the color of my wolf, Corbin is making sure that Colton knows he has no chance with her.

"I'm not yours either!" I spin around and see Jess standing there, she's dressed in her clothes again, but I can still see the tip of my mark poking out of her shirt. "After Saturday, I'm taking my mom and leaving. I want nothing to do with any of this." I can see in her eyes that her wolf is just below the surface ready to break free if she is needed. Jess may not know it yet but come Saturday her life is about to be turned upside down again. I just hope she is strong enough to get through it and if luck is on my side, she will let me explain everything and hopefully she will forgive me or at least not kill me.

"Jess, come on you and I can get some hot chocolate and then have a Twilight marathon." Callie extends her hand to Jess; she closes the distance between her and my sister, she doesn't even spare me a glance. As they turn to head toward the kitchen Jess stops and turns back to look over her shoulder, I knew it. She couldn't not invite me to watch the movie.

"You coming Cole, or you got something else to do?" Cole snorts out a laugh and then turns to me.

"Enjoy your night *alone*, dick." I want nothing more than to punch the little shit, given my status in the pack I should fear nothing except I do--my mom would kick my ass for hurting Cole.

CHAPTER THIRTY
Jessica

I wake the next morning and try to stretch but I'm restricted. I open my eyes and that's when I see them, we must have fallen asleep. I'm sandwiched between Callie and Cole, with Cole's arm draped over my mid-section and Callie's leg thrown over mine. After making hot chocolates and heading back to Callie's room, my new wolf nose alerted me to the fact that I can smell Creed all over me. I decided to have a shower before we watched the movie. I made sure to scrub myself raw to try rid the scent of him from my body. It wasn't until I was in the shower that I realized what a dumb mistake I made, we didn't even use protection. I made a mental note that I needed to get checked out next week, who knows where his dick has been.

Last night was amazing, Cole and Callie never tried to push me for what happened or why my eyes were red and puffy. When I got back from my shower, they had the bed set up for us and junk food waiting, getting lost in team Edward last night was exactly what I needed. I feel Sheba stir inside me and smile. I know it's only been mere hours since I shifted but I feel so in tune and complete with her. I can feel how hurt she is by Creed's actions last night but if I'm honest with myself, I knew it would end that way. Am I hurt and devastated by it---yes. Sheba is distraught and broken-hearted, which is weird to me. She said I would understand come Saturday when the full moon is at its peak, and then I would feel what she feels. Apparently, we can't fully feel each other's emotions until our first full moon as one.

I meant what I said last night, when I get my mom back, we are leaving. I don't care who rules or what happens, but one thing I know for sure, even if I don't want to admit it, I cannot stay here and watch Creed with other girls. I gave him a part of myself that I have never given anyone before, and he threw it back in my face. I feel tears begin to build and try my best to stop them from falling, his rejection hurts more than I care to admit.

I blocked out the pain of being rejected last night because it was easier when I had Callie and Cole constantly distracting me, but now laying here and listening to the silence I have no distraction. Creed treated me like a common whore last night, truthfully, I behaved like one. I have only known him a couple of weeks and I already fell into bed with him, I wish I could blame it on the stress or something, but it wasn't any of those things. It was just me wanting to feel connected to someone and when he placed his hands on me it was the first time all day that Sheba and I felt content and when he was inside me, I felt whole. When he bit me, I saw stars and climaxed so hard I nearly blacked out. What the hell is wrong with me?

"Nothing is wrong with you." I gasp, I didn't mean to say that out loud. I turn my head and face Cole and see so much sadness in his eyes, I don't want him to feel bad for me. I made the dumb decision to let his brother close enough so he was able to hurt me, I am the one to blame. Cole reaches up and cups my face with his hand that was resting on my tummy. His touch feels so intimate, Sheba growls inside my mind and is trying to take control so she can tear his hand away from us. "My brother is an idiot; he shouldn't have treated you like that." His words are my undoing, the tears fall and I'm helpless to stop them.

"I don't know what has gotten into me." I whisper, a sad smile graces his handsome face.

"I wish I could tell you, if you knew the truth Jess you would know why he was able to break down your walls. Creed is an asshole and should have been honest with you from the start." I sniffle and raise my brow in question.

"Honest about what?" A deep menacing growl has us both freezing, I don't have to turn my head to know its Creed. How he can be so quiet and sneak around I have no freaking idea.

"Ever heard of knocking, brother?" I can feel the anger radiating off Creed, but I still won't turn to meet his gaze. I keep my eyes on Cole, he won't look at his brother either.

"Get your hand off her, now!" Creed's voice is rough and coated with so much venom, I've learnt when he sounds like his wolf is partly in control.

"Why?" Oh my gosh, Cole should really stop taunting his brother. I reach up and lift his hand from my face, instead of keeping his hand on his side he decides to wrap it around my waist. I look at Cole in shock, but his gaze is now focused over my shoulder. "I thought you were the love 'em leave 'em type?" The growl that comes from Creed is so loud I feel Callie shift behind me and sit up.

"What the hell is going on?" Her voice is rough with sleep, she releases a long yawn and then I feel her gaze on me and stiffen. This is not a good look at all. "Oh."

"Princess." He growls out, the way he says that one word has a shiver running down my spine. I'd love to say it was from fear but then I would be lying. "If you don't move away from my brother, I will make you." I look at Cole in question; he has a devious smirk on his face. He mouths, *trust me?* I don't have time to register what he means before he leans forward and kisses me! I'm in so much shock that it takes him prodding my mouth with his tongue to snap me back to reality, I gasp, and he uses my moment of confusion to invade my mouth. I raise my hands to push him away from me but don't get the chance, hands wrap around my ankles, and I'm tugged down the bed then hoisted into the air and thrown over a shoulder, I screech in shock but stop when a hand slaps my ass.

"Ouch!" I cry out.

"You will pay for that little brother." Creed turns and marches us out of the room with Cole's laughter following us. I don't even have to see to know we are heading toward his room down the other end of the hall. He kicks the door open and doesn't stop until he kicks open another one and then I'm being pulled from his shoulder and placed on the bench inside his ensuite. Creed pushes my legs apart and then steps between them, he places his hands either side of my head, I lean back against the mirror to try to put some distance between us. He's panting and glaring at me like I planned for his brother to kiss me. This is bullshit, I try to push against his chest so he will let me go, he reaches down and gathers both my wrists in his one and then pins them above my head, my turn to glower now. I release a growl of frustration which just earns me a cocky smile from him.

"Let. Me. Go." I make sure to announce each word so there is no confusion.

"Never."

"Fuck you!"

"You kiss your mother with that potty mouth?" I growl, fuck

him!

"Fuck you Credence!" His face turns cold and hard.

"You already did princess." He sounds like an evil prick, and I hate the fact that my body is coming alive with the way he is manhandling me.

"Yeah well, we all make mistakes, don't we?" His eyes narrow to slits and his upper lip pulls back in a snarl. "I'm done with your games." He leans down until his lips are nearly touching mine, I can see the animalistic look in his eyes, and I gulp.

"We are done when I say we are done." He smashes his mouth against mine and I groan, he explores my mouth with his tongue, and I let him for a moment before clarity returns and I bite down on it, hard. He pulls back and it gives me great satisfaction to see blood dripping down his lip.

"We're. Done." Hurt enters his gaze but he quickly masks it, if I hadn't been staring at him so intently, I would have missed that look. He releases my hands and takes a step back. I sigh in relief and climb down off the counter, I look up at him and shake my head, I want him to see the hurt and disappointment in my eyes. I stand tall and hold my chin high as I turn to leave his room.

"If you go near my brother or any other male for that matter, I will kill them." I turn and look at him over my shoulder and narrow my gaze.

"You would kill your own brother?"

"I would kill anyone who gets in my way." I scrunch my face in confusion.

"Get in your way to what?" A sexy smirk graces his

handsome face, and it takes everything inside me not to groan.

"You princess, I will take anyone out who tries to stop me from getting to you." I roll my eyes and turn to leave, just as I pass through the doorway I turn back and say.

"You should start by taking yourself out, you're the one who blocked your own path to me."

CHAPTER THIRTY-ONE

Jessica

I spend the rest of the day with Callie in her room, it goes without saying that I am avoiding both her brothers. I have no idea what the hell Colton was trying to prove this morning but whatever it was has put a kink in our friendship. I really like Cole just...Not like that. There is no spark or burning desire when I'm near him or when he looks at me, don't get me wrong I wish I was attracted to him and not his brother. With Creed, just his presence has my blood pressure spiking and heat spreading through my body. I don't want to be *that* girl who falls for the guy who is a complete tool and treats her like crap, just the thought of not having Creed has a sharp pain shooting through my chest. Sheba begins to whine and whimper in my mind at the thought.

We can't leave him.

Sheba, he has made his intentions clear. He doesn't want us.

Even thinking those words hurt, I have never felt this way about a guy before, it's frightening.

He does, something is being hidden from us.

What do you mean?

I can tell when they lie.

What the heck, that is a handy thing to know.

Who is lying to us?

All of them, they are all hiding something, and I can't pick up on what it is.

I turn and stare at Callie from the corner of my eye, is she lying to me? Are they all hiding something from me? What in the world could they possibly have to lie to me about though?

Dinner is absolutely awkward; Kane and Meg try to make small talk and Meg is constantly darting her gaze between Cole and Creed in question. Kayla is here and hasn't said a word, I can see her out of the corner of my eye sneaking glances at Creed, and he ignores her.

I help Callie and Meg clear the table while the others head out to do God knows what. I finish drying the last plate and put it away, I exit the kitchen but Meg stops me with her words.

"You kids have fun tonight, don't stay out too late." I turn around and stare at her in question.

"What do you mean?" Her eyes dart to a guilty looking Callie. "Callie?" She refuses to meet my gaze as she speaks.

"It's just a little get together to celebrate your birthday. We wanted to do something nice because we know you have been down about your mom and worried about tomorrow. We just wanted you to be able to have some fun before everything changes, you deserve to have one night off of worrying Jess." My heart swells, she is such an amazing friend. She isn't wrong though I have been so worried about my mom and have been trying to contact her or Jacob to check on her wellbeing but none of my calls go through. Is it selfish of me to go and enjoy one last night of freedom so to speak? I can feel it inside myself that tomorrow everything is going to change for me. I release a long sigh and plaster a smile on my face as I meet my friend's gaze.

"Okay, but you have to help me get ready." Callie squeals

and wraps me in a hug before she drags me out of the kitchen, Meg's laughter follows us all the way to Callie's room.

After I showered and shaved, Callie handed me an outfit, and then I was placed in front of the vanity as she did my hair and makeup. Once she is finished, I stand and go to the full-length mirror in the corner and stare in awe. Callie has transformed me once again, my long blonde hair is curled and cascading down my back, she has done a smoky eye with a subtle wing and nude lipstick. The smoky eye makes my blue eyes pop. I'm in a pair of white ripped jeans and a yellow crop top that shows off my stomach. I refused to wear heels and opted to wear my low-cut chucks.

I try to call my mom's phone again while Callie showers and gets ready, no answer--again. I sigh and push that out of my mind, one more night and then I will be reunited with my mom. I give myself a mental pep talk and hype myself up for a night of fun. Callie tells me that Creed and Cole will both be there, and so will our friends from school. I'm looking forward to seeing Asher and the others but not the Reeves brothers, I want no part of the game they are playing.

Callie and I say goodbye to Meg as we leave, it's dark out and I'm shocked when Sheba tells me to allow her partial control. I do as she says and my vision changes, I can see in the freaking dark! I gasp and turn to share the news with Callie but stop when

I see her smiling right at me.

"Being a wolf is pretty cool Jess, give it a chance and you might even enjoy it." She tries to mask it, but I can hear sadness in her voice which confuses the crap out of me. Callie and I chat on our way to the 'gathering' as she calls it, we walk for about ten minutes before the scent of a bonfire hits my nose, excitement begins to bubble inside me. Thanks to Sheba I can already hear voices and laughter, we enter a clearing of sorts and I spot a lot of people sitting around on logs with red solo cups in their hands. I smile and wave when I see Tommy, Chris, Asher, Selena, Carmi, and Chloe. I have no idea who the other people are, I have seen a few of them around school but that's it. As Callie and I near our friends they each give me a hug and wish me a happy birthday for tomorrow, Asher and Tommy scrunch their noses and look at me funny.

"Why are you both looking at me like that?" They exchange a weird look before turning back to me. Asher begins to rub the back of his neck and smiles at me sheepishly as he asks.

"Have you slept with Creed?" I sputter and choke on air as I gape at my friends; Selena and Chloe stare at me with wide eyes.

"Uh, um, I mean...why?" I feel the blush that heats my cheeks.

"His scent is all over you, almost like--"Tommy's eyes double in size as he snaps his gaze over my head, I don't even need to look to know who he is staring at, I feel his presence before I see him. A second later I feel him press against my back, he wraps an arm around my stomach and pulls me flush against him. I stifle the groan that wants to escape me from his touch but manage to clamp my mouth shut before that can happen. Creed uses his free arm to pull my shirt down slightly and expose the mark he left there, both Tommy and Asher jump back a step and stare at me in shock. I furrow my brow in confusion, Creed leans down and places a feather light kiss against the mark, and I gasp. Holy crap the feeling of his lips against that mark is so intense and has my toes curling.

"Did you--"Creed cuts Tommy off.

"Fuck? Yep." Creed pops the *P* like a child and has me rolling my eyes, my friends gaze keeps darting between Creed and I.

"Are you two mat--"

"No. You know what it means and what will happen to you if you touch." The authority in Creed's voice shocks me, my four friends and even Callie drop their heads as if they are bowing to him. What the hell is going on here? Whatever it is I don't like it, Creed is ruining the vibe. I hate to admit it but as much as I am loving having him plastered against me, I want him to leave so my friends can relax. I pull out of his embrace and turn to face him; he has the most arrogant smile on his face, and it makes my palm itch. I want to slap that look off his face.

"You're ruining the vibe with your presence, please leave." Gasps ring out around us, but no one says a word. Creed's smile splits his face, he closes the distance between us and grips the back of my neck, he tightens his hold until I am forced to look up at him.

"I'll ruin every part of you princess and then relish in your pain as I fix you." I scoff and try to free myself, but his grip is ironclad.

"You're a real piece of work; do you manhandle all your fuck buddies like this or just me?" I hear whispers around us but ignore them and focus on him. My body may crave his touch and his nearness, but my brain knows he is bad news and is nothing but trouble.

"Only you princess, I never kept anyone around long enough to allow them to get under my skin." His words shouldn't fill me with joy, but I would be lying if I said they didn't. I refuse to let him see how much those words affect me, so I keep my face void of all emotion and reach up to run my hand through his hair. He eyes me suspiciously but doesn't comment, I stand on my tip toes, our lips a breath apart. I hear his sharp intake of breath and ignore it as I whisper.

"I don't plan on being around much longer, I heard the best cure to get over someone is to get under another. So go fetch big boy." I use his momentary shock to my advantage and quickly swivel out of his hold and beeline it to Callie. From the smug smirk on her face, I can tell she heard every word I just said and so did my friends.

CHAPTER THIRTY-TWO
Jessica

I don't see him for the rest of the night, which I am thankful for. After our little verbal sparring war my body has been thrumming with need. Sheba has been pacing and been relentless in my mind, she is urging--demanding I find Creed. Callie helped me and taught me how to block Sheba's thoughts from my own. I can feel how pissed she is about it but at least I don't have to hear it. I told my friends about me shifting and how it was sudden, they were all in shock but happy for me nonetheless. Sitting around having a few drinks with my friends I can almost fool myself into thinking this is normal--I'm normal. I let the others know I'm going to get another drink and head over to the keg near the beer pong table. As I finish filling my cup, I feel someone approach me from behind and thanks to my new reflexes I spin around without spilling a drop from my cup. Cole smiles at me sheepishly as he rubs the back of his neck, I have never felt awkward around him--until now. I don't know where I am supposed to look, him kissing me has definitely changed our relationship.

"So...Enjoying your night?" I release a long exhale and try to smile kindly but judging by how his face drops, I failed. "Look, I'm sorry. I shouldn't have done that, but in my defense, I thought I was helping." I splutter and glower at him.

"How on God's green earth did you think you were helping?"

"Well, I know my brother is an imbecile so I thought making him jealous would help him pull his head out of his ass." I honestly have no idea what I am supposed to say to that. You don't go around kissing people just to try and get a rise out of someone, it's...wrong.

"Cole I--"

"Hey Jess, can I steal you for a minute?" I turn to Asher and see him and Tommy standing there shuffling from foot to foot like they're nervous.

"Uh, yeah okay. I'll catch you later Cole." Cole looks royally peeved that our conversation was interrupted but honestly, I'm glad. I turn and walk away with Asher and Tommy. They lead me away from the throngs of people and pumping bass of the music. I'll admit I am grateful to get a break from the loud bass, thanks to my new senses. Sounds are heightened. We stop by an old rickety looking hunting cabin, it's quiet and there is no one around. I begin to panic and worry, why have they brought me here?

"We don't have long Jess; we like you and think you're a cool chick." The tone of Tommy's voice puts me on edge and the way his eyes keep darting around causes me to panic.

"What are you talking about?" Asher and Tommy exchange a loaded look before turning back to me.

"Tomorrow at the summit, it won't go how you think it will. They are all lying to you Jess, this was never about you, it was always about power. Creed isn't doing this for revenge, he is doing this to draw your brother out--"

"Tommy, Asher. What are you doing out here with princess?" I stiffen at the sound of his voice, so much anger and malice drips from his words. Tommy and Asher stiffen and pale at the sight of him.

"Creed, we were just talking I swear we--"A low deadly growl sounds from behind me and if possible, Tommy and

251

Asher grow paler.

"I don't want to hear your bullshit Ash, get back to the party before I change my mind." Asher and Tommy both spare me an apologetic look as they hastily make their getaway. I need them to explain to me what the hell they just meant, what brother? Who is lying to me? I startle from my thoughts when hands land on my shoulders and spin me around. Creed stands there sneering at me with two guys either side of him that I have never seen before. "Leave us." He grits out, the two men give a subtle nod and then disappear back to the party. I shuck out of Creed's hold and try to dash back to the party but before I can get more than a couple of steps his arms band around my waist and hauls me backward. I growl and thrash around, Sheba shatters the block I have in place and tries to take over. I force her back not wanting to go through that pain again.

"Let me go Credence!"

"Never princess, now stop struggling."

"Or what?"

"You will really piss me off." I scoff.

"You're always pissed off! That's nothing new to me." I start smacking his hands until he finally relents and places me back on my feet. I don't stick around; I dash back toward the others and sigh in relief when I see Callie is exactly where I left her and the girls earlier. When she sees me approaching her eyes fill with worry.

"What's wron--"She stops talking as she peers over my shoulder; one guess as to who's behind me. I am getting so over this game of cat and mouse; I release a long growl and spin around. He stands there breathing hard, fists clenched at his sides, his eyes shine with the color of his wolfs.

"Stop. Just stop, you made your point, now leave me alone Credence. I am not an object that you can handle when you feel like it, I'm a freaking person!" I yell the last part and feel so many pairs of eyes on us, but I don't care. Ever since I shifted my emotions have been all over the place, I'm so angry right now, and confused as hell after what the guys just told me.

"My point hasn't even begun to be made." I throw my hands in the air.

"What fucking point?" I feel Sheba simmering just below the surface, my eyesight sharpens, and I know my eyes have changed to the color of hers.

"Jess, maybe we should head back?" I ignore Callie and continue to stare at a brooding male in front of me, I refuse to let him not answer me.

"Tell her!" I see Cole walking toward us out the corner of my eye, Creed stiffens the closer his brother gets.

"Stay out of this Colton." Creed snarls.

"You either tell her or I will. I am over this fucking game and she has a right to know, she isn't lying to us Creed." I dart my gaze between the two brothers, I can see regret and remorse shining in Cole's eyes, but Creed gives nothing away. I'm so tired of this, I hate not knowing, but most of all I'm tired. I am constantly fighting the urge to cling to him when he is near, I'm already hot and bothered by him just having his arms around me.

"You will do no such thing, not until I know for sure." Cole glares at the side of his brother's face, Creed still hasn't shifted his gaze from me and for once I don't cower under the pressure of it.

"Know what?" I ask. Creed's gaze sharpens and his nostrils flare. His gaze darts over my head and then a cruel smile stretches over his face. Before I can spin around and see what has caught his attention his arms snake out and haul me back to him, he spins me around and my back is flush against his chest. Everyone moves so they are standing facing the direction we are, the music cuts out and nothing but growls can be heard. Creed's arms are like a vice around me, I can't move an inch.

"I'm so sorry for my part in all of this Jess." I turn my head and look up at Cole, the sadness in his eyes stuns me. Before I can question him, loud growls break out around us, I turn my head and see figures emerging from the trees. My eyesight zones in on the tall broad figure at the front, my wolf yelps in my mind. I don't have time to ponder her reaction, the man comes closer, and he is illuminated by the light of the moon, his chest is bare, and he only wears a pair of shorts. Tattoo's cover his arms and chest, he's tall, I would guess around the same height as Creed, he has a body to die for! He has long black hair that is slicked back and striking ice blue eyes that sear you with intensity. He has high cheekbones and a straight nose, black perfectly shaped brows, full lips the size women pay money for. This man carries an aura of power with him. He stops a few feet away, I can't stop staring at him, something feels so familiar about him, but I can't think how I would know him.

"You have something of mine Reeves." His voice is husky and low but holds so much power. More people begin to emerge from the woods behind him, two women come to stand either side of him and men fan out around them. The women beside him ooze just as much power as he does.

Kin.

Huh, what do you mean?

Family.

I don't bother replying to Sheba because what she has said doesn't make a lick of sense. Creed bends down until his chin rests on my shoulder and his cheek against mine, his stubble scraps the side of my face and sends warmth through my body. I bite the inside of my cheek to stop myself from thinking about what that stubble would feel like between my thighs.

"You have no business being here." The strange man doesn't take his eyes off Creed and me or even acknowledge that Cole just spoke. When Creed places a kiss on my cheek the man growls and his upper lip pulls back in a sneer. I feel him smile against my cheek before he pulls back.

"Cut the shit little Reeves, your big bro made sure I would receive his messages. You have my attention now Credence, release what is mine and we will be on our way." Creed reaches up and grips my chin in his hand then turns my face so I'm looking up at him. I stare at him in confusion before his mouth is against mine, hell no! I clamp my mouth shut and refuse to open for him, he has been a dick all night and I refuse to let him have this. My body is crying out for me to allow him entry and let him use us, but I ignore that stupid little voice in my head. A frightening growl that promises pain has Creed pulling back and smiling down at me. "Do that again and I'll skin you alive." I snap my gaze back to the man and gasp; his eyes glow a bright yellow and his body is taught with tension, the women either side of him take a step away.

"I will do whatever the fuck I feel like with *her*." Anger bubbles inside me.

"The hell you will!" The man cocks a brow at Creed and wears a smug look on his face, the tension seems to ease from his body with my words.

"You weren't complaining the other night, princess." I gape at him; did he really just say that?

"The fuck did you do to her Reeves?" Creed snaps his gaze to the man.

"Claimed what is mine, don't fucking question me Cairo."

"Don't fucking test me Credence, let her go now." I dart my gaze between the two of them, what the hell is going on?

"She stays with me until the summit."

"There will be no summit Reeves, she isn't going. Hand her over now, or I swear I will break the truce and our pact will mean nothing."

"You will never take her from me!" I still at the conviction and dominance in Creed's words.

"She is my blood; she belongs to me." I gasp and stare at the man named Cairo, his chest rises and falls quickly like he is fighting for control.

"What do you mean *I am your blood*?" His piercing ice blue gaze meets mine, a ghost of a smile hovers over his lips.

"My name is Cairo Cruz, and I am your brother Jess."

CHAPTER THIRTY-THREE

Credence

She stiffens in my embrace; I want to comfort her but can't. Cairo cannot see me as weak; I need him to see me as an equal and agree to my terms. I know what this will cost me, but I made a promise, and I must keep it. I know my brother and sister don't agree anymore and want me to let this go but I can't, it's the only thing that has been keeping me going since she did what she did. I can't forgive her for that, she betrayed us all. Jacob will pay for his part in all of this as well, I know Cairo will help me because he is just as hell bent on revenge as I am.

"B-brother?" She stutters. "I-I don't have a brother, I'm an only child." Cairo looks at me and I shake my head letting him know I haven't told her anything.

"That is what Katherine led you to believe but she lied."

"My mom would never lie to me about this type of thing."

"She lied to you your whole life--"

"No!" Jess sounds more animal than human right now, I stroke her midsection with my thumbs knowing that the contact will calm her. I can feel her anguish through the link. Cairo's gaze snaps to me.

"Get rid of them now so we can talk." I growl out a warning.

"I don't take orders from you Cruz."

"If you want my help, you will do as I say." I glare at him and then mind link the crowd of people around us to leave. I tell Cole, Callie and four of my trusted guys to remain. Cairo waits for everyone to disappear before he moves closer, he stops two steps away from us and smiles kindly at Jess. I want to break his face but tamper the rage inside me, he is of no threat to me.

"Why are you here, now? If you are who you say you are, why have I never heard about you?"

"You look so much like him." Jess jerks back in my hold, I tighten my arms around her. "Because she never wanted you to get mixed up with me."

"Why?" She whispers, I can hear the watery tone in her voice, she is close to crying.

"Because after our father was murdered, I went rogue, I tried to kill Jacob and then was cast out of the pack." Jess gasps.

"I-I...how...I mean..." Cairo shushes her and then motions for us to go sit on the logs by the fire. I release Jess and clasp her hand in mine and lead her over to the logs with my siblings trailing behind us, she doesn't protest or even moan when I sit and pull her onto my lap. Cairo glares at me but says nothing. The two women sit either side of him and constantly keep darting their gaze around making sure no one can sneak up on them. Jess is tense and won't tear her gaze from Cairo, Cole and Callie sit on the log opposite us. Just as Cairo opens his mouth to speak, Jess snaps her gaze to my siblings, they both refuse to look at her.

"You both knew about him, didn't you?" Neither of them look up as they nod their heads. "Creed I can understand lying to me, because he's a dick." Cairo chuckles and I growl in response which just causes him to laugh harder. "But you two, I thought you were my friends." Callie snaps her gaze to Jess.

"We are your friends; we didn't have a...choice."

"There is always a choice, Callie."

"No there isn't, we had to obey orders Jess. We cannot ignore an alpha's command." I release a warning which has my brother clamping his mouth shut. Jess tries to stand but I refuse to let her go.

"Get your hands off me Credence now!"

"No." Cairo stands, I jump to my feet and push Jess behind me. For someone who isn't supposed to care I'm doing a great job of protecting her.

"Touch her again without permission and I'll bury you next to your mother." Before I can respond Callie is on her feet and pushing between us.

"Threaten my brother again and I'll bury you next to your father." I stare at the back of her head in shock.

"Little Callie, if you want to keep breathing, I suggest you stay out of it."

"Threaten my twin again and I'll fucking end you Cruz." Fucking hell, first Callie now Cole. Jess shoves away from me and darts out of reach when I try to grab her, she makes it to Cairo before I can stop her. When she is within reach, he grabs her and pulls her to him and hugs her, I raise my hand to stop my men from trying to get her back. Cairo will never hurt her, he has been searching for her for so long. Cairo pulls back and places his hands on her shoulders as he looks her over.

"I can't believe I finally found you. Come on, it's time for you to come home now." I release a vicious growl in warning, Cairo's men move in closer and the women with him are on their feet standing either side of him.

"She isn't going anywhere." I grit out, his furious gaze meets mine.

"She isn't yours; she is my kin and will come to our pack." Jess looks between us but says nothing, I have to think of something fast or she will leave with him and fuck everything up.

Colton, tell them she is your mate.

The fuck Creed?

Do it now!

Why?

That's an order Cole, right now before she leaves.

I hope you know what you're doing brother.

"She can't go." Everyone turns to face Cole.

"Why?" Cairo snaps, Cole releases a whoosh of air and then looks to Jess.

"Because, she's my mate."

Jess turns pale, her gaze darts between me and Cole, I can see the look of betrayal that enters her eyes. If I was a better man, I'd tell her everything and hope that she would help me but I can't risk her leaving. She opens and closes her mouth like a fish out of water, Cairo looks between me and my siblings. The look in his eyes tells me he doesn't believe a word we are saying.

"If she is his mate then why does your scent cling to her?" I flinch internally but keep my mask of indifference in place and shrug my shoulders and say.

"We fucked." Jess's eyes double in size, Cairo turns his accusing eyes to his sister.

"Did you really fuck the enemy?" Jess gapes at him and splutters before a deafening growl tears out of her. Her eyes change and her posture becomes ridged, Sheba has taken control.

"You may be kin, but you do not question me. I am an alpha heir, and you are beneath me, know your place." I cautiously move toward Jess and Cairo, if I don't defuse this now there will be a bloodbath on our hands. If Jess is anything like her brother, she will have a wolf that will not tolerate insubordination.

CHAPTER THIRTY-FOUR
Jessica

No matter how much I try to pull her back or regain control, Sheba won't allow me. I begin to panic when I feel her anger spike and my body grow taut and tight like a spring ready to snap. Cairo has his gaze locked on me and Sheba is viewing him holding eye contact as a challenge. I don't want to shift or fight; I just want to talk.

Sheba, please don't do this.

He is challenging me; I cannot let him get away with this. We are not weak Jess; we are strong and to be feared.

I am begging you Sheba, let me take control back and I can diffuse this--

No, I will deal with this.

Before I can reply, Creed steps in front of me and ignores Sheba's growl, I sigh in relief. I fear that if he hadn't stepped in Sheba would have shifted and we would have got our asses kicked. Sheba scoffs and relents control back to me, I'm grateful. It is so hard sharing a body with another being and trying to learn balance. Sheba may be a part of me, but she is her own being, she is fierce and strong, while I am meek and reserved.

You are not, you are strong and fearless. You just have to believe it.

Thank you, Sheba, maybe you can help me believe it.

"She is your sister Ro; she is new to all of this." I stare at Creed's back in shock, I never expected *him* of all people to stick up for me.

"I would never harm her." Creed scoffs.

"You could have fooled me; from the way you were just scowling at her." I'm tired of this back and forth, I step out from behind Creed and stand by his side. I fight my bodies need to lean into him.

"I want an explanation."

"Princess, I don't owe you shi--"I cut Creed off.

"I wasn't talking to you Credence; I was talking to *him*." I nod toward a smirking Cairo; I can feel the intense glare Creed is shooting my way but refuse to pay him any attention.

"What do you want to know?" The tone of his voice puts me at ease, don't get me wrong I am still suspicious as hell about him, but Sheba keeps telling me I can trust him.

"Can we sit?"

"You gonna perch on his lap again?" I chuckle and shake my head as I move back toward the logs. Cairo sits next to me, and Creed takes the seat behind me, he sits closer than is necessary, but I don't see the point in commenting, if I do, it will just cause a fight and I would rather get answers right now. I notice the two women sit closer to Cairo and watch the others like hawks. They both look badass and seem like they don't take shit from anyone. "What do you want to know?" I direct my attention back to Cairo and look at him, he has the same color eyes as me but that's about it. He's all hard edges and has an air of dominance about him.

"How are you, my brother?" He doesn't look offended; in fact he smiles kindly and reaches out to clasp my hand in his. We both choose to ignore Creed's subtle growl; I'll deal with him later--and Cole.

"We have the same mom and dad."

"Mom would have told me if she was pregnant or had another child." I can hear the hurt that laces my own voice.

"Katharine isn't our mother Jess." I reel back in shock.

"What do you mean? Why do I feel like there is more to this than you are telling me?" Cairo looks over my shoulder for a moment before nodding and turning back to me. It annoys me that he looks to Creed for permission.

"Kat is our aunt; our mother and father were killed. After they died Kat and her mate took you in and raised you, Kat fled with you after her mate was killed--"

"You're lying!" I hate the look of pity that enters his eyes.

"I'm not Jess, and I think deep down you have always known that something was off about Kat. Did she ever tell you about your birth? About dad?" I open my mouth to protest but he's right, what if he's telling the truth? "Kat is dad's sister, and she did what she thought was right and in reality, she probably saved your life by running." I open my mouth, but no words come out. An arm wraps around my waist and warmth begins to spread through my body. I am beyond thankful for Creed's touch, he snapped me out of my downward spiral.

"Why did she run with me?" I whisper.

"After mom and dad were killed, we had no one else. I couldn't raise you, I was trying to work out how to run the pack. Jacob threatened to kill you if I didn't go rogue, I was so consumed by grief I ran, I knew you would be okay with Kat. It wasn't until years later that I learned Kat fled not long after I did."

"How old are you?" I blurt out, my question doesn't seem to shock him.

"Twenty-six." I gasp.

"So you were only like nine when you ran?" He smiles sadly and nods his head; I can see a range of emotions that swirl in the depths of his eyes. Silence descends and I have no clue how to break it. Cairo seems lost in his thoughts until one of the women stands and comes to his side and places a hand on his bare shoulder. She has blonde hair that is cut into a pixie kind of style, her muddy brown eyes give nothing away. I scan her from head to toe and notice that she is decked out in leathers and has knives strapped to pretty much every part of her body.

"You're not there anymore Ro, we are with you always." I can tell there is a story between these two but at the moment I don't think it is the time to ask, Cairo shakes his head and reaches up to place his hand on top of the woman's and smiles kindly.

"Jess, this is Sky. Sky is my beta and most loyal friend." My eyes double in shock, I didn't see that coming. The woman named Sky nods her head and steps back.

"I'm sorry if I upset you, that wasn't my intention." Cairo nods but I can still see the haunted look in his eyes, and it makes my chest ache for him. If he is my brother, why can't he take over and be alpha?

"It's okay, that was just a rough time for me. Yes, I was just a child, but I had no other choice, if I stayed, I would have died. I didn't think Jacob would try to attack you, but I was wrong, I have been tracking you for years now, and every time I got close, Kat would move. It's a long as fuck story Jess and I want to tell you everything but now isn't the time. I travelled with only a few members of my pack so I wouldn't alert Jacob--"

"Don't go!" I blurt out, if what he says is true, then I don't want my brother to leave me when I only just found him.

"I promise I won't leave you. We have to come up with a plan for tomorrow, I tried to find you before it came to this, but I failed."

"Failed how?"

"The council now knows you live; they won't let you leave Jess. I have managed to stay off their radar so they wouldn't come for me. The council aren't people who you want to mess with, they are strong and old."

"Wait, why won't they let me leave?" Cairo's eyes harden and his body tenses.

"Because I fled, they don't take kindly to deserters. It's like the army once you're in you are in for life. I don't have hard proof yet about what Jacob did but when I find it, I will be able to come home."

"You have to be there tomorrow." Creed cuts in, Cairo narrows his eyes at him over my shoulder.

"Why? What have you got planned Credence?" I want to know how these two know each other, I hate not knowing the full story.

"I plan to take Jacob down and get revenge once and for all." The venom in his voice has me sitting up straight.

"You want revenge, yet you have his daughter on your lands?" Creed's arm around me stiffens.

"Not by choice, she isn't of concern. Jacob will have to relent to me and hand over his pack, Jess is the rightful alpha and has a greater claim to the pack than him." Cairo shakes his head and curses.

"You idiot. He has the council in his back pocket. Why do you think I haven't come back until now? The council will rule in his favor they always do, you just put my sister's life in danger you asshole."

CHAPTER THIRTY-FIVE
Credence

No!

That can't be, I planned everything out perfectly.

I made sure everything was in place, so that the council would be present to watch his demise. If what Ro says is true then were fucked, if he makes a claim to her then the council will grant it. I can't let them do that. All my lies and planning to lure her in will blow up in my face, this will all have been for nothing. I just put my pack and my family in danger all because I made a promise that I refused to break. I grit my teeth and try to calm myself.

We will kill him and the council if they try to take her.

Agreed, we cannot let them win, Corbin.

I feel better knowing Corbin has my back. If what Cairo says is true then I have to convince him to stay, not for me but for her. I meet Cairo's gaze and try to convey to him that I need to talk to him alone--now.

"Jess, do you mind if Creed and I spoke privately for a few minutes?" Jess is in shock that Ro is even asking and not just demanding it. She nods jerkily, I release my hold on her and nod for Ro to follow. I keep walking until we break through the woods and don't stop until I am sure we are out of hearing distance from the others. Ro stands in front of me, the only lighting out here is the moon, tomorrow is the full moon and that's when Jess and Sheba will figure everything out. "What have you done?" A whoosh of air escapes me as I meet his gaze.

"I need you to be there tomorrow."

"Why?"

"Because I'm going to take that son of a bitch down." Ro shakes his head and looks at me like he wants to cuff me.

"How? Your pack isn't strong enough, you can probably take him and his pack but not with the council there as well."

"You owe me this." Cairo's gaze turns frosty, and his posture is now rigid as he meets my stare.

"So, it's like that?" I didn't want to pull that card, but I didn't have a choice, I'm backed into a corner.

"I don't have a choice Ro. I've set too many things into motion to back out." He scoffs and begins to pace in front of me.

"My sister was just a ploy to lure me back, wasn't she? You only want me here for my pack, my sister was just the bait."

"Yes."

"How the fuck did you get Kat back here?"

"I didn't, she knew that the only way to keep Jess safe was to bring her back here and let them see she hasn't shifted." Cairo pauses and turns his accusing stare to me.

"I can smell her wolf; she has shifted already. Why would Kat let that happen? Where is she anyway?"

"She didn't, it just happened. Jacob has her, that's why Jess is here."

"Bullshit, you would have made sure she was here anyway. I know you Creed, I also know Cole. If she was his mate, he would have killed you for touching her, now tell me the fucking truth."

"You already know the truth." Ro growls and tugs at his hair.

"No, no. She isn't staying here..." His gaze meets mine and I see the moment he puts it all together. "You lying sack of shit, you're using her!" He lurches forward and lands a clean hit to my jaw; I stumble back and glare at the fucker. He stands there panting and pointing at me with nothing but loathing in his eyes. "You stay the fuck away from her, she is coming with me. I don't give a fuck about these packs or this land, neither does she! This war has nothing to do with me or my sister." I straighten and rub my jaw as I meet his heated stare with one of my own.

"You try and take her from me, and I will kill you where you stand." A cruel smirk splits his face.

"You gonna kill your best friend? Please, you could never beat me before and you sure as shit can't now. She is innocent. If you do this to her, you are no better than him." I growl.

"Jacob murdered my mother because of your father, he deserves everything he is going to get, and if I have to use your sister to get to him I will. She is nothing to me--a means to an end." Cairo looks over my shoulder and a quick scent of the air tells me I just fucked up, I spin around to see Jess, Cole, Callie and Sky standing there.

"We heard raised voices." I glare at my sister before focusing on Jess. I see the hurt in her eyes. She tries so hard to mask it but fails.

"Why did Jacob kill your mom?" I deflate slightly but I don't get to answer Cairo beats me to it.

"Because their mother was our fathers fated mate--"I cut Cairo off.

"The story Kat and my dad were talking about that day in the office wasn't true, well it was but it was about your father and my mother." Jess gasps and looks to Cairo and then back to me.

"Oh my god...are we...shit...crap...no." When her horrified gaze meets mine again, it dawns on me, I can't fight the smile that breaks across my face as I shake my head.

"No, we are not related in any way princess." The air rushes from her as she nods her head in relief. She darts her gaze between me and Ro before finally settling on me.

"I want to know the truth, about everything. Cole has told me that I will find out everything tomorrow night." I dart my gaze to my brother and glare; he doesn't even give a shit that he has gone against my orders. "Also, after everything is finished tomorrow and I get my mom back, I don't care if you say she isn't my mom, to me she always will be. Her and I will be leaving, Cairo I would love to get to know you and actually sit down and hear about all of this soon if that's okay?"

"Of course." Ro answers, the kiss ass. I stare at her and try to uncover her secrets, why is she not demanding answers?

"Why aren't you pestering us for the truth now?" She cocks a brow and places her hands on her hips as she scowls at me.

"Because I have learnt that all you do is lie and hide things. I don't trust you to tell me the truth, I'd rather wait till tomorrow to know the whole story. Now if you don't mind I'm beat and going to head to bed--alone." She had to emphasize the last part which just makes Cairo and Cole chuckle; I glare at both of them.

CHAPTER
THIRTY-SIX
Jessica

After showering and hopping into bed, I try to force myself to sleep before Callie comes back. But my mind wouldn't shut off, I have a brother. Not only that the woman who I thought was my mom isn't, she is actually my aunt. On top of all that my bio mom and dad were killed and worst of all my bio mom knew my bio dad was boning the triplet's mom! I do not condone cheating at all, point blank no exceptions. I don't care if they are *fated mates* whatever the hell that means. My emotions are all over the place at the moment, I'm hurt by Creed's words but at the end of the day I knew sleeping with him was a bad idea. Don't get me wrong, I enjoyed it and he did dull the burning ache inside me. I'm no sex expert, I have had sex once before and it was terrible and awkward as shit. I groan and roll over trying to clear my mind so sleep will claim me. I don't know what to expect tomorrow and I'm nervous that I may have to shift again but I will gladly go through all that pain again if it meant getting my mom back.

I couldn't sleep after laying here for over an hour, so I decided to count sheep. I was up to 102 when voices outside the door catch my attention.

"We have to come clean."

"No California, what I say goes." Creed sounds like a self-righteous prick.

"Look how well that turned out Credence. Cairo may not even back us tomorrow and if what he says is true then we're fucked. We cannot go against the council; we don't have the numbers."

"Ro said he has an ace up his sleeve Colton, he won't leave Jess. He has spent his whole life trying to find her and now that he knows where she is he won't leave her. He will come."

Anger begins to bubble up inside me, I bit the inside of my cheek to stop myself from marching out there and demanding answers.

"I hope for your sake, she forgives you when she finds out what you have done. Jess is a good person and doesn't deserve this shit."

"You don't think I know that Callie? I thought she was going to be here sooner; It took us two weeks to get this shit done and I don't regret it. Once the bond kicks in at the peak of the full moon, her wolf will override her human side and force her to forgive me." I grit my teeth, like hell will that happen. The conversation stops and I hear them leave. I have no idea what any of that means, but Creed can kiss my natural white ass if he thinks Sheba will forgive him and make me do the same.

I wake the next morning--alone. Callie's side of the bed is untouched, she must have slept somewhere else last night. After having a quick shower and braiding my long hair, I change into a pair of cut-offs and a simple off the shoulder black shirt and pair the outfit with my low-cut Chucks. I leave my face bare of makeup, I don't feel like trying to look my best today. I take a few deep breaths and give myself a mental pep talk and become my own hype man. I open the door and follow the sounds of voices toward the kitchen. As soon as I enter, they all turn to me,

Cole, Callie, Meg and Kane all have warm smiles on their faces. Creed and Kayla refuse to even look at me which is just fine by me.

"Happy birthday sweetie."

"Thanks Meg."

"Eighteen never looked so good." I smile and roll my eyes playfully at Colton as I take the seat between Creed and Callie. Callie nudges me and smiles, I return her gesture.

"Happy birthday, bestie."

"Thanks."

We all dig into the amazing food Meg has prepared for us; they all talk about mundane stuff. I remain silent, so much anxious energy is thrumming through me, and I can't seem to calm it.

"She's anxious because of the full moon, it calls to our beasts." I snap my gaze to Creed, it's the first time he has spoken since I sat down. He has dark circles under his eyes, his hair is a tousled mess, and his eyes have a haunting look inside them that I can't decipher.

"Why?" He shrugs his shoulders and says.

"The moon goddess designed us that way. Each full moon we shift and run as a pack. It's not like movies where we have no choice in the matter but we celebrate every full moon with a pack run. It's good for our wolves to run as a pack, when the moon is at its fullest, we are all at optimum strength." I stare at him in wonder, I never expected him to be so forthcoming with information.

"Will you run tonight, as a pack?" He smiles sadly and shakes his head.

"Not tonight, we have to be at the summit for your ascension."

"What does that mean?" It's then that I notice everyone else has stopped talking and is listening to every word Creed and I are saying.

"It means that tonight you will be named alpha of two packs."

"What if I don't want that?" I whisper, he reaches out and cups my face tenderly in his hand, his touch soothes the chaos inside me. My body begins to heat from his touch, and I stifle the groan that wants to tear out of me.

"You don't have a choice princess. You shifted; there is no escaping your destiny now."

"That's not fair, I didn't choose to shift. It just happened." His brows furrow and he drops his gaze.

"I know, I'm sorry for all of this princess. I wish I could change it but I can't, if things were different I wouldn't--- "Creeds sentence is cut off when the sound of a door slamming open interrupts us. Everyone jumps to their feet; Creed hauls me up and pushes me behind him. I swoon a little at his protectiveness.

"Alpha." A man says, I can't see him thanks to Creed's bulky form in front of me.

"Speak, Kobe." I reel back; the guy said *alpha* so why is Creed speaking and not Kane?

"The council has sent word sir. They have changed the summit time; they want to meet in the next hour." A terrifying growl tears from Creed, I look around to see everyone has lowered their heads almost like they are bowing.

All hell breaks loose after the guy Kobe leaves. Creed begins barking orders at everyone telling them what to do and where to meet. I stand here stunned and just watch as everyone does as they are told. They all hustle out of the house to do as Creed said, while he and I stood there staring at each other. His chest is rising and falling fast, almost like he is trying to contain his anger. I move back as he steps forward and my ass smacks into the table. I can't go anywhere as he closes the space between us and places his arms on either side of me caging me in. He bends down until we are eye level, the look in his eyes has my breath halting.

"Before you run from me, let me explain everything."

"W-why would I run?"

"Because soon enough you will learn that it was all a game, until it wasn't. Let me try to fix this before you flee with Cairo." I shake my head, he reaches up and cups my face between his hands and then kisses me senseless, we're both gasping for air when he pulls back. His forehead rests against mine, his eyes closed and his body is tight with tension. "I'm sorry princess, for all of it."

"Creed, we're ready." His eyes open at the sound of his father's voice and the look he gives me nearly has my knees buckling. He finally drops his mask and lets me see the raw emotions inside of him, sadness, guilt, shame...love. A second later his mask is back in place and his emotions are once again unreadable. He pulls back and looks down at me once more before turning around and storming out of the house, I follow his retreating form until I can't see him anymore.

"Jess?" I shake my head and then turn to face a solemn

looking Kane. "He is a good kid; he means well but---please be patient."

"Huh?"

"Credence didn't mean for it to get this far. He just wants justice for his mother, please try to understand." I see guilt all over his face and it confuses the crap out of me.

"Why does my forgiveness matter to Creed?"

"Because without you he is soulless."

CHAPTER THIRTY-SEVEN

Jessica

I'm sitting in the middle of Callie and Cole, Creed is driving and Kane sits shotgun, I have no idea where Meg is. Kane ushered me out of the house after our little chat and straight into the waiting SUV. We have been driving for around twenty minutes, there are cars following behind us, but aside from them there is no other traffic. If what I am thinking is correct, we are heading to the top of the mountain, I'm afraid of heights so this idea doesn't exactly thrill me! The closer we drive to the peak my palms begin to get clammy, my breaths start to come in short rapid pants. I have no idea what awaits me when we get there and the unknown scares the bejesus out of me. Once we reach the top, I see so many different types of vehicles scattered and parked half-hazardly around the turn around area. Creed slows the car and parks in an empty spot next to an old school Honda.

After he turns the ignition off, we all sit there in tension filled silence for a while, the cars that followed us park and get out. They all stand there and look at our vehicle, my companions show no sign of wanting to get out anytime soon. I spy Callie and Cole out of the corner of my eye. Both of them have their gazes out their windows, I can see how rigid and stiff they are.

Creed and Kane both sit there still as statues staring out the windshield. Creed's gaze shifts to mine in the rear-view mirror, he gives no indication to how he is feeling. His mask of indifference is firmly in place, and he is back to being the cold detached Creed that I hate to know.

"They're ready for us." Creed nods his head. "You got this son, don't let them get in your head." I don't know who Kane is trying to convince more. himself or Creed. Creed's gaze meets mine in the rear-view mirror once again, this time his mask is nowhere to be seen, the intensity in his eyes, makes me hold my breath. I can see the war brewing behind the depths of those beautiful eyes, the look he gives me has my pulse spiking.

I know this meeting is detrimental. I just didn't realize how important it was until this very moment. We hold each other's stare for a long minute, words aren't spoken as Creed and I sit here lost in each other's gaze. The moment is shattered when there is a knock against the window. Creed turns and scowls at the culprit, the poor young man standing there looks like he's about to piss himself from the hard glare Creed gives him. You don't have to be a rocket scientist to know that they're having a mind link conversation that I'm not privy to, once again. Creed gives a sharp nod and then turns to the rest of us, he looks to his brother and sister, each gives subtle nods and then exits the car. I remain sitting in the center and lock eyes with Creed, I try to convey to him with my eyes that I'm scared. The look he gives me in return tells me he can see everything that I'm feeling and as strange as it sounds, I feel like I can rely on him to keep me safe.

After exiting the car, we follow behind Creed, Kane and Cole flank him on either side, Callie and another guy I've never seen before walks behind them. It's like a *mighty duck* V. We continue to trek through these woods with the rest of the pack taking up the rear, I'm starting to wonder why the hell is Creed leading the pack and not Kane? Everyone seems to obey his orders, but he doesn't have to obey anyone, not even his father--the alpha. Little things that I've noticed aren't adding up correctly, I know this is probably the worst time to be thinking about all of this, but let's be real, I am scared shitless and need something to focus on.

We continue to hike up the steep incline and I'm not having a puffing fit or keeling over nearly dying. I know deep down inside it's all thanks to Sheba. I'm slightly unsettled at the fact that she has remained quiet most of this journey and hasn't said one word. I don't know if that's a good thing or a bad thing but right now I just would like her confirmation that what we're about to do is the right thing. Trepidation courses threw me at the fact that I'm going to see my mom or aunt, I don't even know what to call her now. It's a discussion that we need to have once we are safe and out of this place. For the first time Sheba begins to stare inside me.

We cannot leave.

Why not?

We must stay with pack and mate.

Why do you keep saying mate what does that even mean?

It means we found our soulmate.

I gasp and dart my gaze around the clearing that we've just entered looking at each of the men, wondering are they my soulmate? Sheba has only said that once before when we first shifted, my heart begins to beat faster as I lock my gaze on the back of Creed's tall broad frame, could it be?

My thoughts die off once we break through another set of trees and we come to a stop. I peer through the gap and see a large amount of people gathered, tears well in my eyes as I scan the crowd and I see her. Bruises mar her beautiful face, dry blood is crusted down her arms, her clothing torn. Anger wells inside of me, a low growl tears from my chest, her gaze snaps up and tries to find me. I move forward to pass Creed, but his arm snaps out like a viper and stops me in my tracks. I turn and glare up at the broody bastard, he slides his gaze down to me and I see the warning in his eyes. I turn back toward my mom and see her give a subtle shake of her head; I don't know why she doesn't want me to come to her. I search her gaze to try and find a reason why, and when I see fear, I give up and stand tall beside Creed. I make sure to keep my emotions in check and wear a mask of indifference, the last thing I need is for Jacob and his pack to see me as weak. Sheba nods her approval inside my head.

"Thank you for joining us Credence."

"You didn't give us much of a choice though did you, Philip?" I follow Creed's gaze to see him staring at a middle-aged man with salt and pepper hair, dull brown eyes and not very tall; he smiles, and I see he has crooked yellow teeth. He's dressed in an ill-fitted suit that looks too big for him, Sheba growls inside my mind. I'm glad her and I agree that this man is creepy. A group of people surround him, they all appear to be around the same age, but in their eyes, you can see they're older than they appear. Meg told me that shifters age differently to humans, I can see now that she is absolutely right. The man Phillip, makes his way towards the middle of the clearing, the grass crunching beneath his feet. An eerie feeling settles inside me when eight other people follow him to the middle. Sheba startles me when she speaks.

They are the council.

So there are nine of them?

There used to be eleven but somehow, they miraculously died of unknown causes.

Why do I feel like you are hinting that they were murdered?

Because that's exactly what I'm hinting at.

Phillip spins around and looks at each person here, when his gaze settles on me, I feel Creed stiffen beside me. A devilish smirk stretches across his face, he cocks a thick black brow at me. He turns to the others surrounding him, he smiles and nods like they are having a private conversation that none of us are privy to. Creed moves his arm from in front of me and wraps it around my shoulders, he pulls me into his side. I don't fight him, if anything I'm embarrassed to admit I enjoy the safety that his embrace gives me at the moment. I dart my gaze to my mom to see her looking between both of us, I can't get a read on her emotions or gauge what she is thinking.

"Well, look at what we have here. The sort after offspring of two alphas, from rivaling packs, and a female at that." Phillip sounds like a condescending prick. "Never before in the history of our people has there ever been a female alpha. What makes you, Jessica Hastings think you are worthy of this title?" I swallow loudly and dart my gaze to Creed, I'm surprised to find he's staring directly back at me.

"I know I don't deserve it, but I am asking you to trust me right now. Can you do that Princess?" I stifle the gasp that wants to creep out of me from the shock of hearing Creed in my mind.

"I don't think I really have another choice, do I?"

"You always have a choice Princess, but right now in this moment if you wanna get out of here alive with your mother, no you don't. You're going to learn things very shortly that are going

to piss you off, trust in me and I will explain everything once this is over."

"You get my mother out of here alive, then I'll think about listening to you tell the truth for once."

"We're not used to being kept waiting, Miss Hastings." Phillip snaps.

"I don't think she has to answer that Phillip, the fact that she is born of two pure bloodlines is answer enough, don't you think?" Phillips upper lip pulls back in a sneer; his eyes darken as he looks at Creed.

A woman who looks no older than mid-thirties steps forward, she's dressed in a plain shirt and jeans. Her hair is piled on top of her head in a messy bun, something's different about this woman compared to the others. She doesn't look at us like we're beneath her or hostile. She runs her gaze over Creed and then me before settling her gaze on Creed. This woman looks so familiar, I just can't place where I could possibly know her from. When I hear a low growl sound from across the clearing, I'm shocked to see that it's my mom. Her gaze is laser focused on the woman, I see Jacob and Josh standing there with cruel smirks on their faces, their relaxed body language tells me that they are at ease unlike us. I scan the other faces of Jacob's pack; he and his son may look at ease but the rest of the people with them seem like they don't have a choice. As I lock eyes with a plain looking woman to Jacobs far left, I see fear in her eyes.

My mom continues to growl, the woman pays my mother no notice as she continues to stare at Creed. His arm tightens around me, I can feel a slight tremble in his hand. I don't know what it is about this woman that's got my mom and Creed so worked up.

"Credence Reeves, it's been a long time since I have seen you."

"Not long enough if you ask me." The woman chuckles and shakes her head. I don't know what the hell she found so funny about what Creed just said but her laugh has the hairs on the back of my neck standing up.

"Jacob has filled us in on what you have done. Would you care to tell us your side?" I dart my gaze to Jacob and see the evil glint in his eyes, I look to Josh beside him, and the asshole has the audacity to pucker his lips at me, I narrow my gaze and hope he can see how much I loathe him. It gives me great pleasure to see his deformed ear. I turn to my mom next; her gaze is locked onto me. Her eyes hold so much sadness. She mouths the words *I'm sorry*. I furrow my brow in confusion, none of this is her fault I don't blame her for any of this.

CHAPTER THIRTY-EIGHT

Credence

I want nothing more than to wipe that smug look off Shelley's face, the bitch is pure evil. I see now Ro was right, the council has already made up their minds, it doesn't matter what I say.

"I can tell you now that my side is going to be very different from his." Damon and Chris sidle up next to Shelley, they are both kiss asses. "Before I begin though, I want to know why are we all here as if someone is on trial." I can feel Jess's gaze on me but refuse to take my eyes off the council for even a second. They may be the leaders of our kind, but they are slimy bastards and will lie and cheat to get their way, no matter the cost.

"Do not try our patience--"Shelley raises her hand and Damon snaps his mouth shut like the good little lap dog he is.

"No one is on trial; we are here to go through the motions I guess you could say." I feel my dad move forward to stand beside me.

"With all due respect, can we get on with this so we can get the hell out of here?" My dad is one bad motherfucker, Shelley wouldn't dare openly challenge him. She may want to look at him like he is shit under her shoe, but dad has something over her that I don't even know about. Whatever it is must be huge, because there is no way she would ever let him speak to her like that otherwise. Shelley grits her teeth and nods her head stiffly.

"Of course, Kane." Her gaze then shifts to Jess, and it happens so fast I almost missed it, but her brown eyes shone with love before it was quickly masked. What the hell was that about? "Jessica Hastings, you are the first-born female alpha to both packs. We council members wish to know what it is you plan to do with the packs before we continue?"

"I-I." Jess stops and clears her throat before continuing. "I don't know." I release a long sigh, I think the princess just fucked up, Shelley opens her mouth to speak but is cut off when Jess continues. "I may not know what to do right now but I will figure it out. I have recently learnt that my mother and father were killed because of this stupid pack shit." I see Shelley finch but she masks it by acting like she is swatting a fly away. "All I want is for both packs to get along and stop this rubbish." Jacob moves toward the centre of the clearing with Katherine stumbling behind him. He drags her by the back of her neck, the bastard needs to be taught a lesson on how not to touch women. "Get your fucking hands off my mom!" Jess launches forward but I quickly wrap both my arms around her waist and haul her back to me, she slams against my chest and doesn't stop struggling.

"Kitten?" At the sound of her mother's voice, she stops struggling. "I'm okay." A strangled sob tears out of Jess. Now is not the time for her to break down in front of the council, she has to be seen as strong and fearless, not a weak emotional teenager. I open the mind link and say to her.

Stop, if you don't, she will die." She freezes in my arms. *"Trust me to get us all out of here safely.*

After a moment she nods her understanding and I straighten and meet Jacob's gaze, the sly smirk on his ugly face tells me he was hoping for the reaction Jess just gave.

"May I speak?" I grit my teeth and remain quiet as Jacob propositions the council; Chris nods his head to grant Jacob the freedom to speak. "I am not sure if the alpha of the Reeve's pack has told you all, but Miss Hastings has already shifted." Gasps and murmurs ring out around the clearing, the council huddles and begin to talk among themselves. I look to see Jess staring directly at her mom. Katherine looks terrified; something in her gaze sends a cold shiver down my spine. "So, that being said, she doesn't have a choice but to rule and join the packs."

"What the hell are you getting at here Jacob?" Shelley snaps, he darts his gaze to Jess and licks his lips suggestively.

"Since the moment she entered the clearing and my wolf scented her--"I shove Jess behind me and growl long and loud in warning.

"You touch her, and I will kill you."

"With all due respect *Alpha* Credence," I hear Jess gasp behind me. "It is I who should be threatening you for frolicking with my *mate*." More gasps break out, but I ignore them, time for me to admit the truth. I just hope she can forgive me. I stand tall and hold my head high as I say.

"As alpha of the Reeves pack, I Credence Reeves claim ownership of both packs through the mate link. Jessica Hastings and I completed our mate bond the night she shifted." I reach behind me and pull Jess forward until she is standing next to me. She is stiff and refuses to meet my gaze, but I can feel through the mate link that she is angry and hurt by betrayal. I move behind her and pull her shirt down lightly at the collar so they can see the mark on her shoulder, it will never fade or go away like she thinks. It will remain there for the rest of her life, and I didn't even give her a say in the matter. "As you can see, she is marked by me. There is no point for further discussion, Jess and I will both rule the packs starting immediately."

The look of shock and disbelief on Jacob's face is the best

revenge I could have ever asked for. No matter what he says or does he won't be able to rebuke my claims to the packs.

"H-he is lying, she is my mate." He stammers out, I wrap my arms around Jess's waist and ignore how she flinches at my touch.

"If I was lying the mark would have faded within a few hours. Plus, all you have to do is scent her and my scent will be clinging to her. Jess is my mate and nothing you say or do will change that!" Jacob pushes Katherine to her knees in front of him, her terror filled gaze darts to Jess then...me. I can see it in her eyes, Jacob has something up his sleeve and is about to play a trump card I didn't calculate. He pats Katharine like a dog, she flinches each time his hand touches her. Jess trembles in my embrace; I can sense how close her wolf is to the surface. If she shifts now, she will attack Jacob and that will start a war. It is forbidden for one alpha to kill another after they step down outside of battle. Something isn't right, Josh moves toward his father flanked by four other pack members. I turn to my father and see my brother standing beside him, they both stare ahead in nervous anticipation. I open the mind link with my pack and say.

Jacob and Josh are up to something. Stay alert and be ready, something doesn't feel right.

I close the link and lean down to whisper in Jess's ear while keeping my gaze on the sight in front of me.

"Do not shift." If she shifts and challenges Jacob, he has every right to do the same, he will kill her. He is a ruthless son of a bitch and isn't above playing dirty to get what he wants.

"Fuck. You!" I flinch internally at how cold and detached

she sounds. In her mind all I have done is lied, tricked her, and used her. She may be right, but I did all of this to save us and *her.*

Once Josh and the other four stopped by Jacob he turns to face the council.

"Well, I am getting old and who am I to stand in the way of true love?" I tense, something is really fucking wrong. He would never relent that easily. "So, I ask the council to grant me one last request as alpha?"

"What is your request?" Shelley grits out, something is up with her as well. She seems more emotional than I have ever seen her before, and judging from the looks the other council members are giving her they are just as puzzled as I am.

"I have a pack member who deserted their pack and hid the rightful heir. That offence is punishable by death." Jess stills in my arms; I dart my gaze to Shelley who seems to be in shock. I turn back to Katharine to see her looking directly at Jess with tears trailing down her face.

"Granted." Comes from Phillip, Jess thrashes in my arms and it takes all my strength to hold her back.

"Don't you fucking touch her! I'll kill all of you, every single fucking one." Jacob smiles and winks as he turns and clasps Katharine's face between his hands.

"I love you kitten; I would do it all again. Now run--"Her words are cut off when Jacob twists her neck and the clearing is filled with the sickening sound of her neck being snapped. He releases Katharine and her lifeless body falls to the ground with her head at an awkward angle.

Silence, no one speaks. Jess is still in my arms with her gaze on her mother's body, it takes me a second to snap out of my shock. I loosen my grip on her to spin her around toward me so I can shield her from the view of her mother, but I fucked up. She breaks out of my hold and takes off running, she takes three steps before her clothes tear, I'm stunned at how fucking fast she just shifted; I have never seen anyone shift like that on the fly. It takes wolves years to master that and she did it with no effort at all. I snap myself out of my daze and take off after her, Jacob looks gleeful and crouches waiting for Jess's wolf to attack. He killed Katherine knowing that Jess would lose control, if he kills her, he will inherit her claim to both packs.

"Princess, stop!" I yell, she ignores me and when she is two feet away from Jacob she launches into the air, I skid to a stop and wait with bated breath, hoping and praying that she doesn't connect her jaws with him. If she does, he will shift and the council will intervene, they will make sure no one else can aid her in the challenge. My mouth drops open in shock when she veers past Jacob and latches onto her unsuspecting victim.

CHAPTER THIRTY-NINE

Jessica

Numb, shocked, devastated.

I don't know how else I can describe how I am feeling. My gaze is fixed on my mom's lifeless body, she's gone.

My mom is fucking gone!

Red clouds my vision as I look into the eyes of the bastard that took the most important person from me. He fucking killed her. I block out the grief that wants to consume me and focus on my rage. I feel Creed's grip around me loosen and I allow him to think I am so beyond shocked that I will not take the first opportunity he presents to strike back at Jacob. I feel Sheba creep closer to the surface as we wait for his hold to loosen, when it does, I don't hesitate. I bolt toward the bastard, he smiles wickedly.

Allow me control and I will end this.

I want him dead, Sheba!

I will grant you that wish if you allow me control, I don't want to take it from you Jess.

Do it, make him fucking pay for what he did.

I relent control of our body to her, I expect to feel searing pain and wait for it to come but nothing happens. I'm on two legs then a burning sensation takes over and now I'm on four. I'm thankful that Sheba doesn't look toward my mom. Being as close as we are we would be able to see the hollow look in her eyes and that would shatter me. When we near Jacob he drops into a crouch expecting us to attack him, but I feel Sheba's indecision.

What are you doing?

Do you want to break him?

Yes

Then trust me Jess

"Princess, stop!" We ignore Creed's plea and continue on.

I pull back and watch through her eyes as she leaps into the air, Jacob's grin broadens as he waits for us to attack. At the last second Sheba changes direction and latches onto an unsuspecting Josh. It happens in a matter of seconds, I feel his throat in our jaws and then the metallic taste of blood fills our mouth; we land on top of him and Sheba pulls back tearing his throat out, the sickening sound of flesh tearing is a sound I will never forget. Guilt wars inside me, I wanted Jacob to pay not Josh!

"NO!" The anguish I hear in Jacob's voice is gut wrenching. I wanted to hurt him and make him pay; Josh was innocent! Sheba backs up and drops Josh's flesh from her snout, Josh's hands are wrapped around his throat trying to staunch the bleeding, Jacob, his pack and the council members gather around Josh. I look on in horror at what I have done, I can feel Sheba's gleefulness at the sight in front of us.

What the hell did you do, Sheba?

You wanted him to hurt

Exactly, I wanted to hurt Jacob not Josh!

By hurting Josh, we hurt Jacob more than killing him would have

The sounds of footsteps approaching has us swiveling our head, Creed, Callie, Kane and Cole jog toward us and stop when they are two steps away.

"You have to run."

"They will hunt her down, California."

"How do you know that Colton?"

"Enough." Creed snaps, his eyes lock onto mine, he whispers one word, "Shift." I feel Sheba trying to fight the command, but I am forced to intervene and take back control. A minute goes by before she relents, the shift back is painful but not as bad as the first time. I drop forward onto my hands and knees panting, when a hand lands on my back I skirt back and clumsily climb to my feet. Creed's gaze burns with lust, I look down and that's when I notice I am stark naked! Creed shakes his head and then quickly pulls his shirt off and hands it to me, as much as I want to tell him to piss off, I also don't want to stand here butt ass naked, so I snatch the shirt from him and quickly put it on. It's so freaking big on me that the hem nearly touches my knees, I ignore the smirk he gives me because I'm in his shirt.

"We need to move now; Josh's heart just stopped beating." Kane whisper shouts, I'm a sucker for punishment. I turn toward the crowd of people and watch as they begin to step back, Jacob comes into view, and he is hunched over his son's lifeless and bloodied body. I don't stare, I've seen enough. I walk briskly toward my mom, the closer I get the more tears gather in my eyes. I drop to my knees beside her and reach out to run my hand over her hair, it's still soft and silky like it always was. I turn her body over and ignore the odd angle of her head as I gently lift it, so it rests in my lap. I reach up and stroke her cheek, it's still warm. I can't bear to look into her eyes, so I run my fingers down her lids and close them. As soon as I do, the first tear falls, followed by the next and then they just keep coming.

I block out all the noise and chaos around me and focus on her. Her body is still warm and moveable. Pretty soon I know she will turn cold and stiff, looking down at her I can almost fool myself into thinking she is asleep. Except the hole inside my chest and the lump in my throat lets me know she really is gone.

My mommy isn't coming back.

I don't care if she didn't give birth to me, this woman raised me to be who I am today. Katharine Hastings will always be my mother in every sense of the word.

"You need to go." I lift my gaze to see the council woman crouch down in front of me. Her blue eyes look sad and haunted, she keeps darting her gaze around the clearing. From how coiled and edgy she looks; anyone would think she isn't supposed to be telling me this. "If you stay, the council will grant Jacob the right to kill you." She whispers, I give her a dry stare and shake my head.

"I don't care." I utter past the lump in my throat.

"You are our only hope of overthrowing the council and taking Jacob down Jess. You need to run." I glare at the woman, how fucking dare she. "Don't look at me like that, I can scent your brother and his pack in the woods, run now and Cairo will keep you safe." I'm shocked to say the least; I thought they all believed he was dead. "Shhh, no one else knows he is alive. Go now Jess, I will make sure your mother is buried with honor and will send word to you when it is safe."

She's right, we need to go." I turn to the side to see Callie and Cole standing there.

"You're coming?" Both their eyes soften as they look down at me.

"Yeah, but we need to move now while Creed and dad are

distracted." I don't know why but I turn back to the woman, almost like I'm asking her approval or something. She gives a subtle nod and I release the breath I didn't know I was holding. I look down at my mom and place a soft kiss on her forehead and choke out.

"I love you till the end of time and beyond. I'll come back for you mom; I'll make them pay. I swear they won't get away with what they have done."

CHAPTER FORTY

Jessica

FIVE YEARS LATER

On this day five years ago, my whole life changed.

I had no idea when I ran that day with Callie and Cole that my life would be what it is now. The council woman was right; my brother was in the woods. He and his pack took the three of us in and led us to safety, that night though when the full moon rose into the sky, I finally understood what Sheba meant. The mate bond clicked into place, I had to get my brother and the twins--oh yeah, turns out they're not triplets. Callie and Cole are twins and Creed is actually their older brother who posed as a student so he could get close to me. Anyway, I had to get them to lock me up every full moon or whenever I shifted so Sheba wouldn't take off back to Creed. I have learnt so much in the past five years, I learned a lot about the packs and the council and all the laws. I learnt about my bio parents and my mom, I found out about Creed being a lying piece of shit.

Okay let me list this shit off.

- Creed and Cairo are the same age, they went to school together.
- Creed is actually thirty-one now, which means he was twenty-five when I met him.
- My dad and Creed's mom were fated mates.
- Cairo told me that our parents died but there was never a body recovered for our bio mom.
- Katherine Hastings is in fact my aunt, after my parents died, she took on the role as my mom.
- Her mate was killed, not by the Reeves pack but by Jacob-- we just found that out.
- Meg and Mom weren't friends, it was a lie. Creed wanted me

to feel more comfortable and got his mom and mine to lie.

- ℵ Creed knew about me my whole life and had been tracking me.

- ℵ He knew we were mates from the start.

- ℵ He wanted us to mate so that we could rule both packs together and overthrow the council.

- ℵ We learnt that his mother and my father were in fact killed by the council and Jacob.

- ℵ Our dad was the alpha of the Mikaelson pack, but back then it was called the Cruz pack. Our mom is the daughter of the previous alpha from the Reeves pack.

- ℵ Creed was alpha the whole time, he didn't want me to feel intimidated, so he lied and convinced everyone else to lie as well.

- ℵ We have spent the past five years combing through all the bylaws and pack laws to see if we can find a loophole and take the council down.

"Mommy, Co-co is mean." I close my notebook and place it on the seat beside me.

"Why is he mean, baby?" He looks up at me with those big hazel eyes and shakes his head so his blond hair will stay off his forehead, he needs a haircut. The kid refuses to cut his hair, he's always said no since he was two.

"He said I couldn't have a cookie. I want a cookie mommy and Ro-Ro said I can." I look up when the steps on the porch creak and see Cole, Sky, Callie, Cairo and Zeke. I stand and scoop Harlem up into my arms, he is getting way too big for me to carry him. Cole narrows his eyes at my son and then points an accusing finger at my brother.

"See how he looks at me! That's your entire fault, he's a little shit because you allow him to get away with everything." Sky cuffs Cole on the back of his head and narrows her brown eyes at him. "The fuck was that for sunshine?" Sky hates it when he calls her that.

"For being an ass, he's four! Your twenty freaking three, grow up." I hide my smile behind my son's head.

"Yeah Co-co, grow up."

"The Easter bunny isn't real you little demon." I turn shocked eyes to Cole and then turn to my son to see his bottom lip tremble. His watery eyes look to me in question; the look of utter heartbreak on his face nearly causes me to blow up. I turn back to Cole and glare, he at least has the decency to look sheepish, Zeke, Cairo, Callie and Sky look like they want to hit him, "It slipped out; it was an accident I swear." I narrow my eyes at him, but before I can say anything, Ro makes his way over to me and plucks Harlem out of my arms and cradles my son against his chest.

"Don't worry buster, Ro-Ro will make Co-Co pay for that statement." Harlem pulls back and looks up at his uncle, my heart swells. Cairo has been so freaking amazing since I found out I was pregnant, he stepped up and helped me. So did Cole, Callie and the rest of the pack. It's like they say, it takes a village to raise a child and, in my case, it's taken a pack. I couldn't have done this without them, Cole and Harlem are like chalk and cheese but at the end of the day I know they both love each other endlessly.

"Da bunny is real, right?" Ro smiles down at his nephew and nods his head.

"Of course, he is monster, Co-Co is just mad because the bunny doesn't give him chocolate anymore because he's naughty." Cole rolls his eyes and throws his hands in the air.

"Whatever." Cole mumbles as he stomps inside the house.

"He's just antsy because it's a full moon tonight." I turn to Callie and nod; Sky wraps her arms around Callie's waist and rests her chin on her shoulder. I'm so glad that they have each other, it took them no time at all to fall head over heels in love. I envy what they have, I would give anything to have someone love and hold me like that. I watch as Callie turns in Sky's hold and kisses her, how nice it must be to have someone to hold. A throat clearing has me turning to Zeke, he won't meet my gaze and I know shit is awkward with us because I keep rejecting him, but I honestly haven't felt anything toward another man since the mate bond clicked into place five years ago. Ro keeps telling me I have to give it time, I don't think time is the problem. I think the problem is me.

"So, are you gonna join us for the pack run tonight?" Zeke's question doesn't shock me, I've been working up the courage to run with the pack for years. I only shift when I have to or when I'm training with Ro. Ever since Sheba took Josh's life, her and I haven't exactly seen eye to eye. My phone vibrating in my pocket saves me from answering, I fish it out and frown at the unknown number. I push the green button and put it on speaker so the others can hear.

"Hello?"

"Jess?"

"Yes, who's this and how did you get this number?" The woman chuckles before answering.

"I told you I would get in contact when it was safe." I look to Cairo who is passing Harlem to Callie and indicating for her and Sky to take him inside. No one aside from the pack knows about my son, if the council find out I have a male heir, Cairo tells me they will demand I hand him over, so they can raise him in their image and make him rule both packs. I also learnt the reason there is such a war over these two packs is because they are the biggest and strongest in the US.

"You're the council lady?" Ro nods his head and motions for me to keep her talking.

"Yes, Jess I don't have good news I'm afraid."

"What do you mean?"

"After you fled a war broke out. The council is divided and the tension between the packs is at an all-time high. Each alpha thinks the other is hiding your whereabouts, the council is prepared to take control." The shocked look on Cairo's face makes me think that whatever she is saying is bad. "Look, I don't have a lot of time. I have some information that will help your brother's cause." Ro looks taken back and I'll admit even I am a bit flabbergasted to learn the council woman knows that Ro is trying to take down the council.

"What information?"

"I'm not going to say over the phone. You need to come back, if you don't claim the title and your punishment the council will take out both alphas, that isn't good since you are mated to one of them." I look to Ro who mouths that he will fill me in later. Cairo grabs the phone from me and asks.

"Why should my sister believe a word that comes out of your mouth?" The lady doesn't miss a beat.

"Because I don't want to see any harm come to you or her, Cairo. I have done everything I can to cover your tracks over the years and keep the council off your trail. I tried to do the same for Jess but clearly I fucked up there."

"Who the hell are you?" Ro snaps.

"A...friend."

"I don't need any of those, I have enough. If what you say is true, then why should I bring her back to be punished?"

"Credence isn't the monster you all think he is. He has been helping me try to fix this situation and make it safe for Jess and *you* to return home. I'll be in touch again soon, think about what I said Cairo and Jess?"

"Y-Yeah?"

"Keep that baby of yours safe and hidden." I gasp, the woman hangs up and the three of us stand there staring at the blank screen on my phone.

After that ominous as fuck phone call, we head inside and fill the others in. Sky and Zeke left to round up the pack and tell them what's happening while Cairo, Callie, Cole and I stay inside the house and try to figure out a plan. I couldn't tear my gaze from my baby sleeping in my arms. How did she know about him?

"Creed will never hurt you Jess!" Cole shouts,

"Bullshit, he lied and used her just so he could be alpha." Cairo sneers back at Cole.

"Fuck off Cairo, my brother did what he thought was right." Cole snaps back.

"Both of you idiots shut up. Creed fucked up; he shouldn't have done what he did but in his defense, he was blinded by grief. He wanted vengeance for our mom, he still thinks Jacob killed her and that the council had nothing to do with it. What if she is right and Creed is trying to help, shouldn't we at least reach out to him?" Everyone just stares at Callie in silence.

Sheba rears inside of me and heat floods my veins. I gasp and snap my gaze up to the others; I can feel him. The three of them look at me with concern.

"Sis, what's wrong?"

"He's here Ro, I think that woman tracked our call." Callie and Cole look confused; Cairo knows exactly what I'm saying.

"Jess, take Harlem upstairs and wait there until I come for you--"I shake my head and cut him off.

"No brother, he's here for me. If that bitch really did track my call, then he already knows I'm here." I turn to Callie and say. "Take my son and hide, I know he is your brother California but I don't trust him. I need you to protect my son, can you do that?" She may love Creed but her love for Harlem surpasses what she feels for her brother.

CHAPTER FORTY-ONE

Credence

"She's 20 miles south, I sent you the GPS coordinates and Credence?" I grit my teeth and answer.

"What Shelley?"

"If any harm comes to her or Cairo, our deal is off and you're on your own." She ends the call, and a growl of annoyance sounds in the back of my throat. I punch in the GPS location she sent me, and Asher doesn't hesitate to plant his foot to the floor and break every speed limit to get me to her. Three black SUVs trail behind us, my mom and dad stayed back to run things in Rosewood. Shit at home is really dire. Since Jess left things have become bad---really bad. The packs are divided, and my leadership is being questioned. Jacob has made sure the boundaries are being enforced to the letter, no pack member is allowed to attend human school, we must educate our young on our lands now. The council checks in once a month and if we disobey the rules we are punished, they are taking land from us and at this rate the Reeves pack will be no more come next year. We owned half of Rosewood and Jacob the other half, now we are lucky if we even own a quarter. Jess has to come back and claim her birthright. If she doesn't, I fear my pack will be slaughtered and there isn't a damn thing I can do about it with the council watching my every move. Shelley is my ally in the council and is trying to help, I have no idea what her motive is, but I won't look a gift horse in the mouth.

We make it to the location as the sun begins to set. We park the four SUVs down the road and enter through the woods. I would say we have about two or three hours before the moon is at its peak and Cairo's rogues will be in their beast form. They will see me and my pack entering their lands as a challenge.

Asher, Tommy and Kyle walk beside me, and the rest take up the rear. We walk through the woods, and I can smell Cairo everywhere. He has marked this territory thoroughly; I can sense her and my steps falter slightly. I quickly right myself and trudge on, Corbin stirs inside me and yips in excitement, he has been angry at me since we lost our mate. He blames me for Jess running and I can't blame him. I hid so much shit from her all in the name of revenge, my mom was right. If I don't fix this, I will have sacrificed my heart for the pack. The bond has been there for me from the start, it was so hard to keep myself at a distance and not claim her from the first moment I saw her five years ago.

My pack and I have been hunting and tracking her since she left. We haven't been able to pinpoint her location until now. We are in the middle of bum-fuck-no-where, the closest town is nearly an hour away and we have been trekking through these woods for at least twenty minutes.

"This has to be the place, right?" I don't turn to look at Asher as I answer.

"Yeah, Shelley said this is where she pinged her phone." We continue through the woods for another fifteen minutes before we break through, and houses come into view. I see a long dirt driveway and decide not to hide in the shadows and just walk right up to the main house. I'm hoping that by not hiding it won't be seen as much of a threat. My guys follow behind me, I can feel the tension and worry through the pack link. I want to reassure them, but I can't guarantee their safety. They all knew coming with me on this mission there was a chance we wouldn't return, yet they still followed me, and I am forever grateful for that. We pass by rickety looking cabins, and I can't detect any heartbeats so that means there is no one inside. A large wooden house stands at the end of the road, it has a wraparound porch and is in bad need of a paint, I can see from here that the paint is flaking. I feel dozens of eyes on us but keep my gaze forward, the front door of the main house opens and Cairo steps out with two of his pack members, Sky and Zeke, everyone assumes Zeke is the one to watch out for because he is built like a tank, but the real threat is Sky. You won't see that little spit fire coming for you until it's too late.

Cairo rests his arms on the porch railing while Zeke leans against the house and Sky stands like a sentinel next to her alpha. The fifteen men and I continue on to the house under the watchful gaze of Ro and his two betas, I see the look of disdain on his face and choose to ignore it. I didn't expect a warm welcome, and I also didn't expect for him to be giving off hostile vibes. I stop a few meters away from them as I scan the area, I breathe in through my nose to try and scent her. Her scent is being masked, the only way that can happen is if other males rub their scent all over her. A growl of annoyance tears through me without my consent, Corbin is pissed that his mate is being hidden from him and that other males have been rubbing their scent on her. Cairo smirks and tsks me which pisses me off further.

"Problem Credence?" I pull my upper lip back in a snarl, he knows exactly why I am pissed.

"When I find the male or males that are masking *my* mate's scent, I'll kill him." Zeke scoffs and rolls his eyes.

"You're in no position to make threats alpha."

"And why is that Zeke?" I grit out through clenched teeth. Zeke pushes off the wall and comes to stand by Cairo resting his hands on the railing as he glares down at me.

"Because *you* are on our lands and by my count you are severely outnumbered."

"Be that as it may Zeke boy, I am not here to fight."

"Then why the fuck are you here Creed?" It takes everything inside me to calm Corbin and convince him to ignore the threat in Cairo's voice. Corbin hates to be challenged and is a true alpha male.

"I'm here for *her.*"

"She doesn't want you, leave now. You and your pack aren't welcome here."

"I don't give a shit if we are welcome or not, I am not leaving here without her!" I shout, Cairo straightens and then jumps over the railing followed by both his betas. I raise my hand to stop my guys from stepping forward and getting involved. Cairo is maybe ten feet away when I hear the bang of the front door against the house, I don't take my eyes off him though.

"Ro stop." Alpha training 101 don't ever take your eyes off your enemy, but at the sound of her voice I don't care. I stare up at the porch and see her and my breath catches in my throat, my heart beats faster. I scan her from head to toe; she's cut her beautiful long blonde hair. It's now chin length; her blue eyes don't seem as youthful and free as they once did. They look haunted and wiser, her body has changed, her breast strain against her white singlet. Her hips are wider. It's so strange it's almost like her body has stretched but shrunk back down. I snap my eyes back to her face, but she refuses to meet my stare, her gaze is focused on her brother.

"Go back inside Jess, you don't need to bear witness to this." I look to Cairo and see he has stopped a few feet away from me.

"Cairo, back off." My focus immediately shifts back to the porch at the sound of my brother's voice. I stare at him in shock, he hasn't changed a single iota except for his eyes, and his eyes tell the story of what he has been through these past five years. Being a shifter means we age slowly, from the look in my brother's eyes it looks like he has aged ten years. I'm glad to see him safe but I'm also pissed as hell that he chose to flee with our sister and Jess. I could have used his help these past five years while we were under constant attack from Jacob.

"Mind your business Co-Co." *Co-Co?* They have nicknames for each other now. Colton snickers at the name but doesn't say anything, Cairo moves until we are nearly chest to chest. We stare into each other's gazes longer than any shifter should if they don't want to make a formal challenge. I feel Corbin push to the surface ready to fight, if need be, I see Ro's eyes change to the color of his wolfs. I don't make a move; I wait for him to show his cards. I didn't come here for a fight, but if a fight is what he wants I won't back down.

CHAPTER FORTY-TWO

Jessica

I've had enough of this macho bullshit, I brush past Cole and stomp down toward the puffed-up alpha holes and push between them until my back is to Creed and I'm staring up into my brother's angry gaze, his anger isn't directed at me.

"Ro, that's enough."

"He doesn't deserve your forgiveness Jess, not after--"

"I said that's enough!" I feel Sheba rise inside me at the command in my tone. It has been hard to live with my brother and be the lesser, Sheba doesn't do well with him being the superior one in the pack. Sheba is forever trying to challenge him whenever we shift thank God my brother has total control over his wolf.

"Watch it mama bear, you can only poke the bear so much before he snaps." I shake out of my thoughts and drop my gaze to Sheba's dismay. Sky is right, I need to get a better handle on my wolf. Sheba is warring inside of me and wants me to shift so she can be with her mate, Ro must see the struggle on my face. He places a hand on my shoulder and smiles reassuringly.

"Breathe poppet, you're in control not her." I do as he says and take a few deep breaths, it's hard though, because I can feel his eyes burning a hole into the back of my head. The heat I have always felt being near him is present and my body is working against me. It's hard trying to fight your own body's reaction when all it wants to do is go to him.

"Come on sweetheart, I'll take you insi--"Zeke doesn't even get to finish speaking before a vicious growl sounds out from behind me.

"Touch her and I'll rip your fucking arms off." The gruffness of his voice tells me Corbin is more in control right now than Creed. I shake my head at Zeke and then look at Cole, he nods and comes down to join us. He spins me around so we are facing Creed and the others, he keeps his arm wrapped around me ignoring the growls coming from his brother. Ro stands on my other side with Sky beside him, I feel Zeke at my back, and I slowly lift my gaze from the ground to look at Creed. His gaze is focused over my head glaring at Zeke. Creed hasn't changed much; he's filled out more and his brownie-blond hair is cut short, but his hazel eyes still sparkle with mischief and dominance. Even in a plain pair of dark wash jeans and a blue fitted shirt he looks mouthwatering; my heart begins to pound. I know everyone, including Creed can hear the beat of my heart but I can't seem to slow it down. After what feels like an eternity his gaze finally shifts from Zeke to land on me. The angry look he just had is gone, the hard edges on his face begin to smooth out as he looks at me. I see sorrow and pain in his eyes, but I also see longing. His shoulders droop lightly, I see the fight drain from his body, seeing the way he is slightly hunched and hollowness in his eyes has my temperature spiking and Sheba wanting to go to him and comfort our mate. I grit my teeth and steel my spin making sure to keep my emotionless mask in place.

"Why are you here Credence?" I see him flinch slightly from the cold tone of my voice. "If you expected to come here and have me fall to my knees in front of you, you're wrong." A ghost of a smile graces his beautiful face.

"I don't expect you to kneel for me."

"Good, because if anyone is kneeling, it's you. I mean after all I am technically *your* alpha, isn't that right *mate.*" I spit the word *mate* at him like it burns my tongue and judging from the hurt look in his eyes I hit my mark.

"Being that we are mates, technically we are equals." He says with a shrug of his shoulders which just pisses me off.

"Get the fuck out of here Creed and don't come back."

"So you cuss now, how classy." The sarcasm is thick in his voice.

"Fuck off, Credence." I snap as I spin around to head back toward the house but freeze when the front door bangs open, and my son comes running out with Callie hot on his heels.

"Harlem, come here!" She shouts as she chases him down the stairs but it's too late.

"Mommy, mommy." He shouts with a smile on his face, I scoop him up and try to make a hasty exit. Just as I take one step with my son in my arms, growls break out behind me, I spin around to see Cole and Cairo holding Creed back. Zeke and Sky are crouched and ready to fight Asher and Tommy should they attack. I look back to Creed and see his eyes are zeroed in on the little boy in my arms. Growls are the only sounds that can be heard, no one utters a word. Dread pools in my belly, I try to turn s I can flee, but the warning in his growl has me freezing. I look to Callie pleading with my eyes for her to help me, she nods and heads towards her brother. I stand there frozen, stroking the back of my son's head, no one was supposed to see him.

"Brother."

"Sister, nice to see you're alive." Creed growls out.

"Oh, don't be a grump, why don't we let Jess and the monster go inside so we can...chat?" The only answer he gives is a ferocious growl.

"Growl at her like that again and I'll kill you. Alpha or not you do not get to disrespect my mate on our lands." I spin around and catch the shocked look on Creed's face as he darts his gaze between Sky and Callie, a slight blush coats Callie's cheeks but she smiles proudly. Creed stops fighting against Cole and Ro, he straightens with a dumbfounded look on his face. He reaches back and rubs the back of his neck, then a broad proud smile graces his face.

"I'm happy for you sis." He drops his arm back to his side and turns to face Sky. "Well, I couldn't have picked a better mate for my sister. If anything happens to her, I'm coming for you Skylar." A daring smirk graces the spitfire warrior's face as she nods her head. Sky is a badass and wouldn't hesitate to take Creed out if she had to.

"Mommy?" All eyes turn to me at the sound of my son's voice, I look down at him and smile reassuringly.

"You're okay baby."

"Who are they mommy?" I swing my gaze to Creed quickly to see the angry look in his eyes before turning back to Harlem.

"Just someone I used to know."

"Who's the kid, princess?" Creed grits out, I begin to panic. What the hell do I say? I dart my gaze back to him to see his chest rising and falling fast, his fists clenched at his side. I open my mouth, but no words come out. "Who is the kid's father Jessica?" I can hear the threat in his voice, and it sends a shiver down my spine. Cole moves toward me and then plucks Harlem from my arms; he bends down and places a soft kiss on my forehead before turning around to face his brother. He settles

Harlem on his far side and then wraps his free arm around my shoulders. Creed's gaze darts between the three of us, a look of anger then hurt races across his beautiful face.

"He's mine." Cole states, Creed's gaze snaps to his brother and white-hot rage courses through his eyes before he snaps and shifts right in front of us. In the blink of an eye, he went from two legs to four. Cairo is too slow to act, Creed darts past him and heads straight for us. Cole is quicker to act, he turns and pushes Harlem into my chest, I wrap my arms around him as he winks and then jumps away from me. I know he won't shift and fight his brother; Cole has always said from the start he will never stand against Creed if it came down to it. A second later Corbin launches through the air and tackles Cole to the ground, Cole pushes against Corbin's face to stop him from snapping his jaw around his neck. I stand there frozen in horror as I watch Cole try to fend off Corbin's attacks, Ro, Zeke, Callie and Sky rush over to help, but are intervened by Creed's pack mates, next thing you know it ends up in a big brawl. Ro sent our other pack members into the mountains to keep them safe incase Creed came to set us up, but now I wish he hadn't done that.

"Corbin stop, Creed take back control brother!" Cole tries to reason but Corbin won't hear any of it; he just keeps trying to hurt him. Corbin manages to lock onto Cole's arm and he screams out in pain. Harlem begins to scream as he watches his uncle being mauled by a wolf he has never seen before. I have to end this now! I open the mind link that I have kept shut for the past five years and admit the truth. In order to save Cole, I have to trust that Creed will do the right thing for once and protect us.

He isn't Cole's son.

Corbin releases his arm and turns toward me, blood dripping down his jaw.

Who is his father, princess?

I take a deep breath and try to utter the words through the bond, but I can't. He releases an impatient growl which makes me clam up even more. Corbin releases Cole and stalks toward me, Cole is quick to act, he jumps to his feet and runs over, blocking me and Harlem from view. He looks over his shoulder at me in question, I nod my head giving him the okay to tell the truth. He turns back toward Corbin and says,

"He's yours brother. Harlem is your son and your heir."

CHAPTER FORTY-THREE
Credence

"He's yours brother. Harlem is your son and your heir."

I keep playing Cole's words over and over in my mind as I shift back, once I'm in my human skin I stand on shaky legs and stare at my brother waiting for him to tell me that this is a joke. It has to be right? We only slept together once; Jess wanted to go to college not be a teen mom. A loud snarl grips my attention and I turn to see my sister, Cairo, Sky and Zeke in battle with my guys.

"Enough, pull back now!" My pack immediately stops fighting and steps back, Zeke and Cairo release Asher and Tommy, Sky lands one last punch to Brad before she steps back next to my sister and wraps her arm around her waist. Cairo turns to me and shakes his head in disgust, he turns to Zeke and says something, then he takes off around the side of the house. Zeke returns with a pair of basketball shorts and chucks them at me. I don't thank the bastard I just put the shorts on and move toward Jess, Cole steps forward as I get closer, and I glare down at my little brother. He at least has the balls to meet my gaze, when I see pain etched across his features guilt sinks in, I drop my gaze to his arm and shudder. Blood drips to the ground, thanks to his shifter healing I know the cuts will heal in an hour or so, but I still feel like shit for doing that to my own brother.

"He may be yours by DNA, but he is also all of ours." I cock my head to the side confused. "I swore I would never stand against you Credence, but if you hurt the little demon." Cole's eyes take on a hard edge. "All bets are off brother; I will come for you." The dominance in his tone and the fact that his wolf is riding so close to the surface gives me pause. Cole has never stood up to me like this before...ever. I nod my head briskly and wait for him to step aside so I can see my mate and my...son.

Jess cradles the boy to her chest and stares at me with worry and fear. The look of fear in her eyes pisses me the fuck off! How dare she assume that I would hurt my own child, the closer I get to her the tenser she becomes. I stop when there is only a sliver of space between us, I feel Cairo and the others creep in closer. I reach my arms out for the boy, but she turns away and I growl. Her eyes harden as she meets my gaze.

"You do not get to come here and think you can just walk into his life--"

"The fuck I can't! You ran, not me princess!"

"Because you're a fucking liar!" She screams, the boy begins to wail in her arms, and she begins to bounce him and shush him, I look at her in awe. She's not wrong though, if I hadn't of lied and used her, I would have been present in my son's life. Cairo comes toward her and my gaze snaps to him, the look he gives me tells me he is only here to help. He reaches out for the boy and says,

"Let me take him. He doesn't need to hear his parents' crap and all this cussing isn't good for him either." Jess looks reluctant to hand him over. "We're just going to play out back and call the others to come to come home. Unless you plan to ambush us Credence?" I glower at him and shake my head. Jess places a kiss to the top of his head and looks down at him.

"Go with uncle Ro-Ro okay; Co-Co will get you that cookie you want."

"And Z and Sky and Aunt Cal?" Jess smiles warmly and nods her head.

"Yeah baby, be a good boy, okay?" The kid nods his head and reaches out his arms for Cairo to take him. Before they turn to walk away the boy turns back to look at me and my breath hitches.

He has my eyes.

"Hi." He says, I open my mouth to respond but no words come out, his little brow furrows and he whisper shouts. "Ro-Ro, da man is rude." Cairo and Cole burst out laughing as they head out back but not before I hear the snarky remark Cairo makes.

"Yeah, he's a dick but unfortunately you share DNA with him." I growl which just causes them to laugh harder. I turn toward Asher and the boys.

"Go with them and see if they need help with... anything." They smile and go to head out back, but Jess quickly steps in Tommy and Asher's path. She bites her bottom lip shyly as she looks up at her old friends. Tommy sighs and wraps her in a hug much to my dismay then Asher does the same, he pulls back and smiles down at her and says,

"Ain't no hood like motherhood." The three of them laugh while I stand here and wait---impatiently.

"Go meet him, he's amazing."

"And he's also our future alpha." Tommy adds as they walk away, that thought hadn't even crossed my mind until now. Once they disappear and only Jess and I remain, silence ascends, she stands over there scuffing the ground with her shoe. I decide to make the first move and head toward her, her head pops up and when our eyes meet the anger inside me subsides.

"How old is he?" She releases a whoosh of air before she answers.

"Four."

"What's his name?"

"Harlem." I grit my teeth and try to keep my temper in check as I ask.

"What's his full name?" She drops her gaze to the ground and says,

"Harlem Edward...Reeves." Pride swells inside me, she didn't have to give him my last name, but she did it anyway. I reach out and grip her chin between my fingers and lift her head till her eyes meet mine. I want her to see the sincerity in my gaze.

"Thank you." Her eyes round in shock.

"F-for what?"

"For giving him my name." A mischievous glint enters her eyes.

"He has someone else's name before yours." I scowl down at her.

"Who the fuck did you name my son after?" Her mouth drops open in shock and she bats my hand away as she begins to poke my chest.

"He is *my* son. Mine." I smack her hand away and grip the back of her neck and haul her against me and relish in the loud gasp that escapes her.

"*Ours*, he is our son princess. Now who the hell else did you name him after?" A wicked smile graces her stunning face, I can't stop staring at her lips. It takes everything inside me not to kiss her.

"Edward Cullen." I reel back in shock.

"Who the fuck is that douche bag?" She laughs, I missed

the sound of her laugh. She looks so beautiful, and she doesn't even know it.

"Never mind." The laughter is gone from her eyes as she places both her hands on my chest. I shiver from the feeling of having her hands on my bare chest, her tongue darts out to moisten her lips and her pupils dilate. Good, at least I'm not the only one affected here. "Why are you here Credence?" She whispers.

"For you princess."

"Why?" Now is my chance to make up for the bullshit I pulled and try to win my mate back.

"Because I need your help. My pack is being picked off one by one and Jacob has the council in his back pocket."

"So, you're only here because of that?" I can hear the hurt that laces her tone. I bend down so we are eye level and cup her face between my hands.

"No princess. I have been searching for you since you fled, between trying to be alpha and other duties I have slacked as a leader. And now my pack is paying the price for my fuck up."

"How am I supposed to help you? If Jacob has the council then--"

"By taking your rightful position as alpha to both packs."

"I-I can't. The council want me dead after what Sheba did." I shake my head.

"No, they don't."

"How can you be so sure?" I promised myself I wouldn't lie to her again, but if she knew the truth it'll be harder for her to come back.

"Shelley, the council woman has been helping me." She

reels back in shock.

"I knew it, she did ping my phone." I smile sheepishly and nod.

"I wish I could say I feel bad about that, but I don't. I know this is a lot to consider and I want to be better and give you the time that you need to think it over. I can't stay here for long princess. I have to get back."

"Oh, okay. Yeah that makes sense."

"While you're thinking things over, can I...meet my son?" A rush of air leaves her as she smiles and nods.

"Yeah." She tries to move away but I stop her and ask.

"Why didn't you or my siblings tell me about him?"

"I couldn't trust you; Cole and Callie didn't have a choice. I wouldn't let them reach out to you. You fucked my head up...a lot Credence. I wasn't in a good place with just losing my mom and k-killing Josh. The last thing I wanted was you barreling in here and demanding my son--"

"Our son!" I cut in.

"He is mine until you can prove yourself worthy. I will not let you hurt him like you hurt me, no one can know about him Creed. I will not let Harlem be used as a pawn in this sick as fuck battle between the packs."

"I know I fucked up princess but hiding my son from me was fucking low!" I turn and storm around the back of the house to search for my kid. If I stay and talk to her any longer, I will lose my shit and say things I don't mean.

CHAPTER FORTY-FOUR

Jessica

Anger thrums through at his blatant brush off. Who the hell does he think he is to turn his back to me and walks away?

Ah, alpha of the Reeves pack?

Real helpful Sheba. It was just a thought. I know exactly who he is.

Why are you still so angry at him?

Because he lied to me!

Humans and their emotions are so fickle.

I groan and close the link between me and my annoying wolf and follow Creeds retreating form around the back of the house. I slow to a stop and notice Creed's pack members crouched and pretending to hide, Harlem is hunkered down behind a planter box with Callie and Sky, while Cole and Ro stand in the middle of the yard counting out loud. I stop just before I crash into Creed's back, I follow his line of sight and see he is looking directly at Harlem. I wish I could say guilt isn't eating at me for keeping Creed from Harlem, but I didn't have a choice.

"Why Harlem?" He whispers.

"Because I wanted to keep the tradition going." He looks at me over his shoulder in confusion, so I elaborate. "Colton Dallas, California, Credence Utah. Your names are all places and I want him to be a part of that." He cocks a brow in surprise and turns back toward our baby.

"Thank you." I'm beyond shocked, this is the second time in the space of ten minutes he has thanked me.

"For what?" His shoulders sag and he drops his head.

"For giving me a gift, I thought I would never be worthy of. You knew he was mine and yet you still birthed him. You could have aborted--"

"I would *never* have done that; I may hate what you did but Harlem is innocent. If I didn't have him, I don't know if I would have survived the loss of my mom, your lies and learning everything that I have. I am who I am today because of him."

"What about college?" I'm taken back that he even remembers that.

"I take my classes online, having a baby at eighteen wasn't exactly what I planned but we made it work."

"Ready or not here we come!" Cole booms, Creed moves toward Cole and Cairo and both men tense up in anticipation. Creed stops in front of Ro and extends his hand, Ro stares at Creed's hand like it might bite him.

"Thank you for taking care of Callie and Cole, but most of all, thank you for keeping Jess and my...son alive." A proud gleam enters Ro's eyes as he clasps Creed's hand in his own. Ro pulls him for a bro hug and slaps him a couple of times on the back. Creed releases Ro and then turns to Cole.

"I don't need a soppy thank you. If you really want to thank me, don't hide shit from her anymore and be a fucking great dad because he deserves it." Tears well in my eyes, Cole and I have grown so close over the years, he has become a best friend to me--hell a brother even.

"You have my word brother." They are just about to hug but stop when Harlem darts out from his hiding place and asks.

"You have a brother Co-Co?" He spins around and looks at me while placing his hands on his hips. "Momma, I want a brother. Pwwwease, can you go make me one?" I choke on air while everyone else laughs and comes out from their hiding place. I snap out of my stupor and go to my baby; I crouch down in front of him and say.

"Making you a brother is harder than that. A man and a woman have to love each other to make a baby--"

"He can love you; he can make me a brother." My mouth drops open in shock when I realize Harlem is pointing to Creed. Creed looks just as shocked as me, the idiot even points to himself so Harlem can confirm he was indeed meaning him. When Harlem gives him a firm nod everyone bursts out laughing.

"I don't know about the make a baby part but I'm down for--- "I cut Creed off before he can finish.

"I'm not making a baby with him, Buster."

"Too late. You already did." Creed snaps.

"Dude, let her handle this. I don't want to kick your ass for hurting my sister, but I will."

"Shut up Cairo, I'll beat your ass any day." Harlem takes off toward Creed and the others, and when he is within touching distance he strikes out and punches Creed in the...nuts. Gasps ring out as Creed drops to his knees cupping his balls, his face is contorted in pain as he stares at Harlem.

"You don't hurt my Ro-Ro!" Cairo reaches around Creed and fist bumps his nephew; Cairo hasn't nver looked so proud.

"Dude, best freaking nephew ever!" I climb to my feet and pin Ro with a dirty look, I walk over to them and bend down in front of my son.

"That wasn't nice." Creed's breaths are still coming in fast pants as he glares at our son.

"That's it?" Creed wheezes out.

"Well...yeah. What did you want me to do?" His mouth drops open in shock.

"I'm pretty sure that little demon just punched my balls into my stomach and that's all you have to say?"

"If he is a demon then he gets it from you." I quip back.

"Why do I get that from him momma?" Oh shit. I try to think of the best way to break that Creed is his dad to him but I come up blank. I have told Harlem stories about his dad and so has Cole and Callie, but we never said his name. Creed remains on his knees, he reaches out to place a hand on Harlem's shoulder, and he turns toward him.

"Because getting something from me is super freaking cool. Did you know I was the one who taught your aunt and uncle how to shift and fight?"

"No way!"

"Yeah, I even taught your uncle Ro-Ro how to shift on the fly. They each got something from me, and you think they're cool, right?" Harlem nods his head eagerly.

"Yes!"

"See, getting something from me is cool."

"I want something from you, I want something from you." Harlem shouts as he jumps up and down. Creed's eyes soften as he stares at his son.

"You are the best part of me kid." I hear him whisper quietly as he climbs to his feet.

CHAPTER FORTY-FIVE
Jessica

With it being a full moon tonight, Creed and his guys decided to stay behind and run with our pack. I chose to not join the pack run and stay behind with Harlem; I can't trust Sheba to be near Creed. Luckily, she relented when I told her that no one would be able to stay with Harlem, at the mention of him she stopped fighting me and agreed to run tomorrow. I just bathed Harlem and was making our way down stairs when I hear a cupboard shut. I still at the top of the landing and listened then scented the air. Shocked, I quickly race down the stairs and make my way to the old kitchen with Harlem on my hip.

"Shit!"

"Naughty word." Harlem announces, Creed spins around with wide eyes. He has a pot in one hand and pasta in the other.

"I didn't...it slipped out...I thought you were upstairs." I can't help the chuckle that slips through my lips. He looks so flustered and cute---shit, no not cute. "I was trying to make you dinner." My brows jump up in surprise.

"Oh." Is all I can get out.

"I help mommy?" Creed's eyes light up.

"Yeah, you can help me while your mom sits down over there." I stand there stunned, Harlem wriggles in my hold until I snap out of it and put him down. He runs to Creed, who quickly puts the pot in front of his manhood which causes me to laugh so hard I nearly cry. Creed playfully scowls at me.

"Up, up." Harlem says with his arms outstretched toward Creed; he darts his gaze to me in question.

"He wants you to pick him up." It takes a second for my words to sink in and when they do, Creed quickly puts the pot and pasta on the bench and then tentatively reaches down and picks Harlem up like he is made of glass. Creed holds him at arm's length for a moment before he crushes him against his chest and nuzzles his face in the crook of Harlem's neck. Tears well in my eyes at the sight in front of me, seeing them together for the first time---I can't explain it. Harlem wraps his arms around Creed's neck and holds onto him. Guilt eats away at me when I see a stray tear leak from Creed's eyes.

"I promise, I'll be better for you." He whispers and my heart skips a beat. I just hope Creed keeps his promise to our son.

It takes them over an hour to make pasta bake. I sit on the stool quietly and just watched in awe as Creed interacted with him. He's patient and never loses his cool. He takes his time to explain everything he's doing. Harlem helps him set the table, they even did the dishes together.

After dinner Harlem begged us to watch a movie before bed and I'll be honest, I can never say no when he gives me those puppy dog eyes. So here we are, sitting on the couch in the living room with Harlem between us watching *Jungle Cruise*. Creed hasn't stopped staring at him for the past ten minutes, he keeps opening and closing his mouth but says nothing. I can see in his eyes that he keeps jumping from content to angry and I'm not sure why.

Halfway through the movie Harlem falls asleep with his head in my lap and his legs stretched out toward Creed. Creed has his hand resting on Harlem's leg; he hasn't stopped touching him. Creed doesn't realize that I know he has been rubbing up against Harlem every chance he gets, he's marking him with his scent so other males will know. I'd be lying if I said that a part of me didn't soar at the sight of Creed marking our son. The silence between us was comfortable while Harlem was awake but now that he isn't--it's awkward.

I thought it was time to be the grown up here, so I gently move Harlem's head and stand. I reach down to lift him so I can carry him upstairs to bed but Creed lashes out and grabs my wrist. I stare at him in disbelief, he stands then gently pushes in front of me to lift Harlem into his arms. His head lolls to the side on Creed's shoulder but he doesn't even stir. I sigh and then motion for him to follow me up the stairs. Once we reach Harlem's room which is across from mine, I open the door and walk in to turn the bedside light on. Creed moves toward the bed, and I quickly pull the covers back so he can place him in. Creed gently lays him down and I tuck him in placing a kiss on his forehead and telling him I love him. I've never not told Harlem that I love him every night, at the end of the day tomorrow isn't promised so I want him to know he is always loved. I turn expecting Creed to follow me out but stop short when I don't hear his footsteps. He sits on the side of Harlem's bed looking down at him. I lean against the door frame and cross my arms over my chest and just watch. Creed looks so...defeated. Guilt gnaws at me when I look between him and our son. Harlem looks like Creed. There are no two ways about it. But he also has my smile and my dimples. He is the best parts of Creed and me.

I would go through everything that I went through with Creed again if it meant I got my son. I may regret a lot of things in my life, but Harlem isn't one of them. He saved me from my own grief, losing my mom was so fucking hard. She was the only person I wanted when I was in labor. For her to have been there and tell me to breathe and everything was going to be okay, but she wasn't because that son of a bitch took her from me!

"I get that I fucked up Jess and I'm sorry for that. But keeping my own son from me is fucking low." I gape at him, is he serious right now? I know he is serious because he never called me *princess*, he only calls me Jess when he is pissed.

"You have got to be kidding me, right?" I whisper shout. I take a few calming breaths to get a handle on my anger or I risk waking Harlem. Creed turns toward me and the look in his eyes gives me pause. There is no anger in his hazel eyes, just resentment. I wish I could say that look didn't bother me, but it does.

"He's my son, you had four years to get to know him, shit you even named him without me. He doesn't even know who I am!" He stops and takes a few deep breaths and when he seems a bit calmer, he continues. "I won't leave him; he is mine and I want him with me always." Oh hell no, he can go and take a flying leap for all I care. I grit my teeth and motion for him to follow me out of the room. I didn't want to have this heated conversation in my son's room. I close the door and lead the way back down to the kitchen with Creed hot on my heels. I spin around and pin him a glare that I hope sends shivers down his spine. I allow Sheba to rise to the surface, so he knows we are both on the same page.

"You so much as think about taking my son from me, I will kill you. He is mine and will remain with me. You are nothing but a glorified sperm donor!" As soon as the hateful words are out of my mouth his face drops. I can't read his emotions; his mask of indifference is back in place, and he has closed himself off from me. Great. I shouldn't have said what I did but I can't take it back now. He drops his gaze to the floor, his shoulders droop forward and he begins to scuff the floor with the toe of his boot.

"I will never take him from you Jess. I grew up without my mother, remember?" He lifts his gaze to mine and I flinch. I didn't even think about it like that when I snapped at him.

"I'm sorry I shouldn't have said that. I panicked. Harlem is my life and I will not lose him, please don't try to take him from me." Creed surprises the hell out of me when he lurches forward and cups my face between his hands and stares into my eyes imploring me to understand and listen to what he is saying. I stand there quietly, still shocked as hell that he is touching me so freely and I'm not biting his head off.

"When I said I wanted him with me, I was talking about you too, princess. I would never try to take him from you...ever. Am I pissed that you hid my son from me? Fuck yes, I am so angry, but at the end of the day I made my bed and now I have to lay in it. I want to fix things with us princess and be honest with you. I know you may hate me, but please don't take my son away from me Jess."

"Credence, you were frightened of the fact that you had a mate and lied to me about it. Yet now you find out you have a son and you're ready to step up and be a father just like that?" I click my fingers together to annunciate my point. I don't have faith in Creed to keep his word about wanting to be in Harlem's life, but he has to prove himself to me in order for me to even tell Harlem who he really is to him.

CHAPTER FORTY-SIX

Credence

I didn't know how to respond to her statement, so I chose to leave the house. I took a walk around the pack lands aimlessly for so long I lost track of time, when the pack began to emerge from the woods, I knew it must be close to dawn. I found an old set of swings, so I decide to sit my ass down and just look at the sky. Corbin was antsy inside of me, but I can't let him out, not here. Having two shifted alpha wolves together with the amount of tension Cairo and I have is a sure way for a fight to break out. Not to mention the fact that Corbin has been dying to shift since the first moment we spotted Jess. I'm a shallow son of bitch but the moment I saw *my* mark on her neck, a primal part of me relished in the fact that other males would have seen it too.

My mind is so fucked up, I want things to work with Jess. I know she has every right to hate me. I've put her through a lot, and I wish I could have a do-over but that isn't how life works. I thought lying and keeping her in the dark would be best, I was wrong. All I wanted was to seek vengeance for my mother, she didn't deserve the death she got. I love Meg and she *is* my mom in every sense of the word but unlike my brother and sister I actually got to know our real mom. She was kind and sweet and adored the three of us, I have no idea how she could have built a life with dad and not have been with her fated mate. Being away from Jess for five years has been pure agony. Every time I thought I was close to finding her and it turned out to be another dead end, a part of me died each time. I don't agree with my mom and Jess's dad cheating. Katherine was an amazing woman for what she did for Jess, she took her niece in and raised her as her own, her mate was killed by her own pack and yet she still took the heir of that pack in and loved her deeply.

Katherine was buried next to her mate and brother. I know that it killed my dad, but he buried my mom next to her fated mate. A headstone sits on top of Jess's father to represent her mother, but a body was never recovered so she doesn't have her own plot. So much death has surrounded these two packs all of my life and I often wonder why the hell am I even fighting for them. They have caused me nothing but hurt and heartbreak! For fuck sake I even lied and deceived my own mate so I could be alpha of both packs and unite them in peace...What a joke. Who the hell was I kidding. Uniting both packs is all my father has ever wanted me to do.

Anytime I would rebuke him he would threaten to never make me alpha, I have no idea why the hell I wanted to be alpha in the first place. I just wanted to make my father proud. Shit was hard for me growing up, but it got a bit easier when I met Cairo, we were around thirteen, I think. It sounds shallow as fuck but hearing about Cairo and how bad shit was for him, it made me feel better, I mean I had a house and I still had one parent at home. Ro was literally on his own until he met Sky. I shake my head and release a tired sigh. I have to fix shit and make things right or I run the risk of losing my mate. I can't lose Jess; I am so beyond fucking livid at her for hiding my son. No matter how much I fucked up she had no right to keep my own flesh and blood from me. Wolves are family orientated and the fact that I am an alpha makes this worse, my heir should be with me.

Heir?

Do I really want my son to grow up with the pressure that I did? Just because I am fucked up from my upbringing doesn't mean I want that for my own son. I want Harlem to be able to choose if he wants this, not be forced into it, maybe that's it. If I can overthrow the council and get Jess to take her rightful place and throw that piece of shit Jacob out, we could actually make something for our son. With my mind made up, I stand and head back toward the house but stop when I see Cole and Cairo coming toward me. I knew this conversation was coming, hell I expected it earlier. I decide to wait for them and get this over with rather than having this hanging over my head. I know my brother and I have to sort things out, it still burns that he fled with Jess and didn't stay with me. I have known since I first met her all those years ago that Cole liked her, an irrational amount of jealousy surges through me at the thought of her and him being intimate. Would he do that to me?

"She kick you out already?" I stuff my hands in my pockets and shake my head. "Then why are you out here and not inside with my sister and nephew?"

"She isn't ready to let bygones be bygones." I tried to say it light heartedly but judging from the glares they are both shooting at me I don't think they liked my joke.

"You fucking lied to her and used her! My sister isn't a sheep that will follow you Reeves, she is a freaking person. That girl has been through fucking hell, and she still doesn't know that you were hunting her most of her life!" I recoil at the reminder; I just didn't know until I met her that she is my mate.

"Come clean brother. Just be honest with her if you want her to trust you."

"She already hates me!" I snap. Cole shakes his head and looks at me like I'm as dense as a piece of driftwood. Cairo just sighs and runs a hand through his hair.

"I'd be over the moon with joy if she really did hate you. Truth is she doesn't. Ever since *that* night when the moon hit its peak, she has been pining for you--well Sheba has. She has never run with the pack because she knows Sheba will head straight back to you." I stare at him with my mouth open, stunned by his declaration.

"Don't look so shocked, Jess may not like what you have done and wants nothing to do with you, but Sheba does. She needs your help, we have tried--"

"What do you mean? What happened?" I can hear the worry in my own voice. Cairo raises his hand and stops me from spewing more words.

"She is fine, it's just her and her wolf haven't seen eye to eye since Sheba killed Josh. Jess can't forgive her for that. I know Josh was a piece of a shit, but Jess thinks he was innocent." This was all news to me, not bonding with your wolf is bad. After all, you both share one body but have different minds. Josh was so far from innocent, and I have recently learned he was the one who helped Jacob with hurting her mom while she was their captive. I sigh and drop my head, I need to figure shit out fast, and I don't have a lot of time and have to get back to my pack.

"I'll try and talk to her, I don't know if she will listen, but I guess it's worth a shot." With that said, I turn to leave and go in search of Jess but stop when Cairo speaks.

"One more thing." I look over my shoulder, his jaw is clenched tight, and his fists balled at his sides. "You hurt my sister *I'll* be coming for you. You hurt my nephew and my pack will be coming for you. Do not fuck up Reeves, this is your one and only warning, I don't give second chances."

CHAPTER FORTY-SEVEN

Jessica

I wake the next morning stiff, sore, and feeling like I barely slept. After Creed stormed out of the house last night and didn't come back, I gave up waiting for him and went to bed. I reluctantly peel the covers back, not wanting to get up, I'll wallow in self-pity later, but right now I have to get Harlem up and fed. I exit my room in nothing but my sleep shorts and tank top, I open my door and freeze when I see Harlem's door already opened. I pad across the hall and poke my head inside and stifle my gasp, Creed is asleep on the floor next to Harlem's bed. Tears fill my eyes, my heart slams against my chest. I have dreamt of a moment like this but never thought I would ever see it in real life. For years I wished Creed was here to be a father to our son, I had zero faith in his capabilities but seeing him on the hard floor asleep I begin to doubt myself. I hear footsteps down the hall and quietly back out of the room and close the door to let them both sleep a bit longer. I turn to see Cole coming toward me with sleep still clinging to his eyes. Cole is beautiful, don't get me wrong, especially when he's still half asleep and standing in front of me in nothing but a pair of sweatpants.

"He still crashed out?"

"Harlem?" He nods, "Yeah, Creed's asleep on the floor next to him." Cole nods his head.

"Figured, I offered him the couch, but he said he had somewhere better to sleep." I smile like an idiot and follow Cole downstairs to get myself a cup of coffee. Sky, Callie, Zeke and Ro are all in the kitchen eating breakfast and sipping coffee. I bid them all good morning and beeline for the coffee pot.

"Where's the monster?" I inhale half of my coffee before turning and answering Sky.

"Still sleeping." She cocks a perfectly plucked brow at me in question, Harlem never sleeps in---ever. "No idea, might have something to do with Creed sleeping next to him on the floor." Callie snaps shocked eyes to me.

"Creed? As in my brother Creed, slept on the floor?" I fight the smile that wants to split across my face.

"Mm-hmm." Callie looks like a fish out of water. Cole and Sky snicker at her reaction. I break off and talk to Zeke about the pack run last night. I envy them and how they can run as a pack, I have never done it myself. One day I hope that I will be able to join in, Zeke must see my turmoil and wraps his arm around my shoulder and pulls me into his side.

"You'll get there, maybe on the next pack run I'll stay back with you and the monster---"

"Did you just call my son a fucking monster?" I gasp and snap my eyes to Creed who has Harlem on top of his shoulders. The look in Creed's eyes is pure fury, his eyes drop to the arm wrapped around my shoulder and I still. The others have gone silent and watch in rapt curiosity at what will happen next. Creed's upper lip pulls back in a snarl, a deep growl sounds from his throat and his eyes turn blue.

Oh shit.

I try to wiggle out of Zeke's hold, but he just tightens his grip. Creed must sense my distress and pins a deathly glare on Zeke. To his credit though Z doesn't cower or shrink away from Creed's ice-cold stare. Growl after growl comes from Creed, I look up to see Zeke grinning at him like an idiot.

"Zeke, let me go." I grit out through clenched teeth; I feel

Sheba bristling inside me at the way we are being restrained but refuse to acknowledge her.

"Nah babe--"Creed cuts Zeke off.

"Call her *babe* one more time. I dare you!" The threat in his voice sends shivers down my spine.

"You think you can just walk in here and throw your weight around? You are not the alpha here." Zeke must have smoked some green or something, gasps and moans sound out around the room.

"Try me, *Beta*." Creed says *beta* like it is a derogatory word and I bristle at his implication.

"She doesn't want you!" As soon as the words are out of Zeke's mouth Creed's expression changes, so much anger swims in the depths of his blue eyes but I also see hurt. He storms toward Zeke and me, but I quickly wrestle out of Zeke's hold and jump in front of him with my arms outstretched.

"Creed stop, Harlem." At the mention of our son's name, he pauses, and the anger immediately drops from his face. His gaze bores into mine for a moment before he snaps out of it and reaches up to pull Harlem from his shoulders.

"Weeeeeeeeee." Clearly Harlem isn't bothered by the amount of tension in the room and is enjoying his ride down from his father's shoulders. Creed holds Harlem against his chest, and I can see the regret in his eyes. He forgot our son was here and was about to fight another male, before I can get lost in my thoughts Cairo speaks.

"Z, go cool off and come back when you're calm."

"I didn't do anything!" Zeke rebukes.

"You purposely antagonized my brother asshole, get the

fuck out!" The anger that laces each of Cole's words makes me flinch. Cole very rarely gets angry and when he does, he scares the shit out of me. Zeke huffs out his annoyance and storms out of the kitchen, Creed drops his gaze to the floor.

"I'm sorry." I recoil, taken back by his apology, I honestly didn't expect him to say he was sorry. I thought he might have turned it all on Zeke. Harlem turns his head and when he sees me, he squeals and reaches out to me, Creed reluctantly passes him to me with a sigh.

After the incident in the kitchen Creed left with the guys, Callie and Sky followed not long after. I spend the morning playing and reading with Harlem, I finally got him down for a nap and headed back downstairs to clean up our mess of toys and lunch dishes, but stop short at the base of the stairs when I see Creed tidying up the toys in the lounge. I just stand there and stare at him like he is some alien. I never thought I would see Creed being so domestic let alone cleaning up after a toddler. He's bent over cleaning up the train track with his back to me when he says,

"You just gonna stand there and watch me all day?" I quickly snap out of my stupor and rush over to help him clean the remaining toys, then we both wash and dry the dishes in silence. I have no idea what I am supposed to say to him, but I also know I owe him an apology for this morning. Zeke being a dick is on me, he has been trying to get me to go out with him for years. Maybe if I was firmer with Zeke his infatuation with me might have fizzled out years ago. After putting away the last plate Creed turns to leave the kitchen, but I reach out and grab his arm to stop him. He turns and looks down at me in surprise; I blow a long exhale before saying.

"I'm sorry about Zeke."

"Don't be." Huh?

"Uh...What?" He chuckles and that sound has my tummy feeling fizzy and Sheba doing a happy dance.

"Zeke likes you, anyone with eyes can see that." I'm stunned at his calm tone. His eyes crinkle at the sides and I can see the strain on his face as he asks. "Do...Do you like him?" A whoosh of air escapes him when I shake my head. He shocks the hell out of me when he wraps his arms around me and swings me around, I let out a squeak of surprise and quickly wrap my arms around his neck, and he grips me under my ass and hauls me close. As if my body has a mind of its own my legs instinctively wrap around him and we both still, I look down at him in utter fright. This is so not the position we should be in--alone!

Before I can get too lost in my own turmoil, he moves one of his hands from under my ass and grips the back of my neck. Sheba purrs---she freaking purrs like a cat in my head!

He tightens his grip and slowly pulls my face toward his, I don't fight. I wish I could say I was stunned or something but I'm not. Ever since I saw him yesterday a huge part of me wants to kiss him again and see if he still tastes the same. His lips smash against mine; the heat inside me soars to new heights. I explore his mouth with my tongue before I relinquish the control to him, the taste of him has me and Sheba both panting. I run my hand through his hair and tug--hard. He releases a growl of approval and moves so my ass rests on top of the bench, his hands run up and down my body. When he tweaks my nipple through my shirt, I drop my head back and moan, he peppers kisses all over my neck, he reaches down and pulls my shirt off and throws it over his head which causes a girly like giggle to escape my mouth. He reaches around the back of me and unclasps my bra with one hand, the skill in which he does this has doubt creeping in. How many other girls has he done this with since we were last together?

CHAPTER FORTY-EIGHT

Credence

The moment I chuck her bra I see the doubt on her face, Corbin urges me to ignore the look and claim our mate again. As much as I want to sink my cock inside her, and get lost in the ecstasy of being with her, I can't. At least not while she is looking at me like this, I pull back slightly and look down at her.

"What's wrong princess?" She begins to gnaw on her bottom lip and the sight of that has me groaning internally.

"Nothing." She says as she drops her gaze and then brings her arms up to cover her naked chest. I place my hands either side of her face and lift her head until she looks at me.

"The look in your eyes tells a different story." She huffs.

"It's just.... I know I have no right and it's been years and all that--"

"But you want to know if I have slept with anyone else since marking you?" A rosy tinge of red coats her cheeks from embarrassment but she nods anyway. I fight the smile that wants to break free, she is so cute when she is embarrassed.

"No princess, I haven't slept with anyone else." Her eyes round in shock.

"Really?" My smile breaks free this time as I stroke her cheeks.

"Yeah, you're it for me Jess. I know I fucked up and hurt you, but I've changed. Wait." I pull out from standing between her legs and turn to retrieve her shirt and bra and give her space while she changes, then I pick her up and carry her to the lounge room. I plop down onto the couch with her straddling my lap, she tries to move but I grip her hips keeping her exactly where she is.

"What are you doing?" The suspicion in her voice is

tangible.

"Giving you the chance to ask me whatever you want, and I will answer-truthfully...I swear." Intrigue crosses her features.

"Okay, why did you lie to me?"

"I was afraid if you knew the truth you wouldn't help me."

"Well, lying backfired didn't it?" She isn't wrong, five years ago everything I worked so hard to achieve blew up in my face.

"It did."

"If you had told me Creed, I could have helped you."

"I didn't know you then. I thought you would have run."

"Not if you had been honest with me. You lying to me caused me to lose my mom. Why did you do it?" I take a deep breath and for the first time be totally honest with her.

"I'll tell you everything but please no matter how angry or hurt you get let me get it all out before you go off?" She narrows her eyes suspiciously.

"Okay."

"I had been tracking you since you were thirteen." Her mouth drops open in shock, but she remains silent like I asked. "Just so we are clear, I had no idea you were my mate until I met you at school." The tension drains from her body and relief crosses her features. "When you and your mom came to town, I made the arrangements for the school to allow me to attend so I could get close to you--"

"So you were never a student." I shake my head and smile sheepishly at her.

"No, I am the same age as Ro." She cringes but doesn't say anything else. "I knew school was the only place I'd be able to get close to you without your mom around. Your mom is--was a great woman. She fled her pack after the death of her mate and raised her brother's kid, knowing one day you would have to come back and claim your birthright. After your parents were killed there was really no other option for her--"

"Why?"

"Because Jacob wanted to eradicate the Cruz line-- completely. Katharine knew you two would both be next so she ran. When you both came back she got in contact with me and Jacob, what she didn't know was alerting Jacob meant alerting the council."

"Why did it matter if the council knew?"

"Because Jacob and the council are working together, we have found out in the past couple of years that he has paid the old fuckers off to get them on his side. You see the council isn't okay with how we run our pack, women are equal and treated the same as the men. The old fucks believe that women are beneath men and should be used." She flinches but she has to hear the truth.

"But that woman...Shelley, she is a council member."

"Shelley is an anomaly; she is the newest member to the council and seems different. I think if we can get her on our side, we might have a chance of taking the fuckers down once and for all. Anyway, the first time I saw your mom was when you both came to our house. She played the role, she needed to throw you off the scent of her not being your bio mom. My dad never killed her mate, Jacob did. He also never killed your father, your dad and mine were working together to bring the council and Jacob down. Jacob had been trying to overthrow your father for years, especially when Cairo was born."

"What does Ro have to do with this?" A smirk breaks across my face.

"Your brother could never be the alpha of the packs because he cannot be led." She cocks her head to the side, confused.

"Ro can be an alpha but cannot be controlled or led. That is his story to tell, not mine princess." She nods her head and motions for me to continue. "Your father managed to thwart Jacob's moves to take his place but when you, the first female of two alpha lines was born Jacob stopped fucking around and went for the kill shot. For a woman to lead not one but two packs is a huge slap in the face for old schoolers like Jacob and the council."

"Wait, so my mom took me and ran after Jacob killed my parents only to keep me alive so I could overthrow them when I turned eighteen, for revenge for killing my parents and her mate?" I can hear the hurt that laces her voice, I reach up and cup her face.

"No princess, your mother never wanted you to come back." Surprise crosses her features, this is the part she is going to hate--Well, hate me for. "I made her bring you to Rosewood." She pulls back out of my hold and looks at me with devastation, that look has my chest aching and Corbin snapping at me.

"Why?" She whispers, the sound of her voice coupled with the look on her face guts me. I fucked up so bad.

"I needed you here so you could claim the packs and I had hoped to win you over by telling you the truth and what Jacob was up to, but when Corbin scented you and I knew you were my mate everything changed. I was pissed that you had no idea what we were and who you really are, you wanted to leave and be free of Rosewood. I took my anger out on you when I shouldn't have, I wanted to be free like you and never know about any of this. If I could go back, I would princess, I swear."

"So, you brought us to Rosewood because you hoped I would fall for you and what? Make you alpha?" I hang my head in shame.

"Yes. If you didn't, I had other plans." She gasps.

"Oh my god, what were you going to do Creed?" I refuse to meet her gaze because I am a coward.

"I had planned to take both you and your mom as prisoners if you defied me. I was going to force you to choose me as your chosen mate."

"What the fuck! Just so you could overthrow some stupid council and Jacob?" I snap my gaze to her and scowl up at her.

"So I could get revenge for Jacob killing my mom! If it wasn't for your fucking father, she would still be alive." I snap my mouth closed and groan internally, I wasn't supposed to say the last part out loud.

"Wow, so your plan from the start was to use me so I could help you get revenge for your mother's death. So me being your mate was just a bonus, was fucking me part of the plan as well? Oh, what about having a kid with me, is that a bonus too? Are you going to use my son against me?" My anger snaps, I strike out and grip the back of her neck and haul her face an inch from mine and growl, she doesn't back down, she returns a growl of her own in warning.

"I would *never* use *our* son against you! You may have

carried him and birthed him, but he is half me to *Jessica*. Don't ever say that shit to me again, am I clear?" I can hear the anger coating my own tone.

"Fuck. You!"

"Name the time and place princess?"

"Mommy?" I drop my hold on her and she quickly scrambles off my lap as she rushes around the back of the couch to Harlem who is standing at the bottom of the stairs with a confused look on his face. I stand and smile at him reassuringly as Jess kneels in front of him and places her hands on his shoulders.

"Hey monster, you're supposed to be napping." She chides him mildly.

"I was, but then I heard loud voices." Jess flinches slightly.

"Sorry, why don't we--" He turns to me, and cuts Jess off when he says,

"Are you my dad?" Jess gasps and I stand there floundering like a freaking fish.

"Uh, who...I mean what made you ask that buster?" Jess is tripping over her words in shock.

"I heard *weed*." I snicker at the way he says my name but at the same time find it so cute. "Say *our* son." Jess turns and glares at me, I meet her gaze with a look that says I'm not even sorry and shrug. A frustrated sigh escapes her as she picks Harlem up and comes back around to the couch and sits down with him in her lap, I follow her lead and sit at the other end so there is space between us. I remain still and quiet letting her take the lead. I refuse to feel bad that Harlem overheard our conversation. She reaches out and runs her hand through his hair in a soothing motion. "Is *weed* my daddy?" The innocence in which he asks that one simple question astounds me, this kid is so pure. I begin to gnaw on my lip in worry, will this battle between the packs and the council tear that away from him?

"Yes...Creed is your dad." Harlem turns to me and smiles. I don't know what I expected but him looking at me like I'm a-hero wasn't it.

"Mommy says you had to stay away because you were keeping us safe from the bad men." My mouth drops open in shock; I snap my gaze to Jess and stare. The corner of her mouth lifts and she shrugs her shoulders, I turn back to our son and nod like an idiot. I don't know what to say, I had no idea she had even told him about me. "Are the bad men gone now? Can you stay with us?"

I take a deep breath and centre myself before I answer him. "Not yet buddy." His face falls and my chest constricts.

We must end this.

I know Corbin.

We must keep pup and mate safe.

We will, or at least we will die trying.

I reach over and place my hand on his shoulder in what I hope is a comforting move and say.

"When I make *our* home safe, I will come for you...and your mom. I'm not going anywhere."

"So you're gonna stay here with us?" I shake my head and the smile falls from his angelic face again, I'm really fucking this up.

"Buster, Cree--your dad can't stay right now. Remember

how I told you that your dad is an alpha?" Harlem looks to his mom and nods. "Well because he is an alpha he has to go back to his pack and be the boss like Ro-Ro." A sad smile graces his handsome face as he nods, shock ripples through me when he moves out of Jess's hold and jumps on my lap, wrapping his arms around my neck and nuzzling his face in the crook of my neck. I sit there stunned for a second before I snap out of it and wrap my son in my arms. I hear Jess cry quietly but right now my sole focus is Harlem. Renewed determination runs through my veins.

We end this, now.

I'm ready.

When we get back, we take them down and make our home safe for him.

And her.

Yeah Corb, and her.

The sound of the front door slamming open and loud voices shatters this serene moment. I stand with Harlem still in my arms and feel Jess press up beside me, Cole, Cairo and Sky come barreling into the lounge with alarmed looks on their faces. Cole's eyes land on me and the look in his eyes tells me everything I need to know. I turn to Jess and unclasp my son's arms from around my neck and pass him to his mother. Jess looks at me in question and I want nothing more than to soothe her worries, but right now I can't. So I clasp her face in my hands and place a kiss against her lips.

"I've done a lot of shit I regret in my life, princess but meeting you isn't one of them. I'm so sorry for everything I have put you through, if I could take it all back I would. I love you

Jessica Hastings and one day I hope you will love me too." Her eyes widen to the size of saucers. "Now take our son and go and lock yourselves in your room."

"W-what? Why?"

"Jess." She reluctantly tears her gaze from mine to look at her brother. "The council is breaching the pack lands with Jacob's pack, go now and do not come out no matter what." Cairo makes his way over to us and I step back to give him space, he knuckles Harlem's chin as he says. "Remember that game we play, the one where you tell everyone your mom isn't your mom?" Harlem giggles and nods enthusiastically.

"Yeah, I can't tell anyone until you say I can right, Ro-Ro?" My heart breaks at the fact that my four-year-old son has had to be trained like this and taught that this is a game just so some fucker won't hurt him.

"That's right monster, now go with your mom and be good. If anyone asks you who your mom and dad are, what do you say?" I hold my breath in anticipation.

"Aunt Cal and Aunt Sky are my mommies."

"And we are the best darn moms around aren't we buster?" Harlem laughs and nods then gives a sad looking Sky thumbs up. Cairo turns to Jess and places a kiss on her forehead.

"You keep him safe, you run if it gets bad--"

"Ro--"

"No Jess, you run do you hear? You don't stop, you don't help, and you run with that boy and never look back. Do I make myself clear?" A growl sounds within Jess's chest, but we all ignore Sheba's hatred of being told what to do.

"I love you Ro." Cairo's eyes soften for a moment before

he quickly conceals his emotions.

"And I you sister, I'll find you Jess no matter how far or how long it takes. I'll find you." Silent tears trek down her face as she hugs her brother awkwardly with Harlem between them, Sky and Cole both approach, Sky hugs her and Harlem before stepping back. Cole stands there and stares down at her with nothing but...love. Oh my god, my brother is in love with the mother to my child--my mate.

"Keep him safe, don't look back okay." A sob tears out of her, Cole wraps his arms around her and my son.

"Colton, please--"

"Shhhhh, everything is going to be alright, it will all be over before you know it and we'll be telling stories about this epic battle." His words just cause her to cry harder.

"I...love...you Cole." Hearing those words out of her mouth guts me. I don't know if she means it in a brotherly love kind of way or a boyfriend kind of way.

"I love you too, sweetheart." Cole pulls back and then looks down at her, I see it in his eyes. He really loves her; the longing in his gaze guts me.

My brother and I are in love with the same woman.

CHAPTER FORTY-NINE

Credence

I follow Jess upstairs and help her carry some water and food in a pack up to her room in case she needs to run. I make sure the windows are locked and close her curtains.

"Behind the dresser is a set of stairs that leads beneath the basement and there is a tunnel that runs under our land into town." I nod my head; I was actually wondering how the hell she was going to escape. "I-if it comes to that and we have to, you know--please come for us...for him." I turn and look at her in shock. "These past five years have been hell, ever since the bond clicked into place, I haven't been able to breathe properly until...yesterday. I know we have shit to work out, but I want it to work Creed--"I cut her rambling off by marching across the room and gripping the back of her neck to keep her in place as I smash my lips against hers in a heated kiss that has Corbin and I both hot and bothered.

"We have to go now!" I release her at the sound of Cairo's voice. I look down at her beautiful blue eyes and smile.

"I'll always come for you princess, I never stopped searching." I ignore her gasp and kneel down in front of my son who is clinging to his mother's leg. "I need you to be an alpha now." His jaw unhinges and his eyes light up. "You're gonna have to look after your mom for me."

"I'll keep mommy safe." I reach out and ruffle his hair.

"Good man, I'll be back okay." I stand and turn toward Cairo following him out of the room and pause before I close the door behind myself. I look over my shoulder at my mate with our son clutched against her chest, with tears in her eyes and smile. "I love you princess, now keep our prince safe." A tear rolls down her cheek as I close the door and follow Ro out of the house.

Cairo is barking orders for any women and children to head to the mountains with the elderly. Most alphas would make any man or boy stay and fight but not Ro, he won't force anyone to go into battle. He gave his pack the option to stay or leave and hide out in the mountains till this is over. Needless to say, more than half of his pack stayed to fight beside their alpha, I bristle when I see Zeke make his way over and stand beside Cairo. I scan the scattered people before my gaze lands on Sky, and she answers my un-asked question.

"I sent Callie to the mountains as soon as I found out they were coming. She has taken the orphan pups with her." I nod my head.

"Thank you." Her eyes narrow.

"Don't thank me for loving my mate Credence; I will die for her in a heartbeat. She may be your sister, but California is my soul." Hearing the conviction and love in each of her words lets me know that my sister will be okay if I fall. Sky is one badass mother fucker, and I would bet my life on it that out of all the men and women out here, Sky will be the one to walk out of this battle alive, Cairo, Zeke and Cole move toward me and Sky, halting in front of us.

"Sky, take some of the men and women to the woods and stay there until I signal." She nods and then leaves to do as her alpha instructed. Tommy and Asher head toward us and stand on either side of me.

"Brad and the others are going with Sky to help out, we sent word to your dad, and he is sending help but--- "

"They won't get here in time." I finish for Asher.

"We got this Reeves; Zeke take Blake and the other blacktops to the hills and wait for my signal." Zeke does as he is told and heads out. "Cole you're with me, Creed this is my land and my pack. We go on my orders, clear?" Corbin snickers but at the end of the day Ro is right, so I nod my head and do exactly as he instructs.

We stand in the middle of the drive and wait. Asher and Tommy are behind me and the rest of Cairo's men, some of them in human form and some have shifted. Cole and I flank Ro, we chose to stay in human form so we can communicate with the council assholes. We hear their footfalls pound against the earth, they will be here within minutes, the tension in the air is tangible.

"If I don't make it--"

"Ro--"Cole tries to cut Cairo off, but Ro isn't having it.

"Shut it Cole! If I don't make it, both of you better look after my sister and nephew." I can see Ro eyeing me out of the corner of his eye. "You hurt my sister or my nephew Credence I will fucking kill you and make what is happening with the packs look like a game of hide and seek."

"You have my word Ro; I won't fuck up with her again." I hear Cole scoff and it pisses me off. "The fuck is your problem Colton?" My brother turns and meets my glare with one of his own.

"For five years I'm the one who helped her, I changed the fucking diapers and helped with the night time feeds. Whenever Sheba would force a shift to chase you, I was the one who brought her back and helped her heal from the damage *you* inflicted. I did that. I swore I would never go against you or hurt you in any way, but right now--"

"You want to hurt me because you can see Jess is in love with me." Cole grinds his teeth and narrows his eyes to slits. Ro releases a frustrated sigh and turns to my brother then places a hand on his shoulder.

"I know you love her, don't look so shocked Cole everyone knows, well everyone except for my sister that is. My point is, she was never yours to love brother, and she is marked by *him*. The mate bond will always win in the end, if I could have chosen which brother would have ended up with my sister--"

"Finish that sentence and I will break your fucking nose Cairo!" I growl out, the bastard just laughs and shrugs his shoulders.

"Least you know I was always rooting for you bro." He and Cole fist bump each other while I stand there and glare at the fuckers. Now that I have her back, I will never give her up and I need Cole to know that.

"I won't let her go Colton." I feel his eyes on me but keep mine focused in front. "She is my mate and Harlem is *my* son, not yours. I will do right by them and try to make up for my wrongs if she will let me. I know you are the better man--fuck you're the best option for her, but I love her Cole and I'm not prepared to let her go. Jess and Harlem are my ending, I want a life with them." Cole and Cairo stare at me in shock, shit I even feel Asher and Tommy's gaze's burning holes in the back of my head.

"Well, shit Reeves, that was deep as fuck." I don't reply to Ro because they're here, they move out from the woods in a line like soldiers in the army. Shelley is in the front with the other council members, I spot Jacob behind them and a growl. This fucker goes down today, I've had enough of his bullshit. I want this over with, so I can bring Jess and Harlem home, maybe Ro might even come back with her. I spot members from my pack among them. They deserted us because of Jacob and the council eating up our lands.

"Why the fuck is Brenna and Kyle with them?" Cole snaps.

"They left when we lost the eastern border lands." Asher answers.

"What the fuck?"

"You weren't there Cole, shits been hard. We had to fight tooth and nail and live up to their laws just to hang onto the land we have left. Half the pack has left to join Jacob, we don't have the capacity or land now to house what shifters remain." I can hear the hurt and anger that laces Tommy's words, I feel the same way as he does.

"Deal with this shit later." Cairo grits out. Shelley and the other leaders draw near. They all look the same but this time they don't make me nervous. Five years ago, was the last time I was ever scared of the council. "The fuck?" I turn to Ro to see him staring at Shelley like he has seen a ghost.

"Credence."

"Phillip." I grit out when the council and army stop moving, Shelley and Cairo are locked in an intense staring match. Phillip follows my gaze and frowns.

"Who might we have here, Shell?" I see Shelley flinch, but

she masks it by shrugging her shoulders.

"No idea, he looks familiar though." Cairo shields his emotions and gives nothing away. as does Shelley, there is tension between them, but I don't know why.

"Who are you, boy?" Phillip demands. Cairo doesn't tense, he crosses his arms over his chest and levels Philip with a look that would have most men backing down, but not Philip, the egotistical prick.

"I believe you already know who I am." Philip scowls at Ro. Dela, another council member, steps forward. Dela has always been fair and has even sided with my pack on most matters lately.

"You're alive." Philip looks between Dela and Ro with annoyance, clearly not pleased with the fact he isn't in the know with who Ro is.

"I am. I thought you might have put it all together by now Dela." The old man chuckles and shakes his head.

"Would you care to enlighten the rest of us, old friend?" Philip says *friend* like it burns his mouth.

"I believe we just found our fugitive." Phillip's brow furrows, the remainder of the council members and Jacob's pack begin to murmur amongst themselves.

"What fugitive? Spit it out already Dela!"

"Phillip, meet Cairo Cruz. Jessica's older brother." Silence, all eyes turn to Ro. He eats up all the attention with a sly smirk on his face. Phillip manages to pull himself together after a minute and points an accusing finger at Ro.

"You're supposed to be dead!"

"Clearly I'm not, asshole."

"You will watch your tongue, or I'll remove it." Ro drops his arms to his sides and takes a step forward.

"You gonna kill me like you did my father and Creed's mother? Or will you let Jacob have the honors again?" Gasps ring out and Jacob finally steps forward and stands shoulder to shoulder with Philip and Dean. Dean, another council member, has an ugly smile on his face which just confirms they all had a hand in the deaths of my mom and Ro's father.

"You know nothing boy!" Ro pins Jacob with a glare that makes me proud. Jacob bristles under the intense pressure of Cairo's gaze.

"I was there that night you old fuck. I saw *everything*." I dart my gaze to Ro in shock, he has never told me that. How did I not know he was there as well?

"We will discuss your claims when you stand trial." Ro laughs at Philip which causes the fucker to turn a bright shade of red with anger.

"Over my dead body."

"Oh Mr. Cruz, that can always be arranged."

"Shut the fuck up Jacob, you lying fuck." Cole spits out.

"Oh goodie, another deserter. You can stand trial beside your friend here."

"Touch my brother and I'll rip your fucking head off Jacob!" A wicked smirk crosses Jacob's face and I tense. The look in his eyes tells me he is up to something. I dart my gaze to my brother and Cairo, they are both as tense as I am. Jacob moves forward and begins to pace in front of us as he says.

"You see, when *my* mate fled--"Corbin jumps to the surface and releases a long angry growl that has my chest rumbling in its wake. "I knew she would've had help, I just had to do some digging and bribe the right people to get me what I want. You see up until yesterday I had no clue where she was, but when I got a call from one of my sources who was very distraught that she would still harbor feelings for someone else when he was a deceitful piece of shit--"I tune him out and turn to Cairo to find his eyes on me already. I can't leave without raising the alarm, so I mind link Tommy.

"Tommy, head back to the main house and get Jess the fuck out of here."

"Why?"

"Zeke betrayed us, he gave them our location and I have a feeling he is going for Jess as we speak!"

"I'm on it alpha."

I give Ro a nod to let him know it's sorted. "After I paid my source, he sang like a canary and gave up her hiding spot." I manage to catch the last part of Jacobs spiel, Cole steps forward and squares his shoulders.

"So you brought what?" Cole scans over the numerous bodies behind Jacob and the council. "Hundred--hundred and fifty guys with you to take a girl?"

"She isn't just some girl you ingrate, she is my mate!"

"Call her your mate again I fucking dare you!" I snap, he opens his mouth but snaps it closed as a cruel smile stretches across his face. I follow his gaze and watch in horror as Zeke carries Jess fireman style over his shoulder toward us. Ro takes a step forward but stops when Zeke flashes him the dagger in his hand. Where's my son? I begin to panic, and Corbin is fighting for control.

Corbin stop!

Protect mate.

We'll get her killed if we attack now, we're outnumbered.

Zeke moves toward the council and hands Phillip the dagger in his hand and then adjusts Jess, so she lies bridal style in his arms.

"Why?" The command in Ro's voice is awe inspiring.

"Gotta do what you gotta do brother." Ro spits on the ground in front of him.

"You are no fucking brother of mine! I will kill you for this and wear your skin as a coat in the winter to come." Zeke doesn't react just clings to my mate, worry wins out, I move forward and only stop when Jacob places the sharp edge of the blade against Jess. I don't know how he got the upper hand on her or even knock her out. I meet Zeke's gaze and make sure he is able to see the murder in my eyes.

"When I come, you won't even know it. Just when you think you've run far enough or covered your tracks, think again. I will never stop hunting you."

"I wouldn't expect anything less." His answer stuns me but I don't let it show.

CHAPTER
FIFTY

Jessica

It's only been ten minutes and I'm an anxious mess. The only plus side is Harlem doesn't seem bothered by any of this, he's just sitting on the bed playing with his trains. I'm so worried about my brother, Cole, Sky and Creed. Creed just told me he loved me, and I said nothing in return, what if something happens to him and I never get the chance to tell him how I feel? I know that sounds so cliché but right now it's all I can think about. I hear the front door open and tense before I snap out of it and quickly grab Harlem and tell him to hide under the bed. Once I'm sure he is hidden properly I quickly shove his trains behind the pillows and wait, I drop into my fighting stance and call Sheba to the surface. I'm pretty good at shifting on the fly and I'm able to shift within seconds. I strain my hearing and scent the air as I hear footsteps coming up the stairs.

What the hell is he doing here?

The closer his scent gets the more worry seeps into my bones. I have known him for five years and never once has he ever made me question his loyalty. With my decision made I open the door after he knocks and I let him in, locking the door once again. We stand there in silence just staring at each other, the tension in the room is rampant and uncomfortable. I have never felt like this around Zeke before, and the fact that Sheba is uneasy as I am is worrying me. Zeke runs a hand through his short-cropped hair and then pins me with a stare that has all the air rushing from my lungs.

"You're not here to help me, are you?" I whisper, sadness enters his eyes and he drops his head.

"You know I care about you Jess. I would never do anything to bring any harm to you or the monster. I need you to listen to me and please try to understand. We can stop this war from breaking out, this is bigger than Creed's revenge. Let me explain, please?"

"When I come, you won't even know it. Just when you think you've ran far enough or covered your tracks, think again. I will never stop hunting you."

"I wouldn't expect anything less." Zeke answers.

The conviction and threat in Creed's voice is astounding, I have to keep up my act and remain limp in Zeke's arms. I hope I am doing the right thing here, if Zeke is lying to me, I will fucking kill him.

"Now, we thank you for your cooperation. We will leave a member of the council here--"I don't know who is speaking but the tone of his voice sounds gleeful.

"I will remain here to watch over this *pack*." The way the woman spits the word pack is like it is beneath her. "Zeke will take Jess to my car."

"No, the girl comes with me--"

"You dare to question me? You are nothing compared to me Jacob so you will mind your fucking tongue before I rip it out of your fucking mouth." Holy shit, I can tell now that it is Shelley ripping Jacob a new one.

"Very well, you have an hour Shelley. If you have not completed the task and are on the road with the girl in an hour we will return."

"You have my word Phillip."

"I will remain with Shelley to oversee and make sure there are no *loose ends.*" The implication of what he means has me grinding my jaw.

Murmurs break out and then I hear shuffling and footsteps, I'm jostled in Zeke's embrace as he moves. It takes everything inside me to keep Sheba at bay and not allow her to stake her dominance. She is pissed at being carried and playing the damsel in distress.

"Zeke." He pauses and waits for my brother to finish speaking. "Give her to me and I swear to you all will be forgiven." I feel Zeke stiffen and my heart aches for him, if only Cairo and Creed knew why he is doing this.

"I'm sorry Ro, what is done cannot be undone--"

"Except at the peak of the moon on summit night." I hear shock and awe in Cairo's voice, he doesn't try to stop us again as Zeke walks, but I hear growls and crunches, shouts and threats and I know with every fiber of my being that it is Creed going nuts and no doubt Cole will be going off right along with him. After about twenty minutes or so, Zeke stops walking and says.

"You can open your eyes now." I blink my eyes open slowly so they don't hurt from the light, I try to wiggle out of his hold, but he tightens his grip. "If someone does follow our trail its best they only see one set of footprints." I release a sigh and try to ignore the pain in my chest. "I promise you; no harm will come to the monster Jess." Tears fill my eyes at the mention of my son.

"If you're lying--"

"I'm not, I will never go against Cairo. Ro is not only my

best friend he is my brother." The fierce look in his eyes has me believing in him.

"Where are we going?"

"To get Shelley's car. The other council members and the pack have to believe that I am taking you away from the carnage that is about to unfold." I shiver at the venom in his voice.

"Do you mean they want her to kill our pack?"

"Yes."

When we finally reach Shelley's Jeep which is parked out on the main road and it is a good forty-five-minute walk from the house, Zeke places me in the backseat. He tells me to lay down while he drives in case we are being watched. I do as he says and remain still and quiet as we head back to our pack lands, when we roll over a few potholes I know we are getting close.

"We're five minutes out, stay down until I say. I don't trust Jacob not to have left spies behind." Zeke's right, I have learnt so much about Jacob and how he is a cunning son of a bitch. These new revelations I have just learnt from Zeke are so beyond. The minutes tick by so slowly as I wait for Zeke to finally stop the car, when he does a rush of air escapes me. "Your boy is going nuts, give me a minute to check with Shelley and if it's all clear I'll holler out."

"Okay." I wait in the car for what feels like hours. I hear growls, snarls, and raised voices; I bolt upright in the chair when I hear his voice. I peer out the windscreen and see Creed and Cole both in wolf form, Tommy stands behind them with Harlem tucked into his side. Zeke stands next to Shelley with his arms raised like he is surrendering, Creed takes a menacing step toward Zeke, and I wait with bated breath for him to give me a sign that the coast is clear. He has to hurry the hell up or Creed is going to kill him. The back door opposite me wrenches open and I squeal in shock. I launch myself across the seat and wrap my arms around my brother's neck. He hauls me out of the car and holds me tight.

"You're okay now. I got you, and I promise they will pay for--- "

"Ro, no." I pull back and break out of his hold so he can see the seriousness in my eyes. "You have to hear them out, please." Shock colors his features.

"Mommy!" I spin around at the sound of my son's voice, Creed and Cole both clamp their jaws shut and turn toward me. Harlem wiggles out of Tommy's hold and runs as fast as his little legs will carry him, I meet him halfway and scoop him up in my arms and twirl us around in a circle. The sound of his laughter is a balm to my battered heart, I pull him in close and nuzzle his neck absorbing his scent. Sheba and I both release a sigh; nothing beats the scent of our pup. I close my eyes and relish in the moment, if Zeke didn't sacrifice his loyalty I might not be here right now holding my son. I feel his presence at my back, I try to stay in the moment and keep my eyes closed, but when his hands land on my hips, fire blazes inside me. The heat is so intense a small whimper escapes me before I can stop it. He spins me around and peers down at me, the fear and longing in his eyes guts me. He wraps his arms around me and holds on tight, Harlem laughs at the awkwardness of being stuck in the middle of us, I won't lie, I am glad to have him as a barrier between us. Being close to Creed is a bad idea, this man has a hold over me.

"I thought I lost you." The brokenness in which he says those words will haunt me.

"We don't have much time, Credence let her go now." Creed spins and then blocks me and our son from view as he faces Shelley. I try to be serious and focus on the threat I swear, but when I notice he is naked, I can't stop my eyes from checking out his firm, plump ass. I mean he put the *G* in *ghetto booty*.

"I'll kill you." Creed grits out.

"No you won't." I step forward and stand beside Creed, a bit put out to find my brother standing opposite us next to Shelley and Zeke.

"Why are you sticking up for her?"

"You have no idea Credence, I told you to stop looking. I begged you to let this go and live-in peace with Jacob on one side and you on the other. You wouldn't listen! You had to have your revenge and now because of you we will all pay the fucking price!" Oh my god.

"You knew this whole time?" Cairo's gaze snaps to me and the look of guilt in his eyes tells me all I need to know. "You asshole, I trusted you Ro!"

"I'm sorry, I had no choice!"

"What the fuck is going on here?" Creed snaps, I feel his gaze on me, but I refuse to let my brother win and drop his stare. His upper lip pulls back and a growl tears from him. The alpha stare is broken when Shelley steps in front of him, I growl at the bitch, how dare she intervene.

"Jessica Hastings--"Creed steps in front of me again and uses his arm to push me behind him, Cole sidles up next to him and hands him something, when I see him bend slightly, I realize Cole just gave him pants.

"You don't get to talk to her, you speak to us." I bristle at their bullshit alpha male show.

"Actually Credence, I don't need you, because you are the one who endangered her fucking life! I covered her tracks and kept Cairo hidden all these years. I kept them both safe but then you had to go and track her down so she would come back and make you alpha! You stupid shit, there is going to be nothing left in Rosewood!"

"What the hell does that mean?" Cole asks.

"It means, Colton, that if your brother had kept his mouth shut and been a good boy, I could have kept you all safe. His need for revenge and bringing Jess back to make sure he made Jacob pay, is going to cost him."

"The fuck are you on about Shel--"I step out from behind Creed and move so I am slightly in front of them, I stare at Shelley and then peer around her to see my brother. When his gaze meets mine I see it, he knows way more than what he let on.

"Okay, I went with Zeke and left Harlem with Tommy because he told me that you have been helping my brother and are prepared to help Creed. Why do I get the feeling that there is more to this than what Zeke or either of you have said?" Shelley's face becomes stoic and still, she runs her gaze up and down my body and not in a way that is uncomfortable but in a way that makes me feel like she is checking for...Injury. Weird.

Cairo steps forward and stands beside her, I have missed a huge part of something here and I feel like Ro is about to drop a bomb that is going to shatter my reality.

"First, I had no idea Zeke had been recruited. What he says is true though, Shelley has been helping me, Creed and...You."

"How?" Comes from Creed, he steps forward and wraps an arm around my shoulders. His arms make me feel safe and grounded; I switch my hold on Harlem, so he is resting on my hip between Creed and me.

"By keeping the council at bay and away from Cairo and Jess, as well as you, but you wouldn't listen. If you had of let your revenge go then you--- "Cole cuts Shelley off.

"He killed my mother!" Shelley glares at Creed.

"He didn't kill your mother Credence." Creed stiffens beside me.

"What?" The weight in which Cole says that one word astounds me. Cairo releases a long sigh and looks to the brothers.

"Your mother isn't dead."

"How the fuck do you know that Cairo?"

"Colton, your mother is alive and well, I guess you can say."

"Where is she?" I can feel the anger radiating from Creed, if he isn't careful Corbin will break free soon enough.

CHAPTER FIFTY-ONE
Credence

They have to be lying, I saw her die! I saw Jacob kill her with his bare hands after he killed Jess's dad. I know what I saw and what they are saying can't be true, it---just can't be.

"Where is she?" I demand, I can feel Corbin rising to the surface. I tighten my hold on Jess and Harlem. Cole moves forward and stands beside me; we have both been in the dark about all of this.

"You will see soon enough; we have to leave now before Phillip and the others come back."

"Fuck that! Where the hell is my mother and why the hell do you know so much about all of this?" Dela moves forward and a growl of warning sounds from me, he stops his movements and stays beside Zeke.

"Credence and Colton, if we do not leave now, they will come back. They will use any excuse at the moment to get rid of Shelley and I, hiding the fact that you have a child is reason enough. If you want to keep your son safe, then please listen to us."

"Why the fuck should we trust you?" I see out the corner of my eye, Callie moves toward Cairo, Shelley, Zeke and Dela. The gasp that comes from Sky lets me know she has no idea her mate was in on this. Callie won't meet mine or Cole's gaze; she comes to a stop next to Shelley and looks toward Jess.

"I am so sorry I kept this from you. I didn't see another way; all I want is for Harlem to grow up and be free of all this."

"Callie, what have you done?" The pain in Sky's voice makes me hurt for her, she comes to stand on Jess's other side to face off against her mate. Callie's eyes fill with tears when she looks at Sky, a sad smile on her lips.

"I am so sorry, my love. I never meant to hurt you, we all did what we thought was best for the pack and for the monster. Shelley is prepared to help all of us." How the fuck does she know this? Jess scoffs beside me and a small growl reverberates in her chest.

"You promised me you would never lie to me again! You said you were nothing like your brother yet here we stand. I am so fucking sick and tired of everyone making choices for me and thinking they know what is best. I am Harlem's mother and I know what is best for my son not you all!" Hearing that has guilt eating away at me, I can hear the damage my lies have done to her, and I silently vow that I will never do that to her again. I want to help her heal from all the trauma she has endured.

"I know, but that changed the day he was born." Harlem begins to wiggle in her hold.

"Ro-Ro." Harlem calls out, Cairo moves forward but stops when I growl. Cairo shoots me a look that would have a lesser man shitting himself.

"I'm going to get my nephew, and if you try to stop me Reeves, I swear on God's green earth I will fucking put you down. I am of no threat to him."

"But you are to his mother." I counter. Cairo's eyes flash to the color of his wolf. Before this goes any further, Jess places Harlem on the ground and he takes off toward his uncle and squeals happiness when Ro picks him up and chucks him in the air. He maneuvers Harlem so he's sitting on his shoulders and then faces me again.

"I am a lot of things but a threat to my sister isn't one of them. She was safe and free, until you had to go and track her down and drag her back to this shit. She could have had a normal life you selfish son of a bitch. She might of had a boring husband with a boring house and white picket fence with two dogs but you fucked that, not me." His words hit their mark.

"Ro, that's enough." Jess tries to plead with her brother.

"Nah Jess it isn't. He wants to come here and throw his weight around like he is the fucking king, he needs to be knocked down a peg or two."

"Shut up Cairo and leave my brother alone." Cole snaps.

"Enough, we are out of time and have to go. Either you come with us freely or I have my men drag you with us. Which is it going to be?"

"What men?" Cole snaps at Shelley.

"The three hundred men scattered throughout the woods. You really didn't think the rest of the council would leave just Dela and I here did you?" She tsks Cole like he is an idiot and turns to head toward the Jeep. Jess rushes toward Cairo and I follow after her.

"Please don't take him from me." The way she begs her brother causes something inside me to snap.

"You try to take our son from us Cairo, I will burn the fucking world down to find you." Cairo has a disgusted look on his face as he looks between Jess and I.

"I would never take him from you!" Is all he says as he gives Harlem to Jess and stalks off.

Cairo leads me, Jess, Harlem, Sky, Callie and Cole toward his Escalade. The tension between us all is suffocating, I have my hand on Jess's lower back and she has Harlem clutched against her chest. I open the back door for her to slide in, but she stops when Zeke calls out to her. He moves toward her with a bag in his hand but doesn't get a chance to pass it to her because Cole slams his hand against his chest. Zeke glares at Cole but doesn't try to remove his hand---smart boy. He holds the backpack out toward Jess, she eyes it skeptically.

"It has the monster's trains in it, and some snacks and water for the drive." I grab the bag from him and scowl at the beefy fucker.

"Thanks Z."

"Anytime sweetheart." I scoff at his pet name for her and turn to usher her in the car once again. Sky and Callie ride in the back, Jess sits next to me in the middle while Harlem is beside her strapped into his car seat, Cole rides shotgun with Cairo. I have no idea where the hell we are going, I told them I had to call my father, Callie assured me that dad, mom and the rest of our pack will be where we are going. Her and Cairo haven't said another word since then. Callie tries to speak to Sky but has had no luck, Sky refuses to acknowledge her and I honestly cannot blame the woman.

"It sucks doesn't it?" I look at her, her gaze is focused straight ahead.

"What sucks princess?" A sad smirk graces his beautiful face.

"Seeing it from the outside."

"What?"

"I can feel your emotions kind of through the mate link." Wow, since fucking when? "You feel for Callie and Sky, but it wasn't so long ago I was Sky and you were Callie." I gape at her, she's right. Is that why I feel so bad for Sky?

"I don't... I mean."

"Ancient history Credence, it is what it is at the end of the day." Snickers from the front piss me off, I know Ro and Cole are still pissed but when is everyone going to get over it?

"I know I fucked up and I owned that. I told you I will make it up to you, but I have a question for you now princess." She turns and meets my gaze; her blue eyes hold so much defiance.

"Do tell."

"When are you gonna start fucking saying sorry and making it up to me for hiding my son? You kept my kid from me, I missed him growing inside you and watching him come into this world. You robbed me of that and yet you sit here and cry over a few lies I told here and there?" Her jaw unhinges and her eyes round to the size of saucers. "Think about that the next time you want to throw my mistakes in my face. What I did is minimal compared to what the fuck you did!" Her lip pulls back in a snarl.

"That's enough--"

"Shut up Ro. You think what you did is minimal?" A humorless laugh bubbles out of her. "You think I don't know that you spiked my milk with wolfsbane to force my shift early just so you could mark me?"

Oh fuck!

I stare at her in utter disbelief trying to think of a way to save my own ass. "I--how?"

"Oh baby, I know a lot more than what you give me credit for. So the next time you want to come for me, make sure you have more ammo." I'm so fucked, I'm more fixated on the fact that she called me *baby.* The anger that swirls in her blue eyes is turning me on and there is no way I can shift discreetly in this cramped car without everyone knowing my cock is hard as fucking wood.

"That's enough. Sort your shit out when Harlem isn't around, he doesn't need to hear his parents bickering and cussing in front of him." The reminder of our son being present seems to snap Jess and I out of our heated debate. I meet Cairo's gaze in the rear-view and the warning in his eyes pisses me off, so I give him the middle finger and mouth *fuck you,* smart fucker scoffs and says. "I'll pass."

The rest of the drive is silent except for small talk here and there. Jess and I don't talk unless I'm offering to help take Harlem to the restroom when we stop or offering to switch seats with her. I can see why everyone calls him monster now, he has been a terrible passenger the whole way. I find it funny, but the others seem to be over him asking *are we there yet* every five minutes. I can see Jess is tired and getting stressed that Harlem won't settle. After we make another stop because apparently Harlem has to pee every hour, I switch his seat, so he is in the middle and able to see out the windscreen instead of staring at the back of Cole's head the whole time. Jess doesn't say anything as she buckles him back up and claims her seat, Sky and Callie still aren't talking, Cole and Cairo seem to be the only ones getting along. We have been in the car for four hours and even I'm getting over the cramped space, Harlem asks twenty minutes into the drive how much longer and Cairo refuses to answer him, so I decide to cause a bit of shit and say to my son.

"Ro-Ro is just being a control freak and won't tell us where we are going because it makes him feel strong to know something we all don't." I hear Cairo mumbling but ignore him, Harlem smiles up at me and says.

"Ro-Ro is always trying to be strong. My mommy is stronger than him though, Co-Co told me." Cole turns toward Cairo and smiles sheepishly then playfully glares at his nephew.

"I told you that was bro talk! You're not supposed to tell everybody." A distraught look crosses Harlem's face and I glare at my idiot of a brother. I open my mouth to try to soothe my son, but he beats me to it.

"But Co-Co, weed is my daddy. I want him to have bro talks too."

My heart stops.

My gaze snaps to Jess over the top of the car seat to find she is just as shocked as me. I drop my gaze back to my son and find him still looking at Cole, I lift my eyes to my brother and flinch internally. I see envy and hurt in his eyes, my anger flares slightly. Cole has to learn that Harlem is *my* son not his, he also needs to fucking learn that Jess is *mine*.

"You do realize your dad isn't that cool right?" Cairo's light-hearted banter breaks the spell of hearing my son call me *daddy* for the first time. This moment will forever be ingrained in my memory. I have never felt so much pride or love, hearing that one word out of my son's mouth makes my life have a purpose.

"My dad is cool, right mommy?" I dart my gaze to Jess who rolls her eyes playfully and says.

"I suppose."

"See Ro-Ro?"

"Your mom has to say that monster, your dad's kind of it for her." Jess and I both refuse to look at each other or even acknowledge what Ro just said. I know, not the most mature thing but right now we don't need to be having *that* conversation in a cramped car filled with our siblings, son and Sky.

Chapter Fifty-Two

Jessica

It's dark out and I'm stiff and sore from sitting for so freaking long. Sheba is itching to run and right now I want nothing more than to let her. Harlem is finally asleep, Creed kept him occupied most of the drive and it warmed my heart to see how good he is with him. He never got annoyed or pissed that he kept asking so many questions, Harlem asked about his pack and his parents and Creed was all too happy to tell him everything. He even promised Harlem to take him there one day so he can see where he and his aunt and uncle grew up. Harlem's soft snores are the only sound in the car, Cairo turned the radio off an hour ago after it lost reception, being stuck in a car for nine hours isn't my idea of fun at all. I wind my window down and I'm immediately assaulted by the scent of the sea. I snap my gaze to my brother and open my mouth to say something but stop when I hear his voice in my head.

Don't, he'll only lie to you, and it will hurt more when you find out the truth.

How do you know?

I turn toward him and thanks to being a wolf I can use Sheba's vision so I can see at night. Creed looks tired, but looking at him half asleep and his hair all shaggy and tousled he reminds me of Harlem. Harlem looks so much like his father that some days it hurt to look at him and not miss Creed.

Because it's what I would do.

Not everyone lies

So your brother has been honest with you the whole time?

Kiss my ass Credence!

Anytime princess.

You're gross

And yet I can smell your arousal. So, what about my grossness turns you on princess?

I refuse to let my embarrassment show or even acknowledge the fact that he is right, and I am turned on. Seeing how amazing he was with our son has done something to me and all I have thought about for two hours is how good it will feel to have him inside me again.

Where do you think we are going?

I hear him chuckle in my head before answers.

Smooth subject change, I'll allow it this time.

Full of yourself much?

I'd rather be filling you up.

Get your head out of the gutter and answer me!

I have no idea princess; I'm guessing we are catching a ferry somewhere unless this place is by the beach. Would be smart, since we can't track others' scents.

Huh, I actually didn't think of that.

You may not have but if you allowed Sheba to be more present in your mind, she would be able to tell you.

I...it's complicated.

I can relate princess; Sheba did what her instincts told her to.

She killed without my consent!

No, she killed to protect you and avenge your mother. Sheba knew what she was doing and if you had of attacked Jacob, you would have been killed. He is protected by the council and whether or not you want to believe me, Sheba will be able to scent that.

How?

Wolves can scent when another wolf is higher ranked than them.

That is new information to me, and I'll admit it made sense. I have struggled with Sheba since that night and now a part of me is wondering if what Creed says is true?

Princess?

Yeah?

His brows dip low and his eyes cloud, I can feel remorse filtering from him through our bond. He reaches over the top of the car seat and cups my face; his touch ignites a fire inside me. I begin to wonder if there will ever come a time where his touch won't set my body ablaze. I stare into his eyes and wait for him to say what he needs to.

When I thought Josh was putting the moves on you, I took it out on the wrong person, I should have gone after him not you. I want a second chance princess and I know I have no right to ask that of you, but here I am asking anyway.

The sincerity in his voice astounds me. I may be butt hurt over the fact that he lied, but at the same time if it didn't happen, Harlem wouldn't be here.

Okay.

You won't regret this princess.

Somehow I think I might. I say jokingly.

Nah, I won't let you regret it.

Full of yourself aren't you?

Ro begins to crawl to a stop and tension thrums through my body. I don't know why my brother and Callie are hiding things from us, but I refuse to be lied to by them any longer. Ro stops the car in an empty car lot, the other cars pull in and park around us. Before anyone can exit the vehicle, I speak up.

"I am not going anywhere until one of you two tells us what the hell is going on?" The silence that ensues is deafening; the only sounds that can be heard are the other car doors closing and the chatter outside. After a minute of no one speaking an annoyed growl sounds from me, Sheba isn't the most patient of wolves and hates not knowing things.

"I didn't lie." I turn and peer at Callie over my shoulder, the resigned look on her face tells me she didn't want to lie to us, especially Sky. "Well, I didn't mean to. I only found out yesterday. Ro approached me and told me that the council would be coming. and that Shelley would help us."

"Help us how?" Creed cuts in, her guilt-ridden gaze swings to her brother.

"All he told me is that Shelley would help us and keep the monster safe. All I had to do was lead the pack members that couldn't fight to the waiting SUV's at the top of the mountain and come back." I turn toward the front and see Cairo's gaze on me in the rear-view mirror.

"Shelley came to me about a year ago and offered to keep you and Harlem hidden--"

"How the hell did she know about him and you?" I cut in.

"I honestly don't know. I thought she was full of it at the start but as the year went on she came through with info--"

"The raids?" I can hear the disbelief in Cole's voice.

"Yes, the packs that I said were moving into our territory weren't. They were scouts for the council and Shelley would give

411

me a heads up. I swear Jess, I didn't do this for me, I did this to keep Harlem safe."

"Why didn't you tell me Ro?" He drops his gaze and shakes his head.

"She said you were to be kept in the dark. She didn't want you to be a part of it, she wanted you to be free of this shit. That was her one and only condition and let's be real...It wasn't a condition that I wasn't already on board with anyway." I grit my teeth together and try to control my annoyance.

"So basically, Shelley has been your spy and you have followed her orders blindly because she *claims* she wants to keep my mate and my son safe?" Creed scoffs and shakes his head. Creed's not wrong it does all sound a bit far-fetched, what the hell does she have to gain out of this? Cairo growls and turns to meet Creed's gaze with a hardened look on his face.

"What the fuck do you know? I did what I thought was right to keep *my* sister and *my* nephew safe. If you weren't such a fuck up, they wouldn't be in this position to begin with, so wanna tell me again how what I did was wrong?" I can feel Creed's anger and hurt through the mate link and I feel for him but at the same time Ro is right.

"Look, let's not do this right now and wake the monster. Callie and Cairo did what they did with the best intentions. Not the way I would have done things, but still the end result is the same. What the hell do we do now? Can we trust this woman?" Hate to say it but Sky is bang on. What the hell do we do now?

"We don't have any other choice. Our location was burned the moment the council found us. Shelley is offering us a safe haven, and we have to go with her."

"Why the hell should we trust her Cairo?"

"We don't have a fucking choice Cole! I don't have the numbers in my pack to go against Jacob and the council, as far as I am aware Creed doesn't either. Even if we join our packs, we only amount to two-hundred and fifty, Shelley has three hundred with her. The council has the rest of the shifter population behind them, we can't stand against thousands of wolves, we will be slaughtered, and my sister will become Jacob's breeding pet." I shudder at the thought, Creed growls so loud the windows vibrate, and Harlem jolts awake in fright. I quickly undo his buckles and grab him so I can gently rock him back to sleep.

What do you think?

Cairo is right, we don't have a choice, Creed. Better the devil we know, I guess.

"Okay, but I have a condition."

"Name it Reeves."

"Any harm comes to my son Ro, I'll fucking kill you." Cairo's expression turns fierce.

"I will die before I let any harm befall him. If Shelley shows any signs of betrayal, we're out. But I don't think it will come to that. She has nothing to gain from keeping me hidden or protecting Jess and Harlem, yet she helped us out big time today and saved our lives."

CHAPTER FIFTY-THREE

Credence

We all walk toward the jetty; Harlem is asleep in Jess's arms. Cole and I flank her on either side with Cairo, Callie and Sky leading the way to the dock. The rest of the pack follow behind but at a distance, a massive cargo ship can be seen in the distance and that's when I notice the small jet boats heading toward us. Clever Shelley, really fucking clever! I must say I would never have thought about hiding out on a boat, the salt from the sea water will mask our scents. Cairo pulls to a stop a few feet away from Shelley, Dela and Zeke. Zeke seems almost at ease with them, Cairo and Callie may be new to Shelley, but Zeke seems like...holy shit!

"You double crossing motherfucker!" Zeke's gaze meets mine and a ghost of a smile slithers across his face.

"I did what I had to do."

"The fuck does that mean Z?" Zeke meets Cairo's gaze, and a flicker of remorse crosses his gaze before he quickly masks it.

"It means I have been working with Shelley for years. I was the one who told her to approach you with the deal about Jess." Cairo stumbles back in shock, Sky the devil in disguise pulls two daggers from God knows where and is releasing vicious growls toward her former friend.

"You son of a bitch! You sold us out!" Zeke doesn't flinch from the anger in Sky's voice, he shakes his head.

"No I didn't, I did my job. I would never sell you out Sky--ever." Shelley takes a step forward.

"Zeke was planted into your group over a decade ago to keep an eye on you at my request. Zeke went dark for a few years but when he learned that Jess was back in Rosewood he came to his senses and let me know. Ever since that day we have been working on an extraction plan so we could get you all out of here--"

"I trusted you! You're meant to be my beta, you lied to me Zeke!" The hurt and anger that laces Cairo's voice makes me even feel bad for him. Zeke is one of his best friends and he has just found out that he betrayed him and that has got to suck.

"I lied to keep you alive! I did what I did so you wouldn't be hunted like a fucking dog. I kept us safe and hidden." Zeke shouts as he slams his fist against his chest to hammer his point home.

"Enough! We don't have time for this shit. Cairo, your pack will be put into the smaller boats and taken out to the cargo ship. Credence, your father and mother and the rest of your pack are already there, I'm sorry to inform you but only eighty of your pack made it out." I stumble back, shocked, gasps sound out around me but it's all white noise to me. My pack is...gone. Only eighty of my pack members made it out alive, the rest were killed. I should have fucking been there to help them, I'm the goddamn alpha and I deserted my pack when they needed me most. "The council launched an attack on them, Kane and Meg managed to get who they could to safety. Now please get the hell on the boats and hurry up!" I stand here in shock not able to move or speak, the grief at the loss of my pack is nearly crippling me.

"We'll go with you."

"Thank you Jess--"

"Don't thank me Shelley. I'm telling you now, if any harm befalls my son or any member of my brother or Creeds pack, I'll hold you responsible. I don't give a shit about any of this council bullshit or their hierarchy. All I want is to be left the fuck alone and raise my son in peace without any more of these lies and betrayals." A proud smile ghosts across Shelley's face.

"Understood, now let's move."

Cairo and the others went ahead with some of the pack first. Jess, Cole and I waited with the rest. We still don't trust her, so it was better to send Ro first and scout out the boat before Jess and Harlem get there. When he gave the signal, we all piled into the small boats and sped across the water, as we idle next to the ship Jess spins Harlem around, so he is latched onto her front like a baby monkey

"You go first and then I'll pass him up to you." I can see the uncertainty in her eyes, so I rush to say. "I swear princess, I won't let any harm come to him. I'm his father, don't take away my right to care for my son...please." She hesitates a second before she untangles Harlem and places a kiss to his head before passing him to me, he's still half asleep. Once Jess has climbed the ladder and is aboard safely, I clutch my son to my chest and then begin the awkward climb.

No sooner am I over the side of the ship, Jess is there with her arms out for Harlem. I tighten my hold on him and meet her gaze. I want her to see that I can do this. I want to do this. I may have missed four years, but I don't plan to miss four seconds now that I know he exists. Whatever she sees in my eyes has her dropping her arms and nodding.

"Son!" I spin to the left to see my mom and dad standing by one of the cargo containers, I hold Harlem with one arm and then grab Jess's hand with the other and drag her with me to my parents. Callie and Sky are standing by my mom and Cole is by my dad. Five steps away she rushes toward us, but Jess yanks her hand from mine and jumps in front of me to stop my mom, Jess crouches and releases a warning growl. I stare down at her stunned. What the hell is she doing?

Callie rushes forward and gently wraps her arm around my shocked mother, moms gaze darts to me in question but when she notices the sleeping bundle against my chest her eyes round and her hand comes up to cover her mouth. Dad is beside mom in the next second with an angry look on his face, he isn't pleased at Jess's display of anger toward mom. He opens his mouth to say something but stops when mom begins to cry.

"Meg, what's wrong." Mom points toward me and when dad sees what she is pointing at, his eyes widen, and his mouth drops open.

"I-is that...is...I." I reach down and place my hand on Jess's shoulder. She releases a whoosh of air and straightens.

"Mom, dad, I have something to tell you--- "Jess cuts me off before I can finish.

"Meg, Kane I apologize. Sheba took over and went into protective mommy mode."

"I can scent you all over him, but I can also scent my son, why?" Jess drops her gaze to the ship's floor, the chatter around us from the other pack members begins to dwindle as they listen into our conversation. Jess's reaction to my mom caught a lot of attention.

"Because he is my son." Mom and dad both gasp and exchange shocked looks between themselves.

"How?"

"Really dad?" He narrows his eyes at me.

"Yes Credence! How the hell do you have a kid? You haven't been gone that long!"

"Jess and I fucked--- "

"I didn't know I was pregnant when I ran!" Jess cuts in. "It wasn't until a month or two after that I learned I was pregnant. If you want to be angry at anyone, be angry at me but do not take it out on Creed or our son. Creed had no idea Harlem existed until he found me." A moment of silence ensues before my mom moves toward Jess; I see Jess flinch when my mom raises her hand to cup her cheek. A proud smile stretches across my mother's face as she looks at Jess.

"You are so strong my dear. Thank you."

"Huh?"

"You could have chosen a different path, and no one would have known, but regardless of how you felt about our son you still gave birth to our grandson. Now if it is okay with you, I would love to meet said grandson?" A bright smile breaks out on Jess's face as she nods her head.

Shelley had the containers made into rooms--sort of. I mean if you can call a mattress and blanket that, Jess and mom stayed back while dad and I did the rounds to check on our pack. Mom and dad are smitten to say the least with their grandson, Jess was telling mom all about the birth as dad and I left. I'm not ready to hear all of that right now, it's too painful. I know she did what she thought was best, but she kept him from me and there is still some anger and resentment toward her for that.

"What have you got us into this time son?" My dad asks, we're leaning against the railing staring out at nothing but miles and miles of open water.

"Honestly, I don't know."

"We are a pack of eighty now, Cairo has what a hundred and fifty under him and he has told me Shelley only brought fifty of her wolves with her. Why?" I release a long-tired sigh, I have no idea what I am doing.

"Dad, I don't know. I thought I had a plan but that all went to shit five years ago. Shelley said she was leaving the rest behind to keep an eye on the council and report back to her so at least that way we can try and stay one step ahead. As for where the hell we are going I have no freaking idea." A loud squeal has us spinning around to see Jess, mom, Callie, Sky and Cole all sitting there laughing at Harlem doing a dance that has him squealing in laughter. A smile tugs across my face and my heart beats faster at the sight in front of me.

"Being a father is the best and worst thing in the world." I snap my gaze to my dad in shock. "The best thing about it is that you love them so much and they are your everything. The worst thing is that you are the one they depend on, and the worry never goes away. I still worry about you, your brother and sister every damn day. I'm so scared that I'm going to get a phone call and be told one of my children has died. Give up all of this war bullshit son, and let the council have their reign. We have lost enough and don't need to lose more. Be present and be a father to your son because being a parent is the best and most rewarding job you will ever have in your life."

Chapter
Fifty-Four

Jessica

I fell asleep on one of the makeshift beds that Shelley and her guys had made for the packs. I peel my eyes open and jolt upright when I notice Harlem isn't next to me, I look side to side and panic! I jump to my feet and run out of the container and scan the area, I can't see him anywhere.

"Harlem!" I scream out, I run around like a mad woman and screech to a stop when I spot Callie, Cole and Sky. I'm breathless and panting by the time I reach them.

"What the hell Jess?" The worry in Cole's voice is palpable.

"Harlem...Gone." I wheeze out.

"What?"

"Mommy!" I ignore Cole and spin around to see Harlem on top of Creed's shoulders, a look of concern mars Creed's face. Relief washes through me and I stagger toward them with my arms out. Creed pulls Harlem from his shoulders and hands him to me, I crush him against my chest and breathe in his scent. The more I inhale his scent the more Sheba begins to calm inside me. After a few minutes I pull back and stare up at Creed.

"You took him!" His brow furrows in confusion before it's quickly replaced by anger.

"He got up and I thought it would be okay to take him so you could sleep. It looked like you needed it." Shame floods through me, I shouldn't have snapped at him but for fuck's sake we are out at sea, and I thought he might have fallen overboard or something.

"I'm sorry--"

"Save it princess." I recoil at his harsh words; he bends down and places his lips against my ear. "I told you last night, I won't hold back from being his father. You may have done this alone for four fucking years but not anymore. Get used to sharing princess because he's mine too." I stare at Creed in shock as he turns and walks away without as much as a backward glance.

Shelley's has her pack bring around breakfast for each of us and I must say I'm surprised. I didn't think she would have all of this organized but I'm glad to be wrong. Creed hasn't spoken to me since he walked away this morning. Kane, Cairo, Shelley and Creed have been inside the boat having a *meeting* apparently, Sky seems pissed she isn't included but honestly, I'm not bothered. As long as the place we are going to is safe, and I don't have to keep looking over my shoulder everyday I'm happy.

Creed and the others finally emerge after lunch and Harlem takes off toward them. My heart sores when I see a proud and loving smile light up Creed's face as Harlem barrels toward him. I know I need to let him be a dad and have a say, but it isn't easy. All I have known since giving birth is how to be mom and dad and it's not easy having to share now. Creed's gaze meets mine and he jerks his head, I stand and follow him toward the back of the boat where it isn't as busy. Creed puts Harlem down and we stand there and watch as our son gazes out at the ocean.

"Apparently we'll arrive at our destination at nightfall."

"Where are we?"

"I have no idea princess. We have tried for hours to get an answer from Shelley but all she says is it's best we don't know."

"Well that's comforting." Creed turns toward me and to my utter shock he grips the back of my neck and hauls me against his chest then smashes his lips against mine. It takes a second for the shock to wear off and the heat of his touch to scorch through my body and then I'm kissing him back with such hunger that a strangle moan tears from my throat. I reach up and link my arms around his neck, his other hand lands on my ass and pulls me flush against him, I gasp when I feel his hardness against my stomach. Liquid begins to pool between my legs and I'm aching for him to relieve the tension between my thighs.

"Eww mommy!" Creed and I break apart so fast I nearly fall on my ass. Heat colors my cheeks, for a moment I got so lost in Creed I forgot we were on a boat full of people, who have amazing fucking hearing and noses I might add. Plus, our son just saw us making out like a couple of horny teenagers!

Shoot me now!

As daylight turns to darkness and the scent in the air begins to change, I know we are nearing our destination. Creed is tense beside me, and I know he is just as anxious as I am. Cairo, Sky and Creed's family are all sitting by us waiting. The rest of the pack is scattered around the boat and tension from them can be scented as well. We are all on edge and the fact none of us knows where we are or what comes next makes this worse. Shelley has remained inside the wheelhouse the whole day with Zeke, Dela and a few of her other pack members. Trepidation is palpable out here on deck and it's suffocating. We all need to get off this boat fast, wolves don't like to be contained, we like to be on land and free, able to shift and run whenever we want.

If anything happens when we dock, you take Harlem and run. Do you understand?

I turn toward Creed in shock, my heart aches as understanding dawns. He didn't say that out loud because he is giving me the chance to escape with our son and not his own family.

I can't leave you all.

You can and you will.

Creed---

I am telling you now Jessica, you run! You keep our son safe and you fucking run.

I don't give a shit who is around or what they have to say I reach out and pull Creed's face to mine and kiss him. I'm trying to convey to him through this kiss that...I love him.

I love Credence Reeves and I'm done denying it.

I pull back and meet his shocked gaze.

I'll do it for our son.

I'll find a way to make all of this okay, princess.

I know, just promise me that when it is safe, we can try and work on us and become a family?

A smile so bright lights up his handsome face, he doesn't use words. He kisses me so hard he steals the air from my lungs.

"Eww mommy!"

"You can say that again buster." Creed and I break apart and laugh at our son's reaction. Creed just flips Ro off for his comment.

Half an hour later Shelley emerges and each of us jump to our feet. Creed grabs Harlem and hands him to me. Shelley's expression gives nothing away, she is stone faced as she looks to us. Zeke and Dela flank her and they both wear masks as well.

"This is how it is going to go, only you eight plus the boy will come to shore with us and then the pack will follow."

"Why the hell should we do that? It might be a trap!" Cairo voices what we are all thinking.

"I would never do that to you. You may all think you know me, and why I am doing this, but you're all wrong. When we get to shore, and you find out who is there, you will thank me for keeping this moment private for you." Everyone tenses, Creed is coiled so tight I'm worried he is going to snap. I spy Cole out of the corner of my eye and fur dotting his arms. Shit we all have to get off this boat so they can shift or else there is going to be a pack fight *real* soon. I step beside Creed and face Shelley; her gaze is laser focused on me.

"Okay, we'll come with you but on one condition."

"And that is?"

"Callie and Sky stay behind to care for Harlem." Shelley looks to Callie and Sky and then turns back to me.

"You trust them?" Her question is odd, but I don't hesitate.

"With my life."

"Okay, the boy stays with them."

"We stay in the wheelhouse though, if anything happens, I want to make sure I can get the packs out of here safely." Shelley ponders Sky's request for a moment, before she nods. I see Ro smile at Sky from the corner of my eye and I just know that Ro mind linked Sky and told her to say that, my brother is pretty smart I'll admit.

CHAPTER FIFTY-FIVE

Credence

We all pile into one of the small boats; I keep Jess tucked into my side and my arm around her. I don't miss my brother side-eyeing me as he watches Jess and I. I don't have the patience or time to deal with his jealousy right now, so he just needs to get the fuck over it. Shelley, Dela and Zeke accompany us on the boat. I can tell Jess is worried about leaving Harlem behind with my sister and Sky. I know for a fact Sky would never let any harm come to Harlem, Sky is one of the fiercest and most deadly women I have ever met in my life. My sister couldn't have mated with a better woman in my opinion. The boat is silent; dad puts his arm around mom and Cairo is standing on Jess's other side.

I can see lights in the distance and the faint sounds of voices, the closer we get to shore the stronger the scent of death becomes. I look to Ro and see him go rigid.

"Why the hell does it smell like death out here?" Ro snaps.

"Trust me brother, it's better if you see it rather than us telling you." Zeke's ominous reply doesn't help settle my nerves. I look down at Jess and cup her face lifting her head so she can meet my gaze. The terror in her eyes guts me.

I swear I won't let anything happen to you princess.

I just have a really bad feeling Creed.

So do I.

We make it to shore and the scent of death is so overwhelming I have to breathe through my mouth. What in the fuck lives out here? Zeke leads the way with Shelley and Dela following him. We put the girls in the middle of us and flank them with two guys on each side. As we make our way up the little banks the sand gives way to grass and then trees. This is almost like a mirage, there's lights so that must mean there is electricity out here on this island in the middle of fucking nowhere. I clutch Jess's hand in mine and continue to follow the others. The trees give way and then as one we all come to a stop, you know in the movie *Pirates of the Caribbean* how they have that little island Tortuga? Well this is that, there are huts in the trees, bridges that lead from one tree to another, but it isn't rickety or run down it's like...new age. There are buildings and houses on the ground as far as the eye can see, people mill about as if this is nothing new to them and I guess it isn't but I'm in shock. This place is fucking epic! I wish we had more time to look around and take it all in, this place is like the lost city of Atlantis.

We stumble after Zeke and the others and I can't stop looking around, people scatter out of the way and each and every one of them reeks of death, but I just chalk it up to the fact that they live on an island in the middle of nowhere. Some houses are tiny while others are huge and built like houses in suburbia. I never would have thought that houses and buildings like this would ever be found on an island, this place is mind blowing. We continue down what I guess is the main street and the further we get the taller the buildings grow, some look like apartment buildings and others look like office buildings. We see a couple of Whole Foods stores and a chemist; this place has everything. I have no idea how they could have found the materials to build any of this but I would love to meet the person that did all the construction. Z takes a right and we turn down a different road, this part is quieter and almost like this street is just for houses. We walk for another ten minutes before we come to a stop in front of a massive wrought iron gate, either side of them are gargoyles resting atop the massive stone pillars.

"I feel like I'm Dorothy and I just woke up in OZ." I chuckle at my brother and so do the others. Z presses a button on the intercom and seconds later a buzz sounds then and the gates open. We trek up the long drive and my eyes widen at the sheer wealth. This isn't a house, it's a freaking palace!

It has huge windows that go from the ground to ceiling, they're tinted which makes it hard for me to see through even with the help of Corbin's sight. The house stretches out and it looks like the house is made of...what the hell? The house is made up of shipping containers but done in a way that you wouldn't even realize it's classy and sleek. The further we walk the more entranced I am by the house, it curves into a U and as we round the back, I see a patio and chairs set out, a huge tropical garden oasis, if I didn't just spend two days on a boat, I'd swear we weren't on an island, this place is awe inspiring and so unique. The only downside so far to this place is the stench of death and rotting flesh. I snap out of it when Zeke leads us to the patio and motions for us to wait, Shelley opens the sliding door and slips inside the house.

"Dela, where the hell are we?" Dad asks, Dela meets dads gaze but the look in his eyes has me stunned. Dela looks at dad with so much pity and guilt and I can't understand why.

"Just try to be open minded and listen before you all go off the deep end, please." We all exchange a glance and before I can ask Dela what he means my brother speaks.

"What the hell is that smell? Honestly all I can freaking smell is death." The sound of footsteps behind us has us spinning around to see two men fitted out in black jeans and shirt walking toward us. Each of them has a relaxed look on their faces but the way their body is tensed I can tell they are ready to throw down at any given moment. Cole throws his hands up in the air. "Great the MIB are here, just fucking grand." Jess chuckles but tries to mask it by fake coughing. Ro and Zeke don't try to conceal their laughter at all, the two men brush past us and scowl at Cole.

"Don't try to talk about stinks mate, the only ones here that reek are you lot." The guy has an Australian accent and to hone his point he leans forward slightly and takes a deep inhale through his nose then scrunches his face up. "Wet dog, dirt, B.O and you're all in bad need of a shower and for fuck's sake a toothbrush wouldn't go astray." Cole growls in irritation and I spy Jess out of the corner of my eye sniffing herself and cringing. Yeah, can't argue with him there, we all stink and need a fucking bath or two and a gallon of mouth wash. My train of thought is cut off when the door opens and Shelley steps out, her gaze goes straight to my mom and dad.

"What happens next isn't meant to hurt you Meg, or you Kane." My mom and dad seem shocked by her declaration but don't comment. Shelley steps aside and then a woman exits the house mom gasps and reaches out to grip dads' arm to steady herself, dad's mouth hangs open and his eyes are as wide as a dinner plate. After a few seconds he manages to get himself under control and asks.

"How?" Dad utters the word so quietly if we weren't shifters we wouldn't have heard him. The woman stands there with a guilt ridden look on her face, she moves her gaze from my dad to Cole. The way she looks at my brother is weird, almost like she is...awed by him. Her gaze turns to me, I stare back. She wears form-fitting boots that come up to her knees, black jeans that are so tight they look like a second skin, a blue blouse that has the top two buttons undone. Her long brown hair is tied into a high ponytail; she has inflated lips that look fake but you can just tell are real and her small nose sits perfectly straight. When my gaze lands on her hazel eyes... hazel eyes like my own stare back at me.

Fuck no, it can't be!

"Davina?" My dad whispers and my whole world spins on its axis. I drop my grip on Jess's hand and stumble back a few steps. I feel so many pairs of eyes on me, but I can't pull mine from her. She takes a step toward me, but Jess blocks her path and growls.

"Stay the hell away from him." Davina moves her gaze to Jess and smiles wide.

"You must be the girl who hid his baby." Jess flinches slightly but doesn't back down.

"And who the hell are you?" Cairo moves closer to Jess, and I see Cole step toward her as well, but I'm stuck rooted to my spot like an idiot. I can't wrap my mind around this, this has to be a dream this cannot be real! She lifts her gaze from Jess and meets mine as she says the words that I know will change not only mine but my whole family's lives forever.

"My name is Davina Reeves, and I am Credence, Colton, and California's biological mother. I am also Queen to the vampire race and your only chance of surviving the council."

I drop to my knees and ignore the gasps and shouts around me as I clutch my head between my hands. My mother is alive, everything I thought I saw as a child is wrong. She's alive and standing right here in front of me! But worst of all the only fucking thought that keeps playing on a loop in my head is that if vampires are real then does that mean Jess's fetish for this stupid fucking Edward Cullen mean she will leave me for a vampire?

"You're a lying bitch! My mother is dead."

"Colton, that's enough--"

"No dad, mom died years ago she can't be her." It shatters me to hear how broken my brother sounds, we all believed her to be dead.

"I'm so sorry Colton but I am your mother and whether you like it or not I am the only one who can help save your brother's mate and their son."

To be continued...

Thank you!

Holy shit!

Savage Lies was the hardest book I have ever written!
Creed and Jess would not stop nagging me until their story was
written. I have never done a slow burn book before or one
where there is minimal cussing. This one was something very
new to me and way out of my comfort zone, I'm used to writing
smut and cuss words throughout the whole book. This book
tore me apart and only to band-aid me again so I could finish
their story. I hope you enjoyed book 1 of Jess and Creed, book
2 - Brutal Truth will be released soon!

If you would like to stay up to date with all my releases
follow me on the links below. If you loved Savage Lies, please
leave a review on, Amazon, Bookbub, or Goodreads, your
feedback would be much appreciated.

Stalk me on the links below!

Instagram - @author.samantha.barrett
Facebook – author.samantha.barrett
Tiktok - @samanthabarrettauthor
Twitter - @author_sbarrett

Feel free to join my readers group on Facebook – Sam's
Dreamers.

Acknowledgments

I have to give a huge shout out to my mum, due to complications in my personal life my mum stepped up and helped me out by editing Savage Lies. She has never edited before and was super nervous but I had nothing but complete faith in her to smash this editing out and she did not disappoint. Thank you so much mummy, I love you!

Thank you to my girl Amber for all your hard work and everything you do for me and my books! Thank you for putting up with my meltdowns and last-minute changes to formatting and promo stuff, best PA ever!

Shout out to my A team for having my back and pushing me to finish this book even when I wanted to give up. Having you both behind me and supporting me means the freaking world!

To my darling husband and children, from the bottom of my heart I cannot thank you enough for your support. You guys never complain when I'm locked in my office writing or editing, you three truly are the best part of me.

My ARC team! Thank you all so much for reading and reviewing my books it means a lot to me and I apricate each and everyone of you!

To my amazing readers, thank you!

your support and recognition to these characters is the reason that drives me to follow my dreams.

If you loved Savage Lies please leave a review.

Sam. Xxx

About the Author

Samantha is a book lover and writer. She is originally from the land of the long white cloud, New Zealand.

Sam loves anything Twilight and is a TWIHARD proudly.
#TeamEdward

She loves fantasy-romance novels with strong Alpha males.

Samantha loves to write complicated love stories with a twist. A strong and badass heroine is a must!

She lives in Brisbane, Australia with her husband, two children, and four dogs.

If her books leave you wanting more or you feel as if you connected with the characters in some way, she takes that as a win!!
Sam loves writing anything that is out of the box!

If you would like to read Nico and Ryan's journey turn the page to read their blurb.

If you would like to know more about Dom and Soph, turn the page for their book – Redemption.

You can find her on –

Amazon - amzn.to/3vsmuxy

Bookbub – bit.ly/2NvIJl4

Goodreads - bit.ly/2NsCSx2

A Beautiful Dream – Book 1

My name is Ryan Knox.

I thought I was finally free of my past.

I left my old life behind, reconnected with my family, and made all the right choices.

It was supposed to make me happy, until I found out I'm the only one who can save a world I didn't even know existed. My dreams weren't just dreams.

They were the place I fell for someone I had no right falling for.

Now, I need to harness an unknown power inside of me.

The objective is clear—save the Fae realm.

Secrets will need to be uncovered.

Enemies will need to be reasoned with.

And my heart will need to stay out of it.

There's just one problem.

The evil we need to fight, is none other than my twin sister.

A Twisted Fate – Book 2

We were supposed to be happy and free.
They might be, but I'm defiantly not.
I'm supposed to be strong.
An all-mighty hybrid with the power to seal a realm.
But if that's the case, why do I feel so weak?
The man I thought I loved is gone.
There's one problem.
I have to marry in order to unlock my power.

Everything around me is falling apart.
I'm keeping secrets from my friends.
The people closest to me are cursed and need to be saved.
But my sister? I'm not sure I want to save her.

I want to destroy her in every way imaginable.
To take from her the way she took him from me.
To make her feel that unbearable pain.

She wants me dead and after what I've done, I deserve to be.

A Beautiful Nightmare – Book 3

They try to break me every day.
They may break my bones but not my spirit.
My anger builds daily, and I'm determined to make them pay.
After all, the greatest allies can be found in traitors.

I've learnt to fight.
To control the power inside me.
Now, I'm ready to seek vengeance.
It's time to go back and end this.
I will ruin my sister and win the war.
I will avenge my father's death.
I will save my mother by breaking her curse.
I will save the fae realm and set the coven free.
And then I will face the punishment for the lives I took,
Even if it cost me my own.

My name is Ryan Knox,
And I'm prepared to die for what I believe in.

Redemption

My name is Dominic Silver and I am the original hybrid.

After what happened to my mom, I fled New York.
Living in the fae realm with my best friend was great, until I learned his sister is my mate.
But loving Sophia would come at a price I wasn't willing to pay.
My rejection caused her to run, and she was captured by the king of the vampires.
Seventeen years later, she finally escapes.

Seeing her again brings feelings back that I thought had dissipated.
Being near her stirs something inside me that I try to ignore for her safety.
Sophia is a princess and I am the mix breed mutt.
I have nothing to offer her.

When Randall comes back to try and take her again, I need to choose.
Do I accept the mate bond and save her, putting her life in danger?
Or do I deny her again and settle for a lesser evil?

Sophia isn't as innocent as she seems. She's is keeping a secret so big it has the power to change my life. And when the truth comes out, it'll bring me to my knees and my world will crumble around me.